DAVIS, Lindsey
Shadows in bronze

Book#2

32375

SHADOWS IN BRONZE

A Marcus Didius Falco Novel by

LINDSEY DAVIS

BY THE SAME AUTHOR

Silver Pigs

SHADOWS IN BRONZE

A Marcus Didius Falco Novel by

LINDSEY DAVIS

Crown Publishers, Inc.
New York

In memory of Margaret Sadler: a most
dear and trusted friend

Published by Crown Publishers, Inc.,
201 East 50th Street, New York, New York 10022
Member of the Crown Publishing Group.
Originally published in Great Britain by Sidgwick & Jackson Limited
in 1990.
CROWN is a trademark of Crown Publishers, Inc.

Manufactured in the United States of America

Library of Congress Cataloging-in-Publication Data

Davis, Lindsey.
Shadows in bronze : a Falco novel / Lindsey Davis.
p.   cm.
1. Rome—History—Vespasian, 69-79—Fiction.   I. Title.
PR6054.A8925S54   1991
823'.914—dc20   90-25078
CIP

ISBN 0-517-57612-0

10 9 8 7 6 5 4 3 2 1

First American Edition

CONTENTS

DRAMATIS

The Emperor Vespasian	Lord of the World (& short of cash)
His sons:	
Titus	(A treasure)
Domitian	(A trial)
His officials:	
Anacrites	A 'secretary'. (Chief Spy)
Momus	A 'slave overseer'. (Another Spy)
M. Didius Falco	An informer. (Not a Spy)

Disgraced members of a recently extinguished conspiracy:

Gn. Atius Pertinax	(deceased)
Name unknown	A corpse in a warehouse (extremely deceased)
A. Curtius Longinus	Out of town for religious reasons
A. Curtius Gordianus	ditto
L. Aufidius Crispus	Out of town on a sea cruise
Their staff:	
Barnabas	Favourite freedman to Pertinax
Milo	Steward to Gordianus; a large type
'Shrimp'	Milo's sidekick; a small type
Bassus	Bosun to Crispus

Falco's Friends and Relations:

Falco's mother	A force to be reckoned with
Galla (the put-upon one)	A sister, married to a water-boatman
Larius	(A romantic) Son of Galla and the boatman
Maia (the sensible one)	Another sister, married to:
Famia (the vet)	A dark horse
Mico (the plasterer)	*'Just mention my name!'*
L. Petronius Longus	Captain of the Aventine Watch; Falco's best friend. A nice man
Arria Silvia	Petro's wife. An efficient woman
Petronilla, Silvana, Tadia	Their daughters
Ollia	Their daughters' nursemaid
A fisherboy	Their nursemaid's hanger-on
Lenia	Proprietress of the Eagle Laundry
Julius Frontinus	A Praetorian; who knew Falco's brother but wishes he didn't

PERSONAE

Geminus	An auctioneer; who may be Falco's father, but hopes he isn't
Glaucus	Falco's trainer; in other respects a sensible man
D. Camillus Verus	A senator with a problem
Julia Justa	His wife
Helena Justina	Their problem. Ex-wife of Atius Pertinax (*her* problem) and ex'girlfrind of Falco (*his*)
Name unknown	Their door porter (An idiot)

Encountered in the course of Duty

Name unknown	A priest of the Temple of Hercules Gaditanus on the Aventine
Tuillia	A Transtiberina barmaid with big ideas
Laesus	An honest sea captain from Tarentum
Ventriculus	A plumber in Pompeii (fairly honest, for a plumber)
Roscius	An amiable jailor in Herculaneum
S. Aemilius Rufus Clemens	A magistrate in Herculaneum with a very impressive pedigree (and not much sense)
Aemilia Fausta	His sister, once engaged to Aufidius Crispus
Caprenius Marcellus	An elderly ex-consul. Adoptive father of Atius Pertinax (not much sense either)
Bryon	Trainer of the Pertinax bloodstock on the Marcellus estate

Also Encountered:

Name unknown	A Sacred Goat
Nero (aka Spot)	An ox enjoying his holiday
'Ned'	A rather surprised donkey
'Cerberus' (aka Fido)	A friendly farm dog
The Pertinax Bloodstock:	
Ferox	A champion
Little Sweetheart	A joke

PART ONE
AN AVERAGE DAY

ROME
Late Spring, AD 71

'Give your heart to the trade you have learnt, and draw refreshment from it . . . '

Marcus Aurelius, Meditations

I

By the end of the alley the fine hairs in my nostrils were starting to twitch. It was late May, and the weather in Rome had been warm for a week. Energetic spring sunlight had been beating on the warehouse roof, fermenting a generous must inside. All the eastern spices would be humming like magic, and the corpse we had come to bury would be lively with human gases and decay.

I brought four volunteers from the Praetorian Guard plus a captain called Julius Frontinus who used to know my brother. He and I prised off the chains from the backstreet gates, then sauntered around the loading yard while the troopers rattled at the lock on the huge inner door.

While we were waiting Frontinus grumbled, 'Falco, after today, just reckon I never met your brother in my life! This is the last disgusting errand you can expect to drag me on – '

'Private favour for the Emperor . . . Festus would have had a word for it!'

Frontinus described the Emperor with my brother's word, which was not genteel.

'Easy work, Caesaring!' I commented light-heartedly. 'Smart uniform, free living quarters, the best seat at the Circus – and all the honeyed almonds you can eat!'

'So what made Vespasian select *you* to deal with this?'

'I'm easy to bully and I needed the money.'

'Oh, a logical choice!'

My name is Didius Falco, Marcus to special friends. At the time I was thirty years old, a free citizen of Rome. All *that* meant was that I had been born in a slum, I still lived in one, and except in irrational moments I expected to die in one too.

I was a private informer the Palace occasionally used. Shedding a putrid body from the Censor's list of citizens was up to standard for my work. It was unhygienic, irreligious, and put me off my food.

In my time I had operated for perjurers, petty bankrupts and frauds. I swore court affidavits to denounce high-born senators for debauchery so gross that even under Nero it could not be covered up. I found missing children for rich parents who would better abandon them, and pleaded lost causes for widows without legacies who married their spineless lovers the very next week – just when I had got them some money of their own. Most of the men tried to dodge off without paying, while most of the women wanted to pay me in kind. You can guess which kind; never a sweet capon or a fine fish.

After the army I did five years of that, freelancing. Then the Emperor made an offer that if I worked for him he might raise my social rank. Earning the cash to qualify would be next to impossible, but promotion would make my family proud and my friends envious, while seriously annoying all the rest of the middle class, so everybody told me this mad gamble was worth a minor insult to my republican deals. Now I was an Imperial agent – and not enjoying it. I was the new boy; so they saddled me with the worst jobs. This corpse, for instance.

The spiceyard where I had brought Frontinus lay in the commercial quarter, near enough to the Forum for us to be aware of the piazza's busy hum. The sun was still shining; scores of swallows swooped against the blue sky. A skinny cat with no sense of occasion looked in through the open gate. From nearby premises came the scream of a pulley and a workman whistling, though mostly they seemed deserted the way warehouses and timberyards so often are, especially when I want someone to sell me a cheap plank of wood.

The Guards had succeeded in breaking open the lock. Frontinus and I tied scarves round our mouths, then hauled at the high door. A warm stench bellied out in our faces and we recoiled; its gust seemed to push our clothes clammily against our skin. We let the air settle then marched inside. We both stopped. A wave of primitive terror knocked us back.

A dreadful quiet hung everywhere – except where a horde of flies had been zooming for days in obsessive parabolas. The upper air, lit by small opaque windows, seemed thick with scented, sunfilled dust. The light below was dimmer. In the middle of the floor we made out a shape: the body of a man.

The smell of decomposition is milder than you expect, but quite distinct.

I exchanged a glance with Frontinus as we approached. We stood, uncertain what to do. Lifting the cloth gingerly, I started to peel off the toga that had been flung over the remains. Then I dropped it and backed away.

The man had been dead in the pepper warehouse for eleven days before some bright spark at the Palace remembered they ought to bury him. After lying so long unembalmed in a warm fug, the dead flesh was flaking like well-cooked fish.

We retreated for a moment while we braced ourselves. Frontinus gagged hoarsely. 'Did you finish him yourself?'

I shook my head. 'Not my privilege.'

'Murder?'

'Discreet execution – avoids an inconvenient trial.'

'What had he done?'

'Treason. Why do you think I'm involving the Praetorians?' The Praetorians were the elite Palace Guard.

'Why the secrecy? Why not make him an example?'

'Because officially our new Emperor was greeted with universal acclaim. So plots against Vespasian Caesar don't occur!'

Frontinus scoffed caustically.

Rome was full of men plotting, though most of them failed. The stand against fate which this one had taken had been cleverer than most, but he now lay stretched out on a dusty floor beside a blackened patch of his own dried blood. Several fellow conspirators had fled from Rome without stopping to pack spare tunics or a wine flask for the journey. At least one was dead – found strangled in a cell at the grim Mamertine prison. Meanwhile Vespasian and his two sons had been received in Rome with an unconditional welcome, and were settling down to reconstruct the Empire after two years of horrendous civil war. Everything, apparently, was under control.

The plot had been extinguished; all that remained was the disposal of its festering evidence. Allowing this man's family to hold the normal public funeral with a procession through the streets, flute music, and hired mourners prancing around dressed as his famous ancestors had struck the suave Palace secretaries as a poor way to keep a failed conspiracy quiet. So they ordered a minor functionary to arrange a tactful errand boy; this clerk sent for me. I had a large family who relied on me and a violent landlord whose rent stood several weeks in arrears; for flunkeys with unorthodox burials to arrange I was easy prey.

'Well, standing here won't shift him – '

I hauled away the covering, exposing the body full length.

The corpse lay just as it had fallen, yet hideously different. We could sense how its innards were collapsing while maggots seethed within. I dared not look at the face.

'Jupiter, Falco; this bastard was middle-class!' Frontinus looked troubled. 'You ought to know, no middle-ranker passes on without an announcement in the *Daily Gazette* to warn the gods in Hades that the shade of an eminent person is expecting the best seat in Charon's ferryboat – '

He was right. If a body came to light wearing clothing with the narrow purple bands of a Roman knight, busy officials would insist on knowing whose son or father this worthy specimen had been.

'Let's hope he's not modest,' I agreed quietly. 'He'll have to be undressed . . . '

Julius Frontinus muttered my brother's rude word again.

II

We worked fast, fighting down our physical disgust.

We had to hack away two tunics stinking with body waste. Only the roughest wash-and-wear old clothes dealer would pick over these rags far enough to find the embroidered namebands sewn inside the neck. Yet we had to be sure.

Back in the yard, squeezing in gulps of fresh air, we burned all we could; we even charred his shoes and belt. He wore finger rings. Frontinus screwed those off somehow; the gold band indicating middle rank, a giant emerald cameo, a signet ring, and two more, one with a woman's name. They could not be sold in case they reappeared; I would drop them into the Tiber later that day.

At last, looping a rope around the nearly naked corpse, we tugged it across a stretcher we had brought. I went to push him on with my toe, then had second thoughts.

The silent Praetorians kept the alley clear while Frontinus and I staggered along it to pitch our burden down a manhole into the Great Sewer. We listened; there was a splash at the bottom near the stone access steps. The rats would come across him soon enough. When the next summer storm was draining from the Forum, anything that was left of him would be rolled into the river through the massive arch below the Aemilian Bridge, then either lodged up against the piles to frighten passing boatmen or carried on, to be nibbled clean by undiscerning fish in an unmarked, unknown resting place at sea.

The problem was disposed of; Rome would not give its missing citizen another thought.

We strode back; burned the stretcher; sluiced the warehouse floor; swabbed our hands, arms, legs and feet. I fetched a clean bucket of water, then we both washed again. I went out to empty the slops in the street.

Someone in a green cloak with the hood pulled up paused as he saw me alone by the gate. I nodded, avoiding his eyes. He went on up the alley. A respectable citizen walking cheerfully, he continued about his business unaware of the grisly scene he had just missed.

In view of the weather, I did wonder why he was so heavily

muffled; sometimes it seems as if everyone in Rome is sneaking up back alleys on some business that is best done in disguise.

I said I would lock up.

'We'll be off then!' Frontinus was taking his lads for a well-earned drink. He did not invite me to join them – and I was not surprised.

'Thanks for your help. I'll be seeing you, Julius – '

'Not if I see you first!'

Once they had gone I stood for a moment with a heavy heart. Now I was alone I had more time to notice things. In the yard my eye fell on an interesting stack which was buttressing the outer wall beneath a discreet covering of old hides. As an auctioneer's son I could never ignore any abandoned commodity which might be saleable; I strolled across.

Under the hides were a couple of sprightly spiders and numerous ingots of lead. The spiders were strangers but the ingots were old friends; the conspirators had intended using stolen silver to bribe their way into power. All the bars containing precious metal had been recovered by the Praetorians and carried off to the Temple of Saturn, but the thieves who smuggled the bullion out of the British mines had cheerfully cheated by sending the plotters large quantities of lead – useless for bribery. Evidently the lead had been left here for collection by an Imperial waggon train, all neatly stacked with military precision, each row at a perfect right angle to the one beneath. Lead ingots had some value to a man with the right contacts . . . I covered them up again, as an honest state servant should.

I left the gates open while I returned on my own to the manhole over the Great Sewer. Of all the foul corpses of failed entrepreneurs that must be littering Rome, this was the last I would have chosen to treat with such disrespect. Every traitor has a family, and I knew his. His nearest male relation, who should have conducted this funeral, was a senator whose daughter meant a very great deal to me. A typical Falco predicament: faced with a highly important family I was trying to impress, I had to demonstrate my good character by tipping their dead relative without ceremony down a public sewer . . .

Grumbling under my breath, I levered up the cover again, cast in a hasty handful of earth, then muttered the basic requiem: '*To the gods of the shades I send this soul* . . . '

I flung down a copper for him to pay the ferryman, then hoped if Fortuna smiled on me that was the last I would hear of him.

No chance of that. The goddess of fortune only ever grimaces at me as if she had just shut her sacred finger in a door.

Back at the warehouse I kicked at our fire ashes, spreading them about the yard. I coiled the chains over one shoulder, ready to secure the gate. Just before leaving I strolled back inside one last time, my muscles braced under those heavy links.

Everywhere remained bathed in a murky miasma of cinnamon bark. Restless flies were continuing to wheel above the stain on the floor as if still in the presence of an undeparted soul. Motionless sacks of priceless oriental produce sagged in the shadows, filling the air with a dry sweet perfume that seemed to alter the very texture of my skin.

I turned to go. My eye caught a movement. A spasm of terror convulsed me, like a man who has seen a ghost. But I did not believe in ghosts. Out of the moted dimness a muffled figure tumbled straight at me.

He was real enough. He snatched up a barrel stave and swung at my head. He had his back to the light but I vaguely felt I knew him. There was no time to ask what his grievance was. I whirled round, slung the chains viciously against his ribs, then lost my footing and crashed to the floor on my right elbow and knee, dragged down by the weight I was carrying.

With luck I might have grabbed him. Luck has rarely been my ally. While I was flailing in armfuls of ironwork, the villain fled.

III

I had only been away at the manhole for a moment, but I should have been prepared. This was Rome; leave a treasure house unguarded for three seconds and some sneak thief was bound to clamber in.

I had not seen the man's face, though that sense of having recognised him clung persistently. The green hood pulled so securely round his head was unmistakable: the man I had seen while I was emptying the wash bucket. Cursing him, then myself, I limped out to the alley with blood trickling down my leg.

Scattered patches of sunlight threw up a piercing dazzle, while the dense shade was unnervingly cold. The passage at the back of the warehouse was barely three feet wide, with one entrance onto a filthy cutthroat lane. The other way, a crook-shouldered curve hid its exit from view. Lining both sides were dank yards crammed with world-weary trolleys and piles of teetering kegs. Dirty ropes snaked into gaping doorways. Ferocious notices hung by a nail warned visitors away from gates that looked as if no one had opened them for ten years. Surveying this sour commercial hole it seemed impossible that a two-minute walk would bring you to the bright bustle of the Forum – this was Rome. As I said.

No one in sight. A pigeon fluttered on a roof then slipped in through a broken pantile. A gantry creaked once. Nothing else moved. Except my heart.

He could be anywhere. As I looked for him in one place, he would slip off another way. While I busied myself searching, he or some quite unconnected evildoer could jump out unexpectedly and bash in my curly head. If so, or if I fell through a rotting floor in one of these deserted stores, I might lie there undetected for days.

I hopped back. I used an old nail to spring back the teeth of the lock on the warehouse door. I checked the sun-baked yard. Using the military pincers Frontinus had brought, I reapplied the gate chains like a responsible person. Then I left.

The smell of the corpse had infiltrated my clothes. Unable to bear it any longer, I went home to change.

I lived in the Thirteenth Sector. In empty streets it took ten minutes, though at this time of day forcing myself through the crowds occupied

9

three times that. The hubbub seemed worse than usual. I reached home feeling deafened and desperate.

The Falco apartment was the best I could afford, so it was grim. I rented a filthy garret above the Eagle Laundry in a street called Fountain Court (which had never possessed a fountain, and wasn't a court). To reach this impressive location I had to turn off the comparative luxury of the paved Ostia Road, then squeeze down a series of twisting entries that grew narrower and more threatening at every step. The point where they diminished into nothing was Fountain Court. I flailed through several lines of damp togas that were blocking the laundry's frontage, then attacked the long haul up six flights of stairs to the sky-high hovel that served as my office and home.

Once aloft I knocked, for the hell of it and to warn off any wildlife frolicking in my absence, then I told myself to come in and unlatched the door.

I had two rooms, each a bare eight foot square. I paid extra for a rocky balcony but my landlord Smaractus allowed me a discount in the form of natural daylight through a hole in the roof (plus free access to water, whenever it rained). There were multimillionaires in Rome who housed their horses better, though thousands of anonymous individuals fared even worse.

My penthouse was for tenants who went out a lot. Yet for five years this squalid hole had seemed gracious enough, especially since when I was running around for clients I was rarely there. It had never been cheap; nowhere in Rome was. Some of my human neighbours were objectionable types, but an amiable gecko had recently taken up residence. I could entertain four people if I opened the door to the balcony, or five when one was a girl who would sit on my lap. I lived alone; financially I had no choice.

Anxious to discard my insanitary tunic, I stepped quickly across my outer room. There I had a table where I ate, wrote, or thought about the filthiness of life, plus a bench, three stools, and a cooking oven I built myself. In the bedroom stood my lopsided bed, alongside a spare couch, a storage chest which doubled as a washstand, and a perch for when I forced myself to patch the leaky roof.

Stripping off with relief, I used the last water in a pitcher for another good scrub down, then found a tunic that had only torn in two new places since the last time my mother mended it. I combed my hair roughly, rolled up my second-best toga in case I went anywhere respectable later, then pounded downstairs.

While I was delivering my castoffs I heard myself hailed raucously by Lenia, the laundress.

'Falco! Smaractus wants your rent!'

'What a surprise! Tell him we can't all get what we want in life . . . '

I found her in the corner she used as an accounting room, sitting in her greasy slippers while she supped mint tea. Until this pitiful ninny decided to invest in real estate (and real misery) by planning to marry our landlord Smaractus, she had been one of my shabby friends; once I could persuade her to ditch the brute she would be again. Lenia was a sagging drab about five times stronger than she looked, with startling snaggles of henna-red hair which constantly worked free of a limp scarf round her head; she had to poke the strands back in to peer ahead safely when she wanted to go anywhere.

'He means it, Falco!' She had sickly eyes and a voice like forty dried peas rattling in a pannikin.

'Good. I like a man whose ambitions are serious . . . '

By this time my attention was wandering, as Lenia undoubtedly knew. There was another woman with her whom she introduced as Secunda, a friend. We had long passed the time when I saw any advantage in flirting with Lenia, so I spent a few moments giving the glad eye to her friend.

'Hello! I'm Didius Falco; I don't believe I've seen you before?' The lady jingled her arm bangles and smiled knowingly.

'Watch him!' Lenia commented.

Secunda was mature without being overripe; she was old enough to pose an interesting challenge, yet young enough to suggest overcoming the challenge could be very worthwhile. She had a thorough inspection of me, while I gazed back frankly.

I was offered mint tea, but its unappealing grey colour led me to decline on grounds of health. Secunda received my impending departure with fragrant regret; I assumed the expression of a man who might be detained.

'Some ferret-faced scavenger came in for you, Falco,' Lenia scowled.

'A client?'

'How should I know? He had no manners, so he seemed your type. He barged in and asked your name.'

'Then what?'

'He left. I wasn't sorry.'

'But,' Secunda added sweetly, 'he's waiting for you outside, I think.' She missed nothing – if there was a man in it.

Lenia's cubbyhole was open on the street side, except for the clutter of her trade. I tweaked at the laundry until I could look out without being seen. A green cloak with its hood well up was loitering against the open doorflap on Cassius' breadshop two doors down.

'Him in the green?' They nodded. I frowned. 'Some tailor's found himself a gold mine there! Evidently green cloaks with pointed hoods are all the rage this month . . . ' I would soon know; it was my eldest nephew's birthday next Thursday, and if that was the latest fashion Larius was bound to ask for one. 'Has he been there long?'

'He arrived just after you did and has been waiting ever since.'

I felt distinctly apprehensive. I had been hoping that the citizen in green was just an opportunist thief who had noticed something going on at the warehouse and gone in to explore as soon as he thought Frontinus and I had left.

Following me home put his presence in a different light. That degree of curiosity could *not* be innocent. It meant his interest in the warehouse was no coincidence. He must be some character who badly needed to know what had happened there, and to put a name to any stranger connected with the place. This spelt trouble for those of us at the Palace who were thinking we had put the conspiracy against the Emperor to bed.

While I watched, he lost his zest for spying and took himself off strolling towards the Ostia Road. I had to find out more about him. I raised an arm to Lenia, left Secunda with a smile that ought to keep her simmering, then slipped out in pursuit.

Cassius the baker, who must have been keeping an eye on the stranger, tossed me a thoughtful look and a stale bread roll as I went by.

IV

I nearly lost him on the main road. I glimpsed my mother inspecting onions by a greengrocer's stall. Judging by her grim face, the onions, like most of my lady friends, fell short of her standards. My mother had convinced herself my new job working for the Palace involved good money, simple clerical work, and keeping my tunics clean. I was reluctant to let her discover so soon that it was the same old round of trudging after villains who chose to slouch through the streets when I wanted my lunch.

It took deft footwork to avoid her without losing him. Luckily the green cloak was an unpleasant shade of viridian, easy to pick up again.

I trailed him to the river, which he crossed on the Sublician Bridge; a ten-minute hike away from civilisation to the Transtiberina hovels where the street hawkers crowd when they are kicked out of the Forum after dark. The Fourteenth District had been part of Rome since my grandparents' day, but there were enough swarthy immigrants over there to make it feel alien. After my task that morning I did not care if one of them knifed me in the back.

When you don't care, they never try.

We were walking in deep shadow now, through streets overhung by perilous balconies. Thin dogs ran in the gutters. Ragged, lug-haired gypsy children yelled at the terrified dogs. If I let myself think about it, the whole district terrified *me*.

The green cloak was travelling at a steady pace like a citizen going home for lunch. His build was ordinary, with thin shoulders and a youngish walk. I still had not seen his face; that hood stayed up despite the heat. He was too shy to be honest, that was sure.

Although I kept water carriers and piemen between us out of professional etiquette, there was no need. He did none of the ducking and dodging that would have been sensible in this seedy neighbourhood. He never once glanced behind.

I did. Regularly. No one appeared to be shadowing me.

Above our heads limp blankets aired on ropes, and below that other ropes carried baskets, brassware, cheap clothing and rag rugs. The Africans and Arabs selling them seemed to accept him, but exclaimed

13

to each other harshly as I passed; still, they may have been just admiring me for a handsome lad. I caught the scent of new flat bread and sickly foreign cakes. Behind half-open shutters worn women with ugly voices were shouting their exasperation at idle men; occasionally the men lashed out in temper, so I listened with fellow feeling while I quickened my step. In this area they sold intricate little copper knives with spells traced on the blade, addictive drugs distilled from oriental flowers, or boys and girls with limbs like cherubs whose trade in vice was already rotting them with hidden disease. You could purchase the promise of a heart's desire, or a shabby death – for someone else, or for yourself. If you stood on one spot too long, death or some worse crisis might find you without the bother of paying for it.

I lost him south of the Via Aurelia, in an ominously silent street, about five minutes into the Fourteenth.

He had turned up a narrow alley, still marching at that regular pace, and by the time I made the corner there was simply no sign. The place had unhappy doorways let into sheer grey walls, though it was probably not so sinister as it seemed.

I wondered what to do. There were no colonnades to lurk in, and my green friend's siesta might last all afternoon. I had no idea who he was or why we were tailing each other. I was not sure I cared. It was the hottest part of the day, and I was losing interest. If anyone in the Transtiberina suspected I was an informer, I would be found on the pavement tomorrow with some criminal's monogram carved on my chest.

I noticed a sign for a drinking shop, entered its cool gloom, and when the squat-necked, big-bosomed woman who ran it dragged her hulk into view I ordered spiced wine. No one else was there. The shop was tiny. There was one table. The counter was almost hidden in the dark. I felt the bench for splinters then sat down cautiously. It was a place where a drink took ages to come, because even for a foreigner the madam simmered it hot and fresh. This natural hospitality left me churlish, and caught off guard; both feelings were all too familiar.

The woman disappeared again so I sat over my beaker alone.

I laced my fingers together and thought about life. I was too tired to manage life in general, so I concentrated on my own. I rapidly reached the conclusion it was not worth the denarius it had cost me to sit here pondering with my wine.

I felt deeply depressed. My work was dreadful and the pay worse. In addition to that, I was just facing up to ending an affair with a young woman I hardly knew yet and did not want to lose. Her name was Helena Justina. She was a senator's daughter, so seeing me was not quite illegal, though scandalous enough if her friends found out. It was one of those disasters you start knowing it must be hopeless, then end almost immediately because continuing becomes even more painful than breaking off.

I had no idea what to say to her now. She was a wonderful girl. The faith she had in me filled me with despair. Yet she probably saw that I was sliding away from her. And knowing she already understood the situation was not helping me compose my leaving speech . . .

Trying to forget, I swallowed blankly. But the catch of hot cinnamon on the roof of my mouth recalled that warehouse earlier. Suddenly my tongue felt like gravel. I abandoned my winecup, clinked some coins onto a plate and called goodbye. I was on my way out when a voice behind cried 'Thanks!'. After I glanced behind me I lingered after all.

'Don't mention it, sweetheart! Has the woman I saw first been practising witchcraft, or are you someone else?'

'I'm her daughter!' she laughed.

You could see (just about) that she was. In twenty years time this gorgeous little body might look just as unappealing as her mama – but she would be passing through some fascinating stages on the way. She was about nineteen now, and this was a stage I liked. The wineshop woman's daughter was taller than her mother, which made her movements more graceful; she had huge dark eyes and tiny white teeth, clear skin, tinsel earrings, and an air of perfect innocence that was flagrantly false.

'I'm Tullia,' this vivid vision said.

'Hello Tullia!' I exclaimed.

Tullia smiled at me. She was a cuddlesome armful with nothing much to do that day, while I was a man whose low spirits needed consoling. I smiled back at her gently. If I had to lose the sweet lady I wanted, unprincipled women were welcome to do their worst with me.

A private informer who knows what he is doing can soon make a barmaid his friend. I engaged her in harmless banter then eventually broached, 'I'm looking for someone; you may have seen him – he often wears a cloak in a rather evil shade of green.'

I was not surprised when the beauteous Tullia recognised my man; on noticing Tullia, most males in this locality must rapidly join her mother's clientele. 'He lives across the alley – ' She came to the doorway and pointed out the small square window of the room where he lodged. I started to like him. His surroundings looked pretty insalubrious. The indications were that the lad in green lived as miserably as me.

'Wonder if he's there now . . . '

'I can look,' offered Tullia.

'How's that?' She signalled upwards with her eyes. They had the usual arrangement of steps up the inside wall which led to a boarded attic where the proprietors lived and slept. There would be one long window over the shop entrance, to provide all their light and air. A lively young lady with an interest in people would naturally spend her idle moments looking out at men.

Tullia prepared to skip up the steps obligingly. I might have scrambled aloft with her but I guessed her mother was lurking above, which spoiled the fun.

'Thanks! I won't bother him at the moment.' Whoever he was and whatever he wanted, no one was going to pay me for disturbing his lunch. 'You know anything about him?'

She looked at me warily, but I had easy-going manners and all my curls were natural; besides, I had left her mother a decent tip. 'His name's Barnabas. He came here about a week ago – ' As she spoke I was thinking; the name Barnabas had cropped up somewhere else quite recently. 'He paid in advance for a three-month lease – without arguing!' she marvelled. 'When I told him that he was stupid, he just laughed and said he'll be rich one day – '

I grinned. 'I wonder why he told you that?' No doubt for the usual reason men make women wild promises of wealth. 'So what does this hopeful entrepreneur do in life, Tullia?'

'He said he was a corn chandler. But – '

'But what?'

'He laughed at that too.'

'Seems quite a comedian!' Calling himself a grain merchant no longer squared with the Barnabas I was thinking about, who was the freed townhouse slave of a senator, and wouldn't know wheat from wood shavings.

'You ask a lot of questions!' Tullia tackled me slyly. 'So what's your line of business?' I ducked it with a knowing look, which she returned. 'Oh, secrets! Want to leave the back way?'

I always like to reconnoitre a place I may want to come back to, so soon I was flitting through a courtyard at the back of the wineshop, hopping round it fairly smartly since it was part of a private house. Tullia seemed at home there; no doubt the lucky householder had realised her possibilities. She let me out through an unlocked gate.

'Tullia, if Barnabas drops in for a drink, you could mention I'm looking for him – ' Might as well make him feel nervous if I could. In my job you never won a laurel wreath being diffident with strangers who followed you home. 'Tell him if he comes to the house on the Quirinal – I think he'll know where I mean – I have a legacy to give him. I need him to identify himself in front of witnesses.'

'Will he know who you are?'

'Just describe my fine-featured classical nose! Call me Falco. Will you do it for me?'

'Ask nicely then!'

That smile had promised favours to a hundred men before. A hundred and one of us must have decided we could overlook the others. Ignoring a pang of guilt about a certain senator's daughter, I asked Tullia in the nicest way I knew; it seemed to work.

'You've done that before!' she giggled when I let her go.

'Being kissed by beautiful women is a hazard of having a classical nose. You've done it too – what's your excuse?'

Barmaids rarely need an excuse. She giggled again. 'Come back soon; I'll be waiting, Falco!'

'Rely on it, princess!' I assured her as I left.

Lies, probably. On both sides. But in the Transtiberina, which is even more grim than the Aventine, people have to live in hope.

The sun was still shining when I crossed by way of Tiber Island into Rome. On the first bridge, the Pons Cestius, where the current races fastest, I stopped for a moment and emptied my tunic pocket of the warehouse corpse's finger rings.

His emerald cameo was missing; I must have dropped it in the street.

The thought crossed my mind that the barmaid might have stolen it, but I decided she was far too pretty for that.

V

I trudged north. I bought a pancake stuffed with hot minced pork which I ate as I walked. A watchdog wagged his tail at me but I told him to take his smiling fangs elsewhere.

Life is unfair. Too unfair, too often, to ignore a friendly grin; I went back and shared my pancake with the dog.

I was off to a house in the High Lanes Sector, on the Quirinal Mount. Its owner had been a young Senator who was involved in the same plot as the man Frontinus and I had dumped down the sewer. This one was dead too. He had been arrested for questioning, then found choked at the Mamertine prison – murdered by his fellow conspirators to ensure he would not talk.

Now his house was being emptied. Clearing property was a Didius family business, so when the subject came up at the Palace, I volunteered. Besides, the illustrious owner was once married to my special friend Helena Justina, so I wanted to see how they had lived.

The answer was, in lavish style. Seeing it had been a bad mistake. I approached their house in a melancholy mood.

Most Romans are driven demented by their neighbours: rubbish on the stairs and unemptied slop tanks; the rude salesmen with their slapdash shops at ground level and the crashing whores upstairs. Not his honour here; his fine spread occupied its own freehold block. The mansion sprawled on two levels against the Quirinal cliffs. A discreet but heavily armoured door let me in from the street to a still corridor with two porters' cubicles. The main atrium stood open to the sky, so its tasteful wainscot of glazed tiles was sparkling in long shafts of brilliant light. A magnificent fountain in a second courtyard added to the cool and bright effect as it shimmered above exotic palms in shoulder-high bronze urns. Ornate, marble-lined corridors stretched in two directions. If the owner grew tired of his formal reception rooms, various little masculine snugs were hidden away behind heavy damask door curtains on an upper floor.

Before I could settle to my official work in the house, I needed to clear up my worry that the character who had been dogging me that morning had some link with this elegant Quirinal residence.

I turned back to the doorman.

'Remind me – which was that freed slave your master was so fond of?'

'Barnabas, you mean?'

'Yes. Did Barnabas ever own a repulsive green cloak?'

'Oh *that* thing!' winced the porter fastidiously.

Barnabas the freedman had completely disappeared. To put him in perspective, if he had been a missing slave it would hardly be worthwhile posting up his name as a fugitive. Not even if he could read and write three alphabets, play the double-stemmed flute, and was a sixteen-year-old virgin built like a discus thrower, with a willing nature and liquid dark-brown eyes. His master had left behind so much saleable plunder that losing one piece of fine art – human or otherwise – was neither here nor there.

I had been finding it convenient to overlook this Barnabas. The Emperor, in the interests of his own reputation for good nature (a reputation he had never possessed, but wanted to acquire), had decided to honour the dead man's minor personal bequests; I was arranging it. The Senator's little leaving present to his favourite freedman was a cool half-million sesterces. I was protecting it in my bankbox in the Forum, where the interest had already provided a rosebush in a black ceramic pot for my balcony. So until now I had reckoned that when Barnabas needed his legacy he could come to see me of his own accord.

Today's events brought me up sharp. Snooping round that warehouse displayed an unhealthy interest in events any sensible freedman would want to pretend he knew nothing about, and attacking me was a fool's game. I knew I could still not get on with my work with a clear mind, so I bestirred myself to make some more enquiries among the waifs we had not yet sent to the slave market.

'Who knows Barnabas?'

'What's in it for us?'

'Give me something else to think about and I may forget to beat you – '

Screwing facts out of these noodles was hard work. I gave up and hunted down Chrysosto, a Levantine secretary who would sell for a high price once we released him for auction, though at present I was using him to make up inventories.

Chrysosto was a limp bladder with seedy skin and a bleary-eyed look from poking his nose into crannies where a nose is best not applied. He was displaying a white tunic, much too short in the hem, though the legs he was so proud of were just the usual pale shanks that lurk in offices, finished off with hairy knobs for knees and crumpled sandals. You could knock in tent pegs with his hammertoes.

'Stop scribing a moment – what was special about Barnabas?'

'Oh, his honour and Barnabas grew up on the same farm.'

Under my gimlet gaze Chrysosto edged his skinny pins behind a table. He had probably started out with talent, but writing letters for a man with a slow brain and a short temper soon taught him to disguise his initiative.

'What's he like?'

'A Calabrian scruff.'

'Did you like him?'

'Not much.'

'Do you reckon he knew what your master was up to?'

'Barnabas reckoned he knew everything.'

This well-informed Calabrian had been made a free citizen, so in theory if he wanted to moonlight that was up to him. Since his patron was a traitor, I had originally sympathised if he thought skipping from home was a sensible move. Now I wondered if he had taken himself off because he was up to something slippery.

'Any idea why he should run away, Chrysosto? Was he very cut up about your master's death?'

'Probably, but no one saw him afterwards. He stayed in his room with the door bolted; he had his food left outside. None of us had ever got on with him, so no one tried to interfere. Even when he went to jail to ask for the body no one here knew. I only discovered he had organised the funeral when the undertaker brought a bill.'

'Did no one at all attend the cremation?'

'No one knew. But the ashes are there in the family mausoleum; I went to pay my respects yesterday. There's a new urn; alabaster – '

So being an aristocrat had protected the young Senator from being tumbled into a sewer. After he had died in prison his body had been released for expensive funeral rites, even though they were conducted by his freedman, alone and in secrecy.

'One more thing. When your master gave Barnabas his freedom, did he set him up in business – anything to do with importing grain, for instance?'

'Not as far as I know. All those two ever talked about were horses.'

By now Barnabas was causing me considerable alarm. My message through Tullia about his legacy might draw him back here if he wanted the cash. To reinforce it even if he stayed away I sent out a runner to scrawl up a bill in the Forum promising a modest reward for news of his whereabouts. That might entice some friendly citizen to hand him over to a member of the watch.

'What reward shall I put, Falco?'

'Try three sesterces; if someone's not very thirsty, that may buy his evening drink . . . '

Which reminded me, I was ready for one myself.

VI

There was no need to leave the house in search of refreshment. The man who had once lived here was called Gnaeus Atius Pertinax, and he had left behind everything for a comfortable life: there was plenty to drink, and I had ready access.

Because Pertinax was a traitor, his property was forfeit: snapped up by our jovial new Emperor. Some poor-quality farms in Calabria (like the one where he and Barnabas grew up) had already been seized. A few items that still belonged to his aged father were grudgingly returned: some lucrative tenement leases and a pair of handsome racehorses. There were a couple of ships too, though the Emperor was still debating whether to keep those for the state. Meanwhile we had confiscated this mansion in Rome, stuffed with highly desirable contents which Pertinax had grubbed together as such playboys do: through personal legacies, sharp efforts in trade, gifts from his friends, bribes from business colleagues, and successes at the racetrack where his judgement was excellent. The mansion on the Quirinal was being turned over by three imperial agents: Momus, Anacrites and me.

It had taken us nearly a fortnight. We were doing our best to enjoy this drudgery. Every night we recovered, lying in a banqueting room still faintly perfumed with sandalwood, on huge carved ivory couches with mattresses of fine-combed wool, working our way through what was left of the late owner's fifteen-year-old Alban wine. On one of his tripod tables we controlled a silver wine warmer, with a chamber for burning charcoal, a tray for ash, and a little tap for letting off our drink when it was perfectly mulled. Slim lampstands with triple lions' feet burned fine scented oil for us as we all tried to convince ourselves we should hate to live in luxury like this.

The mansion's summer dining room had been decorated by a talented fresco artist; spectacular views across a garden showed the Fall of Troy, but even the garden turned out to be minutely painted stucco on the indoor wall, complete with realistic peacocks being stalked by a tabby cat.

'Our late host's wines,' Anacrites declared, pretending to be a bumptious connoisseur (the sort who makes a lot of noise, but doesn't really know), 'are almost as tasty as his domestic scenery!'

Anacrites called himself a secretary; he was a spy. He had a tense, compact frame and a bland face, with unusual grey eyes and eyebrows so faint they were nearly invisible.

'Drink up then!' Momus chivvied rudely.

Momus was a typical slave overseer: shorn head to deter lice, wine gut, greasy belt, grubby chin, croaky voice from the diseases of his trade, and tough as an old nail stuck in wood. He was clearing out the personnel. He had evicted all the freedmen with little cash gifts to make them grateful, and was now batching up the slaves we had found crammed into barracks at the back of the building complex. The Senator had collected his own manicurists and hair-curlers, pastry chefs and saucemakers, bath slaves and bedroom slaves, dog-walkers and bird-tamers, a librarian, three accountants, harpists and singers, even a squadron of nippy young lads whose sole job was running out to place his racing bets. For a youngish man, with no family responsibilities, he had equipped himself splendidly.

'Making progress, Falco?' Momus asked, using a gilt perfume bowl as a spittoon. I got on well with Momus; he was crooked, filthy, slapdash and devious – a pleasantly clear-cut type.

'Cataloguing a consul's son's homely chattels is an education for a simple Aventine lad!' I saw Anacrites smile. Friends of mine had warned me that he had been poking into my background until he must have known what floor of which crumbling tenement I came from, and whether the room I was born in thirty years ago faced into the courtyard or over the street. He had certainly discovered whether I was as simple as I looked.

'I ask myself,' groaned Momus, 'why anyone with all this loot needed to risk it offending the Emperor?'

'Is that what he did?' I asked, innocently. We three spent more time watching each other than looking for conspirators. Momus, who was a dedicated eavesdropper, went unconvincingly to sleep. His splaytoed feet turned up at a perfect right angle in his black boots, which were rigid, the better to kick slaves.

I was aware of Anacrites eyeing me. I let him get on with it. 'Happy day, Falco?'

'Dead men and eager women all the way!'

'I suppose,' he probed, 'the secretaries at the Palace are keeping you in the dark?'

'Seems the general idea,' I replied, none too pleased by the thought.

Anacrites helped me make up lost time with the Alban nectar. 'I'm trying to place you, Falco. What's your role?'

'Oh, I was the son of an auctioneer until my happy-go-lucky father skipped from home; so now I'm off-loading this playboy's art and antiques onto the fancy goods stalls in the Saepta Julia . . . ' He still looked curious so I carried on joking. 'It's like kissing a woman – unless I'm sharp, this could lead to something serious!'

Anacrites was searching the dead man's private documents; I knew that. (It was a job I would have liked myself.) He was tight-lipped, an insecure type. Unlike Momus, who could carelessly sell off eight Numidian litter-bearers as two poultry-carvers, a charioteer and a fan dancer from Xanthus, Anacrites was examining the study here with the fine detail of an auditor who expects another auditor to be round later checking him.

'Falco, Momus is right,' he fretted. 'Why take the risk?'

'Excitement?' I offered. 'After Nero died, plotting who to make into the next Caeser was a more thrilling game than tossing up knucklebones. Our man enjoyed a gamble. And he was due to inherit a fortune, but while he was waiting for it, one house on the Quirinal may not have seemed too special to a jumped-up junior official who wanted Rome to notice him.'

Anacrites pursed his mouth. So did I. We looked around. The expensive Pertinax mansion seemed special to us.

'So,' I prodded, 'what have you discovered from his honour's papyrus rolls?'

'A pretty dull correspondent!' complained Anacrites. 'His friends were racetrack loudboys, not literary types. But his ledgers are immaculate; his accountant was constantly kept up to scratch. He lived for his cash.'

'Found any names? Details of the plot? Proof?'

'Just biography; half a day with the Censor's records could have winkled out most of it. Atius Pertinax came from Tarentum; his natural father had rank, and friends in the south, but neither cash nor influence. At seventeen, Pertinax put that right by attracting an ancient ex-consul called Caprenius Marcellus who had plenty of status and oodles of money, but no heir – '

'So,' I encouraged, 'this elderly moneybags plucked young Gnaeus fully grown from the Heel of Italy and adopted him?'

'In the best tradition. So now Pertinax *Caprenius Marcellus* had grand ideas and a monthly allowance to pay for them. His new father adored him. He served as a tribune in Macedonia – '

'A safe, warm province!' I interrupted again, with an edge; I did my own national service in Britain: cold, wet, windy – and at that time (during the Great Rebellion) dismally dangerous.

'Naturally! A lad with a future has to look after himself! Back in Rome, as his first stepping stone into public life he marries the serious daughter of a rather dull senator, then promptly gets elected to the senate himself – first attempt; the rich boy's privilege.'

At this point I reached forward and gave myself more wine. Anacrites remained silent, savouring his, so I let myself paint in some colouring I thought he might not know: 'The Senator's safe-looking daughter was a mistake; four years into their marriage she smacked Pertinax with an unexpected notice of divorce.'

'*Really!*' smiled Anacrites in his silky way. It was part of his mystique as a spy to know more about other people than they knew about themselves. Even so, I knew more than he did about the ex-wife of Atius Pertinax.

One thing I knew was that a fortnight ago she seduced a citizen called Falco – much against his better judgement, though not at all against his will.

I drained off my glass. Staring at it, I went on. 'I met Pertinax, once.'

'In your work? What was he like?'

'Describing him politely is more than I can manage without another drink!' This time we both squeezed the sweet amber from its silver samovar. Anacrites, who liked to appear civilised, took warm water in his. I watched him dip his wrist gracefully to regulate the drips from a jewelled jug, then swirl the liquors to mix them in his glass. I had my water the way I like it, in a separate cup.

I enjoyed my wine for a moment, ignoring the water, then said of Pertinax: 'Vicious. A real thresher shark! By the time I blundered into him he was an aedile – ' Junior law enforcement officer, in support of a district magistrate. 'Pertinax had me arrested on a pretext and badly beaten up, then his friendly subordinates wrecked my apartment and tore my furniture apart.'

'Did you make a complaint?'

'Against a senator?' I scoffed. 'And see the magistrate turn out to be his uncle, who would dump me in prison for contempt?'

'So the aedile used his baton on you, and now in return,' Anacrites suggested, glancing round, 'you're rifling through his honour's Macedonian curios!'

'Rough justice,' I smiled, handling the spiralled white stem of my wineglass delicately.

'Apt!' I could see speculation working in his pale eyes. 'So, you met Pertinax . . . ' I guessed what was coming. 'Rumour has it you are no stranger to his wife?'

'I've done work for her. Hasty temper and high principles – not your type!' I insulted him calmly.

'Is she yours?'

'Hardly! She's a senator's daughter. I pee in the gutter, scratch my backside in public, and have been known to lick my plate.'

'Ha! She never remarried. *I* reckon this divorce of theirs may have been some kind of blind – '

'Nix!' I snorted. 'Pertinax was arrested because his ex-wife reported him.'

Anacrites looked sore. 'No one saw fit to warn me of that! I was all set to march in and interrogate the woman – '

'Best of luck!' I said drily.

'Why expose him? Vindictiveness?'

A fair question; yet my hackles rose. 'Politics. Her family supports Vespasian. She never realised that if Pertinax was clapped in prison his cronies would muffle him before he could be interrogated – '

The spy winced; he knew how his enforcement colleagues extracted information in the quiet privacy of a jail cell. 'So, Pertinax Marcellus – Hail and Farewell!' cried Anacrites with mock reverence.

Personally, I'd rather find my way across the Styx with no passport at all, than be handed into Hades with the blessing of the Emperor's Chief Spy.

It was time for Anacrites to report to the Emperor. Momus was asleep, his dirty toes turned out.

Anacrites looked at me from that smooth, cynical face; I decided I could work with him – so long as I always kept one hop ahead.

'You're assessing me for Vespasian,' I suggested, 'while Momus – '

'Puts in a nightly report on us both!' Anacrites breathed with clerkish contempt. His light eyebrows lifted scornfully. 'So, Marcus Didius Falco, where does that place you?'

'Just settling old scores with Pertinax!'

Anacrites could not bring himself to trust me; sensible lad. Nor, needless to say, did I trust him.

Tonight when he got up to leave I unravelled my crumpled toga and tagged along. We went out very quietly, leaving Momus behind, fast asleep.

VII

A warm May night in Rome. We paused on the doorstep, and sniffed the air. A faint spattering of tiny stars hung above the twin peaks of the Capitol. An aroma of hot forcemeat sausage made me suddenly ravenous. Music sounded in the far distance, while the night was alive with the laughter of men who had nothing to regret.

Anacrites and I set off down the Vicus Longus briskly, to deter unwelcome night trade. We passed the Forum on our right and entered the Palatine complex via the Clivus Victoriae. Above us the official suites looked cheerfully lit, though if the Emperor or his sons had been entertaining their banquets had already broken up; our painful new dynasty kept its state in respectable style.

At the Cryptoporticus, Nero's grand galleried entrance, the Praetorians let us through with a nod. We went up. The first people we encountered, and the last I wanted to see, were the Senator Camillus Verus and his daughter Helena.

I swallowed, with one cheek tightening; Anacrites smiled understandingly (rot him!) and made a swift exit.

The Senator had a fluffed-up, formal, newly laundered look. I winked at his daughter affectionately, even in front of him; she gave me a faint, rather troubled smile. Strong looks and a strong character: a girl you could take anywhere – so long as the people who lived there did not mind being told frankly what was wrong with their lives. Helena was austerely swathed in grey, her feet kicking at the heavy, flounced hem of a woman who had been married, her dark head topped by a pointed plain gold diadem. The scroll which Camillus was carrying said they had been here to petition the Emperor, and I could guess their plea: Camillus Verus was a stalwart supporter of Vespasian; he had had a brother who had not been. The brother conspired against the new Flavian dynasty; was exposed, killed, and left to lie where he fell. I had been wondering how long it would take for the Senator to decide his brother's soul was his responsibility. Now I knew: eleven days. He had come to ask Vespasian for the warehouse corpse.

'Here's Falco!' I heard Helena say, chivvying her father. 'He'll find out for us – '

The Senator's wife was a supportive woman but I could see

why it was his daughter he brought today. Beneath her quiet public manner Helena Justina always meant business. Luckily she was still preoccupied after their mission in the throne room and barely reacted to meeting me. Her father explained their presence; he told me the Emperor was being difficult (not surprisingly); then Helena waded in, wanting me to investigate.

'That rather cuts across me working for the Palace – '

'When did that stop you?' Camillus himself assaulted me cheerfully; I grinned, but let their proffered commission drop.

'Sir, if your brother has been bundled into oblivion by a gang of off-duty Praetorians will it really make you feel better if you know?' Helena fell ominously silent. It boded ill for somebody; I guessed who. I tried not to remember the sordid details of her uncle's end, in case she read my face.

I gestured in the direction Anacrites had taken, implying urgent business elsewhere. Camillus asked me to remain with Helena while he organised their transport. He rushed away.

We two stood there, in one of those Palace corridors that was so wide it was almost a room in itself, while occasional officials passed to and fro. I had no intention of ending our tender relationship beneath the tawdry glitter of a Neronian reception hall, so I looked tough and said nothing.

'You know!' Helena accused me levelly, while she was still watching her father out of earshot.

'If I do, I'm not allowed to say.'

She glanced at me with a look that would wither the spines on a porcupine.

While the subject died quietly between us I enjoyed myself surveying her. The cumbersome folds of her matronly stole only emphasised the warm curves they were meant to disguise, and which I had found myself possessing so unexpectedly two weeks before. Her presence tonight had enveloped me with the familiar sense that we both knew each other better than we would ever know anyone else (and yet neither of us had discovered the half of it . . .). 'This is how I like you,' I teased. 'All big brown eyes and blazing indignation!'

'Spare me the disreputable dialogue! I imagined,' her ladyship informed me in a taut voice, 'I might have seen you before this.'

She had on her sweet look of wariness in public places, which always made me step closer protectively. With one finger I stroked very gently from the soft hollow of her temple to the fine contour of her jaw. She allowed it with a stubbornness that implied complete indifference, but her cheek whitened beneath my touch. 'I was thinking of you, Helena.'

'Thinking of dropping me?' It had taken me ten days to make up my mind not to see her again – and ten seconds to decide not to leave. 'Oh I know!' she continued angrily. 'This is May. That was April. I was the girl in *last* month's adventure! All you wanted – '

'You know damn well what I wanted!' I cut in. 'It's another thing I am not supposed to tell you,' I said more quietly. 'But believe me, lady, I thought the world of you.'

'And now you've forgotten,' Helena argued bitterly. 'Or at least, you want *me* to forget – '

Just as I was about to demonstrate how much I remembered and how little I intended either of us to forget, the brisk figure of her illustrious father hove into view again.

'I'll come and see you,' I promised Helena in an undertone. 'There are things I need to talk about - '

'Oh there are some things you *can* say to us?' She deliberately let her father overhear. Camillus must have seen we were quarrelling, a fact he treated with a nervous diffidence which belied his true character. When occasion demanded he was forceful enough.

Before Helena could forestall me I told him, 'Your brother's soul was taken care of with the necessary reverence. If the underworld really exists, he is lounging on the grass in Hades, throwing sticks for Cerberus. Don't ask how I know.'

He accepted it more readily than Helena did. I parted from them tersely, making it plain I had to work.

I rejoined Anacrites, to wait outside the Emperor's room with that tension no one quite loses when visiting a highly important man; being the bugs in favour can easily change. Anacrites groomed a fingernail between his teeth. I felt dismal. Vespasian liked me. He usually showed it by confronting me with impossible tasks for which I earned hardly any cash.

We were called in. Court chamberlains avoided us as if we carried the sores of an Eastern disease.

Vespasian was not one of your spindly, stringy-necked aristocrats, but a burly ex-general. His lavish purple tunic sat on him as casually as brown country frieze. He had a reputation for struggling to power on mortgages and credit, but he loved showing off as Emperor, throwing himself into the work with a grasp no Caesar since Augustus had shown.

'Camillus Verus has been here!' he exclaimed at me. 'And that daughter of his!' The Emperor sounded snappy; he knew my involvement with the lady, and disapproved. 'I said I had nothing to tell them.'

'So did I!' I assured him, ruefully.

He glared at me, as if our predicament was my fault, then settled down. 'What's to report?'

I left Anacrites the subtle pleasure of fibbing to the lord of the world. 'Making progress, sir!' He sounded so efficient my stomach rebelled.

'Found any evidence yet?' crackled Vespasian.

'A denunciation of Pertinax Marcellus by his ex-wife – '

I was furious to see my private information about Helena being paraded, but the Emperor leapt in first: 'Leave the Camillus girl out of it!' (I had not told Anacrites Vespasian and Helena's father were on such friendly terms; he had not asked.)

'Very good, sir.' The spy adjusted his tone. 'After Nero, new Emperors rattled out like barroom dice; I imagine these misguided souls underestimated your staying power – '

'They want a snob with fancy ancestors!' Vespasian scoffed caustically. He was famous for his down-to-earth attitude.

'And a few touches of madness,' I murmured, 'to increase the Senate's confidence!' Vespasian pressed his mouth together. Like most people, he thought my republican passions indicated a cracked brain. A difficult moment prickled us all.

Eventually the Emperor remarked, 'What I will not excuse, is the fact that these traitors tried to seduce my younger son!' It was hard to credit serious contenders with trying to make young Domitian Caesar a puppet emperor; to Domitian, however, who had a popular and virile elder brother, usurping the natural order always seemed a brilliant idea. He was twenty; there were decades of disruption in him yet.

Anacrites and I stared down at the floor. Superior workmanship and oozing with good taste: Alexandrian mosaic – a big, bold, serpentine pattern in black and cream.

'You cannot blame me for defending my own!' the fond father insisted. We shook our heads sombrely. He knew we both thought Domitian Caesar was a toad. The old man restrained himself. Neither Vespasian nor his first son Titus ever criticised Domitian in public with so much as a sour look (though it's my belief they roughed him up fairly frankly behind closed doors).

The fact that Atius Pertinax had been in league with the Emperor's precious son was why Anacrites was tweaking over his papers with silver tongs. For one thing, if we found any evidence against his boy, Vespasian wanted it destroyed.

'So!' he exclaimed, growing bored with speculating. 'The plot's dead: forget it.' The tone of the briefing changed. 'Rome is stuck with me! My predecessor resigned with good grace – '

That was one view of it. The last Emperor Vitellius had been murdered by the Forum mob, his legions surrendered, his son was a babe in arms, and his daughter was swiftly married off by Vespasian with an enormous dowry that would tie her husband up for years, gratefully counting it.

Vespasian sucked his teeth in an angry mood. 'This fiasco has left me with four empty seats in the Senate. The rules are clear: senators must reside in Rome! Faustus Ferentinus has sailed away to drink julep with some ancient aunt in Lycia. I've sent him permission, in deference to the aunt – ' Never imagine that his respect for elderly ladies meant Vespasian was soft; beneath that approachable exterior, a powerful will grumbled dangerously.

'Three other clowns are absenting themselves in the country; Gordianus and his brother Longinus have jumped into distant seaside priesthoods and Aufidius Crispus is sunning himself in the Bay of Neapolis on a yacht. If anyone wishes to greet my accession by retiring into private life,' Vespasian announced, 'I shall not object. But senators *must* account for themselves! Curtius Longinus has been recalled to Rome to give me an explanation, then I suppose I'll be obliged to grant him *a favour he cannot forget* – ' This seemed to be a secret Palace codeword that had never been explained to me. 'He's lodging with the priests of the Little Temple of Hercules Gaditanus overnight and being interviewed tomorrow. Anacrites, I want you there – '

What I hated most about working here was finding myself excluded from whatever was really going on. Scowling, I scuffed my boot heel on the fine Alexandrian floor; then I decided to make my presence felt. 'We may have a problem, sir.'

I mentioned to the Emperor how I had been attacked in the warehouse, how I had tailed Barnabas, and that I thought this link with the Pertinax household could be significant.

The Chief Spy shifted. 'You never mentioned this, Falco!'

'Sorry; slipped my mind.'

I enjoyed watching Anacrites torn between his irritation at me taking the initiative, and wanted to appear the kind of spy who was bound to have found out anyway. 'Just some crack-brained freedman thinking he owes his dead patron a gesture,' was his opinion, dismissing it.

'Could be,' I agreed. 'But I'd like to know whether anything in the Pertinax documentation has pointed to a gambit involving corn chandlery.'

'No,' Anacrites said crisply. 'And I won't commit expensive Palace resources on the word of a Transtiberina barmaid!'

'You have your methods, I'll have mine.'

'Which are?'

'Knowing that riverbank watering holes and Transtiberina wineshops can be the first places to catch the news!'

'Both of your methods are valid,' Vespasian broke in. 'That's why I'm employing you both!'

During our quarrel, the Emperor's brown eyes had grown very still. Anacrites looked embarrassed, but I was angry. Here we stood, discussing treason like trade figures from Cilicia or the price of Celtic beer, but Vespasian knew what I thought. He knew why. Six hours after I fumbled with that sagging corpse, I still had the stench of the dead man's body fat curdling my lungs. My hands seemed to reek still from handling his finger rings. His cadaverous face swam into my memory whenever I let myself relax. Today I had done the Empire no small favour, yet apparently I was only fit for disposals – work that was too sticky for manicured hands.

'If you're spending your time in wineshops, watch your liver!' warned Vespasian with his sardonic grin.

'No point,' I snapped. 'I mean, sir, there's no point me risking my health and innocence in cutthroat bars, collecting information no one will ever act upon!'

'*What* innocence? Patience, Falco. I'm reconciling the senate as my priority – and you're no diplomat!' I glared, but held my peace. Vespasian relaxed slightly. 'Can we lay hands on this fellow Barnabas?'

'I've arranged for him to see me at the Pertinax house, but I'm beginning to suspect he may not come. He's holed up near a tavern called the Setting Sun south of the Via Aurelia – '

A chamberlain broke into the room like a man who has had a good breakfast trotting out to the penny latrines.

'Caesar! The Temple of Hercules Gaditanus is on fire!'

Anacrites began to move; Vespasian stopped him. 'No. You get yourself down to the Transtiberina and apprehend this freedman. Put it to him plainly that the conspiracy has been broken up. Find out whether he knew anything, then let him go if you can – but make sure he grasps that stirring up any more sludge in the duckpond will *not* be well received.' I was supressing a satirical vision of Vespasian as a great frog on a lily pad when he turned to me. 'Falco can go fire watching.'

Arson's a dirty business; it does not require diplomacy.

VIII

I reached the Temple alone. Activity and solitude came like a breath of fresh air.

Whatever the crisis, I had to go alone – and on foot. I wore out my boots, but I was keeping my professional integrity intact.

Every time I paid my shoemender, integrity bothered me less.

The Little Temple of Hercules stood in the Aventine Sector, which was where I lived, so I was able to turn up like any local gawker who had spotted the flames on his way home from a bawdy-house and greeted this spectacle as his second treat of the night. It was a pitiful shrine. It had been poked in between a Syrian bakery and a knife-grinder's lockup booth. There were two worn steps where pigeons stopped to gossip, four front pillars, a warped wooden pediment, and a cranky red roof which bore abundant evidence that it was where the pigeons reassembled when they flew up off the steps.

Temples always seem to be burning down. Their building regulations must omit safety buckets and fire-fighting platforms, as if dedication to the gods brings its own insurance. But evidently the gods get bored guarding altars with unattended perpetual flames.

The fire was well away. There was a lively crowd. I pushed through to the front.

The Aventine vigilantes were leaning in neighbouring porticos while the blaze lit their faces with lurid red. They were a scarred-looking crew, though most had affectionate mothers and one or two could even tell you who their fathers were. Among them my old friend Petronius Longus, a broad, calm, square-browed officer with a baton through his belt, stood thoughtfully cradling his chin. He looked like a man you could drag into a corner for a natter about women, life, and where to buy a hock of Spanish ham. He was captain of the watch, but we never let that interfere with being friends.

I squeezed in alongside. The heat felt strong enough to melt the marrow in our bones. We scanned the crowd in case there was a mad-eyed arsonist still lurking at the scene.

'Didius Falco,' Petronius murmured, 'always first back into barracks, hogging the fire!' We had both done army service in the bitter north: five years in the Second Augustan Legion in Britain. We had spent half our time on the frontier, and the rest on forced marches or camped out in the field. When we came home we had both sworn we would never feel warm again. Petronius married; he decided it helped. Various eager young ladies had tried to assist me the same way, but I had fended them off.

'Been visiting your girlfriend?'

'Which?' I grinned. I knew which. For at least the past fortnight there had only been one. I set aside my vivid recollection of offending her this evening. 'What highly avoidable accident happened here, Petro?'

'Usual fiasco. Temple acolytes off playing dice in a bar down the street; an incense burner left smouldering . . . '

'Casualties?'

'Doubt it; the doors are locked – ' Petronius Longus glanced at me, saw from my face there was a reason for the question, then turned back to the temple with a heavy groan.

We were helpless. Even if his men burst those studded double doors with a battering ram, the interior would explode into a fireball. Flames were already flickering high on the roof. Black smoke with a worrying smell was gusting halfway to the river. Out here in the alley the heat was making our faces shine like glass. No one could survive inside.

The doors were still standing, and still locked, when the rooftimbers caved in.

Someone finally rooted out the fire brigade from a chop-house to douse the shell of the building with buckets. They had to find a working fountain first, and it was the usual ham-fisted effort when they did. Petronius had dispersed most of the crowd, though a few characters with fierce wives waiting at home clung on here for the peace. We hooked grappling irons onto one of the doors and dragged its scorched timbers outwards with an ear-splitting screech; a solidified torso, presumably human, lay huddled just inside. A professional priest who had just arrived told us the molten amulet stuck to the breastbone looked not unlike one Curtius Longinus, the conspirator recalled by Vespasian, always wore.

Longinus had been his house guest. The priest had dined with the man that evening; he turned away looking sick.

Petronius Longus yanked a leather curtain over the charred nugget of flesh. I let him start the questioning while I went on looking round. 'Do you normally lock the doors at night?' he challenged, coughing in the smoke.

'Why should we lock up?' The priest of Hercules had a healthy black beard; he was probably ten years older than us but looked hard as the Citadel Wall. You would only play handball with this stalwart cove if he picked you to play in his own team. 'We're not the Temple of Jupiter, crammed with captured treasure, or the Temple of Saturn

Treasury. Some shrines have to be shut up at dusk to stop vagrants creeping in, but, watch captain, not ours!'

I could see why. Apart from the fact gruff old Hercules Gaditanus probably liked vagrants, there was nowhere to squat in comfort and nothing to steal. It was just a brick-built closet no bigger than a storeroom on a farm.

The terracotta statue of the god which had been laid low by a ton of falling roof tiles had a half-finished air that went with the rough-and-ready place. Even his priest had the famished look of a man who worked in a poor district, dealing all day with brain-battered boxers. Beneath the beard, his oriental face was handsome; he had great sad eyes, as if he knew his god was popular but not taken seriously.

'Who was in charge?' Petronius continued wearily, still upset by the death. 'Did you know this man was here?'

'I was in charge,' stated the priest. 'Curtius Longinus had an interview tomorrow with the Emperor. He was praying in the Temple to compose himself – '

'Interview? What about?'

'Ask the Emperor!' snorted the priest.

'Who keeps the Temple key?' I interrupted, inspecting what was left of the sanctuary.

'We leave it on a wall hook just inside.'

'Not any more!' Petronius corrected angrily.

The hook was there: empty. I stepped over to see.

The priest gazed helplessly at the smoking shards of Hercules' stricken house. Sparks on the inner walls still raced up cracks in the lining cement. He did not want to distress himself surveying the damage while Petro and I were watching him.

'I must write to his brother . . . '

'Don't do that!' I ordered him coldly. 'The Emperor will inform Curtius Gordianus himself.'

The priest began moving off so I prepared to follow. I nodded to Petro, who jerked his head back, annoyed at me for rushing away. I thumped his arm, then clambered out after the black-bearded fellow.

Emerging, we passed an excitable figure who worked for Anacrites; he was so busy making his own presence felt he missed us going by. When I glanced behind he was harassing Petro. Petronius Longus planted his large feet apart and just listened with the faraway look of a tired man who badly needs a drink, planning in advance whether to have half an amphora of his usual crimson rot-gut and a terrible night's sleep, or to broach the delightful Setinum he has been nursing along at the back of a shelf . . . The spy was getting nowhere. Peaceful insolence is a speciality of the Aventine watch.

As the priest set off homewards I skipped along too.

'Did Curtius Longinus arrive back in Rome tonight?' He nodded in silence. Shock had settled on him now; he did not want to talk. His mind was preoccupied but his legs walked automatically with long muscular strides; it took energy to keep up without losing my dignity. 'So he had no chance to meet anyone?' He shook his head.

I waited. He had second thoughts. 'He was called out from dinner to speak to somebody he knew.'

'See who it was?'

'No. He was only away for a moment. I suppose,' decided the priest, who was so pleased with his powers of deduction that he managed to slow down, 'Longinus put off their meeting until later tonight!'

'Here at your Temple! Seems likely. How do you know the mystery person was a man?'

'My servant told Curtius Longinus his visitor's name.'

I breathed a gentle prayer of thanks to Hercules. 'Help yourself and your Temple; tell me . . . '

We stopped on a corner by a fountain that glugged from the private orifices of a melancholy river god.

'How would it help?' fretted the priest.

'When our gracious new Emperor plans his civic rebuilding programme. Rededicating temples gives an Emperor a good name!'

'I understood that the Treasury was struggling for cash – '

'Not for long. Vespasian's father was a tax collector; he has extortion in the blood.'

He had taken out his doorkey. 'You seem fairly free with the Emperor's unearned income!' he commented. 'Who are you?'

'The name's Didius Falco; I act for the Palace – '

'Ho!' He perked up to insult me. 'Why's an intelligent, good-natured son of Rome involved in such shady work?'

'That's what I ask myself! So tell me,' I nudged him again, 'who was this man Longinus knew?'

'Someone called Barnabas,' said the priest.

IX

It was dark now, but since I knew he worked late I wore out more boot leather traipsing back to see Vespasian again.

I waited while he shooed out the flyswatters and wine-fixers who never expect to remain in an audience while anything interesting occurs. Then I waited again, while the high-handed secretarial types got their marching orders too.

Once alone, we both relaxed. I stretched out on an imperial reading couch and gazed at the vaulted ceiling twenty feet above. This room was faced with dark green Brescia panels, divided by pilasters in creamy travertine. The wall sconces were gilt; all shaped like clams; all lit. I was brought up in dark houses where the rafters grazed my curls; looming spaces in elegant colour schemes have made me feel uneasy ever since. I lay on the couch as if I was nervous my body would leave an unpleasant mark on its silk.

The Emperor leaned on one great elbow, scrunching apples. His square, tanned face had that crag of a nose and jolly uptilted chin you see on the coins, with the laughter lines around his eyes. What the average denarius fails to reveal is that Vespasian Augustus had discovered one good source of light relief in me.

'Well, Falco?' He frowned at his fruit. It looked a four-cornered, floury job probably from his own Sabine estate; he never paid for anything he could grow himself.

'Caesar, I'd hate the bog savages to get a good name, but for a really sweet apple Britain beats the world!'

Vespasian had a military career in Britain, which had taken a distinctly glorious turn. My British career was twenty years later, and not glorious at all. Someone like Anacrites was bound to have told him that.

For a moment the old man paused, as if my mentioning the small, crisp russets of Britain that explode on the tongue with such unexpected sweetness had struck old chords. If I had not hated Britain so badly, I might have felt a homesick pang myself.

'What happened at the Temple?'

'Bad news I'm afraid, sir. Curtius Longinus is dead. Luckily for him, cremation is the fashion for Roman funerals nowadays.' The Emperor groaned and pounded his reading couch with a great fist.

'Sir, there's a contract bonus for naming your opponents. Does that include finding the maniac who's frittering them?'

'No,' he said. He knew that was a serious blow to me.

'All the Empire admires Caesar's graciousness!'

'Don't be sarcastic,' he growled menacingly.

In some ways we two were ill-assorted. Vespasian Caesar was an up-country senator from a down-market family, but a traditional aristocrat. I was an outspoken, introverted rough-neck with an Aventine accent and no sense of respect. The fact we could work together successfully was a typical Roman paradox.

While he absorbed my news with an angry frown I took advantage of the lull to report the full story.

'Sir, the missing freedman I told you about had heard Longinus was in Rome. I'm certain they met. It looks as if the freedman caused the fire. Did Anacrites manage to track him down in the Transtiberina?'

'No. The freedman had packed his bags and broken camp. When he lit this fire he must have already been prepared to do a flit. That's clear premeditation. What's he playing at, Falco?'

'Either a crazy campaign of vengeance for his patron's death in jail – or some more dangerous development.'

'You mean, either Barnabas blamed Longinus for having Pertinax killed – or Longinus had to be silenced before he saw me tomorrow because of something he might say? *Did* Curtius Longinus cause the death of Pertinax?'

'No, sir. The man I dropped in the Great Sewer for you this morning probably arranged that.'

'So what could Longinus have had to tell me?'

'I don't know. Perhaps his brother can enlighten us.'

The big man brooded glumly. 'Falco, why do I gain the impression that the moment we bury one conspiracy, a new one crawls to light?'

'I suspect because one has.'

'I'm not the type to waste my time running in fear of assassins.'

'No, sir.'

He grunted. 'I need you for something, Falco,' he offered. 'This reflects very badly on my administration – I want people to know I send for them in good faith! It's unsafe to invite the other Curtius brother to Rome, but someone had better get down there fast to warn him. There's not much involved. Carry him my condolences. Remember he is a senator; they are an old family, of good standing. Just tell him what happened, put him on his guard, then ask him to write to me – '

'A messenger boy! Caesar, *you* asked me to work here! Yet I have to squeeze out commissions like drips from a dry cow – ' The look on his face stopped me. 'What about warning the yachtsman Crispus in Neapolis?'

'Fancy bearding him on his boat?'

'Not much; I get seasick, and I can't swim. But I want real work to wrestle with.'

'Sorry,' he shrugged, crabbily offhand. 'Anacrites is looking forward to the seaside breezes serving that writ.'

'So *Anacrites* gets to gambol in the playgrounds of the rich, while *I* do three hundred miles on the back of a frisky mule then take a sock on the jaw when I tell Gordianus how he was bereaved? Caesar, am I at least empowered to negotiate for his return? What you call offering *"a favour he cannot forget"*? What if he asks me about it? What if he tells me what he wants?'

'He won't, Falco – well if he does, use your initiative.'

I laughed. 'What you mean, sir, is that I have no meaningful authority; if I do win him over some snooty court chamberlain may thank me, but if anything goes wrong I am all on my own!'

Vespasian nodded drily. 'That is called diplomacy!'

'I charge extra for diplomacy.'

'We can discuss that if your attempt works! The challenge,' he explained more quietly, 'is to find out from Curtius Gordianus why his brother Longinus has got himself killed.'

Into his last apple now, he queried, 'Are you free to leave Rome at once? How are you coping with the Pertinax estate?'

'Quite a good house clearance! The luxury stuff has all been dispersed; we're doing table sales in flea markets now: job lots of jugs with loose handles and dented custard pans. Even the best homes turn up basketfuls of blunt old knives with none that match – ' I stopped, because from what I had heard this sounded like the kitchen sideboards in Vespasian's family house before he became Emperor.

'Getting good prices?' he asked eagerly; I grinned at him. The Imperial skinflint's idea of a good price was pretty steep.

'You won't be disappointed, sir. I'm using an auctioneer called Geminus. He treats me like a son.'

'Anacrites thinks you are!' Vespasian tossed across. It startled me that Anacrites was so sly. My father left home with a red-headed scarfmaker when I was seven years old. I had never forgiven him and my mother would be mortally insulted if she thought I dealt with him nowadays. If Geminus *was* my father, I didn't want to know.

'Anacrites,' I told Vespasian shortly, 'lives in his own romantic world!'

'Hazard of his job. What do you think of Momus?'

'Not much.'

Vespasian grumbled that I never liked anyone; I agreed. 'Pity about Longinus,' he mused on the verge of concluding our interview. I knew what he meant; any Emperor can execute people who don't agree with him, but leaving them free to attack him again takes style.

'You do realise,' I complained, 'the brother Gordianus will think you ordered today's inferno? When I turn up with my happy smile he'll suppose I'm your private exterminator – or am I?' I demanded suspiciously.

'If I wanted a tame assassin,' Vespasian answered, letting me insult him as if he was pleased by the novelty, 'I'd use someone who makes fewer moral judgements – '

I thanked him for the compliment, though he had not intended it, then I left the Palace cursing the chance of a contract bonus which I had lost through the priest Longinus finding himself a fiery end. To qualify for the middle rank, I needed four hundred thousand sesterces invested in Italian land. Vespasian paid my out-of-pocket expenses, plus a meagre daily rate. Unless I could earn some extra, this would bring in a bare nine hundred a year. It cost me at least a thousand just to live.

X

Despite the dangers of the streets at night, I hoofed it back to the Pertinax house. I managed to reach the Quirinal with nothing worse than a bruised arm after a drunk with no sense of direction crashed straight into me. His sense of direction was better than it looked; as we pirouetted madly he relieved me of my purse: the one I carry full of pebbles for footpads like him.

I quickened my step for several streets, in case he rushed after me to complain.

I arrived at the house without further mishap.

Because of the curfew restrictions in Rome we could only bring wheeled vehicles onto the Quirinal after dark; being an executor was ghostly work. Four carts were standing outside now while the auctioneer's men loaded them with satinwood couches and enamelled Egyptian sideboards, wedging in lamps to stabilise the loads. Indoors I helped the porters by putting my shoulder to a screwdown clothes press they were manhandling through the hall.

'Falco!'

The foreman Gornia wanted me to see something. Our footsteps echoed as we turned down an empty red corridor to a ground-floor bedroom I had not been in before. We stepped through a panelled door, set between two basalt portrait busts.

'Oh *very* nice!'

A lady's room: sumptuously quiet. Five times as big as any room I had ever lived in, and half as high again. The dado was painted to imitate dove-grey marble, with upper wall panels in celestial blue, outlined with fine pastel ribboning and finished with central medallions. The floor mosaic had intricate patterns in shades of grey, planned for the room of course, with a designated space for the bed; the ceiling had been lowered there, creating a cosy niche for sleeping in.

The bed had gone. Only one item remained. Gornia pointed to a small chest carved in oriental wood, which stood off the ground on four round painted feet.

'Indian import? Is there a key?' Gornia handed me a hunk of cold brass, with an uneasy look as if he feared we were about to find a mummified baby. I blew at the dust and opened up.

Nothing valuable. Old letters, and some casual strings of amber beads, all uneven shapes and mismatched colours, like something a girl full of hope might keep in case she ever had a child to play with them. The top document looked tasty: *Turbot with Caraway Sauce.*

'Nothing for Anacrites. Keep the box; I'll see to it – ' Gornia thanked me, and two porters removed the chest.

I stayed behind alone, sucking my lower lip. I had realised who lived here once. Helena Justina: the conspirator's ex-wife.

I liked this room. Well; I liked her. I liked her so much I had been trying to convince myself I had better not see her again.

Now some old box that once belonged to her had set my heart thumping like a lovelorn twelve-year-old.

All that remained here was a massive chandelier on a great gilt boss. A draught among its expensive tapers created leaping shadows which led me through a folding door into a private courtyard garden – a fig tree and rosemary. Helena would have enjoyed sitting there, drinking her warm tisane in the morning or writing letters in the afternoon.

I came back and just stood, imagining how this beautiful room must once have been, littered with the paraphernalia of her life: a high bed and the inevitable wicker chairs and footstools; display cabinets and shelves; perfume jars and oil flasks; silver cosmetic casques; sandal-wood boxes for jewellery and scarves; mirrors and combs; coffers for clothes. Waiting maids moving to and fro. A harpist to entertain her when she felt sad. (Plenty of time for that: four miserable years of it.)

Pertinax had had his bedroom in a separate wing. That is how the rich live. When Pertinax had wanted his noble young wife to grant his matrimonial privileges, a slave summoned her down two chilly corridors. Perhaps sometimes she had gone to him of her own accord, but I doubted that. Nor would he ever have bothered to surprise her here. Helena Justina had divorced Pertinax for neglecting her. I hated him for it. He wallowed in luxury, yet his sense of values was grotesque.

I strolled back to the atrium with a pain in my gullet, and happened upon Geminus.

'You look seedy!'

'Picking up tips on decor.'

'Get yourself a proper job and earn some decent cash!'

We had cleared out the statues, but while we were gossiping a new one turned up. Geminus valued the artwork privately then openly leered at the wench. She was superbly carved, then cast in bronze, a joy to inspect: Helena Justina herself.

I whistled softly. It was a clever work of art. I wondered how it was possible to capture in metal that sense of angry outrage always waiting to break out, and the hint of a smile at the corner of her mouth . . . I flicked off a huddle of woodlice from the angle of her elbow, then patted her neat bronze behind.

Geminus was the auctioneer Anacrites had libelled as the parent who inflicted me on the world. I could see why people might think so. (Just as, looking at my family, I could see why my father had chosen to escape.) He was a stocky, secretive, moody man, about sixty years old, with rampant grey hair, all curls. He was good-looking (though less good-looking than he thought). His profile swooped in one strong line without a ledge between the eyes – a real Etruscan nose. He had a nose for a scandal and an eye for a woman that had made him a legend even in the Saepta Julia where the antique dealers congregate. If one of my clients had an heirloom to sell, I pushed it his way (if the client was a woman, and I happened to be busy, I pushed her too).

We stood playing at art critics. Helena's statue was unsigned but had been made by a good Greek sculptor, from life. It was magnificent, with gilding on the headdress and tinted eyes. It showed Helena at about eighteen years old, with her hair folded up in the old-fashioned style. She was formally robed – in a way which cleverly hinted how she looked underneath.

'Very nice,' commented Geminus. 'A very nice piece!'

'Where had they hidden this beauty?' I asked the porters.

'Shoved in a cubbyhole, next to the kitchen latrine.'

I could cope with that. I did not fancy Pertinax brooding over her in his private suite. (All the fool had kept in his bedroom and study were silver statuettes of his racehorses and paintings of his ships.)

Geminus and I admired her stately workmanship. He must have noticed my face.

'Castor and Pollux! You chasing her, Marcus?'

'No,' I said.

'Liar!' he retorted.

'True.'

In fact, when her ladyship had wanted a closer acquaintance she chased me. But that was no business of his.

Women change a lot between eighteen and twenty-three. It was painful to see her untouched by her trials with Pertinax, and to wish I had known her first. Something in her expression, even at that age, made me uneasily aware I had been flirting too busily elsewhere today – and all my life.

'Too submissive. He's missed her,' I murmured. 'In real life the lady glares out as though she'd bite your nose off if you stepped too close – '

Inspecting my snout for damage, Geminus reached to give it a possessive tweak; my arm jerked up to fend him off. 'So how close do you generally step?'

'Met her. Last year in Britain. She hired me as her bodyguard back to Rome – all perfectly straight and free from scandal, see – '

'You losing your touch?' he mocked. 'Not many noble young ladies could ride fourteen hundred miles with a likely lad and not allow themselves some consolation for the rigours of the road!' He peered at her. I felt a moment of uncertainty, as if two people I cared about had just been introduced.

I was still clutching her recipe.

'What's that?'

'How to cook Turbot in Caraway. No doubt her husband's favourite midday snack – ' I sighed grimly. 'You know what they say: for the price of three horses you may buy a decent cook, and with three cooks you can possibly bid for a turbot – I don't even own a horse!'

He eyed me evilly. 'Want her, Marcus?'

'Nowhere to keep her.'

'That statue?' he asked, with a broad grin.

'Oh the statue!' I answered, smiling sadly too.

We decided it would be highly improper to sell a noblewoman's portrait in the public marketplace. Vespasian would agree; he would make her family buy it back at some exorbitant price. Geminus disapproved of emperors as much as I did, so we omitted Helena Justina from the Imperial inventory.

I sent the statue to her father. I wrapped it myself for transit, in a costly Egyptian carpet which had not been inventoried either. (The auctioneer had tagged it for himself.)

The brain can play strange tricks, late at night in an unfurnished house.

Gornia and his porters had already departed; Geminus went ahead of me. I stepped into a reception room to collect my crumpled toga; when I came out I was rubbing my eyes from weariness. The lamplight was dim, but I half noticed someone in the atrium – one of the slaves, presumably.

He was looking at the statue.

In the moment when I was turning to close the door of the room behind me, he disappeared. He was a light-haired, slender man of about my own age, with sharp features that reminded me of someone I had once met . . . *Impossible*. For one chilling moment I thought I had glimpsed the ghost of Atius Pertinax.

I must have been brooding too much lately; I had a fertile imagination and was overtired. Thinking about dead men all day had turned my brain. I did not believe that dispossessed spirits ever returned resentfully to stalk their silent homes.

I strode to the atrium. I opened doors but failed to find anyone. I returned to the bronze figure and stared at her boldly myself. Only her face showed, above the hem of the carpet I had earlier furled round her.

'So it's you, me and him; sweetheart. He's a ghost, you're a statue, and I'm probably a lunatic . . . '

The grave image of the young Helena looked back at me with bright, painted eyes and the suggestion of a smile that was ethereal, sweet and true.

'You're all woman, princess!' I told her, giving her carpet-wrapped posterior another playful spank. 'Thoroughly unreliable!'

The ghost had melted into some marble panelwork; the statue looked superior. The lunatic shivered, then hurried out after Geminus on his way home.

XI

It's my opinion Rome's best houses are not the fine shuttered mansions on Pincian Hill, but the character dwellings that line the Tiber's bank in my own sector, with their quiet steps down to the river and wonderful views. Geminus lived there. He had money and taste and had been born in the Aventine; he would.

To make me feel better he always said they flooded. Well; he could field enough slaves to sweep the Tiber out again. And if an auctioneer finds his furniture wet, he can easily get more.

He was travelling back tonight in his normal quiet style – a lordly litter with six massive bearers, a gaudy troop of torchmen and his two private bodyguards; I hitched a lift. On the way he whistled through his teeth in the annoying way he had, while I hardly spoke. When he dropped me off two dirt tracks from home, he gave me a dark stare.

'Stick with your roots, Marcus; keep the nobility for fleecing, not flirting!' I was in no mood to argue. Besides, the man was right. 'Talk about it?'

'No.'

'You want to find yourself – '

'Please don't tell me what I want!' I sneered unpleasantly. I climbed out.

Geminus leaned after me to ask, 'Would money help?'

'No.'

'You mean, not from me – '

'Not from anyone.' I stood stubbornly in the street while his litter moved off.

'I never understand you!' he grumbled back at me.

'Good!' I said.

Reaching my apartment block, I heard the sinister cackle of Smaractus my landlord being entertained with raw wine and ribaldry by Lenia. I was exhausted. The sixth floor seemed a mile away. I had intended to bunk down at laundry level in some hamper of grubby togas, but the self-assurance of Smaractus had fired me with so much bad temper I went surging upstairs without a second thought.

A shutter flew open below me. 'Falco?' I could not face another quarrel about my unpaid rent, so I leapt to the next landing and kept going.

Six flights later I had just about calmed down.

As I opened my door in the dark I heard one or two astute roaches rustle off. I lit a rush and lunged about, batting hopefully at the rest. Then I squatted on a bench, resting my tired eyes from the glitter of rich men's marble as I gazed at the grey slatted walls of home.

I suppressed a curse, then unsuppressed it and let rip. My gecko shuffled on the ceiling, looking shocked. Halfway through the oratory I noticed an iron skillet sitting on my cooking bench; it was half-full of yesterday's veal cutlet stew. When I went over to peer under the upturned dish which I was using as a lid, the stew looked so clammy I could not face eating it.

A document had been left for me on the table: good quality papyrus and Vespasian's seal. I ignored that too.

Thinking of my talk with Geminus, the only statue I had room for was one of those three-inch clay miniatures people leave at shrines. There was nowhere for a fully-grown wench who needed space to keep her dresses and somewhere to sulk in private when she found herself offended with me.

Fighting my weariness, I stumbled out onto the balcony and watered my plants. It could be windy up here, yet my hanks of dusty ivy and pots of blue scillas flourished better than I did. My youngest sister Maia, who looked after them when I was away, said that this gardening was meant to impress women. Our Maia was a shrewd little bun, but wrong about that; if a woman was prepared to climb six flights of stairs to see me, she knew in advance what kind of cheapjack hero she was climbing those stairs for.

I breathed the night air slowly, letting myself remember the last young lady who visited my eyrie, then left with a flower in her shoulder brooch.

I was missing her badly. No one else seemed worth bothering with. I needed to talk to her. Every day without Helena seemed somehow unfinished. I could manage the hurly-burly, but the evening stillness reminded me what I had lost.

I fell indoors, too tired to lift my feet. I felt drained, yet Vespasian's letter got the better of me now. As I wrenched at the wax I was automatically assessing today's events.

A conspirator in a dead plot had died unnecessarily; a freedman who ought not to be important suddenly was. This idiot Barnabas provided an irresistible challenge. Smiling, I unrolled the document.

a) Under the authority of Vespasian Augustus; M. Didius Falco to escort the funeral ashes of A. Curtius Longinus, senator (deceased), to his brother A. Curtius Gordianus (priest), believed to be at Rhegium. Departure; immediate.

b) Travel documents herewith.

It sounded crisp. Needless to say, the ashes were missing; I would have to endorse someone's docket to get those released. For *Rhegium* read *Croton*. (Palace scribes are never accurate: they don't have to make the forty-mile detour over mountain roads when they get it wrong.) As usual, they had forgotten to enclose my travel pass, and there was no mention of my fee.

A vigorous snake in the margin in the Emperor's own hand exclaimed:

c) Why am I rebuilding the Temple of Hercules? Can't afford it. Please explain!

I found my inkpot behind half a cabbage and wrote on the back:

Caesar!

a) The priest has been loyal.
b) The Emperor's generosity is well known.
c) The Temple was not very big.

Then I resealed the letter, and readdressed it to go back.

Under the cabbage (which my mother must have left for me) I noticed another important communiqué: from her. She stated darkly,

You need new spoons.

I scratched my head. I could not tell if this was a promise or a threat.

The Palace had had its money's worth; I went to bed. The normal procedure was simple; I stood my favourite winecup on the corner of the blanket box, then peeled off my tunic, rolled under the hairy counterpane and drank my drink in bed. Tonight I just fell down on top and kept all my clothes on. I managed to think about Helena long enough to share all my worries, but just as I reached what might happen after that I could feel myself falling asleep. Had she been there in my arms events would probably have taken the same course . . .

Informing is a drab old business. The pay's filthy, the work's worse, and if you ever find a woman who is worth any trouble you don't have the money and you don't have the time; if you do, the chances are you simply don't have the energy.

I could no longer remember leaving my house that morning; I had come home tonight too exhausted to eat my dinner and too depressed to enjoy a drink. I had passed by my best friend without a chance to gossip; I had forgotten to visit my mother and let Helena guess my ghastly involvement in the disposal of her relative's corpse.

I had shared my lunch with a watchdog, swapped insults with an Emperor, and thought I'd seen the ghost of a murdered man. Now my neck ached; my feet hurt; my chin needed shaving; I was longing for a bath. I deserved an afternoon at the races; I wanted a night on the town. Instead, I had committed myself to travelling three hundred miles to visit a man I was not allowed to interview, who would probably refuse to see me when I arrived.

For a private informer, this was just an average day.

PART TWO
A TOURIST IN CROTON

SOUTHERN ITALY
(Magna Graecia)
Several Days Later

*' . . . Croton, a very ancient city, once the foremost in Italy . . . If you are
a sophisticated type and you can take incessant lying, you are following the
right road to riches. You see, in this city no literary pretensions are honoured,
eloquence has no standing, sobriety and decent behaviour are not praised
and rewarded . . . '*

Petronius, The Satyricon

XII

Vespasian had signed a travel pass for me. I screwed this treasure out of his clerks and picked up a state mule from a stable at the Capena Gate. The ancient watchtower still stands at the start of the Appian Way, though the city has expanded beyond into a quiet suburb, popular with the more discerning type of millionaire. Helena Justina's father lived hereabouts so I delivered her box of recipes and I dare say she would have had me in for a few words of thanks, but she was a sociable lady with a life of her own and the door porter claimed she was not there.

Young Janus and I had had run-ins before. The Camillus family never needed a floor mosaic to say beware of their dog; this two-legged specimen of human mange drove off enquirers before they edged a sandal in the door. He was about sixteen. He had a very long face, which gave plenty of scope for his current flush of acne, with a very short brain cavity on top; the brain inside was an elusive piece of plasma. Talking to him always made me tired.

I refused to believe these were Helena's orders. She was capable of dispatching me on a one-way ferry to Hades, but if she wanted to do it she would tell me herself. Still; it solved one problem. Telling her I was not going to see her again would be difficult if they never let me in.

I asked where she was; sonny didn't know. I informed the porter pleasantly that I knew he must be lying because even when she becomes a batty old harridan with no hair or teeth, Helena Justina will be much too well-organised to sail off in her sedan chair without a word to her staff. Then I left friendly greetings for the senator, left Helena's box, and left Rome.

At first I went south on the Appian Way to avoid the coast, which I hate. At Capua the Via Appia took its route towards Tarentum in the Heel of Italy while I turned west, heading for the Toe. Now I was on the Via Popilia, for Rhegium and Sicily, aiming to strike off it just before the Messana Strait.

I had to cross Latium, Campania and Lucania, and go deep into Bruttium – half the length of Italy; I seemed to be travelling for days. After Capua came Nola, Salernum, Paestum, Velia, Buxentum, then a

51

long hike close against the Tyrrhenian shore until the road to Cosentia in the far south. There the ground climbed abruptly as I peeled off the highroad to cross the peninsula. It was then the mule I had picked up at the last staging post turned tetchy on me, and I saw I had been right to dread a mountain rollicking.

Cosentia: provincial capital of the Bruttii. A hunchbacked collection of single-storey shacks. It was up in the hills, hard to get at, and had not been as important as the Bruttians' second city, Croton, for several hundred years. Still, Cosentia was their capital; odd tribe, the Bruttii.

I stayed a night at Cosentia, though I hardly slept. This was *Magna Graecia*: Greater Greece. Rome had conquered Magna Graecia long ago; in theory. But I rode through its sullen territory with care.

The roads were almost empty now. At Cosentia only one other traveller stayed at the inn – the man I never saw. This fellow had his own pair of horses, which were what I recognised; a big roan that narrowly missed the grade as a flat-racer, and a skewbald pack animal. We had been running parallel from Salernum, if not longer, but I was always up and on the road before he appeared in the morning and by the time he caught up at night I had fallen into bed. If I had known he was still with me at Cosentia, I would have made an effort to stay up and make friends.

I hate the south. All those old-fashioned towns with massive temples to Zeus and Poseidon; all those schools of philosophy that make you feel inferior; all those sombre-faced athletes and the broody sculptors sculpting them. Not to mention their sky-high prices for strangers and their awful roads.

If you believe the *Aeneid*, Rome was founded by a Trojan; as I travelled the south my scalp crawled as if these Greek colonists had me marked as their ancient enemy in a Phrygian cap. People seemed to have nothing to do but lurk in their dusty porches watching strangers down the street. Cosentia was bad enough; Croton, thinking itself more important, was bound to be worse.

Crossing over to Croton involved serious alpine work. The temperature dropped as my road went on rising. Thick forests of chestnut and Turkey oak covered the Sila plains, then beeches and silver fir, while alders and aspens grappled onto the granite crags. Locals called this a good road; it was a wild and winding track. I never travelled after dusk; even in daylight I thought I heard mountain wolves. Once, when I was eating lunch in a sunny clearing full of wild strawberry plants, a viper slipped away behind a rock, eerily emerging from beneath my outstretched boot. I had felt safer swapping insults with the cutthroat Roman call girls at the Circus Maximus.

Snowcaps still lay on the peaks but the naval contractors had started trekking up for seasoned logs, so smoke from their bonfires sharpened the thin air. My nose dribbled as I drew off the path among wayside violets to overtake oxen with long waggons that swayed under the boles of mighty trees. The crumpled plain rose a thousand feet and higher above the sea. In Rome summer was approaching, but here the climate lagged. Everywhere was dripping in the thaw; furious torrents rushed along deep river valleys and icy spring water quenched my thirst.

I forged alone through this rough terrain for a couple of days. Above the Neaethus Valley a spectacular view opened onto the Ionian Sea. I descended among cultivated olives and vines, yet the landscape became scarred with erosions and pimpled with weird cones of clay, stranded there by the summer rush of waterways which had dragged away all the looser topsoil, stripping the dry scenery like a savagely sucked fig. At length my road switchbacked again and I reached Croton, which lurks like a very painful bunion, just underneath the ball of Italy's big toe.

This place Croton had been Hannibal's last refuge in Italy. I reckoned if a heathen like Hannibal passed through here again, Croton would still be prepared to give him a free splash in the municipal baths and honour him into exile with a banquet at the town's expense. But there was no friendly welcome for me.

I rode into Croton with a stream of sweat between my shoulder blades. The landlord at the official *mansio* was a lean laggard with eyes like slits who assumed I had come to check his records for the Treasury auditor; I declared haughtily I had not yet sunk so low. He examined me closely before he condescended to let me book in.

'Staying long?' he whined furtively, as if he hoped not.

'I don't expect so,' I answered, implying with pleasant Roman frankness that I hoped not too. 'I have to find a priest called Curtius Gordianus. Know anything about him?'

'No.'

I was certain he did. In Magna Graecia lying to Roman officials is a way of life.

I was in my own country yet I felt like a foreigner. These dry old southern towns were full of fine dust, ferocious insects, lumbering bylaws, and tight-knit corrupt local families who only honoured the Emperor if it suited their own pockets. The people looked Greek, their gods were Greek, and they spoke Greek dialects. When I strolled out to get my bearings in Croton, I found myself in trouble in the first half-hour.

XIII

A toga would have been out of place in Croton. Only the magistrates at the courthouse even possessed formal clothes. Luckily I never insult a strange city by appearing overdressed. I had an unbleached tunic beneath a long storm-grey cloak, with plain leather sandals and a soft cord for a belt. The remains of a good Roman haircut were discreetly growing out, but no one could object to that since my head was well-hidden under swoops of white cloth. I was not frightened of sunstroke; I was disguised as a priest.

A forum is the place to find people. I walked towards it, politely allowing the citizens of Croton the shadier side of the street. They were a pushy lot.

Croton was a shabby sprawl, full of buildings that had been shoved askew by earthquakes. Sour smells seeped out from cluttered alleys where peeling walls carried election notices for men I had never heard of. Dogs that looked like wolves from the Sila mountains scavenged alone or raced through the byways in yelping packs. On second-floor balconies overweight young women with bulging jewels and narrow eyes waited until I passed by, then passed lewd comments on my physique; I refused to answer back because these ladylike daughters of Croton were probably related to the best men in the town. Besides, as a priest I was too pious for witty street chat.

I was led to the Forum by the babble and a strong smell of fish.

I wandered through the market. Everyone else had a good stare. Their eyes followed me from stall to stall, while knives hesitated over swordfish far too long before crunching them into steaks. As I paused in the colonnade, I glimpsed a youth flitting round a pillar with a distinct air of having no real reason to be there; I squinted directly at him, so if he was a pickpocket he would know I had spotted him. He disappeared.

The racket was appalling. They had some healthy produce though. There were sardines, sprats and anchovies all shimmering as brilliantly as new pewter candlesticks, and fresh vegetables that looked plump enough even for my mother, who grew up on a Campagna small-holding. The usual disasters too: piles of ever-so-shiny copperware that would stop looking special as soon as you got it home, and streamers of cheap tunic braid in unattractive colours that would bleed in the wash.

After that came more mounds of watermelons; squids and sea snakes; fresh garlands for tonight's banquets and laurel crowns left over from yesterday at glossy knockdown prices. Crocks of honey; plus bundles of the herbs that had fed the bees.

All I did was ask the price of liquorice. Well, so I thought.

In Magna Graecia, everyone spoke Greek. Thanks to an exiled Melitan moneychanger who once lodged with my mother and paid my quarterly school fees (one of life's little bonuses), I had received the scratchings of a Roman education. Greek was my second language; I could strike up a pose then recite seven lines from Thucydides, and I knew Homer was not just the name of my Uncle Scaro's dog. But my thin-bearded Thracian schoolmaster had left out the practical vocabulary a man needs for discussing razors with a barber in Buxentum, requesting a spoon with a snail-pick from a half-asleep waiter in Velia – or avoiding offence in Croton when bartering for aromatic herbs. I felt confident I knew the word for liquorice root; otherwise even for my mother (who expected a present from the south and had thoughtfully recommended what to buy), I would never have made the attempt. In fact, I must have inadvertently used some ripe old Greek obscenity.

The stallholder was a dwarf broad bean who had been left on life's vine until he turned leathery in the pod. He let out a yowk that attracted attention from three streets away. A tight crowd assembled, penning me against the stall. Elbowing forwards came some local layabouts whose idea of a good market day was beating up an unarmed priest. Under my tunic I had a safe-conduct signed by Vespasian, but down here they probably had not even heard yet that Nero had stabbed himself. Besides, my passport was in Latin which seemed unlikely to fill these shantytown bullies with respect.

I could not move because of the crowd. I assumed a haughty expression and pulled my religious veiling more securely over my head. I apologised to the herbseller in my best formal Greek. He jabbered more wildly. Stumpy Crotonese joined in. This was clearly the sort of friendly southern marketplace where peasants with shiny expressions and two left ears were just looking for a chance to set upon a stranger and accuse him of stealing his own cloak.

The rumpus was growing uglier. If I jumped over the stall they would grab me from behind, a cheap thrill I preferred to avoid. I kicked up one heel behind me to investigate the stall; it was just a trestle covered with cloth, so I dropped to the ground, gathered up my priestly garments, and scuttled under like a reclusive rat.

I came out between two piles of conical baskets, with my nose against the stallholder's knees. He seemed deaf to reason, so I bit him on the shin. He hopped back, shrieking; I scrambled out.

I now had one rickety table between me and a premature funeral. One glance at the multitude convinced me I really needed my little phallus amulet against the evil eye. (A gift from my sister Maia; so embarrassing I had left it at home.) The crowd swayed; the table lurched, then I crashed my hip so it toppled over towards the Crotonese. As they all jumped back I held up both hands in prayer.

'O Hermes Trismegistos – ' (I'll pause here to mention that since I had been bound to tell my mother I was leaving Rome, the only divinity who *might* be watching my progress was Hermes the Thrice Great in his role as the patron of travellers, who must have been having his ear bent painfully by my ma.) 'Aid me, wing-footed one!' (If things were quiet on Mount Olympus he might be pleased to have an errand here.) 'Offer the protection of your sacred caduceus to a fellow messenger!'

I stopped. I hoped curiosity might encourage the by-standers to leave me alive. If not, it would take more than a loan of a winged sandal to hop free of this predicament.

No sign of young Hermes and his snaky staff. But there was a puzzled lull, another surge, then out of the surge leapt a bronzed, barefooted man in a curly-brimmed hat who vaulted the trestle straight at me. I was unarmed of course; I was a priest. *He* was flourishing a monstrous knife.

Yet I was safe. In a trice this apparition had his weapon at the liquorice merchant's throat. The blade was twinkling sharp – the sort sailors keep for slicing through dangerous tangles of rope on shipboard or murdering each other while they enjoy a drink ashore. He was more or less sober, but gave the impression that cutting out the livers of people who looked at him too closely was they way he relaxed.

He bawled at the crowd, 'One step closer, and I stick the herbalist!'

Then to me: 'Stranger – *run for your life!*'

XIV

Clutching swathes of my religious get-up, I hared past the courthouse without stopping to enquire if the magistrate would hear my case. Before the third dark alley I heard my rescuer's bare feet pattering behind.

'Thanks!' I gasped out. 'Well met. You seem a handy type!'

'What had you done?'

'I've no idea.'

'Usual story!' he exclaimed.

We took the road out of town and soon afterwards were sitting in an eating house on the shore. He recommended the shellfish pottage with saffron sauce.

'A mélange of shellfish,' I commented cautiously, 'at a tavern with no nameboard, in a strange port, is a risk my mother taught me to avoid! What else do they do?'

'Shellfish pottage – without the saffron!'

He grinned. He had a perfectly straight nose which was attached to his face at an unfortunate angle of thirty degrees. His left side had the uptwitched eyebrow of a bright, comical fellow, and his right the downjerked mouth of a moody clown. Both halves of his face were fairly presentable; he just lost ground on the composite effect. His two profiles were so different I felt compelled to stare at him, as though he were deformed.

We both ordered pottage, with. Life's short enough anyway. May as well drink deep and die in style.

I paid for a flagon while my new friend called up side dishes; a trug of bread, a saucer of olives, hard-boiled eggs, lettuce salad, whitebait, sunflower seeds, gherkins, slices of cold sausage, and so on. Having fixed a few nibbles, we introduced ourselves.

'Laesus.'

'Falco.'

'Captain of the *Sea Scorpion*, out of Tarentum. I used to do the Alexandria run, but I gave it up for shorter hops with fewer storms. I'm in Croton to meet someone.'

'I've ridden down from Rome. Arrived today.'

'What brings you to Bruttium?'

'Whatever it was, it now looks like a bad mistake!'

We raised our cups and tackled the hors d'oeuvres. 'You never mentioned what you do, Falco.'

'Quite right.' I broke off some bread from a circular loaf, then concentrated on cleaning an olive stone between my front teeth. 'I never mentioned it!'

I spat out the stone. I was not so discourteous as to keep secrets from a fellow who had saved my life; Laesus knew I was teasing. We pretended to let it drop.

The place we had come to was surprisingly busy for mid-afternoon. Seafront canteens are often like that, catering for sailors who have no idea of time. Some customers were drinking at the counter indoors but most were packed onto benches in the open air, like us patiently waiting for their food.

I told Laesus that in my experience quayside tavernas are like that too; you sit for hours imagining they are filleting a fresh-caught red mullet just for you. The real truth is: the cook is a lackadaisical noddy who has disappeared on some errand for his brother-in-law; on his way back he quarrels with a girl he owes money to, then stops to see a dogfight before helping along a game of soldiers at a rival restaurant. He arrives in a filthy temper halfway through the afternoon, warms up a sickly bumper-fish in yesterday's rascasse broth and hurls in some mussels which he can't be bothered to clean, then an hour later you heave up your dinner into the harbour because you drank far too much while you were waiting for the cook . . .

'Console yourself, Laesus: a meal on a quayside never stays around long enough to poison you!'

He just smiled. Sailors get used to listening to strangers' fantasies.

Our pottage came. It was good, in a hearty, harboury way. I had just mastered filtering it across my tongue to field the chunks of crab claw, when Laesus niggled slyly, 'Since you seem shy of telling me, I'll guess . . . You look like a spy.'

I was hurt. 'I thought I looked like a priest!'

'Falco, you look like a spy who's *disguised* as a priest!' I sighed, and we drank some more wine.

My new friend Laesus was a queer phenomenon. In a place where I had no reason to feel confidence in anyone, he seemed utterly trustworthy. Both his eyes were black and beady like a robin's. He always kept his sailor's hat on. It had a round, felted crown surrounded by a twirling brim so that it looked like an upturned field mushroom.

The company thinned out. We were left with two old seamen and a few travellers who like me had fled for the sleepy port. Plus a trio of young ladies called Gaia, Ipsyphille and Meröe, with faded personalities and low-slung frocks, who went to and fro a lot. In the absence of fresh grapes or roasted chestnuts, these squeezy fruits were available upstairs as dessert.

Gaia was surprisingly attractive.

'Want to try your luck?' Laesus asked, intercepting my gaze.

He had a generous attitude; he seemed eager to keep my place at table if I went off with one of the girls. I shook my head slightly, with a lazy smile, as if it was simply too much effort to shift. Then I closed my eyes, still smiling, as I remembered another handsome girl I knew – and her scathing look if she was to catch me considering a cheap thrash with a harbour whore. The elegant and dignified Helena Justina had eyes the rich, dark browny-gold of palm dates from the desert – plus a snort like a bad-tempered camel when her highness was annoyed . . .

When I looked up, the girl called Gaia had gone upstairs with someone else.

'Tell me,' I suddenly asked Laesus. 'If you come from Tarentum, did you ever encounter a senator called Atius Pertinax?'

He finished a mouthful. 'I'm not on boozing terms with senators!'

'He was a shipowner; that was why I asked. While I was riding through the Sila forests, it struck me that since Pertinax was born a southerner he might have had his ships built here – '

'I'm with you!' Laesus said. 'Is he in trouble?'

'Oh, the worst kind; he's dead.' Laesus looked startled. I gulped my wine callously.

'So,' he ventured, recovering. 'What was he like?'

'Couple of years short of thirty. Lean build, thin face, nervous temper – he had a freedman called Barnabas.'

'Oh I know Barnabas!' Laesus flung down his spoon. 'Everyone in Tarentum knows Barnabas!' I wondered if they knew he was a murderer now.

Laesus remembered that four or five years earlier Barnabas had been busy at Tarentum on his master's behalf, having two new merchant vessels built. '*Callypso* and *Circe*, if I recollect.'

'*Circe* is right. She's impounded at Ostia.'

'Impounded?'

'Ownership inquest. Know any more about these two?'

'Not in my line. Did this Pertinax owe you money, Falco?'

'No; I've got some cash for Barnabas. It's his master's legacy.'

'I can make enquiries in Tarentum if you like.'

'Thanks, Laesus!' I did not mention the freedman's recent habit of roasting senators alive, since Vespasian wanted the political aspects hushed up. 'Listen, friend; I'm curious about these two for my own reasons. Were they popular locally?'

'Barnabas was an uppity ex-slave. People he cadged drinks from hoped Rome would give him his comeuppance.'

'Rome may yet! What about Pertinax?'

'Anyone who owns ships and racehorses can convince himself he's popular! Plenty of flatterers wanted to treat him like a great man.'

'Hmm! I wonder if he found Rome different? He was involved in a piece of stupidity; that could explain why – he wouldn't be the first small-town boy who went to show Rome how big he was, but his reception disappointed him.'

The people who had been sharing our table were leaving, so we both stretched our feet across to the opposite bench, spreading ourselves more comfortably.

'So who are you meeting here in Croton, Laesus?'

'Oh . . . just an old client.' Like all sailors he was highly secretive. 'What about you?' Laesus asked with a sidelong look. 'In the marketplace you called yourself a messenger – you mean to Barnabas?'

'No, a priest. Curtius Gordianus.'

'What's *he* done?'

'Nothing. I've just brought him some family news.'

'Spying,' he commented, 'seems a complicated trade!'

'Really, Laesus; I'm not a spy.'

'Of course not,' he answered, being very polite.

I grinned. 'I wish I was! I know one; all he does is office work and field trips to popular seaside resorts . . . Laesus, my good friend, if this was an adventure tale by some scurrilous court poet, you'd now exclaim, *Curtius Gordianus – what a coincidence! The very man I shall be dining with tonight!*'

He opened his mouth as if he was about to say it, paused long enough to milk every ounce of suspense – then collapsed.

'Never heard of the damned fellow!' Laesus declared agreeably.

XV

The sea captain Laesus was a wonderful find; though it has to be said that having rescued me, he took me to an eating house that made me horrendously ill.

I found my way back to the mansio, awash with saffron pottage, though not for long. There must have been a bad oyster in my soup. Luckily I have a finicky stomach; as my family often joke, when they decide they have waited long enough for their legacies, poisoning me is the last solution they will try.

While my fellow travellers were gnawing at the landlord's unspeakable boiled bellypork, I lay on my bed groaning privately; later I had a slow scrape in the bathhouse, then sat out in the garden with something to read.

About the time the meal ended, other guests straggled out to enjoy jugs of wine in the last light of day. I just had a beaker of cold water to aid my recovery.

There were plenty of tables in the recreation area; it saved the landlord, who was the usual idle scamp, from filling the spaces with flowerbeds that would require his attention. Most of these tables were empty. No one needed to invade my privacy, so when people did head towards me I froze into the character of a man who would rather give himself eyestrain over his holiday reading than look up and let strangers insist on making friends.

This had little success.

There were two of them. One was a bad dream on legs – the legs were like elm trunks, below a mass of well-organised muscle with no visible neck; his sidekick was a whiskery shrimp with a mean look and rickety build. Everyone else in the garden hid their noses in their wine beakers; I nuzzled my scroll short-sightedly, though without much hope. The new arrivals glanced around, then fixed on me.

The two of them sat at my table. They both had that knowing, expectant air which means the worst. An informer needs to be gregarious, but I tread warily with locals who seem so sure of themselves. The other customers studied their drinks; no one offered to help.

It is quite common in the south for tricksters to smile their way into a mansio, settle round some quiet group, then bully them out for an evening in the town. The travellers get off lightly if they escape with just a headache, a beating, the loss of their money, a night in a jail cell, and a sordid disease they pass on to their wives. A man on his own feels safer; but not much. I looked scholarly; I looked reserved; I tried hard to project the impression that the pouch on my belt was too empty to cope with a long night drinking sour red wine while a swarthy maiden with a tambourine danced at me.

Thanks to the market pickpocket, the empty pouch was true. Fortunately it was my decoy purse again; I kept my serious funds with my passport, round my neck. So far I still had them. But Vespasian's retainer was too puny to tantalise a tambourinist with grand ideas.

I stuck things out long enough to make a feeble point, then laid a piece of dried grass in my scroll to keep my place and tucked its baton under my chin while I rerolled what I had read.

Both my new cronies wore white tunics with green binding; it looked like household livery, and from their confident expressions must have been the livery of some minor town councillor who thought himself big in the neighbourhood. The large one was surveying me like a farmer who had turned up something slimy on his spade.

'I'd better warn you,' I tried frankly, 'I know when a stranger comes to town men of enterprise plunder his life savings in the high spots while sinful women tickle his chastity in low dives – ' There was more hope of extracting a flicker of expression from a pair of archaic statues in a deserted tomb.

I drank my water thoughtfully, and let events take their course.

'We're trying to find a priest,' the large one growled.

'You don't strike me as devoted types!'

Taking my advice from Laesus about changing my appearance, I had snuggled into an old dark-blue tunic after my bath. With my open-backed felt slippers, this indigo disaster completed a comfortable ensemble for a night staying in for a good read. I probably looked like a sloppy philosophy student who was thrilling himself silly with a collection of racy legends. Actually I was dipping into Caesar on the Celts, and any interruption was good news for my sore gut because the lofty Julius was beginning to enrage me; he could write, but his sense of self-importance was reminding me why my crusty ancestors so distrusted his high-handed politics.

It seemed unlikely these visitors wanted to discuss Julius Caesar's politics.

'Who's this priest you're after?' I offered.

'Some fool of a foreigner,' the big terrorist shrugged. 'Caused a commotion in the marketplace.' His small friend sniggered.

'I heard about that,' I admitted. 'Used a naughty word for liquorice. Can't imagine how. Liquorice is a Greek word anyway.'

'Very careless!' the strong man groused. He made it sound as if being casual with language was a crucifixion crime. That's one opinion though not mine and not, I thought, a debating point this monster himself chewed over by a roaring country fire on long winter nights. 'You've been asking for someone we know; what do you want with Gordianus?'

'What is it to you?'

'I'm Milo,' he told me proudly. 'His steward.'

Milo stood up. I decided Gordianus must have something to hide: his household steward was built like the door porter of an extremely shady gambling hall.

Croton is famous for its athletes, and the most famous of all had been called Milo. The Gordianus steward could easily have modelled for the souvenir statuettes I had resisted in the market. When Croton captured Sybaris (the original sin city, further round the Tarentine Bay), that Milo had celebrated by sprinting through the stadium with a bull across his shoulders, killing the beast with one blow of his fist, then eating it raw for lunch . . .

'Let's go inside,' this Milo told me, looking at me as if he quite fancied half a hundredweight of uncooked sirloin.

I smiled like a man who was pretending he could handle the situation, then let myself be led indoors.

XVI

Milo told shrimp-features to keep watch outside.

The steward and I crammed into my allocated cell; I certainly would have enjoyed myself more enduring a sleazy night out in Croton with some light-fingered, moustachioed dancing-girl. There was no doubt what was going to happen to me here; the only question was when.

There were three beds, but few tourists could face a summer excursion to Croton so I had the room to myself. At least it saved anyone else getting hurt. Milo filled most of the extra space. I found this Milo something of a trial. He was big. He knew he was big. He spent most of his time enjoying how big he felt crowding ordinary people in small rooms. His heavily greased muscles gleamed in the light of my rush. Close to, he had an oddly washed-out, antiseptic smell.

He pressed me down onto a three-legged stool with the effortless pressure of two massive thumbs which were itching to inflict more intimate pain. To worry me he prodded at my stuff.

'This yours?' he demanded, fingering my *Gallic Wars*.

'I can read.'

'Where did you steal it?'

'Auctioneer in the family. I get first pick of the second-hand stalls in Rome – '

I watched unhappily. The volume had seemed a real bargain, though I would have to sell it back to obtain the next scroll in the set. It had well-cut edges and cedar oil still protecting the paper, while one of the bosses on the roller retained traces of gilt. (The other boss was missing originally, but I carved a replacement myself.)

'Caesar!' Milo noted, with approval.

I felt lucky I was reading military history, not some soft subject like beekeeping. This oaf used his massive body for moral crusades. He had the cold stare of a brute who had convinced himself it was his private vocation to snuff out the lives of prostitutes and poets. Just the sort to idolise a dictator like Caesar – too stupid to see that Caesar was a proud snob with far too much money who would despise Milo even more than the Gauls (who at least had sensational rites of human sacrifice, druids, and Atlantic-going boats).

Milo set my Caesar down awkwardly, like a thug who had been house-trained not to damage expensive things – except perhaps when his master specifically told him to frighten some victim by smashing a priceless ceramic in front of his eyes.

'Spying pays!'

'I doubt it,' I told him patiently. 'It doesn't pay me. I'm not a spy; I'm a dispatch carrier. All I get is a sestertius a day and the chance to find out the hard way how the magistrates in Bruttium never repair their roads . . . '

Still mooning over Caesar, Milo turned away. I rescued my scroll, then winced as my oil flask cracked onto the floor when he tipped out my luggage from its two frugal mule panniers. He called himself a steward, but I would not have trusted him to fold a pile of tablecloths. Six snarled tunics, one distressed toga, two neck scarves, one hat, one sponge, one bathscraper and a box of writing stuff later, he found the knife I had worked into the wicker of one of the panniers.

He turned to me. Drawing my knife from its scabbard, he tickled my chin with it. I jerked uneasily as he yanked the thong round my neck so he could pull out my petty cash and travel pass. Then he had to put down the knife, to hold the pass with both his stubby paws while he slowly studied it.

'M. Didius Falco. Why have you come to Croton?'

'Message for Gordianus.'

'What message?'

'A private one.'

'Spit it out.'

'It's personal; from the Emperor.'

Milo grunted. In Croton this probably passed for an elegant expression of logical thought. 'Gordianus won't see a hick courier!'

'He will when he knows what I've brought him.'

Milo rounded on me again. It was like being menaced by an overplayful plough ox who had just noticed that a hornet had stung him five minutes ago. Patiently I lifted my gaze to a shelf where the landlord had left some extra fleas nesting in rolled-up counterpanes. The shelf was close to the ceiling, which stopped you banging your head but meant you could waste a lot of time on a freezing southern night trying to find spare bedding in the dark. Up there now stood a fine porphyry vase, over a foot high and topped by a prettily fluted lid which I had secured with a spider's web of twine; knowing what was inside, I did not want the contents leaking out among my underwear.

'Get it!' Milo said.

I straightened slowly, then reached above my head. I seized the two handles, steadying my grip. The vessel was expensive green stone from the Peloponnese, and solid stuff; its contents weighed next to nothing, though your shoulders know when they are supporting a porphyry vase overhead like an unstable male caryatid. The stone is almost impossible to work, but Vespasian had paid a great deal for this; it was a smoothly-sculpted masterpiece and if it slipped through my grasp it would make quite a dent in the floor.

'Look!' I grunted, still with my arms up, 'this is something personal for Curtius Gordianus. I don't recommend you to uncover what's inside – '

Milo had a simple approach when anybody told him not to do something; he did it.

'What have you brought him?' He lunged closer, intending to look.

'His brother,' I said.

Then I crashed down the funeral urn on Milo's head.

XVII

About twelve miles south of Croton a headland called Cape Colonna rounds off a long stretch of desolate coastline at the north end of the Gulf of Scylacium. Right on the shore, in a typical Greek location, stands a huge Temple of Hera with an uplifting view straight over the aching dazzle of the Ionian Sea. It is a grand sanctuary in classic style – or to a man in trouble (say Curtius Gordianus, hotfoot from a narrow brush with the Praetorians), a good safe spot, a long way off from Rome.

Gordianus held the title of Chief Priest here. Great temples often have local patrons who sweep the poll at elections for their priesthoods. Until I terrified Milo's shrimp at the mansio, I had not expected to learn that the hereditary Chief Priest had lodged himself in active residence. For a senator, trimming up altars in person is hardly the point.

Even in glaring sunlight the cold clear air raised goosebumps on my arms, while the fierce ocean atmosphere stretched the skin across my cheekbones and a strong breeze tore my hair back from the scalp. The Temple stood glazed with light from sea and sky. Entering the hot stonework of the Doric colonnade, its overpowering quiet nearly flattened me.

In front of the portico, at an altar in the open air, a veiled priest was conducting a private sacrifice. The family whose birthday or good fortune he was celebrating clustered round in their best clothes, pink-cheeked from the strong sun and the wind off the sea. Temple servants held fine boxes of incense and glittering censers to burn it in; sparky boy assistants who had been chosen for their handsome looks wielded bowls and axes for the sacrifice while they flirted thin moustaches at the family's young male slaves. There was a pleasant scent of applewood to attract the goddess's attention, plus a nasty whiff of goat hair which the priest had just ritually singed in the altar fire.

They had a white she-goat standing by, with garlanded horns and a bothered expression; I winked at her as I jumped down from the colonnade. The goat met my eye; she gave vent to a frantic bleat, then bit her adolescent handler in his sensitive young groin and bolted down the shore.

Milo's shrimp launched himself after the nanny. The priest's assistants tumbled cheerfully after him. The heartbroken pilgrims

67

whose great occasion lay in ruins propped their expensive laurel wreaths against the altar where they would not be stepped on, then streamed away along the beach as well. The goat had already spurted a stadium's length. I was wearing my religious robes; it would have been undignified to cheer.

It was going to be some time before the cavalcade returned. The Chief Priest exclaimed in annoyance, then walked to the Temple steps. I followed, though his attitude was discouraging; a poor start for my new diplomatic role.

Aulus Curtius Gordianus was in his late forties, slightly taller than me, with an untidy, ill-tended build. Like an elephant, he had large webby ears, small reddish eyes, and bald wrinkled skin with an unhealthy greyish tinge. We both sat on the edge of the platform hugging our robed knees.

The pontiff sighed irritably, shading his eyes as he squinted after the circus that had by now diminished into skirmishing dots a quarter of a mile away.

'Oh this is ridiculous!' he fumed.

I glanced at him briefly, as if we were two strangers brought together by an amusing accident. 'The sacrifice must come willingly to the altar!' I reminisced helpfully. (I had been through a seriously religious phase when I was twelve.)

'Quite!' He was acting the cheerful social manner of a temple professional, but the tartness of an off-duty senator soon showed through. 'You have the air,' he remarked, 'of a messenger who expects his arrival to have been foretold to me in a dream!'

'I imagine you heard about me from the busybody on a donkey I just passed riding back to Croton. I hope you thanked him with a denarius. I hope when he gets back to Croton he finds it's a forged one!'

'Are you worth a denarius?'

'No,' I admitted. 'But the eminent personage who sent me rates quite a few.'

I waited until Gordianus swivelled to look at me properly. 'Who's that? Who are you? A priest?'

He was very abrupt. Some senators are. Some are shy; some were born rude; some are so weary of dealing with the ditherers in politics they sound intolerant automatically.

'Let's say I'm serving my turn at the altar for the state.'

'You're no priest!'

'Every man is chief priest in his own household,' I intoned piously. 'What about you? Self-exile at your rank is not allowed!' I could feel the sun's heat burning into me from the great stones behind as I continued to taunt him. 'Chief Priest here is a fine, honourable sinecure – but no one expects a senator with a million in his bankbox to carry out the daily grind of skinning goats in the raw sea air! Not even if serving the Lady of Olympus was bequeathed to you along with your family olive groves –

or did you and your noble brother buy these priesthoods outright? Tell me; what's the premium now for a corking post like this?'

'Too much,' he interrupted, visibly restraining himself. 'What do you have to say?'

'Senator, with a civil war just ended, your place is in Rome!'

'Who sent you here?' he insisted coldly.

'Vespasian Augustus.'

'Was that his message?'

'No; that's my opinion, sir.'

'Then keep your opinions to yourself!' He moved gathering his robes. 'Unless divine intervention trips up that goat, I see nothing to stop her fleeing north round the whole Tarentine Gulf; we can discuss your business now.'

'Is it proper to interrupt a sacred occasion, sir?' I demanded sarcastically.

'The goat has done that,' he capitulated with an air of weariness. 'Assisted by you! These unfortunate people will need to start again tomorrow with another animal – '

'Oh, it's worse than that, senator.' In most temples a death in his family is held to pollute the priest; I told him quietly, 'Curtius Gordianus, they will need another priest.'

Too subtle: I could tell from his expression that he completely missed the point.

XVIII

The Chief Priest at Colonna had a house adjoining the Temple. It was a simple affair – in a spacious, sun-lit, well-appointed, seaside way. Outside, the stonework looked bleached and the balustrades weathered. The windows were small and protective; the doors heavily porched. Inside they had gilding on the candelabra, light furniture they could move outdoors on favourable days, and storm lanterns for blustery nights.

When the door slammed several slaves popped their heads out looking flummoxed, as if Gordianus had come home too early for lunch. The bright atmosphere did not reflect the style of the so-called steward Milo, so I guessed these busy females really ran the house. They had the whole place aired, as fresh as lavender. I heard brooms swishing on wet floors and noticed the scent of frying liver – perhaps titbits the pontiff had allocated himself in the course of a previous sacrifice. (Any priest who knows his business captures the choicest cuts: the best reason I know for doing your civic duty as a priest.)

Gordianus led me swiftly into a sideroom. Cushions lay everywhere, with little vases of wild flowers among the silver bowls and flagons on the sideboard displays. The wages of treason: an attractive country life.

'Sir, I'm Didius Falco.' No flicker of recognition showed. I presented my passport; he glanced at it. 'I've left your steward in Croton, tied to a bed.'

Gordianus threw off his robes. Still in charge so far, he looked pained. 'Will somebody find him?'

'Depends how often the mansio staff count their blankets.'

He became more thoughtful. 'You overcame Milo?'

'I hit him with a lump of stone.'

'Whatever for?'

'He thought I was a spy,' I complained, letting the priest see that his steward's incompetence made me seethe with rage. 'Milo is a credit to his cheap gymnasium, but his brain needs exercise! Being a Palace messenger is a thankless task. I have been set on by the Homeric heroes who sell chickens in Croton market, then assaulted by your dim-witted staff – '

I was enjoying this tirade. I needed to establish my authority. His noble birth meant Gordianus could always count upon the senate to

70

support him; I worked for Vespasian, and if I upset a senator – even a traitor – I could not count on his Caesarship at all.

'Milo claims you will not see me. With respect, sir, that is pointless, and insulting to the Emperor. Shall I go back to Rome with nothing to tell Vespasian except that his townships in Magna Graecia need a good stamping on while the pontiff at the Temple of Hera is too stubborn to hear his elder brother's fate?'

'What fate?' Curtius Gordianus was glaring at me with contempt. 'Is my brother a hostage? Does Vespasian send me threats?'

'Too late for that, sir. You and your brother picked a quarrel with someone far less delicate.'

Then, having finally achieved his full attention, in one brisk sentence I described the Temple fire.

He was sitting in a long casual chair. His awkward body tended to sag into the nearest place he could prop himself with minimum effort. As I told him Curtius Longinus was dead he jerked involuntarily, swinging his heavy legs to the floor. Then he was crippled by an onslaught of emotion at his brother's appalling end. He stayed, twisted uncomfortably, unable to absorb the tragedy with a stranger watching him.

Adopting good manners, I went out quietly, leaving him alone while I fetched the porphyry urn. For a few moments I stood outside beside my mule, stroking the beast quietly while I watched the sea and soaked in the sun. The bereavement that had struck this house was nothing to do with me, yet announcing it left me feeling drawn. I removed the twine that was fastening the two parts of the great vase, peered inside, then replaced the lid hurriedly.

The ashes of a human being look very slight.

As I re-entered, Gordianus struggled to his feet. I cleared a small table in order to set down his brother's funeral urn. A flush of anger coloured him but then he readjusted his face to hide his distress.

'Vespasian's response?'

'Sir?' I was looking round for somewhere to deposit the inkpots and bowls of pistachios which I had shifted to accommodate the urn.

'My brother was called to Rome to explain our position – '

'The Emperor never spoke to him,' I interrupted. I edged the clutter onto a shelf. 'Vespasian ordered your brother an honourable funeral, and he himself,' I mentioned drily, 'paid for this urn. When you can bear it, I'll try to explain – '

The Priest of Hera seized a small bronze handbell which he rang with bitter violence. 'Remove yourself from my house!'

Well, I never expected to be asked to stay to lunch.

Members of his household were tumbling into the room; they stopped at the intensity of the priest's agitation. Before he could order them to frogmarch me out, I made him hear the facts:

'Curtius Gordianus, your brother fell victim to a freedman connected with Atius Pertinax Marcellus. You will be aware how Pertinax died. Apparently blaming his old master's associates, this Barnabas has killed your brother; he may come for you next! Sir, I am here to convey Vespasian's offer of his good will. You will need the nine days of formal mourning; I hope to see you after that.'

Out in the hall I bumped into Milo, just arrived. He had a gloomy bruise surrounding a vivid cut.

I tutted gently, 'That's a nasty knock! Don't worry about the urn; I washed off the blood!'

I bounced out of the door before he could reply.

I reappeared at the Temple as a tired procession stumbled up the beach. The goat was leaning back obstinately all the way. Something about her predicament aroused my fellow feeling; I too spent most of my life bleating and being led towards certain doom.

There was nobody else in authority, so the senior suppliant consulted me.

'Go home,' I commanded, inventing cheerfully. 'Sweep out your house with cypress twigs – '

'What about the goat?'

'This goat,' I pronounced with dignity (thinking of tasty ribs, roasted in the open air with sea salt and wild sage), 'is sacred to the Goddess Hera now. Leave her with me!'

The pilgrims collected their wreaths then trekked away homewards; the acolytes scampered into the Temple to get up to whatever horrible young servitors play at together when they find themselves unsupervised. With a grin, I took charge of the goat.

The animal shuddered woefully on a long piece of rope. She was a pretty little thing. Luckily for her, although I had nothing to eat, as a priest I suddenly felt much too pure-minded to contemplate devouring Hera's sacred goat.

Better own up; I was incapable of slaughtering any creature who looked up at me with such melting, mournful eyes.

XIX

I can never remember if the nine days of formal mourning apply from when a person dies or from when you hear the news. Gordianus reckoned the latter; wretched for my hygiene, but it gave him longer to recuperate.

For nine days I roamed the foreshore, while my goat investigated driftwood and I lectured her on the finer things in life. I survived on goats milk and wheatcakes off the altar. To sleep I snuggled in between my mule and the goat. I bathed in the sea, but I still smelt of animals and there was nowhere for a shave.

When people visited the Temple I kept out of the way. No one wants to find a shrine they are attending for religious reasons inhabited by a bearded derelict and a runaway goat.

After two days a deputy priest turned up to stand in for Gordianus. By then I had organised the acolytes into handball teams and was running a league on the beach. Once the lads were exhausted, I used to sit them down and read aloud from my *Gallic Wars*. Fresh air and Vercingetorix kept them out of trouble for most of the day though I preferred not to investigate their habits at night.

After dark when everywhere lay silent, I usually went into the Temple alone and sat before the goddess of Matrimonial Love, thinking about nothing while I munched her wheaten cakes. I requested no favours, and the Lady never destroyed my scepticism by appearing as a vision. She and I had no need to communicate. The goddess Hera must have known that Zeus her thunderous husband had failings in common with private informers; too much free time – and too many fancy women suggesting ways of using it.

Sometimes I stood at the sea's lisping edge with my feet in the water, thinking about Helena Justina who knew this too. Remembering that young porter at the Senator's house refusing me admission on a flimsy excuse, insight smote me; she was sensible and far-sighted. *Helena Justina had left me!*

I strode back into the Temple and stood angrily before the goddess of Matrimonial Love. The Queen of Olympus surveyed me with a face of stone.

* * *

On the tenth morning, when I was light-headed with starvation and solitude, one of the acolytes came down the shore to see me. This sinful little minnow was called Demosthenes – a typical altar boy, old beyond his years yet visibly unwashed behind the ears.

'Didius Falco, people are getting bad ideas about you and your goat!'

'Nonsense,' I rallied miserably. 'This goat is respectable!' Demosthenes gazed at me with fathomless eyes in a handsome, untrustworthy face. So did the goat.

The acolyte sniffed. 'Curtius Gordianus is at the Temple, Falco. He says you can use his private baths. Want me to scrape your back?' he suggested offensively. I told him accepting favours from him would only cause me problems with my goat.

I had learned to live with Croton's lack of amenities. I went straight to the Temple, tied my nanny in the portico, then marched up to Gordianus in the sanctum.

'Thanks for the chance of a bathe!' I cried. 'I admit that by now I'd sell myself into slavery to some one-eyed Nabataean camel-drover if he promised me an hour in a hot steam room first! Sir, we need to talk about your being here – '

'Domitian Caesar approved my travel leave – '

'I meant, whether Croton is safe for you. The Emperor will uphold your leave of absence.' He looked surprised. 'Imperial policy is to support Domitian Caesar's official acts.'

'What about his unofficial ones?' he laughed bitterly.

'Oh the policy is to tut at him fiercely – then smile and forget!'

We walked outside to the steps.

Gordianus moved slowly, drugged with exhaustion after his bereavement. He sat and sagged like sour dough in a crock, almost visibly shrinking, then gazed at the ocean as if he saw in its shifting lights and currents all the world's philosophies – saw them with a new understanding, but a deep new distaste.

'Yours is an unenviable job, Falco!'

'Oh it has its attractions: travel, exercise, meeting new people from all walks of life – ' The goat strained at the end of her string so she could chew my tunic sleeve. I held her off with both hands; she bleated with a foolish look.

'Acts of violence and announcing misery!' Gordianus scoffed. I watched him over the goat's forelock, while I stroked her wide white ears; she knelt down and settled to munching at the end of my belt. 'Falco, what do you know about this mess?'

'Well; let's be discreet! There are many people – apart from supporters of the late, not-much-lamented Emperor Vitellius – who view the new Imperial dynasty less than wholeheartedly. But it's clear the Flavian circus is here to stay. The Senate fully ratified Vespasian. He is halfway to becoming a god, so all wise mortals are putting on a more reverent face . . . Are you willing to tell me what your brother intended saying to the Emperor?'

'He was speaking for both of us. We had, as you put it, put on a reverent face for the Flavians.'

'That's hard,' I sympathised, falling in with his low mood. 'So your brother's accident must seem a bitter blow – '

'His murder you mean!'

'Yes – so tell me, what could he have intended to say to the Emperor that someone wanted to prevent so badly?'

'Nothing!' snapped Gordianus impatiently. I believed him. Which meant one thing: it was something Longinus had only found out after he returned to Rome . . . While I was pondering, Gordianus frowned painfully. 'You must reckon we had only ourselves to blame.'

'Not entirely. Curtius Gordianus, you can die by misadventure in a thousand ways. A clerk in the Censor's office told me once that lead pipes, copper saucepans, mushrooms cooked for elderly men by young wives, swimming in the Tiber, and womens' face creams are all deadly dangerous; but perhaps he was a pessimist – '

Gordianus rocked on the step restlessly. 'My brother's suffocation was deliberate, Falco. And a horrific way to die!'

I stated at once very quietly: 'Asphyxia is very swift. As far as anybody knows, it is not a painful death.'

After a moment I sighed. 'Perhaps I see far too many deaths.'

'So how do you stay humane?' he demanded.

'When I look at a corpse I remember, *he must have parents somewhere; he may have had a wife.* If I can, I find them. I tell them what happened. I try to be quick; most people want time to react alone. But some of them come back to me afterwards and ask for the details all over again. That's bad enough.'

'What's worse?'

'Thinking about the ones who want to ask, but never come.'

Gordianus still looked hunted. I could see that once he had drummed up the grit to oppose Vespasian, failure utterly deflated him.

'My brother and I,' he explained with a struggle, 'believed Flavius Vespasianus was a Sabine adventurer from an untalented family, who would bring the Empire into ruin and disrepute.'

I shook my head. 'I'm a staunch republican – but I won't run Vespasian down.'

'Because you work for him?'

'I work for the money.'

'Then opt out?'

'I do my duty!' I retorted. 'My name is on the tax roll, and I never fail to vote! More importantly, here I am, trying to reconcile you and Vespasian to give him breathing space to rebuild the ruins he inherited from Nero.'

'Is he capable?'

I hesitated. 'Probably.'

'Hah! Falco, to most of Rome he'll still be an adventurer.'

'Oh I believe he knows that!'

Gordianus went on staring out to sea. He had slumped like a sea
anemone, a soft grey blob clinging to the stonework, weakening as
the sun moved onto us.

'Do you have any children?' I asked, fumbling for a way to reach him.

'Four. Plus my brother's two now.'

'Your wife?'

'Dead, thankfully – ' Any woman with much about her would want
to kick his anklebone; I was thinking of one in particular. Perhaps he
saw it in my face. 'Are you married, Falco?'

'Not exactly.'

'Someone in mind?' When the people who asked were not entirely
cynical, it was easiest for a bachelor to pretend. I paused, then nodded.
'No children then?' he went on.

'Not as far as I know – and that's not flippancy. My brother
had a child he never saw; it won't happen to me.'

'What happened to your brother?'

'Casualty; Judaea. A hero, they tell me.'

'Was this recent?'

'Three years ago.'

'Ah . . . you can say then: in this situation, how do we cope?'

'Oh, we tolerate the crass intrusions of people who hardly knew
them; we set up expensive memorials which fail to impress their real
friends! We honour their birthdays, comfort their women, make sure
their children grow up with some parental control – '

'Does this help?'

'No, not really . . . No.'

We both smiled grimly, then Gordianus turned to me.

'Evidently Vespasian sent you because he considers you persuasive,'
he sneered. I had won his confidence, though what happened to my
brother in the desert was nothing to exploit. 'You seem to be genuine;
what do you recommend?'

Still thinking of Festus, I did not answer at once.

'Oh Falco, you cannot imagine what has been going through
my head!' I could. Gordianus was the sort of tormented defeatist
who could easily put his whole brood to the sword, then persuade
some loyal slave to butcher him too. I imagined it clearly; everyone
sobbing and making a mess of good floor rugs with their pointless
blood – his type should never attempt treachery. If he brazened this
out, he had done no worse than many senators contemplate every day
over lunch.

Of course, that was why these people mattered. That was why the

Emperor was treating them so carefully. Some plots are dreamed up over Tuesday's cold artichokes but fade out by Wednesday's anchovy eggs. Curtius Gordianus displayed a mad insistency. He had ganged up with amateurs who were pressing on in defiance long after self-preservation would steer anyone else back to respectable pastimes like drinking and gambling and seducing their best friends' wives.

'So what alternatives are left, Falco?'

'Vespasian will not object if you withdraw to your private estate – '

'Retire from public life!' A true Roman, the suggestion shocked him. 'Is he ordering that?'

'No. Sorry – '

Caught out by my mistake, I was starting to lose patience. He shot me a quizzical look. I remembered his brisk attitude when he first greeted me as Chief Pontiff; I decided this squashed pillow needed plumping up with a public role.

'The Emperor was impressed by your adopting a religious post, though he would prefer you to accept a more demanding place – ' I sounded like Anacrites; I had been working at the Palace far too long.

'Such as?'

'Paestum?'

Now Gordianus sat quiet. After exile on this bleak shore, the mighty complex of temples at Paestum represented sheer luxury. 'Paestum,' I continued seductively. 'A civilised city in a delicate climate, where the violets are the sweetest in Europe, and all the perfumers' roses bloom twice every year . . . ' (Paestum: on the west coast in Campania – well within Vespasian's reach.)

'In what position?' Now he was talking more like a senator.

'I have no authority to confirm that, sir. But during my journey here I did learn they have a vacant post at the great Temple of Hera . . . '

He nodded at once.

I had done it. Everything was over. I had hooked Curtius Gordianus back from his exile, and with luck earned myself a contract bonus. (Or, being realistic, I would earn it if Vespasian agreed to the solution I had suggested, if we ever managed to agree what that solution was worth to the Empire – and if he paid.)

I stood up, easing my spine. I felt grimy and tired; familiar hazards of my trade. Lack of decent conversation had left my speech sluggish. I became aware of countless scratches stinging my legs from forging through maritime brushwood at the whim of my goat. I was a wreck. I had ten days' ferocious stubble; I must look like a mountain bandit. My hair had coarsened and my eyebrows stiffened with salt.

While I watched Gordianus beginning to gloat at his own good luck, I blotted out the irony of my own predicament. If I did earn this bonus, it would be one small instalment towards the four hundred thousand sesterces that might have helped me approach Helena. *Informing is a drab old business. The pay's filthy, the work's worse, and if you ever find a woman you don't have the money, or the time, or the energy* . . . And she leaves you anyway.

I told myself I would feel better once I enjoyed a long and steamy hour, with decent hot water in ample quantities, in the pontiff's private baths. A good bathe when you really need it can get you over almost anything.

Then I remembered that clumsy bastard Milo had broken my favourite oil flask at the Croton mansio.

XX

I was clean at last, well scraped and starting to relax, when the commotion occurred.

As the bathhouse was private, several glass and alabaster jars of interesting oils lived permanently on a marble shelf. I dipped in discreetly and had my eye on a particular green flagon of hair pomade for a final therapeutic touch . . .

As I unwound in the luxurious hot steam room, I felt I had the measure of what had been going on. The Curtius brothers owned a family tree so ancient that Romulus and Remus had carved their names in its moss. To them Vespasian was a nobody. His good generalship meant nothing; nor the forty years of service he had already given Rome. He had no money and no famous ancestors. You cannot let people who own nothing but talent rise into the highest positions. What chance is there then for the upper-crust bunglers and fools?

Longinus and Gordianus, two impressionable boobies with more status than sense, must have been easy prey for stronger men with wickeder ideas. Longinus had paid for it cruelly, and all Gordianus really wanted now was an escape he would be able to explain away to their sons –

At this point heavy running footsteps interrupted my reverie.

As I rushed out with the slave who had come to fetch me, a stricken figure was being carried from the Temple to the house on a makeshift sling. Milo was arguing fiercely with Gordianus in the porch; when I appeared, all wet curls and wonderful unguents, and wrapped in a skimpy towel, the Chief Priest exclaimed icily, '*Falco* was in the bathhouse!'

I said, 'Thanks for the alibi; so what was the crime?'

Gordianus, whose normal greyish pallor had become a sickly white, nodded as the unconscious man was hurried past us indoors; the deputy priest, the one who had been in charge while the pontiff was in mourning. The veil that would have covered his head at the altar was still tangled round him, soaked in crimson.

'Poor fellow was found bleeding from a head wound. He had been felled with a lampstand. Someone had left your goat there in the Temple – '

'If that was an attempt to implicate me, it's clumsy!' I interrupted angrily. 'I never take her inside the Lady's sanctum, as you well know!' A slave had brought me a tunic so I fought my way into it, with some difficulty since I was still wet.

'Falco, the blow was badly aimed; he may live – but if so he will be fortunate – '

'Stop wondering; the blow was meant for you!' I plucked at my clinging tunic as I turned from Gordianus to his steward, who was giving me a cross-eyed scowl. 'Milo, I kept away from the Temple while pilgrims were there. Were you on watch?' The huge oaf looked uncooperative, still remembering how I had brained him at Croton. 'Think, Milo! This is urgent! Has there been anyone who looked less than genuine? Anyone asking questions? Anyone who for any reason sticks in your mind?'

It was stony-hard work, but I extracted details of a visitor who sounded possible. This man had insisted his sacrifice be conducted by Gordianus himself. The staff at the house had turned him away, saying the pontiff would not officiate until today.

'And was he here again this morning?' Milo thought so.

'What makes you sure?' Gordianus himself rapped out.

'The horses,' mumbled Milo. I looked up rapidly.

'Horses? Not a skewbald effort and a twitchy-eared roan?' Grudgingly, Milo agreed.

'Do you know this villain, Falco?' Gordianus cried indignantly, as if he thought I must be in league with the man.

'He followed me down here, at least from Salernum; possibly from Rome – ' Our eyes met. We both thought the same.

'*Barnabas!*'

I gripped the priest by the elbow and wheeled him indoors where, rightly or wrongly, he might feel more safe.

To me, there could be no doubt that the attacker was long gone, but we sent out Milo and various household minions to scour the countryside. We saw a ship close to shore, which fuelled our suspicion that the attacker may have had accomplices who fetched him off by boat, horses and all. Gordianus groaned, his head in his hands. He was letting himself imagine how his deputy, anonymously veiled, had been bludgeoned as he stood in prayer with his hands on the main altar . . .

'I left my family in Rome, Falco – are they safe?'

'From Barnabas? I'm not an oracle, sir. I don't sit in a cave chewing bay leaves; I simply can't put myself in a trance and prophesy his next move – ' He bit at his lower lip desperately. 'He murdered your brother,' I reminded him patiently. 'Vespasian insists he answers for it. Now he has tried to attack you; when he learns his mistake he may try again.' He stared at me. 'Sir, this proves what I suspected – somehow your brother Longinus posed a threat. So do you, apparently. Whatever it was your brother knew, he could have sent you a message between meeting the freedman at the priest's house and going to the Temple of Hercules that night; Barnabas must be afraid he did so. If anything does arrive from Longinus, it will be in your interests to tell me – '

'Of course,' he promised, unconvincingly.

Forgetting myself, I grasped his shoulders and shook him. 'Gordianus, the only way to be safe is if I reach Barnabas first! The freedman will be dealt with, but he must be found. Can you tell me anything that may help?'

'Are *you* chasing him, Falco?'

'Yes,' I said, because although Anacrites had been assigned this doubtful privilege, I was determined to beat him if I could.

Still shocked by today's graphic proof of his own danger, Gordianus continued to look vague. 'You and Pertinax were on close terms,' I insisted. 'Do you know his freedman? Was he always so dangerous?'

'Oh, I never dealt with his staff . . . Does he frighten you?'

'Not much – but I do take him seriously!' I eased my tone. 'Not many freedmen would consider that their duty to their patrons included murder. Why this exaggerated loyalty?'

'Barnabas believed his master had a golden destiny. So, for that matter, did Pertinax! His adoptive father filled him with a stupendous notion of his personal worth. In fact if Pertinax had remained alive, *he* would have been the dangerous one.'

'Ambition?' I scoffed quietly. Dead or not, anything about this Pertinax niggled me, because of his marriage to Helena. 'Did Pertinax covet power for himself?'

'Pertinax was an inadequate boor!' Gordianus grated with a sudden bellow of impatience. I agreed. 'Did you know him?' he asked in surprise.

'No need,' I answered glumly. 'I knew his wife.'

Having allocated Helena Justina's ex-husband a place on the chain of humanity that was less than a stag beetle in a cowpat, I could hardly believe the man had held Imperial ideas. But after Nero some odd candidates had emerged: Vespasian for one. If the freedman believed the death of Pertinax had robbed himself of the chance to be the Empire's Chief Minister, his vindictiveness became understandable.

Curtius Gordianus stood in silence, then he said, 'Take care, Falco. Atius Pertinax had a destructive personality. He may be dead, but I don't believe we have seen the end of the man's malign influence!'

'What does that mean, sir?' If the Chief Priest wanted to be mysterious, I could not be bothered to take him seriously.

Suddenly he smiled. It wrinkled his face unpleasantly, and his teeth were the type to keep for strictly private use – badly chipped and stained. 'Perhaps I chew bay leaves in the afternoon!'

Well that explained the teeth.

I had to leave the subject there, because the searchers had returned – needless to say, without our man. But they had found one thing that might be useful. Kicked to the back of the sanctum in the Temple was a pocketbook that seemed more likely to belong to the assailant than the deputy priest: it contained a few notes which appeared to be sums checking tavern bills (*hay: one as; wine: two asses; food: one as* . . .). These calculations seemed to belong to some careful type who was suspicious of innkeepers – well, that gave me a wide choice! What caught my eye in particular was a list on the front page which seemed to be dates (mainly in April, but a few in May), with names alongside them (*Galatea, Lusitania, Venus of Paphos, Concordia* . . .). Not horses, who would be all 'Fury' and 'Thunder'. Works of art, perhaps – a dealer's auction list? If those were statues or paintings which had all changed hands in the space of six weeks, it must have been a famous collection which had been broken up; Geminus would know. Another alternative, and the one I eventually favoured, was that it sounded like a sailing list, and the stately symbolic names represented ships.

There was nothing else for me to do at Cape Colonna. I was anxious to leave. Before I left, Gordianus said sombrely, 'This freedman is too dangerous to tackle alone. Falco, you need help. As soon as Milo has installed me safely at Paestum, I shall send him to join forces with you – '

I thanked him politely, promising myself to avoid this stroke of fortune if I could.

When I arrived back in Croton I bumped into Laesus, though I had not expected to see him again and *he* looked pretty surprised at seeing *me*. But I discovered that while I had been paddling on the beach at Cape Colonna this excellent spark Laesus had sailed to Tarentum. My honest new friend told me he had made enquiries about Barnabas at the old Pertinax farm (now part of the Imperial estate).

'Who did you ask?'

'Who was bound to know? His mother, ghastly witch. Zeus, Falco!' Laesus complained. 'The wicked old baggage chased me out of her home with a pan of smoking fat!'

I tutted gently. 'Laesus, you have to charm them before they reach the hearth. Throw a purse in over the threshold but remember, your average granny can tell at twenty yards if a purse is only stuffed with mountain rocks!'

Laesus dashed on heedlessly: 'She didn't want money, only my blood. The revolting crone started life as a slave but she's free now and people look after her – I suppose Barnabas took care of it.'

'Her loving boy! What was she like?'

'She smelt frowsty as a tiger's armpit and had no sense of time. But if the barmy old basket knows anything at all, you can hang onto the freedman's cash yourself. As far as I could gather, his mother thinks he's dead.'

I laughed.

'Laesus, I'll bet mine thinks the same; but it only means I haven't written home for a week!'

Events at Cape Colonna had shown Barnabas was very much alive.

I ought to have gone to see this angry old Calabrian bat myself, to sort out the real story. But life's too short; you can't do everything.

I showed Laesus the notebook we found in the Temple of Hera.

'Look at this list: Nones of April, *Galatea* and *Venus of Paphos*; four days before the Ides, *Flora*; two days before May, *Lusitania, Concordia, Parthenope*, and *The Graces* . . . Mean anything? *I* think these are ships. I think it's either a docking list, or, more likely at that time of year, a record of sailings . . . '

Laesus looked at me with those bright black robin's eyes of his. 'Nothing I recognise.'

'You said you used to sail to Alexandria yourself!'

'This doesn't mention Alexandria!' Laesus argued, with a pinched appearance at being caught out in his own professional sphere. 'It was a long time ago,' he admitted, understandably shamefaced.

I grinned at him remorselessly. 'A long time, and a lot of wine jugs if you ask me! Alexandria was a hunch.'

'Well, leave me the list and I'll ask around – '

I shook my head, tucking the notebook away in my tunic. 'Thanks; I'll keep it. It may be nothing important anyway.'

It says much for his lopsided charm that although I feel queasy just peering into rockpools I almost agreed to travel in his ship with Laesus round to Rhegium. But you can die of being seasick; I preferred to stick on land.

I made Laesus a present of my goat. I guessed she might end up barbecued on the shore. I felt bad about it afterwards. But there are two things a private informer is better not lumbered with: women and pets.

I never mentioned she was sacred. Killing a sacred beast brings horrible misfortune but only, in my experience, if you know what you have done. When you don't know you don't worry, so you stand more chance.

The goat went with Laesus quietly: a fair-weather creature – like most of my friends. I told her if she had to be eaten by a sailor, I could not entrust her to a nicer man.

XXI

So; back to tell the Emperor how well I had done in Bruttium.

That week I spent in Rome was disastrous. My mother despised me for failing to fetch her liquorice. Lenia bullied me out of three weeks' rent. Helena Justina had left no messages. At the Camillus house I learned that she had left Rome to spend high summer in some country retreat; I was too proud to ask the door porter where. Her father, who was a pleasant man, must have heard I had come calling; he sent a house slave after me inviting me to dine, but I was too miserable to go.

Against this depressing background it was with some trepidation that I entered the Palace to report. Before I encountered Vespasian I tracked down Anacrites to compare notes.

I found him in a poky office, studying invoices. I managed to extract a confession that he failed in his mission to find Aufidius Crispus, the conspirator who had fled to Neapolis. It also emerged that he had done nothing about Barnabas either; even my news that the freedman had made another attack on a senator failed to rouse him. Anacrites was now auditing the contractors who had organised the Emperor's Judaean Triumph, so his mind was on tenders and daywork rates; he seemed to have lost all interest in plots.

Cursing him for a short-tempered, introverted scarab, I slouched off to see the Emperor, feeling very much alone.

After I finished my story Vespasian pondered for some time.

'Caesar, I hope I have not overstepped the mark?'

'No,' he answered eventually. 'No, that's all right.'

'Will you install Gordianus at Paestum?'

'Oh, yes! Decent of him to be satisfied with that . . . '

Opposing the Emperor was a highly productive racket! Gordianus had enjoyed all the excitement of plotting with his cronies, then afterwards he had just settled back munching pan-fried sweetbreads off the altar at Colonna while he waited for his reward. I said nothing, though what I thought may have shown in my face.

We had a short, inconclusive discussion about money, then Vespasian continued to stare at me in a way I found odd. The feeling of being excluded from secret court protocol started to grate again but

84

just when my indignation made me want to run off to herd sheep on Mount Etna for six months, he mentioned wryly, 'I should have sent you after the yachtsman too!'

I took a moment to realise this could be an offer of work.

'Oh?' I asked (casually).

'Hmm!' he said (with a grim smile). 'Anacrites did his best, he tells me, but had to bring back my letter to Crispus marked "address unknown".'

'Oh what bad luck!' I exclaimed.

The feeling I was getting now was one which I much preferred. The Emperor may have been aware of that.

'I imagine,' suggested Vespasian cheerily, 'you will not be too keen on leaving Rome so soon after your return?'

I shook my head, looking grave. 'I have an elderly mother, sir, who likes to keep me here! Besides,' I added, lowering my voice because this point was serious, 'I hate jobs where some other mucker has already swanned in and spoiled all the trails.'

'I appreciate that. But Aufidius Crispus owns half Latium,' Vespasian told me, not without a tinge of jealousy. 'So I feel obliged to worry when he fails to communicate.'

Latium was long-established farming country, rich in olive oil and wine. A new Emperor who was jostling his opponents into order would pay careful attention to anyone who was big in Latian wine.

I grinned at the Emperor. Neither of us mentioned the sacred word 'diplomacy'.

'Well, sir, lots of people would dart away if they were saluted by a Palace spy!'

'He may find himself saluted by someone worse than that. As a gesture from me, I want you to warn Crispus. Find him, Falco; and find him before Barnabas does!'

'Oh I'll find him. I expect what it needs,' I offered, helpfully, 'is a new face, someone who looks completely unlike a public official – '

'Exactly!' said Vespasian. 'The letter's with my secretary. It's first-quality papyrus, so when you do encounter Crispus, try not to drop it in the drink.'

I pointed out that prices on the Bay of Neapolis were notoriously expensive, yet I failed to persuade him to upgrade my daily fee.

'But you can travel at public expense,' was the best he would come up with. 'There is a ship called the *Circe* I want to return to Pertinax's father; I gather she used to be based at Pompeii, so you can sail her back there for the old man.'

I reckoned I would arrange transport overland for myself. Yet having access to a merchant vessel did offer possibilities; I remembered a certain abandoned commodity which might enhance my livelihood while providing a handy disguise . . . I would turn up in Campania as a traveller in lead.

On my way out, I popped my head into Anacrites' closet where he was still scowling over a pile of boring bills. I made sure I gave him a big happy grin and a wave to cheer him up.

Anacrites shot me a look in return which implied that I had made myself a lifelong enemy.

Despite Anacrites, I was starting to feel more cheerful as I prepared for my trip to Neapolis. I had tracked down one ex-conspirator without too much difficulty. This second one appeared no worse. Finding men, like chasing women, was my way of life. I had learned to approach both in a relaxed mood.

If I had known about the *other* man I would be hunting in Campania, my mood might have been different.

And if I had known about the woman I would find there, I might not have gone at all.

PART THREE
A QUIET FAMILY HOLIDAY

THE BAY OF NEAPOLIS
The end of June

' . . . orgies, love affairs, adultery, trips to Baiae, beach parties, dinner parties, musical entertainments, boating parties . . . '

Cicero, **In Defence of Caelius**

XXII

Crossing the Plain of Capua we had one of our emergencies.

By then my friend Petronius Longus the watch captain had remembered that the last time we went on holiday he had said never again. I was working, using Petro's brood for cover. One of my numerous nephews, Larius, who was just turned fourteen, had been sent with us because his mother said he was going through a difficult phase. My sister thought he needed supervision. He was unlikely to get it. My view was that the seaside existed to let me act irresponsibly.

I had made that quip in front of Arria Silvia, Petro's wife; one of several mistakes already, and we were still ten miles from the sea.

The atmosphere was becoming more coastal. Both Petronius and Silvia assumed we were headed for Baiae, the best resort on the Bay, but Baiae was further north than I needed to be. I was wondering when I could safely mention this.

We had already skirted Capua. The white-scarred crags of the Apennines continued on our left, but the rain-soaked hills on the right had petered out. Up ahead, the flat-based valley merged into a low grey oceanic horizon. We were watching for Mount Vesuvius to separate from the main range near Neapolis.

Petronius had the reins. I did my whack, but he enjoys driving and since it was his family swarming in the back it seemed natural for him to be in charge. We had come in an ox cart: three adults, three little girls, hampers, plenty of amphorae, enough clothing for a six months' tour, several kittens at the springy, exploratory stage, my dismal lad Larius, and a fifteen-year-old neighbour Silvia had brought to help. This teenager was a lumpen creature, given to wild sobbing moods. Her name was Ollia. She was a maid with a dream, but she could not decide what it was.

I had warned Silvia that Ollia was bound to be seduced on a beach by some wily fisherboy. Silvia only shrugged. She was tiny and tough. Petronius endured her with his easy good temper, but she terrified me.

Petronius Longus had acquired his wife five years before. She was a copper-beater's daughter. As soon as we came home from Britain I had watched Silvia and her father settle on Petro like two old women in a market selecting a fresh sprat for their festival treat. I said nothing. There was no point upsetting him. He had always been attracted to dainty girls with flat chests and scornful voices who ordered him about.

So far the marriage was a peculiar success. Silvia's father had set them up in a way that showed how grateful he was to be rid of her. (Petronius, who was a scoundrel in his quiet way, had all along been eyeing up the copper-beater's cash.) The two of them must have quarrelled, but they kept it to themselves. When they produced Petronilla, Silvana and Tadia in rather short order there was no evidence that Petro had only done it to gain the honours of a three-times father to improve his civic rights. He adored his children; I had a hunch he even felt romantic towards his wife. But although Silvia thought the world of him in some ways, to her he was always just a sprat.

Petro's approach to fatherhood was pretty calm; he carried on with whatever he wanted to do while his rumbustious tots mountaineered all over him. The two eldest were scrambling up his powerful back, then slowly sliding down again, murdering his tunic braid. Tadia, the littlest, was viewing the countryside from my lap. Since she knew she ought not to be sucking her thumb she was gnawing one of mine. Private informers are iron-jawed, hard-hearted brutes who treat women like casual flotsam, but Tadia was only two; she did not yet appreciate that her friendly Uncle Marcus would pick up any pretty girl and play with her, then toss her aside as soon as the next one smiled at him . . .

Petronius had stopped the cart.

Tadia had a wide-eyed, panicky, whimpering look. Her father reproached me coldly, 'She obviously wants a lavatory, so why can't you mention it?'

Petro's Tadia was famous for enduring miseries in silence; just the sort of woman I longed to acquire but never could.

By then we were all tired, and all starting to wonder if this trip was a wise idea.

'Well, I've stopped,' announced Petronius. (He was a single-minded driver who resented interruptions, though with three children under five we had had plenty of those.)

No one else moved. I volunteered to put her down.

The Plain of Capua has no public facilities. Still, no one was going to mind if a two-year-old in trouble watered their crops.

Petronius Longus waited with the ox cart while Tadia and I stumbled about the local scenery. We were in the most fertile region of Italy, whose thriving vineyards, neat market gardens and well-gnarled olive groves extend from the great Vulturnus River to the sweet Lactarii Mountains, where the flocks of sheep run to six hundred ewes at a time.

We might as well have been in the deserts of Arabia Petraea. We had to look for a bush. Our immediate location offered only thin scrub. At two, Tadia was a woman of the world, which meant she refused to attempt a public performance so long as anyone within a five-mile radius might be buried in a foxhole watching her.

Finding Tadia's camouflage took us so far we could hardly see the road. It was rapturously peaceful. A cricket scraped at us from a sprig of flowering broom and there was a woozy scent of warm, bruised thyme underfoot. Birds were singing everywhere. I would have liked to dawdle and enjoy the countryside but Petronius held the rigid view that a family on a journey has to rush on.

Tadia and I gave her bush a thorough dousing, then emerged.

'Hmm! Tadia Longina, that's a pretty butterfly; let's wait here and watch him – ' Tadia watched the butterfly while I stared nervously towards the road.

I had glimpsed a dark, surly flurry. Men on horseback flooded round our companions like sparrows mobbing a crust. Then the slight figure of Arria Silvia stood up in the cart, apparently delivering Cato the Elder's speech to the senate on the need to destroy Carthage . . . The riders galloped off, somewhat hastily.

I seized Tadia, sprinted back to the road, recaptured a loose kitten, then vaulted up beside Petronius, who started the ox.

Silvia sat in pinched silence while I tried to betray no excitement as Petronius drove on. He was steering as he always did, except when he spotted a narrow bridge ahead or some squabble among his children was making him tense. He held the reins loosely in his left hand, leaning forwards on one knee, while his right arm lolled on his diaphragm. He looked as if he was nursing the first murmur of a heart attack, yet it was just how he relaxed.

'What was all that about?' I murmured discreetly.

'Oh . . . ' He stretched his shoulders slowly before he spoke. 'Half a dozen foul-mouthed countrymen in armour-plated helmets looking for some idiot who had stamped on their toes. They pawed our kit and threatened us all until Silvia gave them a piece of her mind – ' Sampling Arria Silvia's mind was as tricky as letting a midge fly up your nose. 'I pretended I was just a Roman tourist who had stopped beside the highroad for an argument with his wife – ' I wondered what they were arguing about; knowing them, probably me. 'They rattled off towards Capua. The sour green cloak in charge said I was the wrong man anyway . . . '

'Who did they want then?' I meekly enquired.

'Some stupid bastard called Falco,' Petronius growled.

XXIII

Late June: everyone who could manage it had left Rome. Some visited their country villas. Most of those who chose the seaside must have arrived two days before us. The crowds gave my predicament more urgency; I wanted to be safely behind doors.

At least I knew where I stood: Barnabas was still skulking about in that horrid viridian cloak. He was here in Campania – and now he was looking for me.

There were plenty of towns and villages around the Bay but we ruled out some, and the rest rejected us. Neapolis itself, with its fine summer palaces, seemed too pretentious to afford, while Puteoli, which had been the main landfall for Rome until the development of Ostia thirty years before, remained a noisy commercial port. Misenum was lousy with officials, being home to the fleet. Baiae, the fashionable watering hole, was commoner but full of dirty lodgings which refused to welcome children. Surrentum straddled a marvellous ravine which had to be reached by sea or miles of winding road; if a demented assassin was pursuing me, Surrentum could form a dangerous trap. Pompeii was too brash, Herculaneum too prim, and the thermal spa at Stabiae chockablock with wheezing old gentlemen and their snooty wives. There were villages on the slopes of Vesuvius, but the children had been promised the sea.

'If one more bare-arsed Campanian landlord shakes his head at our kittens and chamber pots,' Petronius confided in a dangerous undertone, 'I reckon I'll lose my temper unpleasantly!'

'How about Oplontis?' I suggested, trying to assume an air of casual innocence.

Oplontis was a small fishing hamlet in the centre of the Bay where the pervading scent of grilled mullet spoke well of the amenities. It boasted an immensely elegant villa complex, heavily boarded up. The smugglers were drinking peacefully and the beach boys pretending to mend their nets while they stared at us. This looked suitable. It looked cheap. It looked small enough to be safe; if an armed troop clattered in from Herculaneum, a curious crowd would flock out from every cottage on the beach. Oplontis (as it happened) was where I wanted to be.

We found a gap-toothed old biddy in black who hired us two scrappy rooms on the first floor of a faded hostelry. I noticed Petronius working out how if anybody sinister entered the front courtyard we could evacuate his family through the stable at the rear.

No one else was staying there; we could see why.

'We can manage for a night,' Petro tried to convince himself. 'Then find somewhere better for tomorrow – ' He knew once we settled in we would be fixed for our whole stay.

'We ought to have stopped in Baiae!' Silvia complained. Even when the rest of their tour party are tired as dogs, other peoples' wives can always find the energy to whine. Larius kept sniffing; he had noticed an intriguing smell. Seaweed, perhaps. Or perhaps not.

'Oh Larius, put a peg on your nose!' I snapped. 'Wait until you sample the public latrines in Stabiae and Pompeian drains!'

There was a courtyard with a well and a thin vine struggling on a pergola. Larius and I had a wash and sat on a bench while Silvia organised the beds. It was obvious she wanted to quarrel with Petro. One of our rooms had a window covered by a hide, allowing Larius and I to overhear the family violence; the phrase *'nothing but trouble!'* cropped up several times: that was me.

Petro's pretty little turtledove informed him that at first light next morning they would take their children home. His reply was too quiet to catch. When Petro swore he was astonishingly vulgar, but in a savage undertone.

Eventually things grew less intense; then Petro came down. He dashed a bucket of water over his head, hesitated, then joined us on the bench; his need for solitude was evident. He produced a smokey-green glazed flagon, gulping straight from it like a traveller who had driven further than he intended, and put up with a lot of abuse.

'How's the billet?' I ventured, though I guessed.

'Ropey. Four beds and a bucket.'

'Is Silvia upset?'

'It'll blow over.' A faint, tired smile touched Petro's lips. 'We've put the children and Ollia in one room; you two will have to be with us.'

Sleeping our large party on the cheap posed tactical problems: worst for Silvia and him. I offered to take Larius out for an hour; Petro merely grunted irritably.

He pulled again from his flask, which he did not offer round. Being clean again in a quiet place (with a drink) soon mellowed him sufficiently to go onto the attack: 'You ought to have warned me, Falco!'

'Look, I'll find a different dosshouse – '

'No. If some mob-handed bully boy is chasing you, I want you in sight!'

I sighed, but said nothing because his wife came down.

Silvia seemed quieter now. She took a spiteful pride in remaining efficient whatever the crisis, so had carried down a tray of cups. Larius got hold of the flask; I left it alone. I was looking forward to sampling the famous wines of Surrentum and Vesuvius, though certainly not tonight.

'Falco, you ought to have warned us!' Arria Silvia accused me bitterly, as if she really thought Petronius would have omitted saying it.

I sighed. 'Silvia, I have work to do. I'd like to stay unobtrusive in a family group. As soon as I can meet the man I need to interview, I'll be off. Petronius is not involved – '

Silvia snorted. Her voice grew more tense. 'Oh I know you two! You'll leave me alone with all the children in this terrible village while you do what you like. I won't know where you are, or what you're doing, or what any of it is about. Who,' she demanded, 'were those men this afternoon?' Silvia had an accurate grasp of whatever her male companions were trying to conceal.

I must have been weary. I was beginning to feel I could no longer cope; a typical holiday mood.

'The one in green must be a freedman with a grudge called Barnabas. Don't ask me who loaned him the cavalry. Someone told me he was dead – '

'Ghost, is he?' Petronius rasped.

'Matter of time!' Petro gave me his sardonic smile; I decided to concentrate on Silvia. I poured her a drink; she had a prissy way of sipping wine that made my teeth grate. 'Look, you know I work for Vespasian. A certain group have hung back from welcoming him to the purple; I'm persuading them that that is a bad idea – '

'*Persuading*?' Silvia interrogated.

'Apparently,' I said drily, 'the new diplomacy consists of reasoned argument – backed up by hefty bribes.'

I was too tired to argue and far too much in awe of her. Silvia reminded me briefly of Helena at her worst, but a tussle over nothing with her ladyship had always given me the mental satisfaction some men find in playing draughts.

'Earned any real cash from Vespasian yet?' Petronius niggled. My reply would have been ill-natured but we were supposed to be here to enjoy ourselves, so I held back. In a scruffy lodging house beside the Bay of Naples you get no thanks for restraint.

'I want to know what you are doing here?' Silvia broke in.

'My fugitive is on a boat that was spotted in this neighbourhood – '

'Spotted where?' she insisted.

'Oplontis actually.'

'So,' Silvia deduced inexorably, 'our staying at this disgusting village is no coincidence!' I tried to look suave. 'What will you do when you find the boat, Falco?'

'Row out to speak to him – '

'You don't want my husband for that.'

'No,' I said, cursing inwardly. I can row. But I had envisaged Petronius doing the hard work while I jumped off at landing stages and steered. 'Unless,' I started with a cautious glance, 'you can spare him to come to Pompeii to help me unload a cargo of ingots I'll be using for my disguise?'

'No, Falco!' Silvia raged.

Petronius made no attempt to speak. I avoided his eye.

Arria Silvia shot me a look that was as poisonous as aconite. 'Oh, what's the point asking me? You'll both do as you like!'

It seemed a smart idea to take Larius upstairs to inspect the accommodation and unpack.

This did not delay us long. We found our rooms up a dark corridor. We were hiring two stuffy cubicles with crumbling wattle walls. The beds had uneven softwood slats where they had lost their suspension ropes. Larius and I bent up our pallet to look for bugs but there was nowhere a bug who liked his comforts could make a nest, just a coarse cover, waxy with ancient dirt, which held together a few matted lumps of straw that would poke into our backs like mountain scree.

I changed my boots for sandals and headed downstairs, intending to suggest that we left Ollia with the children while the rest of us went out to eat. Larius was fiddling secretively in a satchel; I told him to follow me. At ground level I stopped, waiting to bawl up at him when the absent-minded sparrow forgot to come.

Across the courtyard Petronius Longus sat where we had left him, with his head back against the pergola, his long legs stretched out, and a pain-free expression as he absorbed the evening peace. He hated quarrels, yet could let them slide over him. Now he had finished driving he was, despite everything, starting to enjoy himself. His familiar brown hair looked more ruffled than usual. His winecup lolled at an angle; it was obviously empty, its weight in his hand merely comforting. His other arm was crooked casually round his wife.

After five years suffering the hazards of marriage these two managed in private with less fuss than their public mask implied. Arria Silvia had edged in beside Petronius. She was weeping, reduced to a disappointed young woman who felt exhausted beyond her strength. Petro was letting her snuffle on his great shoulder while he went on dreaming to himself.

Just when I had impressed myself with this clever dissertation on marriage, Silvia dried her eyes. I watched Petro rally his attention and wind her in closer. I had known him for years, and had seen him kiss more women than his wife would want to hear about; I could see the old reprobate was taking much more trouble now than a mere peck to keep the peace. Afterwards he said something to her, very quietly, and she answered him. Then they both got up and walked out towards the road with their arms round each other and their heads close.

I felt an internal wrench that had nothing to do with lack of food. Larius appeared. I told him I had changed my mind about dinner, then dragged him back indoors.

One aspect of my nephew's difficult phase, I noticed, was that wherever anyone took him the young curmudgeon looked as if he wished he had stayed at home.

XXIV

Next day the sun was shining; in my mood, this came as a surprise.

I strolled out to take stock; to the right and left the two arms of the Bay lay shimmering in a fine grey haze. Ahead, Capri was entirely hidden by mist, and when I glanced back over my shoulder the cone of Vesuvius loomed as a mere blur too. But even at that early hour the light off the sea was beginning to dazzle; this soft, all-pervading haze would precede a hot, blue, brilliant day.

I felt dismal. My nephew had slept soundly, despite our rocky mattress. Petronius snored. So (I discovered) did his wife.

'Falco looks jaded. We must find him a girlfriend!' Arria Silvia chirruped brightly at breakfast, piercing a peach with her vixenish front teeth. I told myself that at least we had not been away long enough for people to collect stomach disorders and start comparing notes on them while we ate.

'Give him five minutes in Pompeii,' quipped Petro, 'and he'll find one for himself . . . ' For a moment I thought he meant a stomachache.

I could not concentrate on pointless domestic chat. I felt thoroughly preoccupied. Here I was in Campania in the holiday season. As we drove in yesterday I had sized up the laughing faces on all sides – frank young women in the pink of condition, relaxed and plumped up in the warm seaside air, each one wearing very little and just looking for a reason to take it off . . . So here was I, a handsome devil in a nearly-new mustard tunic (a snip from a second-hand stall, jollied up by my mother with two rows of crinkled braid). And if a woman who looked like a Venus of Praxitiles had jumped out of a fountain straight into my lap wearing nothing but a pair of fancy sandals and a smile, I would have tipped her off and stomped away to brood on my own.

Breakfast was water and fruit. If that was not what you were used to at home, you could omit the fruit.

We men slunk off to Pompeii the same day.

Just out of town at the mouth of the Sarnus lay a small harbour which also served the larger centres at Nola and Nuceria. We left the cart at the port; the Marine Gate was too steep to take it up. Larius wanted to stay watching the boats but I could not face telling my sister that her first-born had received a rude awakening on the River Sarnus quayside from a barrel-waisted bosun, so we dragged him along with us. Petro and I went through the pedestrian tunnel on the left of the Gate; there was a separate slope for pack animals, which Larius pointedly scuffled up by himself. As we waited at the top, we could hear him muttering scornfully.

Pompeii had wine, grain, wool, metalwork, olive oil, an air of thrusting prosperity, and ten smart watchtowers set in vigorous city walls.

'A place that intends to last!' One of my sharper remarks.

All right; I do know what happened at Pompeii – but this was eight years before Mount Vesuvius exploded. Any student of natural science who did notice their local mountain was shaped like a volcano deduced it was extinct. Meanwhile, the Pompeian playboys believed in art, Isis, Campanian gladiators, and ready cash to purchase gorgeous women; few of the flashy bastards were great readers of natural science.

At that time Pompeii was famous for two events: a riot in the amphitheatre when the Pompeians and Nucerians set about each other like hooligans, leaving quite a few dead: then a devastating earthquake. When we visited, eight years after the quake, the whole place still resembled a building site.

The Forum was rubble and ruins, mainly because the townsfolk had made the mistake of commissioning their architects to rebuild it on a grander scale. As usual, given this excuse, the architects dreamed and spent their fees, oblivious to the years that passed. A freed slave who was out to make a name for himself reconstructed the Temple of Isis and the citizens had propped up their amphitheatre in case they ever wanted to beat up their neighbours again. But the Temples of Jupiter and Apollo stood shrouded in scaffolding with their statuary stored in the crypt, and it was hard work forcing a path round the contractors' wheelbarrows to get ourselves up past the provision markets, under one of the ceremonial arches, and on into town.

This seemed an educational spot for Petronius and me to bring young Larius. Having Venus as their patroness, the town councillors wanted her to feel at home. Once they rebuilt her own Temple it would dominate the Marine Gate, but she hardly needed that. The fashionable marker for every Pompeian's elegant vestibule was a wall painting of Priapus with his tireless erection; the richer they were, the more immense the welcome the god of procreation extended at their door. It was none too easy for strangers to distinguish the commercial brothels from private homes. (Judging by the town's racy reputation, it might not matter if you got it wrong.)

Spotting my nephew staring about with his sweet air of astonishment, a prostitute outside a genuine bordello grinned at him through her few blackened teeth. 'Hello, sonny! Want to meet a pretty girl?'

In a chalk sketch on their wall the lord of fertility, visibly virile yet again, demonstrated what was required of a lad, though the madam did not inspire much confidence. She was quite revolting under the clogging layers of kohl.

'We're just looking round at the moment,' I apologised sociably as Larius dodged back under my wing. 'Sorry, grandma – ' For some reason the old bag of bones started shrieking abuse. Petronius grew flustered so we dived into the safety of an open-air winery.

'Don't expect me to lead you into bad ways,' I muttered to Larius. 'Your ma thinks I'm looking after you. Ask your father when you get home.'

My sister Galla's husband was a lazy river boatman whose main advantage was the fact he was never at home. He was a hopeless womaniser. We could all have coped if my sister had not minded, but Galla was unusually fastidious and she did. Sometimes he left her; more often Galla threw him out. Occasionally she relented 'for the sake of the children' (that tired old myth); the family's father stayed with her a month if she was lucky, then he drifted off after his next short-sighted garlandseller, my sister produced another unhappy baby, and the whole brood were left on their own again; when they were stuck, the poor things were sent to me.

Larius was looking morose as usual. I could not decide if it was being stuck, or being sent to me.

'Cheer up!' I chivvied. 'If you want to waste your pocket money ask Petro what to pay. He's a man of the world – '

'I'm happily married!' Petronius protested – though he then revealed to my nephew that he understood a fairly basic service could be had for a copper as.

'I wish,' Larius pronounced haughtily, 'people would stop ordering me to cheer up!' He stalked off to lean over the fountain at the cross-roads, scooping up an abstemious drink of water by himself. A pimp spoke to him and he scuttled back; Petro and I pretended we had not seen.

I leaned on the counter with my nose in my beaker, facing up to the fact that I had half a score of nephews, of whom Galla's gloomy Larius was only the first to throw off his boyhood tunic at fourteen. Thanks to my own elusive father, I was acting head of our family. Here was I, meddling with high politics, scouring the coast for a renegade, dodging a murderer, booted into oblivion by the woman I had set my heart on – yet I had also promised my sister that sometime during this trip I would enlighten her boy on whichever facts of life he had failed to pick up already from his dreadful friends at school . . . Petronius Longus is always kind to a man in a crisis; he clapped me on the shoulder and treated us by paying for the wine.

As we went out I found myself glancing behind, afraid I might be followed by a grim wraith in a green cloak.

XXV

We had come to meet a man. As usual in these circumstances we suspected he would lead us a merry dance then rob us blind. Since he was a plumber, it was a virtual certainty.

We found our way north past the Temple of Fortuna Augustus towards the water tower beside the Vesuvius Gate. The Pompeians provided sensible raised walkways but at the hour we turned up they were using all the pavement space themselves, so we three honest strangers tramped through their rubbish in the road. While we concentrated on planting our sandals out of the stickiest mule dung it was difficult to inspect the street scenery, but from the back alleys we could glimpse the tops of trellises and walnut trees above high garden walls. Fine, spacious, two-storeyed houses faced onto the main thoroughfares, though there seemed to be a depression: so many were being converted into laundries and warehouses or let out piecemeal as apartments over shops.

Until the earthquake, the town's water system had relied on the aqueduct which brought water from Serinum to Neapolis, a handsome artefact with a subsidiary branch which came in here to a big square tower which had three arches of brickwork decorating its outer walls. Large mains used to lead off, one for the public fountains and two others for business premises and private homes, but the quake had cracked the cistern and broken up the distribution pipes. The man we wanted was tinkering with the reservoir half-heartedly. He wore the usual one-sleeved workman's tunic, two little warts beside his chin, and the whimsical, slightly tired expression of a man who is much brighter than his job requires.

'Been at it long?' I asked, trying to hide my amazement that in the country it took eight years to cement a leaky tank.

'Still waiting for a town-council order.' He clanked down his basket of chisels and wrenches. 'If you're buying a house in Pompeii, sink a deep well in your garden and pray for rain.'

I owed our introduction to my brother-in-law the plasterer; it took the form of that death's head phrase, *Just mention my name* . . . His name was Mico. I mentioned it extremely cautiously.

'Mico's name,' I admitted, 'sends even hard-bitten foremen with thirty years' experience rushing off to the nearest fountain to drown themselves – I dare say you remember him?'

'Oh I remember Mico!' observed the plumber, through gritted teeth.

'I reckon,' suggested Petronius, who knew my cack-handed brother-in-law and despised him as we all did, 'that after enduring a riot and an earthquake, being visited by young Mico proves the proverb that disasters come in threes!'

Mico's plumber, whose name was Ventriculus, was a quiet, calm, honest-looking type who managed to give the impression that if he said you needed a new cistern it might almost be true. 'He was pretty bad,' agreed the plumber.

'Torture!' I said, starting to smile for the first time this trip. Heaping abuse on my brothers-in-law always cheers me up. 'A painter in Latium lost an eye when his brush bounced off a tumulus in Mico's bumpy skim. He received no compensation; the judge said, if he knew he was following *Mico* round he should have been prepared for hummocks . . . ' I stopped, then we all grinned. 'So you're a friend of Mico's?'

'Isn't everyone?' murmured Ventriculus, and we all grinned again. Mico is convinced anyone who meets him loves him. The fact is, they just stand there trapped by his awful great-heartedness while he buys them drinks (he does buy the drinks – he buys plenty; once Mico gets you stuck in a tavern he keeps you squirming there for hours). 'Why,' Ventriculus teased me, 'would any loving brother give his sister to this Mico?'

'My sister Victorina gave herself!'

I could have added that she gave herself to anyone with the bad taste to have her, usually behind the Temple of Venus on the Aventine, but that cast a slur on the rest of the family which we did not deserve.

The thought of my relations was upsetting me so badly that I launched into what I wanted Ventriculus to do. He listened with the mild demeanour of a man who had waited eight years for his town council to draw up a specification for emergency repairs. 'We do have spare capacity; I can take on a foreigner . . . '

So we all trooped back through Pompeii and out to the port. The plumber plodded along in silence, like a man who has learned to be polite to lunatics through dealing with civil engineers.

Thinking about my nephew, I had forgotten to check my ship's arrival, but when the Emperor says a vessel will be moved from Ostia to the Sarnus you can reckon that the sailors will set off immediately and not stop to dice for any sea nymphs on the way.

The ship called the *Circe* was waiting in the harbour. This was one of the Tarentum galleys built for Atius Pertinax – a huge, square-sailed merchantman, thirty foot deep in the hold, with two great steering paddles either side of a high stern which curled up and over like the slim neck of a goose. She was sturdy enough to have braved the Indian Ocean and float back with sweet cargoes of ivory, peppercorns, gum tragacanth, rock crystal and luminous sea pearls. But since her maiden voyage she had led a harder life; Pertinax had been using her last year to thrash round Gaul. Now she was laden to the gunnels with a cold Atlantic shipment – long, four-sided ingots of British lead.

Ventriculus whistled admiringly when we all piled on board.

'I told you what they were,' I said as he inspected the ingots in amazement.

'I do hope,' he queried bluntly, 'these are not lost Treasury stock?'

'Just separated out from the system,' I replied.

'*Stolen?*'

'Not by me.'

'What's their history?'

'They were part of a fraud I investigated. You know how it is. They might have been useful for evidence so they were parked in a yard while the higher-ups all wondered whether they wanted a court case or a cover up.'

'What's the decision?'

'Nothing; interest faded out. So I found them still lying around . . . There's no documentation attached to them, and the Treasurer at the Temple of Saturn will never spot the loss.' Well; probably not.

'Any silver still in these?' Ventriculus asked, and he looked disappointed when I shook my head.

Petronius was gazing into the open hold with the grey face of a man who bitterly remembered being posted to a frontline fort in a province at the end of the world: Britain, where whichever way you turned, somehow the filthy weather always met you in the face . . . I saw him square his shoulders, as if they still felt damp. He hated Britain almost as much as I did. Though not quite. He still reminisced about the famous east coast oysters, and his eye sharpened keenly after women with red-gold hair.

'Does Vespasian know you've palmed this stuff?' he muttered in an anxious tone. He had a responsible job with a respectable salary; his wife liked the salary almost as much as Petronius loved his job.

'Special franchise!' I assured him cheerfully. 'Vespasian enjoys making a quick denarius on the side.'

'Did you *ask* him to chip in with you?'

'He never said no.'

'Or yes either! Falco, I despair of you – '

'Petro, stop worrying!'

'You've even pinched the ship!'

'The ship,' I stated firmly, 'is due to be returned to the indulgent millionaire who bought it for his son; when I've finished I'll inform the old duffer where his nautical real estate is berthed. Look, there's a fair weight to be shifted here; we had better get on . . . Oh Parnassus! Where's that lad?'

With a sudden pang of fright I sprang out on deck, scanning the harbour for Larius, who had disappeared. Just then the half-baked lunatic came roaming along the quayside with his characteristic lope and a vacant expression, gawping at the other ships. I caught sight of him – not far from a wrinkly stevedore with what looked like ninety years of sunburn lacquering his features, who was sitting on a bollard watching us.

XXVI

We had a hard day of it.

We spent the morning unloading ingots into our ox cart. Ventriculus rented a workshop in the Theatre quarter; the Stabian Gate was nearest but so steep that instead we trundled all along to the Nuceria Road Necropolis, chipped off the corners of a few marble tombs, and turned into town there. Our ox, whom we called Nero, soon looked sick. He had a charitable nature but evidently thought hauling great baulks of lead went beyond the call of duty for a beast on holiday.

Ventriculus started work at once. I wanted him to turn the ingots into water pipes. This meant they had to be melted down, then rolled out into narrow strips about ten feet long. The sheet lead was cooled, then curved around wooden battens until the two edges could be pinched together and soldered with more melted lead. (Making this seam is what gives pipes their pear-shaped section if you look at them end on.) Ventriculus was willing to provide various widths, but we concentrated on a regular-sized bore: *quinariae*, about a digit and a quarter in diameter – the handy household size. Water pipes are unwieldy objects: even a ten-foot quinaria weighs sixty Roman pounds. I had to keep warning Larius, who was short on concentration, that he would know all about it if he dropped one on his foot.

As soon as we had transferred all the ingots to the workshop and the plumber had produced a batch of pipes, we sent the cart back to Oplontis; Ventriculus threw in gratis a sack of bronze taps and stopcocks, which shows what kind of profit *he* was making on the deal. The plan was that I should take round samples and make on-the-spot sales, but wherever possible I would fix up major contracts for Ventriculus to carry out at a later date. I wanted to take a large instalment back to Oplontis now, which meant only one driver and no passengers; Petronius would drive the load. He was big enough to protect himself, and got on well with Nero. Besides, although he had never complained I knew Petro wanted to speed back early, to placate his wife. I felt a real public benefactor when I sent him off.

I treated the plumber and Larius to a splash in the Stabian baths. Then before our hike home the lad and I trooped off via the harbour so I could have a last word with the captain of the *Circe*. I showed him the notebook I had brought home from Croton,

and told him my theory that the list of names and dates referred to
ships.

'Could be, Falco. I know *Parthenope* and *Venus of Paphos* as Ostia
corn transports . . . '

While we were talking I lost sight of my nephew yet again.

I had left him mooning on the quayside. Scratched graffiti of
two gladiators gave witness to where he had been amusing himself
last: instead of the pimply-kneed rabbits we had seen adorning tavern
walls in town, my scallywag's doodles had powerful lines; he could
really draw. But artistic talent is no guarantee of sense. Keeping track
of Larius was like house-training a chameleon. Ships exerted a special
fascination; soon I was dreading that he had slipped aboard one as a
stowaway . . .

Suddenly he sauntered back in sight: gossiping with the well-tanned
crow's-nest type I saw spying on us with such interest earlier.

'*Larius*! You flea-brained young punk, where in Hades have you
been?' He opened his mouth casually to answer, but I cut him short.
'Stop dodging off, will you? It's bad enough looking over one shoulder
for some manic assassin, without constantly scouring the horizon for
you!'

Perhaps he intended to apologise, but my fright had made me
so annoyed I just nodded to the curious stevedore then dragged
my nephew away by one ear. Remembering Barnabas brought another
cold sweat under my tunic. Snatching a final glance around the port
as if I feared the freedman might be watching us, I stormed off in the
direction of the hole we were calling home.

Oplontis was a way station on the road to Herculaneum. It was not
far, though more than anybody wanted to tramp after a day of lugging
lead to and fro. Pompeii was sited on rising ground (an ancient lava
field I suppose, though we had no reason to guess that then); as we
turned north in the warm twilight a complete panorama of the shore
confronted us. We stopped.

It was almost July. The nights grew dark without ever growing old.
It was dusk now, with the steep cone of Vesuvius just vanishing from
view. All along the beautiful Bay, from Surrentum to Neapolis, where
the tycoons of Campania and various important Romans had built their
seaside villas over the past fifty years, twinkled the lanterns that lit their
fanciful porticos and romantic colonnades. At this time of year most
were in residence. The entire sweep of the coastline was dotted with
dancing yellow lights from bonfires on the beach.

'Very picturesque!' Larius commented wryly. I had paused for
breath, allowing myself a moment of enrapturement. 'Uncle Marcus,
this seems a good chance to have our embarrassing chat. "*Larius*," he
mimicked, "*why does your daft mother say you're being difficult?*"'

He was half my age and twice as despondent but when he stopped being miserable he had a wonderful sense of fun. I was very fond of Larius.

'Well, why does she?' I grunted, irritated at being interrupted in a fit of reverie.

'No idea.' In the second it took me to bring out the helpful question he had reverted to being a morose lout.

While my nephew gazed at the scenery, I scrutinised him.

He had an intelligent brow under an unkempt swathe of hair that drooped into solemn, deep-brown eyes. Since I saw him throwing nuts at his little brothers last Saturnalia he must have shot up three digits in height. His body had stretched so fast it had left his brain trailing behind. His feet, and ears, and the parts he was suddenly too shy to talk about, were those of a man half a foot taller than me. While he was expanding into them, Larius had convinced himself he looked ridiculous; in all honesty he did. And he *might* fill out handsomely – or he might not. My Great Uncle Scaro looked like a listing amphora with out-of-proportion jug handles all his life.

In view of his surly answer, I decided a man-to-lad talk would be unprofitable tonight. We started to walk again but after another ten paces, he heaved a dramatic sigh and fetched out, 'Let's get it over with; I promise to cooperate!'

'Oh thanks!' I was trapped. Casting round in despair I asked him conventionally, 'What does your schoolmaster think of you?'

'Not much.'

'That's a good sign!' I heard his head turn doubtfully. 'So what's causing your mother all this grief?'

'Didn't she tell you?'

'She was well-primed for a torrent but I didn't have three days to spare. Tell me yourself.'

We must have marched on for half a minute. 'She caught me reading poetry,' he admitted in the end.

'Good gods!' I burst out laughing. 'What was it – rude verses from Catullus? Men with big noses, vindictive whores in the Forum, grubby lovers chomping at each others' private parts? Believe me, there's more pleasure, and much better nourishment, in a decent lunch of goat's cheese and bread rolls . . . ' Larius shuffled. 'Your mother may have a point,' I murmured more kindly. 'The only person Galla knows who scribbles elegies in notebooks is her peculiar brother Marcus; he's always in trouble, short of cash, and usually has some scantily clad rope dancer in tow . . . She's right, Larius: forget poetry. It's just as disreputable, but much more remunerative, to sell green-tinted love potions or become an architect!'

'Or be an informer?' Larius jibed.

'No; being an informer rarely brings in cash!'

Out in the Bay other faint lights were bobbing, as the night fishermen uncovered their lamps to lure their catch. Much nearer at hand a single ship had appeared unnoticed while we walked; she must have come from the direction of Surrentum, hidden in the twilight as she hugged the shore below the Lactarii Mountains, but now she emerged proudly into the centre of the Bay. We could just make her out. She was much smaller than the *Circe*, altogether a different craft from Pertinax's huge merchantman. This was the sort of toy every rich man who owned a villa at Baiae kept tied up to his landing stage – like the other pleasure boat I had in my life at the moment, the one the conspirator Crispus had fled aboard so conveniently.

Larius and I both slowed our steps. Gliding in silence the ship made a lovely, slightly melancholy sight. We watched, enthralled, as this slender vision crossed the Bay – no doubt some plump young barrister proud of his senatorial ancestors was bringing home a dozen high-class girls with low-grade morals from a beach party on the Positanum coast; his expensive caïque was sliding gracefully with a silver wake back towards one of his coastal properties . . .

My nephew exclaimed with a thrill of speculation he could hardly keep in, 'I wonder if that's the *Isis Africana*?'

'And what,' I asked him levelly, 'is the *Isis Africana*?'

And still bursting with the prospect, Larius piped up: 'She belongs to that man Aufidius Crispus. It's the name of the yacht you're looking for . . .'

XXVII

We quickened our pace again, our eyes still following the boat, but it grew darker and she was lost from us out in the Bay.

'Very clever!' I scoffed. 'I owe this to your tar-stained nark on the quayside, I presume?' Larius ignored me. I tried to contain my anger. 'Larius, we ought to have tipped him a denarius to stop him warning the owner that we asked.' We kept striding on. I made an attempt to restore peace. 'I apologise. Tell me I'm an ungrateful, bad-tempered swine.'

'You're a swine . . . It's just his age; he'll grow out of it!' Larius announced to the ocean balefully.

I laughed, ruffling his hair.

'Being a private informer,' I confided, twenty paces later, 'is less glamorous than you think – it's not all hard knocks and easy women, but mostly bad dinners and ruining your feet!' Fresh air and exercise were doing the boy good, but I felt glum.

'What shall we do when we find her, Uncle Marcus?' he fetched out unexpectedly. I had no idea what had brought us back on friendly terms.

'The *Isis Africana*? I shall have to decide my tactics when I've had a quiet look. But this Crispus sounds tricky – '

'What's tricky about him?'

'Big ideas.' I had done my homework before I left Rome. 'The illustrious Lucius Aufidius Crispus is a senator from Latium. He owns estates at Fregellae, Fundi, Norba, Formiae, Tarracina – good growing land in famous areas – plus a huge villa at the Sinuessa spa where he can sit in the sun and tot up his accounts. In his career in public service he landed jobs in all the wrong provinces: Noricum, for heavens sake! You've been to school; where's Noricum?'

'Go up to the alps and turn right?'

'Could well be – anyway, when Nero died and Rome came up for auction, nobody had heard of Noricum and nobody had heard of him. Despite that, Crispus sees imperial purple in his horoscope. What would be tricky is if he persuaded Fregellae, Fundi, Norba, Formiae and Tarracina to glimpse it too.'

'Local boy making good?'

'Right! So he's dangerous, Larius. Your mother will never forgive me if I let you become involved.'

Disgust silenced him briefly, but he was too inquisitive to sulk for long. 'Uncle Marcus, you always called politics a fool's game – '

'It is! But I was tired of helping bad-tempered women divorce feeble stationers' clerks, and working for the clerks was even worse; they always wanted to pay me in bottom-grade papyrus you wouldn't use to scribble a curse. Then I was invited to drudge for the Palatine. At least if the Emperor honours his commitments, there should be good pickings.'

'For the money then?' Larius sounded puzzled.

'Money is freedom, lad.'

If he had not been too soft to take the knocks and too shy to handle the women, this Larius would have made a good informer; he could persist with a line of enquiry until the person he was questioning wanted to thump his ear. (Also, his outsize puppy feet were bearing up to the Oplontis road far better than mine; I had a badly sore toe.)

'What do *you* want money for?' he grilled me relentlessly.

'Fresh meat, tunics that fit properly, all the books I can lay my hands on, a new bed with all four legs the same length, a lifetime's supply of Falernian to guzzle with Petro – '

'A woman?' he interrupted my happy flow.

'Oh I doubt it! We were talking about freedom, weren't we?'

A vaguely reproachful silence ensued. Then Larius murmured, 'Uncle Marcus, don't you believe in love?'

'Not any more.'

'There is a rumour you were smitten recently.'

'The lady in question left me. Due to my shortage of cash.'

'Oh,' he said.

'Oh indeed!'

'What was she like?' He was not even leering; he sounded genuinely intrigued.

'Marvellous. Don't make me remember. Right now,' I suggested, feeling older than my thirty years, 'what I'd settle for is a big copper bowl full of piping hot water to soak my tender feet!'

We trudged on.

'Was the lady – ' persisted Larius.

'Larius, I'd like to pretend I'd drag off my boots for her, and walk barefoot over a cinder path for another hundred miles. Frankly I stop feeling romantic when I get a bulging blister on my toe!'

'Was she important?' Larius finished stubbornly.

'Not very,' I said. (On principle.)

'So not,' persisted Larius, '"*she whom, through living, gives your life its sweet reason*" . . . ? Catullus,' he added, as though he thought I might not know. (I knew all right; I had been fourteen myself once, and stuffed to the gills with dreams of sexual conquest and depressing poetry.)

'No,' I said. 'But she could have been – and for your private information, *that's* a Falco original!'

Larius murmured quietly that he was sorry about my sore toe.

XXVIII

As we approached the inn at Oplontis, I saw two skulking figures on the dark beach outside.

I said nothing to Larius, but led him round in the shadows to slip in through the stable block. We found Petro bedding down the ox. Poor Nero was almost asleep on his cloven feet; after hauling my lead he was too tired even to bend his neck to the feeding trough so Petronius Longus, the hard man of the Aventine watch, was ticing whisps of hay into the beast's huge mouth with murmurs of loving encouragement.

'Just a bit more, precious . . . ' we heard him coax, in his tone for spooning broth down a sad child. Larius giggled; Petro was unabashed. 'I want to take him home in good condition!'

I explained to my nephew that Petronius and his brother (who was a tireless entrepreneur) had formed a syndicate to buy this ox with three of their relatives; it always caused bad feeling when Petro popped up at his country cousins' farm to borrow his investment.

'How is Nero meant to be shared then?' Larius asked.

'Oh the other four tell me it's a leg each for them, and I get his balls,' Petronius replied gravely; the big-city innocent. He shoved in a last sheaf of hay then gave up.

Larius, who was sharp but not yet sharp enough, squatted down to check, then leapt up proclaiming, 'He's an ox! He's been castrated; he hasn't any – '

Catching sight of our faces, he clammed up as the joke slowly dawned.

'Anyway,' I commented, 'this ox must be four years old; what lunactic named him Nero while the Emperor was alive?'

'I did it,' Petronius answered, 'when I picked him up last week; the others call him Spot. Apart from the fact he has a curly topknot and heavy jowls, whoever clipped his equipment bungled it, so he shares with our glorious late Emperor indiscriminate lechery: bullocks, heifers, five-barred gates; the fool will jump on anything – '

Petronius Longus had fierce views on government; trying to keep public order among citizens who knew they were ruled by a mad lyre player had filled him with frustration, though this was the only open political gesture I had seen him make.

111

Trailing a long dribble of saliva, Nero, who hardly looked equal to jumping on anything, closed his dun-coloured eyelids and leaned against the stall; changing his mind, he lunged forward fondly towards Petronius. Petro jumped back, and we all jammed up the gate, trying to look nonchalant.

'One bit of news,' I told Petro. 'Our ship is called the *Isis Africana* – Larius has been using his initiative.'

'Intelligent boy!' Petro applauded, pinching his cheek (knowing Larius hated it). 'And I've got something for you, Falco. I stopped by a turning to one of those upland villages – '

'What had you stopped for?' Larius interrupted.

'Don't be nosy. Picking flowers. Falco, I was asking one of the locals about who is important hereabouts. Do you recollect that antiquated ex-Consul we investigated in connection with the Pertinax conspiracy?'

'Caprenius Marcellus? His father? The invalid?'

I myself had never met him but I certainly remembered Marcellus: one of Rome's elderly senators, with seven previous consuls in his glorious pedigree. He had possessed an enormous fortune and no heir, until Pertinax caught his eye and was taken on as his adopted son. (Either he was *very* shortsighted, or being descended from consuls did not make a senator astute.)

'I saw the old bird at Setia,' Petro reminisced. 'Good wine country! But he was rich as Crassus. He owns vineyards all over Campania – one up on Vesuvius.'

'Officially,' I mused, 'Marcellus was cleared of conspiracy.' Even though he owned the warehouse the plotters used for storing their bullion, having a good pedigree and a massive fortune had largely protected him; we had made routine enquiries, then respectfully backed off. 'He's supposed to be much too ill for politics – and if so he won't be here; he couldn't travel if the story's genuine. His place might be worth a visit though – '

It struck me that this villa rustica could be harbouring Barnabas. In fact, a villa on Mount Vesuvius whose owner was ill elsewhere could provide a perfect hideaway. I was sure Petronius reckoned the same, though in his cautious way he said nothing.

Changing the subject, I mentioned the two secretive figures I had noticed earlier on the beach. Planting Larius behind us, Petro and I armed ourselves with a lantern and marched out to look.

They were still there. If they were lying in wait, they were completely unprofessional; a murmur of surreptitious voices met our ears. As our footfalls disturbed them, the smaller shadow detached itself and ran into the inn with a squeak. My nose twitched at rancid, second-rate rose-water, then I glimpsed a familiar top-heavy bosom and anxious, moon-shaped face. I chuckled.

'Ollia's quick off the mark! She's found her fisherboy!'

She had too. He sauntered up past us with the self-assured, curious stare these gigolos always possess. A dim girl's dream. He had the lovingly tended haircut, short sturdy legs and brawny brown shoulders that were made for showing off to city girls as he practised hurling nets.

'Goodnight!' Petro called firmly, in the voice of a watch captain who can handle himself. The young lobster-catcher sloped off without answering. His features were not up to much by Aventine standards, and I guessed that as a boatman's apprentice he was pretty slovenly.

We left Petronius in the courtyard: a man who took life seriously, strolling round to see that all was in order before he turned in.

As Larius preceded me up to our room, he turned back to whisper thoughtfully, 'He can't have a girlfriend, not with his family here. So *who* is he picking flowers for?'

'Arria Silvia?' I suggested, trying to sound neutral. Then my nephew (who was growing in sophistication daily) squinted down at me sideways, in a way that had me snorting with helpless laughter all up the stairs.

Arria Silvia was asleep. Through the tangled spread of her hair on the pillow her face looked flushed. She was breathing with the deep contentment of a woman who had been wined and dined, then walked home through the summer night and warmed up again afterwards by a husband who was famous for his thoroughness. Beside her bed she had a large bunch of dog roses, stuck in a dead fish-pickle jar.

As he came upstairs later we could hear Petronius humming to himself.

XXIX

Every householder knows the hazard; a man and a boy at the door selling something you don't want. Unless you feel strong, these whey-faced inadequates land you with anything from fake horoscopes or wobbly iron saucepans to a second-hand chariot with mock-silver wheel finials and a very small Medusa stencilled on the side, which you subsequently discover used to be painted crimson and had to have its bodywork remodelled after being battered to all Hades in a crash . . .

Larius and I became a man and a boy. Our load of black-market fitments gave us carte blanche to enter private estates. No one sent for the vigilantes. We shuffled round the coast, taking Nero up clinkered carriage-drives and sometimes back down them again five minutes afterwards; surprisingly often though, our visits took longer and our list of orders was longer when we left. Plenty of fine villas around the Bay of Neapolis now have British water pipes, and most did not acquire the goods as official ex-government stock. Several people took advantage of our cheap rates to renew their entire supplies.

I was not surprised; we had come knocking at the Corinthian portals of the rich. Their great-great-grandfathers may have filled the family coffers through honest toil in their olive groves or awards for political service (foreign booty, I mean), but subsequent generations kept themselves in credit by haggling for bargains kept under the counter after being smuggled into Italy without paying harbour-dues. They were matched in iniquity by their household stewards. These snooty rascals were getting new pipework for the price of cobnuts (and then creaming off a premium from their masters' accounts), but they still tried to slip us old iron rivets and funny Macedonian small change when they paid.

After a few days completely tongue-tied, Larius found his voice and worked up a sales patter that sounded as though he had been born in a basket under a market stall; what was more, I could trust him with the arithmetic. Soon we were quite enjoying selling pipes. The weather stayed wonderful, Nero was behaving, and we sometimes managed to arrive at a friendly kitchen door just as they were serving lunch.

Information seemed harder to come by than corn-meal cakes.

We had called at almost every maritime villa between Baiae and Stabiae. Even the friendly ones denied knowledge of Crispus and his boat. I had wasted hours allowing arthritic door porters to reminisce about marching through Pannonia with some low-grade legion led by a syphilitic legate who was later cashiered. Meanwhile Larius was sauntering along piers to look for the *Isis Africana*; any day now some lad with a fishing line would suspect him of immoral overtures and push him in the drink.

Against such a negative background, huckstering lead began to pall. This was the dreary side of being an informer: asking routine questions which never produced results; wearing myself out while I strongly suspected I had missed the real point. My work dragged. Because of it I could never relax and enjoy my friends' companionship. My stomach felt queasy. All the mosquitoes in the Phlegraean marshes had discovered my presence and homed in for their seasonal treat. I missed Rome. I wanted a new woman, but although there were plenty available I never liked any I saw.

I was trying to keep cheerful in front of Larius, though his basic good-nature was coming under strain. One day it rained as well. Even when the skies cleared, dampness seemed to hang around our clothes. Nero became bad-tempered; controlling him was such hard work we soon let him amble aimlessly.

In this way we found ourselves on yet another dusty Campanian road that led between lush vineyards and vegetable allotments. Healthy cabbages stood to attention in little hollows dug round them to conserve the dew. Distant labourers poked at the black soil with long-handled hoes. Nearby there was a trellised arch marking the entrance to an estate, with a flurry of brown hens around its feet, and an extremely pretty country maiden climbing out over a field gate in a way that showed us most of her legs and a lot of what went on higher up.

Nero had stopped to talk to the chickens while Larius gawped at the girl. She smiled at him as she approached.

'Time we made a call,' Larius decided, with a deadpan face. The lassie was too short, too young and too rosy for my taste, but a heart-stopper otherwise.

'That's your assessment is it, tribune?'

'Absolutely, legate!' Larius exclaimed. The girl passed us; she seemed used to being sized up admiringly by racketeers in carts.

'If she goes in,' I decided quietly. She went in.

Larius told me to amble on ahead; his intestines were suffering the twitchiness that makes being away from home such a joy. I set off to soften up his ladyfriend while he got himself fit. As I passed under the entrance arch the pallid sun ran behind another ominous cloud.

Something told me hobbledehoys hawking clothes pegs probably gave this establishment a miss. It was a run-down, beaten-up tip, full of dirt and disease, seeming to consist of out-buildings that had been knocked together from broken doors and planks; as I strolled in among them I was met by a woff of goats' pee and cabbage-leaves. From all quarters came a drone of fat, warm flies. The hen coops looked delapidated, and the byres a foot deep in mud. Three stove-in beehives leaned against a wattle screen; no neat, clean bee would zoom in here.

The girl had disappeared. Beyond the initial squalor some absentee landlord's tumbledown farmhouse, which he probably bought as an investment and had never even seen, was gradually dying from lack of management.

I never made it to the house. Common sense overruled: there was a horrendous dog with a matted tail, who was chained to a rocky post and raising havoc. The studs on his collar were as big as Indian emeralds. The links of his twelve-foot-long chain must have weighed two pounds apiece, but Fido was tossing the metalwork around as lightly as a banquet wreath of rosebuds while he raced from side to side, evidently thinking his next banquet might be me. In response to the racket, round a corner loomed a black-chinned lout with a cudgel. He went straight towards the dog, who redoubled his efforts to tear at my throat.

Without waiting to be told that the mutt was only being friendly I turned round, plucked my boot out of a cowpat, and set off back to the road. The man left his dog, but thundered after me. He was gaining fast as I burst out through the arch, bawling for Larius, and saw he had already turned Nero round for a quick getaway. I fell aboard. Nero mooed anxiously and set off. Larius, who had stationed himself in the back of the cart, was swinging an off cut from a quinaria wildly from side to side. The farmer could easily have grabbed the lead pipe's end and grounded Larius, but he soon gave up.

'Bit of luck!' I grinned, when my sister's pride and joy climbed over to join me on the front.

'It had struck me she might have a husband,' Larius answered demurely, getting his breath.

'No chance to ask . . . Sorry!'

'That's all right. I was thinking of you.'

'Nice lad, my nephew!' I commented to the countryside at large. (Though barley-fed pullets with red cheeks and straws in their hair had never been my type.) I lapsed into sadness, recalling women who were.

Larius sighed. 'Uncle Marcus, the omens seem hostile; shall we give up for today?'

I considered this option, glancing round to get my bearings. 'Damn Crispus! Let's drive up the mountain, find a cheery Vesuvian vintner, and get ourselves roaring drunk!'

I turned Nero off the coast road and up towards the mountain above Pompeii. According to what Petronius had told us, unless we found a winery first we would be driving past the farmland owned by Caprenius Marcellus, that rich old consul who once made the mistake of adopting Atius Pertinax.

It was about midday, but I think I had already realised the Villa Marcella was not a place where Larius and I would be offered a free lunch.

XXX

A shrine to my old friend Mercury, patron of travellers, marked the entrance to the Caprenius Marcellus estate. The god's statue surmounted a flat-sided pillar, carved from soft Pompeian lava-stone. This roadside herm wore a wreath of fresh wild flowers. Every morning a slave rode out on a donkey to renew the wreath; we were in rich man's territory.

I consulted my nephew, who looked glad to avoid a hangover; in any case, Nero took the initiative and boldly entered the track. The ex-Consul Marcellus was fabulously wealthy; the approach to his Vesuvian villa gave visitors ample time to find an envious expression before they turned up offering their respects. Passers-by who were calling to beg for a drink of water would die of dehydration on the way up.

We trundled through vineyards for about a mile, occasionally noticing weathered memorials to family freedmen and slaves. The track broadened into a more imposing formal carriage-drive; Nero expressed approval by lifting his tail and squirting out explosions of liquid manure. We passed geese in a mature olive grove, then a gallery of cypress trees brought us alongside a riding range dappled with shade; two desolate mountain nymphs with rather worn stone drapery acted as major-domos to a row of topiary peacocks who were looking out longingly over landscaped garden terraces.

Here, on the lower slopes of the mountain where the climate was most pleasant, stood a farm complex which must have gone back twenty generations; attached to it was a grand, much more recent villa in the handsome Campanian style.

'Quite nice!' sniffed my nephew.

'Yes, a tasteful plot! You stay here; I'll poke about. Whistle if you spy anyone.'

We had arrived at the noontide siesta. I winked at Larius, glad of a chance to explore. I trod quietly; as a consul Caprenius Marcellus had once held the highest magistracy in Rome, and after the distress of his son's political disgrace he was likely to be feeling sensitive.

I assumed the great house would be locked up, so I tackled this older villa rustica first. I strolled into the courtyard. The surrounding buildings were constructed of ancient rough-cut stone; white doves slept in the sunlight on red pantiled roofs which were holding up to the centuries well, yet sagged on their battens with comfortable ease. To the left were living quarters, lying quiet. Everything about the place looked well clipped and thriving, so there must be at least one bailiff who had read his Columella's *Country Matters*.

I entered the block directly opposite, through a handy open door. A short corridor contained various small rooms, once part of the old farmhouse but now given up to storage. I found an inner court containing olive-crushers and oil-presses; they looked scrupulously clean and had a faint, rich smell. Glancing over a half-door at the end of the passage, I saw a great barn with a threshing floor in front; a slim brindled cat was twining itself over a sack of grain. Somewhere a donkey brayed; I could vaguely hear a grindstone. I turned back.

The swimming scent as I passed the doorway had already told me that the unexplored rooms accommodated wine vats – in substantial quantities. Twenty transit amphorae lolled in the outside passage, partly blocking my path; the threshold was stained with a rich damson colouring. Within, the first compartment held presses, awaiting the new season's crop; in a larger room beyond would be the vats. I heard movements, so as I broached the inner sanctum I knocked, in order to appear respectable.

It was the usual happy scene of kegs and alcoholic smells. There were no windows in the solid walls, so this darkened area kept itself at a cool, even temperature. A blackened candle-end burned in a red dish on a rough wooden table among pipkins and tasting tots. Equipment that looked as if it belonged in a military hospital hung round on wall hooks. A very tall elderly man was funnelling last season's wine into a household flask.

'One of life's delights!' I murmured. 'A vintner racking off the home-farm special reserve, and looking pleased with it!' Without speaking, he let the slow trail from the demijohn run on. I leaned in the doorway peacefully, hoping for a taste.

The large flask suddenly gushed to the brim. He tapped his funnel, rocked back the demijohn and stuck a bung in it, then straightened up and smiled at me.

In his prime he must have been one of Campania's tallest men. Time had stooped him and left him desperately gaunt. His wrinkled skin had a floury, transparent look, and he wore a long-sleeved tunic as if he felt continually cold, though at present its sleeves were pushed back for his work. Whether his face was handsome could never have been an issue, for its features were completely dominated by a massively jutting nose. It was pitiful; he could have launched a pirate's trireme down the slipway of his great snout.

'Sorry to disturb you,' I apologised.

'Who did you want?' he enquired pleasantly. I stood back to let the nose go first, then we both started out to the yard.

'That depends. Who's here?'

His glance sharpened. 'Farm business?'

'Family.' We had reached the yard and crossed most of it. 'Is the Consul at Setia? Does he have an agent here?'

The man stopped dead as if some spasm of anguish had crippled him. 'You want to see the Consul?'

'Well, I'd *like* to – '

'Do you or don't you?' the tall man snapped.

O Jupiter; the Consul was in residence! (The last thing I expected, yet just my luck.)

My companion swayed slightly, gathering his resources with visible pain. 'Give me your arm!' he commanded imperiously. 'Come with me!'

It was difficult to back out. I could see Larius waiting in the cart, but the vintner was clinging hard to my arm. I relieved him of the wine flask as he tottered along.

So much for sampling a tot of his fiery Vesuvian jollop while I discreetly picked his brains, then scarpering before anybody found out I had been here . . .

As we turned the corner to the front of the main building, I discovered it was a massive two-storey villa with a central belvedere. Certainly it was not locked up! Bed linen was airing out of upper windows in the fitful sun, whilst in the dark shade between the pillars stood square plant tubs, still dripping where they had been watered shortly before. There were two immensely long wings, extending either side of a theatrical entrance; beyond this grand piece of masonry smoke wreathed, from a bathhouse furnace probably. The nearer wing supported a roof garden; craning up I glimpsed fan-trained peach trees, and exotic flowers entwining the balustrade. Instead of the inward-looking design of a town house, here graceful porticos with the best view in Italy faced straight out over the Bay.

I heaved at a handle-ring in the bronze mouth of a whiskery lion's head, so my companion could push ahead through the main door. He stood in the airy atrium regaining his strength. The hall had an open roof, above a rectangular pool with a marble rim and a dancing figurine. There was an air of high tradition. To the right was the strongbox. On the left stood a small shrine to the household gods; a posy of blue and white flowers sat in front of them.

'Tell me your name!'

'Didius Falco.' Five or six slaves appeared, but hung back when they saw the two of us conversing. Suddenly certain, I smiled at the tall man. 'And you must be Caprenius Marcellus, sir!'

He was just an old crosspatch in a natural wool tunic; I could have been wrong. Since he did not deny it, I was right.

The ex-Consul was scrutinising me down that nasal promontory. I wondered if he had heard of me; there was no way I could tell from his austere face.

'I am a private informer on an Imperial assignment – '

'That's no recommendation!' Now when he spoke I had no difficulty spotting the clean vowels and confident delivery of an educated man.

'Forgive me for barging in like this. One or two matters I need to discuss – ' His resistance was growing. His slaves moved discreetly nearer; I was about to be thrown out. I waded on quickly, before Marcellus could signal them. 'If it helps,' I claimed on a lucky impulse, 'your daughter-in-law was a client of mine quite recently – '

I had heard that he was fond of Helena, but he surprised me with results: 'In that case,' the Consul answered, with a cool expression, taking back his wine flask from my hand, 'be so good as to follow me . . .'

Walking with less difficulty now, he stomped off past the Lararium where his chipper household deities were pointing their bronze-booted toes at the bud-vase which some reverent member of the household had placed on the shrine. Two minutes later I guessed who might have done that. We entered a side room. It had doors which stood open onto a courtyard garden where a low table was arrayed with a country lunch. I could see at least ten waiting-slaves with napkins on their arms, standing about among the potted plants. I was not invited to the cold buffet, however. The ex-Consul had a guest that day, but someone much higher class than me.

At a grey marble pedestal a young woman with her back to us was adjusting a floral display with a swift, firm touch that said when she arranged a vase of flowers, they stayed arranged. My eyes half closed as I recognised the soft curve of her neck. She heard us. I had trained my face never to show surprise, but a smile that cracked the dry skin of my lips started even before the lady turned around.

It was Helena Justina.

She was the same height as me. I could look straight into those startled cantankerous eyes without stirring a muscle. Just as well; my legs had lost all their strength.

Since I last saw her, her own clear skin had deepened its colour in the country air, while her hair had developed a redder richness in which nothing so natural as country air had played any part. Today she had her hair bound up with ribbon, in a sweet, simple style that must have taken two or three maids an hour and a half and several attempts to fix. She was wearing white. Her gown looked as fresh as a great candida lily that had opened in that morning's sun, while the golden lady it was enhancing drew all my attention as the heavy lure of pollen draws a bee.

'Juno and Minerva!' she raged at the Consul. 'What's this then; your local rat-catcher – or just a passing rat?'

All the colours in the room grew brighter as she spoke.

XXXI

I was really stuck now. When Helena's feelings were getting the better of her she had more light and character in her face than many women with famous looks. My heart started running at a harder pace, and showed no sign of steadying.

'This trespasser claims you will vouch for him,' Marcellus suggested, sounding as if he doubted it.

'Oh she will, sir!'

Her dark-brown eyes raked me with contempt. I grinned happily, ready to roll over at her feet like a ticklish dog pleading for more.

As a prize for a senator's daughter I was not at my best. For selling the lead with Larius I wore a workman's one-sleeved red tunic and around my waist a deeply creased dirty leather pouch where I kept Vespasian's letter to Crispus plus my lunch; today Silvia had sent us out with apples, which at groin level produced an intriguing effect. Whenever I moved a folding metal rule and set square tied on my belt clanked together stupidly. My torso was displaying broad red tracts of recent sunburn, and I could not remember when I had last had a shave.

'His name is Marcus Didius Falco.' She pronounced it like a wronged widow denouncing a thief: a widow who was *well* able to stand up for herself. 'He'll spin you more fables than the Sybil of Cumae; don't employ him unless you have to, and don't trust him if you do!'

No one I had ever known was so rude to me; I beamed at her helplessly, drinking it in. The Consul laughed indulgently.

Marcellus was attempting to reach a long chair, the sort used by invalids. Slaves had followed us in – ten or twelve flat-footed country cream clots, all looking so respectful it made me ill – and as he began struggling the circle tightened formation; but it was Helena who moved to him. She pulled the chair nearer, then held it firm, allowing him to sink onto it in his own time.

A man could look forward to growing old with Helena Justina in charge: plenty of scope to enjoy writing your memoirs while she made you eat sensibly and kept the household quiet for your afternoon nap . . . Refusing to look at me, she rescued the wine flask and carried it outside.

'Wonderful creature!' I croaked at the old man. He smiled complacently. A cheeky half-naked artisan could only admire their strong-willed lady from afar; it was understood that her life and mine would never touch.

'We think so.' He seemed pleased to hear her praised. 'I have known Helena Justina since she was a child. It was a famous day for this family when she married my son – '

Since she had divorced Pertinax, who was dead now anyway, I found difficulty answering. Fortunately she returned (all dancing crimson ribbons, and the sweet sharp spice of some highly priced fragrance from the Malabar Coast . . .).

'So the villain is called Falco!' the Consul declared. 'An informer – is he good at his job?'

'Very,' she said.

Then, for an instant, our eyes met.

I waited, trying to gauge the scene. I sensed a slight atmosphere; nothing to do with Malabar perfumery. Her ladyship took herself off to another chair some distance apart, extracting herself from our business affairs like a well-bred young woman. (This was nonsense; Helena Justina interfered in everything if she could.)

'Matters to discuss?' Marcellus prompted me. I apologised for not visiting him in formal dress and offered my condolence on the death of his adopted heir. He was up to it; his face showed no alteration that I could detect.

Next I stated in the same neutral voice how I had been appointed an imperial executor for the Pertinax estate. 'Insult piled on injury, sir! First some negligent jailor finds your son strangled; then the five fellow senators who had pounded their intaglio rings on his will as witnesses are bumped aside by Vespasian's agents taking over as executors – a fine waste of sealing wax and three-stranded legal thread!'

The Consul's expression remained inscrutable. He made no attempt to disown Pertinax: 'Did you know my son?' Interesting question: could mean anything.

'I had met him,' I confirmed carefully. It seemed easiest not to mention that the testy young bastard once had me badly beaten up. 'This is a courtesy visit, sir; a vessel called the *Circe* is being returned to you. She is docked on the Sarnus at Pompeii, ready to be claimed.'

An oceangoing merchantship: a life-saver to a poorer man. To a multimillionaire like Marcellus, simply a fleet vessel his chief accountant sometimes reminded him he owned. Yet he burst out at once, 'I thought you people were impounding her at Ostia!'

I felt a flutter at his intimate knowledge of the Pertinax estate. Sometimes in my business the simplest conversation can give a useful hint (though an excitable type can easily miscalculate and convince himself of a hint that was never there . . .).

As he noticed me speculating I reassured him quietly, 'I had her sailed down here for you.'

'I see! Shall I need repossession documents?'

'If you let me have writing equipment, sir, I'll give you a

certificate.' He nodded, and a secretary brought papyrus and ink.

I used my own reed pen. His people were shifting in surprise that a scruff like me could write. It was a good moment. Even Helena was glinting at their mistake.

I signed my name with a flourish, then smudged my signet ring onto a wax blob which the secretary grudgingly dripped for me. (The smudge made no difference; my signet in those days was so worn all anyone could make out was a wobbly one-legged character with only half a head.)

'What else, Falco?'

'I am trying to contact one of your son's household who is owed a personal legacy. It's a freedman who originated on his natural father's estate – fellow called Barnabas. Can you help?'

'Barnabas . . . ' he quavered weakly.

'Oh, you know *Barnabas*!' Helena Justina encouraged from across the room.

I paused, looking thoughtful, while I tucked away my pen in a fold of my pouch. 'I understand Atius Pertinax and his freedman were extremely close. It was Barnabas who claimed your son's body and arranged his funeral. So are you saying,' I asked, remaining non-committal, 'that afterwards he has never been in touch?'

'He was nothing to do with us,' Marcellus insisted coldly. I knew the rules: consuls are like Chaldaeans who read your horoscope and very pretty girls; they never lie. 'As you say, he came from Calabria; I suggest you enquire there!' I had intended to ask about the missing yachtsman Crispus; something made me hold back. 'Nothing else, Falco?'

I shook my head without arguing.

This interview had raised more questions than it solved. But a con-frontation served no purpose; it seemed best to withdraw. Caprenius Marcellus had already excluded me. He began a tortured fight to raise his long shanks from the chair. Clearly he was an invalid who enjoyed fuss; after only half an hour of him I no longer trusted the way that his pains came and went so conveniently.

Attendants closed in. Helena Justina was also making herself busy with the old man; I nodded once, in case she deigned to notice, then I left.

Before I reached the atrium the swift light step I knew so well came following me.

'I have a message from my father, Falco; I'll come to the door!'

Somehow I was not surprised. Aggrieved women are a hazard of my work. It was not the first time one had rushed after me, intending to back me into a corner for some vile tirade.

It was not the first time either that I had hidden a sly grin at this prospect of free entertainment.

XXXII

Decorative plaques hung with wind chimes were suspended between the great Doric pillars in the white-stepped portico. Their trembling tintinnabulation added to my sense of unreality.

Larius, who never let grand mansions intimidate him, had just parked our ox at the elegant Marcellus carriage stop; my nephew sat there picking at his pimples while Nero, who had brought a spinning cohort of cattle flies, nibbled into the neat edge of the lawn.

Behind them lay the astonishing blue half-circle of the Bay. In the middle distance a bevy of gardeners were scything a piece of greensward large enough to exercise a legion at full strength; their heads all popped up as Nero bellowed at me. Larius merely gave us a sombre stare.

Her ladyship and I stood together above the steps. Her familiar perfume hammered my senses as neatly as a metal mallet on bronze. I was dreading some new reference to the burial of her uncle. The subject never came up, though I sensed Helena's anger still tingling just below the surface as we talked. 'Here on holiday?' I croaked.

'Just trying to avoid you!' she assured me serenely.

Fine; if that was her attitude – 'Right! Thanks for seeing me to my ox – '

'Don't be so sensitive! I came to console my father-in-law.'

She had not enquired about me, but I informed her anyway. '*I'm* trying to trace Aufidius Crispus – working for the Emperor.'

'Are you liking it?'

'No.'

Her ladyship tilted her head, with a frown. 'Restless?'

'I don't talk about it,' I told her brusquely – then because it was Helena I immediately relented: 'It's hopeless. The Palace doesn't like me any more than I like them. All I get is pottering errands – '

'Will you give it up?'

'No.' Since I had taken this on for her sake, I stared her out. 'Look; will you be discreet with Marcellus about my interest in his son?'

'Oh I do understand!' Helena Justina responded, with a hint of rebellion. 'The Consul is a frail old man who can hardly move – '

'Settle down; I'm not harassing the poor old bird – ' I stopped. A large attendant came out from the house and spoke to Helena;

he claimed to have been sent by Marcellus, bringing her a parasol to ward off the strong sun.

I pointed out coldly that we were standing in the shade. The slave stuck fast.

My hands began clenching at my sides. He had size, but his body was so soft he wore wristbands like a gladiator to convince himself he was tough. It took more than a few buckled straps to convince me. Here on the Consul's estate he was safe enough. But anywhere off his home ground, I could have doubled him up like a piece of human guyrope and fastened him in a cleat.

My temper reached straining point.

'Lady, I may have all the social breeding of a cockroach in a wall crack, but you don't need a bodyguard when you're talking to me!' Her face set.

'Wait over there please!' Helena Justina instructed him; he looked truculent, but did shuffle off out of earshot.

'Stop sounding so brutal!' she ordered me, with a look that would etch cameo glass.

I restrained myself. 'What does your father want?'

'To thank you for the statue.' I shrugged. Helena was frowning. 'Falco, I know where that statue used to be; tell me how you came by it!'

'There's no problem with the statue.' Her air of interference was beginning to annoy me. 'It's a good piece, and your father seems the best man to appreciate it.' Her father had trouble controlling her, but he was very fond of Helena. A man of taste. 'Did he like it?'

'It was father who commissioned it. A gift to my husband . . . ' She folded her arms, reddening slightly.

I chose to avoid this glimpse of the courteous Camillus family honouring Atius Pertinax as they betrothed him to their young daughter. Helena was still looking troubled. I finally realised why: *she was afraid I had stolen the thing*!

'Sorry to disabuse you; I happened to be in your ex-husband's house for legitimate purposes!'

I walked down the steps, anxious to get away. Helena was following me. As I reached the ox cart she muttered, 'Why do you want the freedman Barnabas? Is it really because of his legacy?'

'No.'

'Has he done something wrong, Falco?'

'Probably.'

'Serious?'

'If murder is.'

She bit her lip. 'Shall I make enquiries here for you?'

'Best to keep out of it.' I forced myself to look at her. 'Lady, take care! Barnabas has caused at least one death – and may intend more.' Mine for instance, but I omitted that. It might worry her. Or worse, it might not.

We were standing in full sun now, which gave that lump with her parasol an excuse to come down. Pretending to turn away I confided, 'If you know Barnabas, I need to talk to you – '

'Wait in the olive grove,' she urged in a hurried undertone. 'I'll come after lunch . . . '

I began to feel badly harassed. Larius was gazing seawards, so discreet it made me cringe. That inquisitive hulk Nero nosed around me shamelessly to see what was going on, dribbling down my tunic sleeve. Then the bodyguard stationed himself alongside the lady as he held up the parasol. It was a huge yellow silk affair with a trailing fringe, like a monstrous jellyfish; at the Circus she could have obstructed spectators for at least six rows behind.

Helena Justina herself stood here in her brilliant white dress and ribbons, like a light, bright, highly decorated Grace on a vase. I stepped up into the cart. I looked back. Something drove me to announce, 'By the way – I realised that sooner or later you would give me the bum's rush, but I thought you were well-mannered enough to mention it!'

'Give you the *what*?' The woman knew exactly what I meant.

'You could have written. No need for a full oration; "*Thanks and get lost, punk*" would express the right idea. Writing "*Goodbye*" would not have tired your wrist!'

Helena Justina drew herself up. 'No point, Falco! By the time I decided, you had already tripped off to Croton without a word!'

She shot me a look of spectacular distaste, dodged out from the parasol, then skipped up the steps and back into the house.

I let Larius drive. I reckoned if I tried my hands would shake.

She unsettled me. I had wanted to see her but now I had, everything about the occasion left me shifting in my seat.

Nero was plunging straight towards the olive grove, eagerly showing off how well he knew the way. Larius sat with one arm on his knee, unconsciously copying Petronius. He turned sideways to inspect me.

'You look as if you'd been poked in the ear with a broom.'

'Nothing so subtle!' I said.

'Excuse me,' Larius goaded heartlessly. 'But *who* was *that*?'

'*That*? Oh, her in the ribbons? The honourable Helena Justina. Father in the senate and two brothers on foreign service. Married once; one divorce. An adequate education, a passable face, plus property worth a quarter of a million in her own right – '

'Seemed a pleasant sort of woman!'

'She called me a rat.'

'Oh yes, I gathered you two were very close!' my nephew declared, with the candid, casual sarcasm he was honing to perfection nowadays.

XXXIII

My brain was wanting to race, and I was trying to prevent it. All the way down to the olive grove I scowled in silence. Larius whistled jauntily through his teeth.

Rather than think about Helena, I considered Caprenius Marcellus. He might not be active politically now, but he was still keenly alert. He must have known all about his son's plot while Pertinax was alive – and probably encouraged it. I bet he knew where Aufidius Crispus was too.

I wondered if Marcellus had invited Helena to visit him in order to pick her brains about developments on the official side after his son's death.

Meanwhile I had no doubt Helena had abandoned me. I could hardly believe it. Six weeks before things had been so different. Remembering, a slow, rich warmth spread into me, fixing me where I sat . . . And what would that smart young lady be thinking now? Whether to have a pound or two of Lucanian sausage or a great fat conical sheep's cheese from the Lactarii Mountains for her lunch. Helena had a spanking appetite; she would probably need both.

Larius and I ate our apples in the olive grove.

I prepared for a lengthy wait while the Consul dawdled through his three-hour snack and washed it down; his honour had filled himself a substantial wine flask for one old man and a wench who was, as far as I had ever found out, abstemious with drink. Marcellus looked like the kind of invalid who made the most of his convalescence.

To fill time before Helena could escape from the villa, I began another talk with Larius.

He had a better grip of the facts of life than I ever had at fourteen. Modern education must be more advanced; all I learned at school was the seven elements of rhetoric, bad Greek and simple arithmetic.

'I'd better give you some tips on handling women, Larius . . . ' I was devoted to women, yet cynical about my success.

Eventually we reached the point where I was imparting certain practical information, though trying to keep a heavy moral tone. Larius looked shifty and unconvinced.

'You'll find a girl! Or more likely a girl will find you.' He was certain it was hopeless, so I spent some time trying to revive his confidence. He was a charitable soul; he heard me out patiently. 'All I ask is be sensible. As head of the family I have enough soulful orphans wanting porridge in their feeding bowls . . . There are ways to avoid it: holding back manfully in moments of passion, or eating garlic to put the women off. Garlic at least is supposed to be good for you! Some people swear by a sponge soaked in vinegar – '

'What for?' Larius looked puzzled. I explained. He pulled a face as if he thought it sounded unreliable (true: due to the problem of finding a young lady who would bother to go through the procedure on request).

'My brother Festus told me once, if you know where to go and are prepared to afford it, you can buy scabbards sewn from fine calfskin to guard delicate parts of your anatomy from disease; he swore he had one, though he never showed me. According to him, it helped prevent the arrival of curly-haired little accidents – '

'Is that right?'

'Young Marcia's existence does argue against it; but perhaps his calfskin doings had gone to the laundry that day – '

Larius blushed. 'Any alternatives?'

'Get too drunk. Live in a desert. Pick a girl with a conscience who gets lots of headaches – '

'Sharp practitioners,' proclaimed a light, scathing, female voice, 'go for senators' daughters! They give their services free, while in the event of a 'curly-haired accident' the lady is *bound* to know someone who knows how to procure an abortion – and if she's rich she can pay for it herself!'

Helena Justina must have let her lunch go down hiding under a tree and listening to us. Now here she came: a tall girl with a bite like Spanish mustard, whose scorn any wise informer could learn to live without. Her face was white as a shell; she had a sharp, withdrawn expression that I remembered from when I first met her, when she was dismally unhappy after her divorce.

'Please don't get up!' Larius and I made a half-hearted attempt to raise our backsides, then fell down again. Helena sat there on the dry grass with us, managing to look rank conscious and remote. 'Who's this, Falco?'

'My sister's son Larius. His mother reckons he needs cheering up.'

She smiled at my nephew in a sweet way she had refused to smile at me. 'Hello, Larius.' She had a direct approach to young people which I could see attracted him. 'Someone should warn you, your uncle's a hypocrite!'

Larius jumped. She gave me an irritating smile. 'Well, Falco leads a dangerous life, of course. In fact one day he'll die of a brain tumour when some furious woman breaks a big stone pot on his head – '

By now Larius was looking seriously alarmed. I jerked my head and he made himself invisible.

It was no business of a senator's daughter to invade the scene when I was trying to do my duty as a substitute father.

'Lady, that was harsh!' I watched as she tore at the grass beside her, breathing furiously again.

'Was it?' She stopped torturing the fescue and turned on me. 'Do private informers come from some barbarian tribe whose gods let them fornicate without the normal risks?' Shocked at her language, I started to speak. 'Your advice to the boy,' she overruled me with some malice, 'was a complete farce!'

'Oh that's unfair – '

'Wrong, Falco! Sponges in vinegar, Falco? Calfskin scabbards? *Holding back manfully?*'

I experienced a surge of reminiscence that was embarrassingly physical . . . 'Helena Justina, what happened between us was – '

'A great mistake, Falco!'

'Well, slightly unexpected – '

'Once!' she scoffed. 'Hardly the second time.'

True.

'I'm sorry – ' She heard my apology arching her strong eyebrows in a way that made me furious. I forced myself to ask, 'Is anything wrong?'

'Forget I spoke,' she answered bitterly. 'Rely on me!'

There was nothing safe to say to her, but after a desperate moment I tried anyway: 'I thought you understood, *you* could rely on me!'

'Oh for heavens' sake, Falco – ' In her usual crisp style Helena abandoned it. 'What have you dragged me all the way out here to say?'

I leaned against a gnarl in the olive tree behind. I felt drugged; starvation perhaps.

'Enjoy your lunch? Larius and I had apples; mine was the one where a maggot had got at all the best bits first.' She was frowning, though probably not because she wished she had brought us a basket of scraps. Seeing a woman looking anxious over my appetite generally makes me relent. 'Don't worry about us . . . Tell me about Barnabas!'

Immediately the tension between us eased.

'I knew him of course,' Helena said at once. She must have been thinking it over while she had lunch. Her expression flooded with interest. She loved a mystery. And I always felt more cheerful when I had her to help. 'He could easily be here. He and Gnaeus often came here in summer; they kept racehorses on the farm – ' It was nothing to do with me, yet it always jarred when she called her vile ex-husband by his personal name. 'What has the fool been up to, Falco? Not really murder?'

'Misguided vengeance campaign, according to the Palace, though

I have stronger views! Don't ever approach him; he is much too dangerous.' She nodded: an unexpected treat. I had rarely been able to influence the lady (though that never stopped me giving her advice). 'When you knew him, what was he like?'

'Oh I hated having him round the house; he seemed to despise me, and I thought that affected my husband's attitude. He had a dreary effect on my marriage. Even at home we never had a meal in private; Barnabas was always there. So he and my husband talked about their horses and pretty well ignored me. They went everywhere together – have you discovered why they were so close?'

'Because they grew up together?'

'It was more than that.'

'Then I don't know.'

She was looking at me so gravely I smiled at her. Once a girl strikes you as attractive, it's difficult to forget. She looked away. I felt the smile fade.

'Barnabas had been born to a female slave on the Pertinax estate; my husband was the legitimate son of the house. They shared one father,' Helena informed me levelly.

Well, it was common enough. A man keeps slaves to serve his physical needs: all of them. Perhaps, unlike Larius, Pertinax senior had lacked an elder relative to educate his habits. More likely, when sleeping with a slave why should he care? A birth only meant one more entry in the plus column of his accounts.

'Is it important?' Helena asked me.

'Well, the facts don't alter – but they certainly make more sense.'

'Yes. There were no other children; these two were tumbled together from infancy. My husband's mother died when he was five; I suspect no one gave him much attention after that.'

'Was there rivalry?'

'Not much. Barnabas, who was older, became very protective and Gnaeus was always ferociously loyal to him – ' She poured her story out; she would go on puzzling over it for hours by herself, but she wanted to share it with me.

She stopped. I didn't speak.

She started again. 'They were as close as twins. Castor and Pollux. Little room for anybody else.'

Her mood darkened with an old sadness, regretting her wasted years. Four of them; not so much in the human span. But Helena Justina had gone into that marriage as a dutiful young girl; she had wanted to make it work. Though she finally opted for divorce, I knew her sense of failure had left permanent scars.

'Pertinax *was* capable of affection, Falco; Barnabas and the Consul were the two people he loved.'

'He was a fool then,' I grated before I could help it. 'There should have been three!'

XXXIV

A ladybird landed on Helena's dress, which gave her an excuse to catch it on her finger and watch it instead of me. The ladybird was prettier anyway.

'I beg your pardon.'

'There's no need,' she said; I could see that there was.

After a short silence she asked me what to do if she found any trace of Barnabas, so I explained how I was staying in Oplontis, and the best time to catch me was in the evenings when we ate. 'It's not far; you could send a slave with a message – '

'Are you staying in Oplontis on your own?'

'Oh no! Larius and I have a lively female entourage – ' She looked up. 'Petronius Longus is here. He has a bevy of little girls.' She had met Petro; she probably thought him respectable (which, in the presence of his wife and children, he generally was).

'Ah, you're with a family! So you're not lonely?'

'It's not my family,' I snapped.

She frowned over that one then started again. 'Are you not enjoying your beach party?'

Defeated by her persistence, I finally sighed. 'You know me and the sea. Sailing on it makes me sick; even staying alongside makes me nervous in case any of my jolly companions suggests a joy ride on the waves . . . I'm here working.'

'Aufidius Crispus? How far have you got?'

'I've sold a lot of good people new sets of water pipes; hence the dreadful garb.' She made no comment. 'Look, when do you expect I'll hear from you about Barnabas?'

'Today I shall have to let this commotion you've caused settle; tomorrow I had planned going to Nola with my father-in-law.' Helena seemed to hesitate, then she continued. 'Perhaps I can help you with Crispus. I may know people he visits when he comes ashore.'

'Your father-in-law for instance?'

'No, Falco!' she replied sternly, rejecting my suspicion of political skulduggery up at the villa.

'Oh pardon me!' I wriggled against my olive tree and gave her a twisted grin. 'I'll find him eventually,' I assured her.

Helena was looking thoughtful. 'Listen, try the magistrate in Herculaneum. His name is Aemilius Rufus; I've known him for years. His sister was engaged to marry Crispus once. Nothing came of it. She was keen, but he lost interest – '

'Trust a man,' I contributed helpfully.

'Quite!' she said.

I sighed slightly. I was feeling melancholy. 'It seems a long time . . . '

'It is!' she retorted crossly. 'What's the matter?'

'Thinking.'

'What?'

'You . . . Someone I thought I knew so well, yet will never know at all.'

Now there was a silence that said if I intended to be objectionable, the whole conversation was closed.

'You were going to come and see me, Falco.'

'I know when I'm not wanted.'

A tired expression crossed her face. 'Were you surprised to find me here?'

'Nothing women do surprises me!'

'Oh don't be so conventional!'

'Excuse me!' I grinned. 'Princess, if I had had the slightest inkling *you* featured on today's job list, I would have spruced up my togs before I came barging in. I do prefer to look like a man whose departure a woman might regret!'

'Yes, I realised you wanted to leave me,' Helena stated suddenly.

The ladybird flew off, but she soon found some other six-legged friend to study on the back of her hand. She was sitting extremely still, not to disturb the bug.

I thought of all the things I ought to say; none of them came out. I managed to ask, 'What do *you* think?'

'Oh . . . it does seem best.'

I stretched my chin and studied the space ahead of my nose. Somehow the fact she was making no difficulties only created more. 'People were going to get hurt,' I insisted. 'Two of them were people I particularly cared about: me and you.'

'Don't worry about it, Falco . . . just a passing fling.'

'A special one,' I told her gallantly, having problems with my throat.

'Was it?' she queried, in that thin, light voice.

'I thought so . . . Are we still friends?'

'Of course.'

I smiled miserably. 'Ah that's what I like about senators' daughters – always so civilised!'

Helena Justina rapidly shook the wildlife off her hand.

There was a scuffle behind us and my nephew tumbled into the grove.

'Sorry, Uncle Marcus!' His diffidence was pointless since there was nothing going on. 'I think that pest with the sunshade is coming down!'

I rocked to my feet fast. 'Your new bodyguard seems a persistent type!' I offered my hand as Helena scrambled up too but she ignored it.

'He's not mine,' she said shortly. I felt an uneasy twinge, as if a drunk in a bar had lurched to his feet, staring straight at me.

We all headed back to the track. At the ox cart, Helena urged us, 'Drive under the trees and stay out of sight – '

I nodded to Larius to drive under cover. Still no sign of her minder. Abruptly I grasped her shoulders, confronting her. 'Listen lady, when *I* was your bodyguard, there were no conflicts of interest. I took my orders from you – and when you wanted your privacy I stepped back!'

A splash of colour moved among the cypresses above. I shot a warning glance then dropped my fists as I let her go. Her left hand brushed through mine – but made no attempt to answer my pressure as she slipped free.

Something had been bothering me; I realised what.

On the finger where people display their wedding rings a twist of metal had run beneath my thumb like an old friend. It was a ring made of British silver which I had given to Helena myself.

She must have forgotten it. I said nothing, in case she became embarrassed and felt obliged to take it off now our affair was supposed to be at an end.

I started to turn away under the trees, then came back. 'If you're going to Nola – no; it's nothing.'

'Don't be so irritating! What?'

Nola was famous for its bronze. My mother expected a present from Campania so had tactfully suggested what to get. I told Helena. The Senator's elegant daughter gave me a cool look.

'I'll see what I can do. Goodbye, Falco!'

Larius and I sat under the olive trees while I counted off the time for a tall girl, striding furiously, to storm up past the terrace and the riding range, then back into the house.

'Are you seeing her again?' my nephew quizzed.

'Sort of.'

'Assignation?'

'I've sent her out to buy something.'

'*What?*' Suspicion was already darkening his romantic soul as he guessed I had done something outrageous.

'A bronze bucket,' I confessed.

XXXV

Just before we reached the road we passed an aristocratic litter borne by half a dozen slaves, progressing at a stately pace towards the house. Talc windows hid the occupant but his slaves' gold-braided livery and the spanking crimson carriagework said it all. Luckily the Marcellus approach road was wide enough for both of us, since my nephew made it a point of honour never to give way to anyone of a higher rank.

All the way back to Oplontis Larius was so annoyed at my treatment of Helena that he refused to speak to me. Damned romantic!

Still in silence we bedded Nero down.

We went in to change our grimy clothes. Our landlady had been dyeing her wardrobe a deeper shade of black so the filthy stink of oak gall extract pervaded the whole inn.

'You'll never see her again!' Larius exploded, as his disgust finally broke.

'Yes I will.'

She would buy me my bucket; then he would probably be right.

The Petronius offspring were all in the inn courtyard, crouched in the dust with their heads together, playing elaborate games with myrtle twigs and mud. They turned their backs as a sign we should not interrupt the intensity of their play. Their kittens lolloped round them. No one appeared to be in charge.

We strolled outside. The nursemaid Ollia was lying on the beach while her fisherboy displayed his glossy pectorals alongside. He was talking, as they like to; Ollia stared out to sea, stuck with listening. She had a wistful look on her face.

I gave the girl a grim nod. 'Petronius?'

'Gone for a walk.'

Her fisherboy was no older than my nephew; he had the kind of moustache I really hate – a skinny black lugworm stitched on above his feeble mouth.

Larius skulked along with me. 'We ought to rescue Ollia.'

'Let her have her fun!'

My nephew scowled, then to my surprise abandoned me. Feeling my age, I watched him lope over to the pair then squat down too. The

135

two lads glared at each other while young Ollia continued to stare at the horizon, an overweight, overemotional mollock, paralysed by her first social success.

I left this awkward tableau and kicked my heels along the shore. I was thinking about Pertinax and Barnabas. I was thinking about Crispus. I was wondering why I had started to feel that Crispus and Barnabas had me constantly struggling at some tangent to the truth . . .
   After that, I was thinking about other things, irrelevant to work.

I hunched irritably on the tideline, playing with a desiccated dogfish eggcase, until I gradually began to feel like Odysseus in Polyphemus' cave: a huge single eye was watching me balefully.
   It was painted on a ship. Scarlet and black, with the shameless elongation of a painted Egyptian god; there was presumably a matching one around the vessel's haughty prow but she lay sideways to shore, so without a tame dolphin to tow me out behind there was no way I could check. She was riding at anchor, safely beyond the reach of holiday-makers' curiosity. Apart from reeking of the kind of happy affluence that loves to be viewed by wide sectors of the public while supposedly enjoying its privacy, she was not the kind of precious toy to be brought in and belted against the ratty bales of straw which formed a rough-and-ready bump rail on the Oplontis mooring stage.
   Whoever designed this nautical beauty had a statement to make. There was *money* written all over his ship. She was forty feet of blatant artistry. She had a short, single bank of red ochre oars which were perfectly aligned at rest, dark sails, a mainmast for her square rig plus a second for a foresail, and lines so suave they hurt. Somehow the shipwright had managed to combine a slim keel like a warship with enough cabin and deck space to make life aboard a pleasure for the financier who possessed the stupendous capital that had created her.
   At a slight shift of the incoming evening breeze, the gilding on her duck tail stern and her masthead goddess flashed restlessly. There was a nippy little bumboat trailing behind in a perfectly matching rig – identical steering paddles, identical toy sail, and the same painted eye. While I gawped, the bumboat was pulled closer and after some distant activity I watched it set off shorewards, sculled at a fast and elegant pace.
   Cheered by this happy accident, I walked onto the landing stage and waited my chance to introduce myself to what I was convinced would be the Crispus ménage.

There were two tykes aboard: a lean, wide-awake sailor standing astern to row, plus a substantial chunk of bellypork taking his ease in the prow. I hung about, ready to make myself useful catching their mooring rope. The oarsman touched; I gripped the bumboat's prow;

the passenger stepped out; then the deckhand pushed off at once. I tried not to feel superfluous.

The man who landed wore soft doeskin boots with copper half-moons jingling on their thongs. I had heard the sailor call him Bassus. Bassus clearly thought a lot of himself. He was the type of mighty transit barrel who rolls through life clearing a wide swathe. And why not? Far too many feeble whingers with all the dye bled out of their characters skulk on the sidelines of existence hoping no one will notice them.

We walked towards the beach. I weighed him up. He probably kept a bankbox in all the great ports from Alexandria to Carthage and Massilia to Antioch, but like a wary seaman he always carried sufficient good gold on his person to bribe his way out of seizure by pirates or tangling with small-town officials when he went ashore. He had earrings, and a nose stud, and enough amulets to ward off the Great Plague of Athens. His Sun God medallion would have caved in the chest of a lesser man.

He was not even the captain. The whip through his belt told me this was merely the bosun – the overseer who striped the hide of any oarsman on the *Isis* who upset her tranquil motion by catching a crab. He had the silent confidence of a man whose bulk can dominate a tavern from the moment he enters it, but who knows the first officer on a sleek lugger like the *Isis* never needs to cause a fuss. If this was just the bosun, Aufidius Crispus the owner probably thought himself foster brother to the gods.

'You've come from the *Isis*!' I commented, giving the ship an admiring eye but not bothering to annoy him with the obvious statement that she was a superb rig. Bassus condescended to flick me a glance. 'I need to see Crispus. Chance of a word?'

'He's not aboard.' Short and sweet.

'I know better than to believe that!'

'Believe what you like,' he returned indifferently.

We walked up the beach, as far as the road. I broached him again, 'I've a letter to deliver to Crispus – '

Bassus shrugged. He held out his hand. 'Give it to me if you like.'

'That's too easy to be true!' (Besides, I had left the Emperor's letter upstairs at the inn, when I changed my clothes.)

The bosun, who had been fairly passive so far, finally formed an opinion of me. It was unfavourable. He did not bother to say so. He simply suggested that I should get out of his way, which, being an accommodating type, was what I did.

While Bassus was disappearing over the horizon, I strode up to Larius and instructed him to find Petronius as quickly as he could. Without waiting, I retraced my steps to the edge of the sea where I stared out again at the tantalising prospect of Aufidius Crispus' ship.

I have to admit, this was one occasion when being a non-swimmer became slightly inconvenient.

XXXVI

The beach at Oplontis was the usual litter of dank seaweed, broken amphorae, snaggles of stiffened fishing net and scarves left behind by girls who were intent on other things. Wasps homed in on half-gnawed melon rind. Walkers risked deadly hazards from rusty daggers and dress brooches. There was the usual left boot which always looks just your size and perfect, but when you trudge across to have a look has half its sole missing. If people managed to fend off the cynical urchins touting overpriced fishing trips, a jellyfish that was not as dead as it was pretending would sting them instead.

Now it was early evening. A subtle diminution in the brash daytime light, an imperceptible cooling of that glorious heat, and shadows which suddenly ran out to ridiculous lengths were giving the atmosphere a magical tinge; it almost made being at the seaside acceptable. People who were tired of working stopped. Families who were tired of quarrelling left. Tiny dogs stopped terrorising mastiffs and settled for raping any bitches they could manage to climb onto, afterwards running round in glorious circles to celebrate their productivity.

I looked back towards our inn. Larius had loped off to find Petronius, and Ollia was gone too, along with her briny swain. The beach lay unusually empty. Apart from the dogs and me, a party of off-duty shop boys were making a lot of noise with a shuttlecock while their girlfriends dragged together driftwood for a barbecue fire. The fishermen who were normally cluttering the place had either sailed off with their lanterns to raid tuna shoals after dark, or had not yet returned from their more lucrative trade running tourists out to look at the rock on Capreae from which Emperor Tiberius had thrown people who offended him. All they left for me was a single skiff, upended above the tideline, growing silvery in the sun.

I am not a complete idiot. This broad-bellied cockleshell looked as if it had been lying here a long time. I did carry out a thorough inspection for stakes stuck through its planking, or bungholes with missing plugs. There was nothing wrong with my convenient coracle – or at least, nothing a highly cautious landlubber could see.

I found a spare oar leaning against someone's worm-eaten mooring post, then another paddle under the skiff when I managed to lever it right side up. I shouldered it down to the water's edge, helped by the shop boys' girlfriends, who were happy to fill time respectably before it grew dark and their lads started getting ideas. I tossed a last look back for Larius or Petro but there was no sign, so I climbed in, swayed on the prow with an effort at bravado, and let the girls shove me off.

It was a clumsy piece of carpentry. The clod who built it must have been feeling off colour that day. It bobbed in the wavelets like an intoxicated fruitfly dancing at a rotten peach. It took some time to get the hang of keeping this mad thing pointing forwards, but in the end I began to make some progress from the shore. The breeze in my face was slight, though not helping much. My purloined oar had a bitten blade, and the other paddle was too short. The glare off the sea added a new glaze to my sunburn while it also made me squint. I didn't care. The reluctance Aufidius Crispus had demonstrated to facing an innocent interview fired my determination to get on board the *Isis* and find out what the big mystery was supposed to be.

I dug deep and pushed out steadily until I had halved the distance from Oplontis to the ship. I congratulated myself on my spirit and initiative. Vespasian would be proud of me. I came near enough to read her name, painted high on the prow in angular Greek lettering . . . At about the same time as I grinned triumphantly, a completely different sensation impinged on me.

My feet were wet.

Almost as soon as I noticed the cold, I was standing in seawater up to the ankles and my luckless skiff was foundering. Once the Tyrrhenian Sea discovered it could seep through the dried planks, it rushed in on all sides and my vessel sank beneath me rapidly.

There was nothing I could do but shut my eyes, hold my nose, and hope some sea nymph with a nice nature would pull me out.

XXXVII

Larius pulled me out. Wallowing with a Nereid would have been more fun.

My nephew must have seen me set off and been on his way after me before I sank. Remember his father was a boatman; Larius had been dandled in the Tiber even before he was weaned. He could swim when he was two. He never used the sinister, silent, Batavian crawl which the Army teaches. My nephew had a horrible style, though a thrashing turn of speed.

When I came round, with the feeling of having been violently engulfed then flailed against a concrete wall, I could tell how Larius had achieved my rescue by the agonies I had acquired as a result. I had a bruised throat where he had heroically gripped me, and a gashed ear where he had crashed my head against a mooring stage. The backs of my legs were raw from being dragged over the pumice up the beach, and I was being pumped back to life by Petronius Longus, applying his full bodyweight. Afterwards, I felt perfectly happy to lie still for a long time, considering my sore windpipe and pummelled flesh.

'Think he'll live?' I heard Larius ask; he sounded more curious than concerned.

'Reckon so.'

I let out a grunt to inform Petronius that he could now feel free to amuse himself with jokes at my expense. His unmistakable fist thumped my shoulder.

'He's been in the Army. *Why* can't he swim?' That was Larius.

'Oh . . . the week we did watersports in basic training, Marcus was confined to barracks on fatigues.'

'What had he done?'

'Nothing serious. We had a high-handed junior tribune who got the idea Marcus had been playing around with his girl.'

There was a pause. 'Had he?' Larius eventually enquired.

'Oh no! In those days he was much too shy!' Untrue. But Petronius does not believe in corrupting the young.

I rolled over away from them. I peered seawards for the *Isis* through swollen eyes, but she had gone.

The low evening sun savaged my legs and shoulders, as it came glancing through my lightly bloodstained marinade of brine. I lay

140

face down on the beach thinking about death by drowning and other cheerful things.

Far away at the water's edge I could hear Petro's three young daughters shrieking with delight as they chased each other fearlessly in and out of the dreadful sea.

'Anyway!' Petronius chaffed Larius. 'How come you're always extricating this fool when disaster strikes?'

Larius blew his nose. He took his time answering but when he did I could tell he was enjoying it.

'I promised his mother I'd look after him,' he said.

XXXVIII

Next day my friends decided I must be taught to swim.

It was probably a bad idea for them to try giving lessons to someone who still went rigid at any possibility of going under with seawater filling his lungs. Still, they all took it seriously so I attempted to cooperate.

It was hopeless. Petronius could hardly hold me up by the back of my tunic as he did with his children, and when Larius tried making water wings from inflated wineskins he just wore himself out blowing them up.

Nobody laughed, however. And nobody condemned me when I climbed back out of the water, walked up the beach, and sat down alone.

I stayed by myself, morosely flipping pebbles at a hermit crab. I skimmed them to miss, since I was not in the mood for outright cruelty; the crab found a shell of his own and started to build an extension to his house.

IXL

We were eating when Helena came.

We had left Ollia with the children, apart from Tadia who had been badly stung by a jellyfish so we brought her with us, still flushed and miserable (the poor mite had sat on it). Larius stayed with Ollia; I overheard the two of them discussing lyric poetry.

We ate at an open-air winery where they also served seafood. Petronius had inspected the kitchen at Silvia's behest; I won't pretend the proprietors welcomed him, but he had the knack of getting into places wiser men would have left alone, then being treated for ever as a friend of the management.

Helena had seen us and was out of her sedan chair by the time I came up. I heard her instruct the servants to amuse themselves with a flagon and come back for her later. They stared at me, but I had little Tadia half-asleep in my arms so I looked harmless.

'Personal delivery, ladyship?'

'Yes – I'm having a mad burst of energy – ' Helena Justina sounded breathless, but that may have been the effort of extracting herself and my mother's new bucket from the sedan chair. 'If I were at home I'd be tackling those jobs everyone avoids, like spring-cleaning the pantry where we keep the fish-pickle jars. In someone else's house it seems impolite to suggest their kitchen amphorae may leak . . . ' She was dressed plainly in grey though her eyes were very bright. 'So I may as well deal with you – '

'Oh thanks! Like a nasty sticky ring on a floor slab, waiting to be scrubbed away?' She smiled. I muttered grittily, 'When you smile you have beautiful eyes!'

She stopped smiling. But she still had beautiful eyes.

I looked away. Out to sea. Round the Bay. Up at Vesuvius – anywhere. I had to look back. Those eyes of hers finally met mine directly.

'Hello, Marcus,' she said carefully, like someone humouring a clown. And I answered, 'Hello, Helena.' So sensibly she blushed.

When I introduced the Senator's daughter I tried to spare her embarrassment, but she was carrying a bucket and my friends were not the type to miss an eccentricity like that.

'Brought your own feeding pail, young lady?' Petronius has a typically Aventine line in ribaldry. I caught his eye as he watched his curious wife inspecting Helena.

Arria Silvia had already twitched her whiskers at the prospect that my stately guest might be more than a business acquaintance. 'I'm very fond of Falco's mother!' Silvia stated regally when the bucket was explained (establishing that she and Petro knew me first).

'Lots of people are,' I breezed. 'So am I sometimes!' Helena gave Silvia a pale, commiserating smile.

Helena Justina became withdrawn in noisy public places, so she sat down at our table with hardly a word. We had been devouring shell-fish; I had once come all across Europe with her ladyship, one Hades of a journey where we had had nothing to do but swap complaints about the food. I knew she liked to eat so I skipped asking and ordered her a crayfish bowl. I gave her my napkin and the way she accepted without comment may have been one of the clues Silvia sniffed out.

'What happened to your ear, Falco?' Helena could be pretty curious too.

'Got too friendly with a jetty.'

Petronius, looking relaxed as he winkled the legs off his prawns, related how I had tried to drown myself; Silvia added a few humorous details of my failure to get afloat today.

Helena frowned. '*Why* can't you swim?'

'When I ought to have been learning, I had been confined to barracks.'

'Why?'

I preferred to leave this open but Petronius helpfully passed on the tale he had spun Larius, 'We had a tribune who thought Marcus had been playing around with his girl.'

'True?' she grilled, adding scornfully, 'I suppose so!'

'Of course!' Petro gladly confirmed for her.

'Thanks!' I remarked.

Then Petronius Longus, being basically good-natured, swigged the juice from his bowl, stuffed a bread roll in his mouth, poured wine for us, left some money for the meal, gathered up his weary daughter, winked at Helena – and took himself off with his wife.

After this performance I cleaned my bowl slowly while Helena was finishing hers. She had turned up her hair the way I liked, parted in the centre then twisted back above her ears.

'Falco, what are you staring at?' I gave her a look that confessed I was wondering if I dared nuzzle her nearest ear lobe – so she shot one back which said I had better not try.

An uncontrollable grin took possession of my face. Helena's expression informed me that being flirted at by a love-them-and-leave-them gigolo was not her idea of a holiday treat.

I lifted my cup, gently saluting her; she sipped hers. She had taken more water than wine when I first served her, and had drunk very little when Petro refilled her cup. 'Had your ration up at the villa rustica?' She looked surprised. 'Is your father-in-law a heavy drinker?'

'A glass or two at mealtimes to help him digest. Why?'

'That day I came, the flask he collected would have done duty at a gladiators' victory thrash.'

Helena considered it. 'Perhaps he likes to leave some on the table for the slaves who wait on him?'

'Perhaps!' Neither of us believed it, as both of us knew.

Time to talk business, since flirting had been ruled out. 'If you've already been to Nola and back, you've had a busy day. So what's so urgent?'

She flashed a tired, rueful smile. 'Falco, I owe you an apology.'

'I expect I can bear it. What have you done?'

'I told you Aufidius Crispus had never been to the villa – then the enfuriating man arrived as soon as you left.'

I gloomily used my thumbnail as a toothpick. 'In a litter with a fancy gold prong on top, and slaves in saffron livery?'

'You passed him!'

'Not your fault.' She ought to have known by now that if I was ever annoyed she had only to expose me to that grave, apologetic look. I was not annoyed but she did know, judging by her expression, which was having a tricky effect on me. 'Tell me about it?'

'It appeared to be a sympathy call. I was told, he had come to talk to Marcellus about his son.'

'Prior arrangement?'

'Looked like it. I think my father-in-law rushed his lunch with me so the men would be able to talk in private when Crispus arrived.' Modest women expect to be excluded from male get-togethers; Helena was openly annoyed. 'They took the flagon,' she acknowledged. 'You never miss much!'

I grinned, enjoying the flattery. I also enjoyed her secret glint as I let her manipulate me – then her swift, sweet, honest laugh when she noticed I knew. 'Don't suppose old Marcellus told you what they discussed?'

'No. I tried to hide my interest. He passed the visit off with a comment about Crispus making himself agreeable . . . Ask me why I went to Nola with Marcellus?'

I leant closer with my chin on my hands and requested obediently, 'Helena Justina, why did you go to Nola?'

'To buy you a bucket, Falco – *and you've never even looked at it!*'

XL

It was a highly desirable bucket – a handsome shape, good capacity, the bronze gleaming like sunshine on Lake Volsinii, its rivets secure, and a ring-moulded handle to give a firm grip.

'Superb. How much do I owe?'

'You could pay a lot more, for much less – ' She told me and I paid up, pleased with the bargain she had got for me.

'Very few people can buy a good bucket. I told Larius I could rely on you.'

'Talking of him – ' She dived under her stole, which she was keeping in the bucket while the evening stayed mild. 'I bought this to help you cheer him up.'

It was a miniature stag, also in bronze, small enough to sit in the palm of my hand and beautifully modelled. I made the right noises, but Helena Justina could spot insincerity at a stadium's length: 'Is something wrong – are you offended?'

'Jealous,' I confessed.

'Fool!' Laughing, she dived in again. 'Your mother asked me to look out for these for you.' Next she gave me a parcel about six inches long, heavy, and wrapped in cloth.

It was a set of spoons. Ten. Bronze. I tried the balance: beautiful. They had pleasing egg-shaped bowls, slightly elongated in the length. The hexagonal handles were straight, then turned down and curved into a rat-tail fixture on the bowl; they had moulded knops by the elbow joints, picked up by a complementary finial . . .

'Well, my cold gruel should taste a lot better out of these!'

'Wipe them with a cloth when you wash them, so they won't mark – do you like them?'

They were superb. I told her that. Whatever they cost must be more than my mother could possibly afford; I was reaching for my funds again, with a sharp pain in the purse area, when she muttered, 'Those are from me.' It was just like her. No one in the Didius family had ever possessed a full set of matching spoons. I was overcome.

'Helena – '

'Just enjoy your gruel.'

She was playing with a finger bowl. I lifted her free hand – the left – kissed her palm, then gave back the hand. A bracelet of spindle-shaped blue faïence beads shivered on her wrist. Nothing else. No silver ring.

So that was it.

I held my ten spoons tenderly, though I felt like a noblewoman's plaything who had been bought off. I made no attempt to control my face. I should have done. Because as I sat in resentful silence the Senator's daughter turned to look at me. And she immediately realised what I thought about the reason for her gift.

I had made a mistake.

One of those moments. Two seconds, to destroy an entire relationship. One stupid, wrong expression that shatters your life.

XLI

In the following few minutes I watched more doors close against me than I had ever even noticed were ajar.

'I have two pieces of information, Falco.' Her flat tone confirmed that assisting me had withered to a distasteful public duty. 'First, my father-in-law went to Nola because Aufidius Crispus had invited him as his personal guest at the Nola Games.' She looked as if she had just wasted an hour on a manicure for an important dinner party, then broken a nail against the doorlatch on her way out. 'Crispus was the host all round; he paid for the Games.'

'A good show?' I asked carefully. It was not the first time I had insulted a friend – or a woman – but I normally liked to minimise the damage this did to myself.

'Athletes, chariot races, thirty pairs of gladiators, a bullfight – '

'So can I expect to find Crispus at Nola?'

'No; it was a one-day spectacle.'

'Ah! Is he very public spirited – or standing as a magistrate?'

'Neither.'

'But he *was* courting support?'

Teasing information from Helena had never been harder. Luckily the chance of putting me in my place made her slightly more talkative: 'It's obvious, Falco. Campania, at the height of the holiday season. What better opportunity for an ambitious man to approach influential Romans – quite privately? Half the Senate will be here at some time this summer – '

'So Crispus can entertain, coerce, *manipulate* – all without attracting suspicion! In Rome if he gave public entertainments half the Forum would be taking bets on what he wanted – '

'Exactly.'

'Yet here he only looks like a great-hearted, gregarious type enjoying his holiday!' This time she merely nodded. 'Well! That explains why Crispus won't ingratiate himself with the new Emperor; the man is planning regal moves himself. Vespasian may not be the only voter in Rome who does not go along with it – '

'Oh I wish I believed that – ' Overcoming her reticence, Helena Justina beat one hand on the table. '*Why* must people have so little faith in the Flavians?'

'Vespasian and Titus are a credit to Rome. There's no scandal; and that's no fun.'

'Don't be so fatuous!' She rounded on me bitterly. 'The only decent Emperor in our lifetime! But Vespasian will be pushed out of office, won't he? Before he has started, before anyone even gives him a chance to show what he can do – '

'Don't despair yet.' By nature Helena was a fighter and an optimist; I dropped my hand over the one she had smacked down. 'This is not like you!'

She broke away restlessly. 'Aufidius Crispus is wickedly powerful. He has far too many well-placed friends. Falco, you must stop him!'

'Helena, I can't even find him!'

'Because you're not trying.'

'Thanks for the flattery!'

'I don't need to boost your confidence; you have a high enough opinion of yourself!'

'Thanks again!'

'What have you achieved chasing Crispus? You're pottering in the sunshine on this lead-selling lark – you *enjoy* pretending to be an entrepreneur! I suppose you've been showing off to all the women who run wayside wineshops – '

'A man needs some pleasure!'

'Oh shut up, Falco! You must find out what Crispus intends and prevent it – '

'I will,' I said briefly, but she went storming on.

'If you won't do it for the Emperor, at least think of your own career – '

'That stinks! I'll do it for you.'

Too late I saw her flinch. 'I'm not your tribune's girlfriend making herself available to the new intake of recruits; Falco, spare me the cheap dialogue!'

'Cool down. I'm doing my best. What you call 'pottering' is a methodical search – '

'Well have you found anything?'

'Aufidius Crispus goes nowhere and sees no one – according to them. There's a conspiracy of silence among the well-heeled seekers of sea air – ' I watched her anxiously; women of her rank were well taken care of, yet her eyes had a heaviness which even discreet cosmetics had failed to disguise. Paint can be a cruel friend. I risked seizing her hand again. 'What's bothering you, treasure?' She escaped from me angrily. 'Helena – *what's the matter?*'

'Nothing.'

'Oh cobnuts! Well, what was the other thing you had to say?'

'Never mind.'

'Nice girls don't quarrel with men who buy them langoustines!'

'There was no need for that!' Her face set, hating me for what

she saw as false concern. 'You and your friends had shrimps; I don't
expect special treatment – '

'If you did, you wouldn't get to eat with my friends – '

'I like shrimps – '

'That's why you like me . . . Lady, I thought we were talking
about the peace of the Empire – tell me your story!'

She took a deep breath and abandoned our spat. 'When Aufidius
Crispus left the villa rustica after seeing Marcellus, I happened to
walk through the room where they had been, before it was cleared.
The flagon was empty. And on the tray were *three* winecups.'

'All used?'

'All used.'

I considered it. 'Maybe Crispus brought someone with him; his
litter was closed – '

'I was on our roof garden when he left; he was alone.'

Sweet thought: a senator's daughter spying over balustrades and
discreetly counting cups! 'Could this mean Barnabas?'

'I doubt it, Falco. My father-in-law never allowed Barnabas the
run of his house. While I was married, staying with Marcellus was
the only time I enjoyed normal family life; he excluded the freedman
and allowed me my proper place – in fact he still does. He *might* grant
Barnabas shelter, but he would never include him at a private meeting
with a senator.'

'Don't discount the possibility,' I warned. 'Could Marcellus be
entertaining some secretive house guest?' She shook her head. 'Helena
Justina, I need access to explore the villa rustica – '

'First find Aufidius Crispus!' she interrupted fiercely. 'Find Crispus
– do what Vespasian is paying you for!'

Scowling, I paid up; then we left the restaurant.

We walked slowly on the road by the shore while we waited for
her bearers to reappear. The hard note remained in her voice: 'Do
you want me to introduce you to Aemilius Rufus in Herculaneum?'

'No thanks.'

'So you won't go!'

'I'll go if I find I need to.' She exclaimed with annoyance as I tried
to rally her. 'Look, let's not fight . . . Here are your chair men. Come
on, fruit – '

'*Fruit?*' That got her, bursting into her rare, sweet, unexpected laugh.

'Did Pertinax have a pet name for you?'

'No.' Her laughter subsided instantly. No comment seemed necessary. Then she turned to me with a deliberate look. 'Will you tell me
something? Was it when you were working at my ex-husband's house
that you changed your mind about us?'

My face must have answered her.

I remembered the comfortable stylishness of that house on the

Quirinal, which I knew had been a wedding gift from Marcellus to Helena and Pertinax. Only the gods could say what other sumptuous luxuries had been showered on the young couple by their relations and friends. Geminus and I must have catalogued some of it. Tortoiseshell bedheads. Mosaic glass serving bowls. Gold filigree plates. Exotic embroidered coverlets Queen Dido might have slept under. Polished maple table tops. Ivory chairs. Lampstands and candelabra. Camphorwood chests . . . and innumerable perfect sets of spoons.

'Marcus, surely even you could understand that if a *house* was all I wanted, I would never have arranged my own divorce from Pertinax?'

'Just being realistic!'

Helena slipped from my side and into her chair before I could even consider how to say goodbye. She closed the half-door herself. The bearers were stooping to the carrying poles; I grasped at the door, wanting to hold her back. 'Don't!' she commanded.

'Wait – shall I see you again?'

'No; there's no point.'

'There is!' There had to be.

I gestured the bearers to stop but they would only take orders from her. As the chair lurched when they raised it, I glimpsed her expression. She was comparing me with Pertinax. Rejection by a husband who was too crass to know what he was doing had been bad enough; though since no senator's daughter has much say in the choice of her husband, Pertinax was simply a false entry in life's ledger that could be cursed and written off. To go straight from him to a cynical lover who left her after the most casual kind of usage was entirely her own mistake.

Of course, I could have told her it happens every day. Women who *know* they know better frequently cast themselves at treacherous men whose sense of commitment only lasts as long as the rascally smile that gets them into bed . . .

Unlike Helena Justina, most women forgive themselves.

Just when I was prepared to be totally honest in order to keep her, she dragged the window curtain right across and shut me out. I had no need to consult the Sybil at Cumae to realise my exclusion from Helena's life was intended to be permanent.

I stood there, still with my mouth open to tell her that I loved her, while the bearers sneered at me churlishly and carried their lady away.

PART FOUR
HARPING IN
HERCULANEUM

THE BAY OF NEAPOLIS
July

*'Perhaps you may be expecting a troupe of Spanish dancers,
Gypsy girls, with their wanton songs and routines . . .'*

Juvenal, Satire XI

XLII

The town of Herculaneum was very small, very sleepy, and if any interesting women lived there, they were hidden behind locked doors.

There was no rubbish in the streets. At Pompeii the town council had to provide stepping stones to help pedestrians cross the dubious substances which seeped and stagnated in their roads; the Herculaneum councillors believed in wider pavements – wide enough to hold a hot-piemen's convention, only it was a place which frowned on pies. And at Herculaneum rubbish never showed its face.

I hated Herculaneum. It had tasteful, well-scrubbed houses owned by people of little character who thought a lot of themselves. They lived in prim little streets. The men spent their days counting their money (of which they had plenty), while their good ladies were carried in closed litters from their own safe doorsteps into the homes of other respectable women, where they sat around plates of almond cakes and talked about nothing until it was time to go home again.

Unlike Pompeii, where we had to bawl to make ourselves heard, in Herculaneum you could stand in the Forum at the top of the town and still hear the sea gulls at the port. If a child cried in Herculaneum its nursemaid dashed to gag it before it was sued for a breach of the peace. At Herculaneum the gladiators in the amphitheatre probably said '*I beg your pardon!*' each time their swords did anything so impolite as landing a nick.

Frankly, Herculaneum made me want to jump on a public fountain and shout a very rude word.

We had left this hive of mediocrity until last because I despised it so heartily. Now our friend Ventriculus in Pompeii had informed me he would use up most of my lead on the orders we had already obtained. (The news came earlier than I calculated, though I was not surprised; I expected the plumber to cheat me a little, according to the customs of his trade.) So this was my last chance. We were here, with Nero and one last cartload of samples, hoping to prise out further details of Aufidius Crispus' plans (or even, if my luck took a special turn, to discover where the elusive sardine had parked his pretty ship).

I had no intention of visiting the magistrate Helena Justina had mentioned. I was sharp; I was tough; I was good at my job. I did not need a self-appointed supervisor. I would find my information for myself.

While I nosed round Herculaneum looking for it, I admitted to Larius that we had reached the limit of the expenses Vespasian would want to pay.

'Does that mean we have no money?'

'Yes; he's mean with failure.'

'Would he pay you more if you found something out?'

'If he thought it was worth it.'

Some people might panic; I felt shifty myself. But Larius uttered stoically, 'We'd better make sure we discover something quick!'

I liked my nephew's attitude. He saw life in simple terms. Once again I mused how his tenacious approach would make Galla's eldest an asset in my line of work. I mentioned it, as Nero approached Herculaneum's wide main street (it was called the Decumanus Maximus, which is what every two-goose town in Italy calls its main street). Larius responded to my careers advice by telling me about a wall painter Ventriculus had introduced who was offering him summer employment sketching figures on a frieze . . .

I knew nothing about this; I was highly annoyed. I told my nephew what I thought of artists. His chin jutted, with the irritating tenacity I had previously admired.

This particular Decumanus Maximus was the cleanest and quietest I ever saw. It was partly thanks to an immaculate vigilante who marched up and down there so respectable locals who needed to know if their dinner would be ready could ask him the time. His other method of serving the community was pointing out to layabouts like us that on the main boulevard at Herculaneum wheeled traffic was not allowed.

When he roared it out I had just noticed the bollards standing up like mileposts to block our way. We had been cruising towards the courthouse (I could see the sun glinting off a bronze charioteer outside this elegant basilica). There was an arch across the road ahead, which probably led to the forum, a row of shops alongside us, and a fountain which Nero was treating to a tentative sniff.

I hate disciplinarians. This one ordered us away from the Decumanus with the good breeding I expect from a country official, which was none. For a bone bodkin I would have told him where to stuff his swagger stick, even if it meant we were run out of town . . . Larius caught my eye.

'Just tell him we're sorry and we'll go!'

I could not altogether blame the man for abusing us. My nephew and I had made the mistake of buying cheap holiday haircuts, with the usual preposterous results. We had gone to an open-air barber by the gladiators' barracks in Pompeii, who had taken three hours of sombre snipping to turn us out like murderers. Also, we were now eating pilchards wrapped in vine leaves, which no one from Herculaneum would *dream* of doing in the street.

We turned downhill towards the port. There were side streets to either hand; Herculaneum was built on a pedantic Greek grid. To save me the trouble Nero chose a direction himself. It was a picturesque scene of overhangs and pilastered walkways; a basket-weaver dreaming on his stool, and an old woman who had been out for a lettuce who stood decrying modern society to another old baggage who had been out for a loaf. Into this maelstrom of the Herculaneum highlife our mad ox eagerly plunged.

The disaster happened quickly, as disasters love to do.

Nero swung off to the right. There was a packman's donkey tethered outside a dosshouse, a strong young male with sleek ears and a pert backside: Nero had spotted the grand passion of his life.

As he turned he rammed the cart hard against a pastry cook's portico. The weight of lead held us fast, so he broke free. The vibrations from his joyful bellow brought down four rows of roof tiles. Stoneware went flying under his hooves as he ditched us and skittered through some potter's produce with that special dainty, high-stepping tread of a bull on the loose, all set to swerve on the spot with a horn at the ready if approached. The parts of him that were supposed to be deactivated were swinging heavily, with perilous implications for the donkey.

Women burst onto first-floor balconies. In colonnades at street level little children squealed in terror then stopped, fascinated by the scene. I grabbed the rope we kept for winding round the ox's horns and bounded after him, reaching Nero just as he reared and dropped onto his new friend. Young Ned wheezed, and squealed rape. Some misguided cookshop boy caught hold of Nero's tail. Next minute all the breath was smashed out of me as a thousand pounds of copulating ox swung round to free his rear end and sideswiped me against the dosshouse wall.

The wall, which was made of cheap rubble in a wicker frame, sagged under me enough to prevent broken bones.

I rebounded out of the house wall in a shower of stucco and dust. By now Larius was darting about on the sidelines, squeaking useless advice. What I really needed was a harbour crane. I would have run away to hide, but one fifth of this maniacal bovine belonged to Petronius Longus, my best friend.

People were trying to rescue Neddy with anything to hand. Mostly they hit Larius and me by mistake. I walked face first into a hastily flung pail of water (or something), while my nephew took a nasty thwack from a marrow on the tender part of his neck. The donkey was trying to kick up his hind legs with some evidence of character, but once he got stuck underneath he could only brace himself for a painful surprise.

At Nero's moment of glory fortune rescued us. His victim's legs gave way (I had been frightened for his heart). Ass and ox collapsed to the ground. Ned scrambled up trembling, with a wild look in his eye. I swiftly lassooed Nero round a back leg, Larius sat on his head, and our big boy wrestled savagely beneath us – then quite suddenly gave in.

We should have been the heroes of the hour. I did expect a tussle over compensation for damaged shop fronts, and perhaps a claim under some lesser-known branch of the Augustan marriage laws, for permitting a draught animal to spike a donkey adulterously. What happened was *much* more interesting. The vigilante from the Decumanus Maximus had noticed us shouting at our ox with an Emperor's name. We assured him he had misheard. We called Nero 'Spot'; the fool ignored us. We called Nero 'Nero' and he ignored it too, but apparently that didn't count.

Larius and I were both arrested. For blasphemy.

XLIII

The lockup for vagrants was a converted shop at the side of a temple.

'Well, this is a new one!' I chortled.

My nephew reassumed his old moody look. 'Uncle, how are you going to tell my mother I've been in jail?'

'With great difficulty, I expect.'

The jailor was an amiable duffer who shared his lunch. His name was Roscius. He had a grey spade-shaped beard and side whiskers; we gathered from his easy-going attitude that Herculaneum was the sort of inferior town which frequently arrested innocent visitors. He did keep a cellar, where he dumped anyone who looked a bit foreign, but we two had the honour of being chained to a bench where he could chat.

'Know a senator called Crispus?' I asked, mainly to impress Larius with my unflappable professional expertise.

'No, Falco.' The jailor was a man who spoke, then slowly thought about it. 'Not *Aufidius* Crispus? He had a house in Herculaneum; sold it to buy that boat – '

'Seen him lately?'

'No, Falco.' He thought; then opted for caution this time.

Larius felt things were unproductive. 'Show Roscius your pass!' I fetched it out; Roscius read it and handed it back.

Larius closed his eyes in desperation. I returned the pass to Roscius. 'Aha!' he said, not getting the point, but noticing that there might be one.

'Roscius, my friend, could you float that the way of a magistrate? If there's one named Aemilius Rufus, better choose him.' It still went against the grain, but whoever provided the jailor's lunch had used cold meat which turned up at the edges with a sinister dark rim. Our own relations were too far away to send provisions in. I reckoned I had about three hours before my nephew's hungry stomach gained the side effect of a very nasty attitude.

Roscius sent the pass to Helena's friend. We took turns with his flagon and all got slightly drunk.

Towards the end of a peaceful afternoon two slaves turned up to say that one of us lags had to stay locked up, but the other could come with them. I explained to Larius that he would have to be the hostage, since Rufus was the friend of a friend of mine.

'Just hurry up, will you?' Galla's treasure snarled. 'I could murder a bowl of Baian beans!'

The house of Aemilius Rufus was a modest affair, though he probably owned a stack of gracious architecture elsewhere. This one had the atmosphere of an unvisited museum. It was furnished in a heavy style with wall friezes of battle scenes and grand spiky furniture, formally arranged, which I would never dare sit down on in case I nudged a leg out of line. It was a house without the grace of children, pets, the trickle of a fountain, or growing plants. If there was a gecko on the gloomily lacquered ceilings, he kept his head well down.

His honour was on a sun terrace, which at least had the sprawling untidiness most sun terraces achieve. Its occupants had been murmuring politely, though when I shuffled out into the sunshine they seized on the excuse and stopped. After a hard day trying to stay awake in the courthouse, Rufus was relaxing at full stretch with a large goblet clasped to his chest: a hopeful sign.

He had with him a thin noblewoman who must be his sister, and another lass. They were positioned at a wicker table which held the inevitable pastry plate. The magistrate's sister picked at the sweetmeats spasmodically, while her visitor cheerfully tucked in. It was Helena Justina. She did me the supreme honour of letting my arrival put her off her food.

Unavoidable: as soon as you say goodbye for ever, you trip over the lady wherever you go. So now mine was on a Herculaneum sun terrace, licking ground almonds off her fingers, with a tantalising smear of honey on her chin which I would have enjoyed licking off for her myself.

She was wearing white, which was how I liked her, and she stayed very quiet, which was not. She ignored me, though I refused to be demoralised by that.

The illustrious Sextus Aemilius Rufus Clemens, son of Sextus, grandson of Gaius, of the Falerna voting tribe; tribune, aedile, honorary priest of the Augustales, and currently ranking praetor, leaned around the back of his day bed; I stiffened. I was being greeted by a good-quality copy of a Praxiteles Apollo. If I stood him on a plinth with his clothes off and a thoughtful expression, Geminus would buy him like a shot. A classic face; assertive intelligence; painfully fair colouring in a rare, superb combination with extremely dark brown eyes. Helena Justina's friend was so good-looking I wanted to spit on him and see if any of the artistry washed off.

He had taken a fast run at public life. I put him not far beyond thirty. In five years he would be commanding a legion in one of the better provinces, and make consul easily in ten. Since he lived with his sister I guessed he was a bachelor, though it had not held him back in collecting votes. The reason he stayed single was probably being spoiled for choice.

He picked up my pass from a small silver table, read it, then surveyed me with limpidly dark eyes as I approached. 'Didius Falco? Welcome to Herculaneum!' He gave me a frank, open smile like a man who dealt honestly, though I supposed he was no better than all the rest. 'I gather someone has a shocked little donkey who will never be the same again . . . So what exactly *is* the name of your ox?'

'Spot!' I declared stoutly. He smiled. I smiled. The friendliness would never last. 'My nephew and I,' I insisted, sticking up for us, 'have spent a humiliating morning and we intend filing a claim for wrongful arrest. Nero was one of the few Emperors who managed to avoid the honour of being decreed divine.'

'He's sacred in Campania, Falco; he wed a local girl!'

'Pigswill! Didn't Poppaea Sabina come to grief when he kicked her in the stomach during a pregnancy?'

'A domestic tiff which good Campanians prefer to forget!' Herculaneum's golden magistrate grinned at me, with an attractive flash of teeth. 'I agree. Blasphemy seems a trumped-up charge. Suppose I ask instead about your unorthodox deliveries of lead?' His apologetic tone was upsetting. I prefer blunter questions, accompanied by a soldier's knee in my soft extremities.

'Problem, sir? How can I help?'

'There have been,' Rufus offered, with a gentleness that made my liver curl, '*complaints!*'

'Oh I don't understand that, sir!' I protested in outrage. 'It's top-quality stock from Britain, and we make every effort to ensure all our installations have good workmanship to match!'

'It's not your customers who complain,' Rufus stated. 'It's those with official franchises who are being undercut.'

'Tough,' I said. I was losing a battle I could not control; tiring work. The magistrate shrugged. 'Any more of this lead?'

'No sir; that's the last.'

'Good. You can pick up your ox from the livery stables, but unless you show me proof of ownership, I have to confiscate the lead.'

For a man with a handsome profile, his business acumen was admirably sharp.

Now that he had pinched my samples, we became best friends. He waved me to a stool and made free with the wine he was drinking himself: a clean-flowing vintage my expert friend Petronius would admire.

'Very generous of you, sir – are the ladies joining us?'

His two refined companions had kept aloof, though we knew they were listening. Rufus veiled his eyes, entrusting me with a hint of male conspiracy, as they deigned to squirm sideways towards us, chinking their bangles to indicate the inconvenience.

'My sister Aemilia Fausta – ' I gave her a solemn bow; her friend looked wise to it. 'Helena Justina you know, I believe. She has been telling us what she thinks of you – '

'Oh he's a typical man!' scoffed Helena wittily, unable to miss this chance. 'He has dreadful friends, silly habits, and his antics make me laugh!'

Rufus shot me a bright, curious glance; I gravely asserted, 'The daughter of Camillus Verus is someone I hold in the highest esteem!' It sounded unreliable; the truth so often does.

Helena grumbled something under her breath, so Rufus laughed. He rolled up his napkin and threw it at her; she biffed it back with the easy informality of old family friends. I could imagine their adolescence shared in long summer holidays here, swimming and boating and picnicking. Sailing to Surrentum. Trips to Capreae. Baiae. Lake Avernus. Stolen kisses in the Sybil's Cave at Cumae . . . I pictured the effect such a glorious hunk of glowing masculinity must have had on Helena Justina while she was a growing girl.

Perhaps he still did.

The rough wine at the jailhouse plus the smooth wine on the sun terrace were filling me with a pleasant sense of irresponsibility. I beamed at the ladies, then sat back in the sunshine enjoying my drink.

'You work for Vespasian,' the magistrate broached. 'So what brings you here?' He was playing the innocent, well-mannered host, while swiftly ascertaining my interest in his patch.

Banking on Helena's good judgement in sending me here, I said, 'The Emperor wants to find a senator called Crispus. He is somewhere in this area, though people seem reluctant to admit to seeing him – '

'Oh I've seen him!'

'You never told me that!' For the first time, the magistrate's sister spoke: a sharp, almost petulant voice.

Rufus looked at her. 'No,' he said; his tone was not quarrelsome, though without apology. I remembered Helena saying Aemila Fausta had wanted to marry Crispus, but he had declined to complete the contract. Crispus backing out could look like an insult to her family; her brother was bound to disapprove of her continuing interest. He turned back to me. 'Aufidius Crispus contacted me recently; we met at the baths at Stabiae.'

'Any particular reason for him getting in touch?'

'No,' said the magistrate levelly. 'Nothing particular.' Well; nothing a spruce young aristocrat would tell a hangdog like me.

'Special friend of yours, sir?'

'A friend; not special.'

I gave him a gracious smile. 'I don't mean to pry. I know he has a connection with your family. Marriages planned between persons of rank are public events.'

I sympathised actually; I had sisters myself. Besides, I was feeling hot, and on the verge of getting drunk again.

He stiffened, then acknowledged it. 'My sister had a disappointment there. We shall have to find her new interests to compensate. Aemilia Fausta was hoping to take up music this summer, though I'm afraid I have failed to find a harp teacher so far . . . '

'Bad luck!' I murmured innocently.

'I've heard you are a man of many talents, Falco. I don't suppose you play?' Rufus had confiscated my livelihood. He must have deduced how badly I needed to find another one.

I took a thoughtful look at his sister, then tried to avoid revealing the pessimism I felt.

Aemilia Fausta carried a defeated expression no one could blame her for; it must be sorry work being the fairly ordinary sister of a fabulously handsome artefact who attracted all the attention wherever they went. She matched their house – antique and undisturbed, like an old, aloof Greek statue which had gathered dust in a viewing gallery for many years. The knack of giving pleasure had passed her by through no fault of her own. She was given to wearing robes the colour of second-rate gemstones – the grubby yellow of tourmaline or that sour, olivine green which jewellers know as peridot. Her complexion looked sickly, beneath a varnish of cosmetics that crinkled in the heat like a puppet's mask. Even here, on a high balcony where a pleasant breeze was rising off the sea, no hair on her sleek, pale head wafted out of place and she would evidently be annoyed if it tried. Her hair was the wrong shade of honey to be interesting.

For all that she was a young woman. Too old to remain single without a good reason, yet twenty-five at most. Her brother had cornered the family share of bone structure, but she must be educated and rich, and unlike her friend Helena she could be taken out in public without demolishing every plate of almond cakes that strayed within her reach. If she ever risked a smile she might be modestly attractive to a man in the right mood. Blow that dust off her, chase her about in the fresh air, pinch her in cheeky places until she jumped and squeaked a bit – something marginally tasty might be made of the noble Aemilia . . .

Helena Justina was looking daggers of disapproval, so I piped up at once that I would be happy to take the job.

XLIV

I had better things to do than hang about in the hope of a word with a woman whose only word would be 'goodbye'. I hoofed off back to the jail to free Larius. I took him to a cookshop, then he and I rescued Petro's disgraced ox. Nero had made friends with the horses and mules at the stable. He was like a child at a party; he did not want to go home.

'He looks tired,' commented Larius, as we butted the brute outside so we could harness him.

'Well he might!'

I set Larius on the road back to Oplontis with the cart. Since no man wants his apprentice around while he's teaching a lady the harp, I agreed that my nephew could take himself off painting walls. I stressed it was a temporary arrangement; Larius nodded unconvincingly.

As a harp tutor I lived in the magistrate's house. It saved on rent. Yet I grew to dread its cold, unlived-in smell. Doorways which I would have left open to show life going on in family rooms were grimly sealed with curtains. All the couches had sharp edges looking for a shin to bark. By day there was always a riot in the kitchen and at night there were never enough lamps. Rufus usually ate out; he must have noticed that his cook couldn't cook.

I armed myself for action with some musical manuscripts I found in the town. Aemilius Rufus had been right when he said the Emperor Nero still commanded loyalty here. Within a week of his suicide all the shops in Rome had swept their shelves clear of Caesarly tunelets and sent them out to the markets for wrapping fish. But there were plenty in Campania. For a beginner, Nero's tosh seemed ideal. His compositions were stupendously long, which gave Fausta plenty of practice; they were slow, which was good for her confidence; and without being unpatriotic, they were simplicity to play.

A lyre would have been easier, but with typical obstinacy Aemilia Fausta had set herself the professional challenge of a cithara. It was a lovely thing; it had a deep resonance box decorated with mother-of-pearl, then the sides swept up into elegant horns, with an ivory crosspiece to take the seven strings. How well I could play the cithara is a question I'll leave blank (though when I was in the army

164

I did own a flute with which I managed to create a fair amount of annoyance). Aemilia Fausta was not wanting to run away from home to join a pantomime band; for showing off to drunks at dinner parties, I reckoned I could get her up to scratch. And it would hardly be the first time a teacher had bumbled through a lesson on the basis of some hasty reading up the night before.

The noble lady did possess the sceptical strain I would expect in a friend of Helena's. She once asked me whether I had played much.

'Madam, music lessons are like making love; the point is not how well I can do it, but whether I can bring out the best in you!' She had no sense of humour. Her owly eyes stared at me anxiously.

Teachers who can play well are pretty self-involved. She needed someone like me: gentle hands, a sensitive nature – and able to explain in simple language where the lady I was with was going wrong. As I said: like love.

'Are you married, Falco?' she asked. Most of them do. I gave her my innocent bachelor's smile.

Once that had been clarified, Aemilia Fausta trundled on through her latest Imperial air, while I footled around with a forthcoming lecture on diatonic scales. (A subject on which I admit I could not expound with much fluency.)

We had our lessons indoors. Not to annoy the neighbours. (They never paid for tickets. Why give them a free treat?) A lady's maid sat in with us, for propriety, which at least allowed me to eye up the maid improperly during boring passages.

'You seem to have cracked this one, madam. Try it again, leaving out the repeats . . . '

At that point that maid, who was sewing the sides of a tunic, gave a cry as she upset her pot of pins. She went down on her knees to pick them up so I scrambled round on the floor to help. People who go to the theatre may suppose the maid would take this chance to slip me a note. She wasn't in a comedy, so she didn't; and I was not surprised. I live in the real world. Where, believe me, ladies' maids very rarely hand private informers secret notes.

Still, the knees she was down on were lusciously dimpled, she had fluttery black eyelashes and slender little hands – so I had no objection to spending a few moments with her on the floor. Aemilia Fausta played her harp more vigorously. The maid and I managed to find most of her pins.

When I got up, the noble lady dismissed her maid.

'Alone at last!' I cried gaily. Fausta humphed. I stopped her in mid chord and lifted the harp away with an air of suggestive, tender concern which was part of my stock in trade. She looked alarmed. I gazed deliberately into her eyes (which were, to be frank, not the best eyes I ever gazed into in the line of work). 'Aemilia Fausta, I must ask, why do you always look so sad?'

I knew perfectly well. The magistrate's sister spent too much time dreaming bitterly of lost opportunities. She lacked confidence; probably always had. What really annoyed me was the way she let her dressers paint her twenty-year-old features with a forty-year-old face. For all the silver hand mirrors in her well-stocked bower, she could never have looked at herself properly.

'I'm happy to listen,' I encouraged smoothly. My pupil allowed herself a poignant sigh which was more promising. 'The fellow is not worth it if he brings you such unhappiness . . . Will you talk about it?'

'No,' she said. My usual measure of success.

I sat quietly, looking snubbed, then pointedly offered the harp again. She took it, but made no move to play. 'Happens to everyone,' I assured her. 'The ones who hang around are deplorable dogs, while those you want won't look at you!'

'That's what my brother says.'

'So what's our hero's name?'

'Lucius.' Keeping me in suspense while she pretended to misunderstand my question almost made her smile. I braced myself for those heavy layers of red ochre to crack, but her normal spiky melancholia took charge. 'It is Aufidius Crispus. As you well know!'

I ignored the indignation, and let her settle down. 'So what went wrong?' I asked.

'We were to be married. He seemed to be delaying for a long time. Even I had to accept the delay would be permanent.'

'These things happen. If he was unsure – '

'I do understand all the arguments!' she declared in a light, too rapid voice.

'I'm sure you do! But life's too short for suffering – '

Aemilia Fausta gazed at me, with the dark, tired eyes of a woman who had been unnecessarily miserable most of her life. I really do hate to see a woman as sad as that.

'Let me help ease your troubles, madam.' I gave her a long, sad, significant look. She scoffed wryly, under no misapprehensions about her own allure.

Then I dropped into the silence, 'Do you know where Crispus is?'

Any sensible woman would have brained me with the harp.

There was no need for drama; I could see she really did not know the yachtsman's whereabouts.

'I don't. I wish I did! If you find him, will you tell me?' she pleaded.

'No.'

'I have to see him – '

'You have to forget him! Play your harp, lady!'

The lady played her harp.

She was still playing, and there was still a slight atmosphere which a stranger might misinterpret, when a cheery voice cried, *'I'll see myself in!'* and Helena Justina arrived.

I was demonstrating fingering. The best way to do that is to sit beside your pupil on a double seat, and put both arms round her.

'Ooh, lovely! Don't stop!' cooed Helena in a facetious tone which nearly made me choke. Aemilia Fausta played on stolidly.

It was a warm day so I and my pupil were casually clad in a few light drapes of nothing much. For my musical role I always adopted a laurel wreath; it tended to slide down over one eye when I bent towards my pupil (as a harp teacher has to). Helena Justina was sensibly wrapped in several layers, though with a rather odd sunhat on (it looked like a folded cabbage). She let the contrast between herself and us speak a lot.

She leaned on a marble pediment oozing queenly distaste.

'I never knew you were musical, Falco!'

'I come from a long line of self-taught strummers and squeakers. But actually this is not my instrument.'

'Let me guess – panpipes?' she mocked derisively.

Feeling left out, Aemilia Fausta twanged into her rather stately version of a whirling Bacchic dance.

I assumed the ladies wanted to gossip so I waited long enough to show it was my own decision, then I left. I returned to my menial's cubicle and did some desultory reading for Fausta's lesson the next day. I could not settle, knowing Helena was in the house.

Feeling peckish, I set off in search of sustenance. The food here was poor and pedestrian. On the other hand, the food was free, and if your stomach could take it they let you eat what you liked. (The magistrate kept a personal physician, in the event of really serious aftereffects.)

I came into the hall, whistling breezily since I was employed to bring music to the home. An old crone with a mop fled to complain about me to Fausta looking appalled. The ladies were in the inner garden; I could hear the chink of spoons in pretty custard bowls. No place for me. I decided to go out.

Life is never all black. As I went past the porter's corridor, Aemilia Fausta's maid pushed her hand out through the curtain and slipped me a note.

XLV

I stood in the street, reading my message with a faint smile.

'You look shifty!' Camillus Verus' stately daughter, at my back.

'Trick of the light . . . ' I lifted my shoulder to stop her looking over it, then managed to screw up and drop the note as if that was what I had intended all along. I grinned at her. 'Aemilia Fausta's waiting maid has just made me an offer I shall have to refuse.'

'Oh *shame!*' mouthed Helena gently.

I hooked my thumbs in my belt and slowly swaggered off, letting her come if she chose. She did.

'Thought we were strangers; can't you leave me alone?'

'Don't flatter yourself, Falco. I wanted to see Rufus – '

'Bad luck. He's deploying the fabulous Apollonian profile in court. Two sheep rustlers and a slander case. We reckon the sheep stealers did it, but the slander's a put-up; plaintiff's nephew is a barrister who needs to show off – '

'You're well at home! I would not have thought Aemilia Fausta was your type,' she found it necessary to add.

I walked on, replying peacefully, 'She has a scrawny appeal. I like blondes . . . And there's always the maid.'

'Oh you won't see her again!' chortled Helena. 'If Fausta spots her girl making overtures, she'll be sold before you get back from our stroll.' I gave her my hand into a colonnade as a handcart laden with marble creaked past. 'Don't waste your time, Falco. Aemilia Fausta never notices rugged types with wicked grins.' She jumped off a pavement with an impatient twirl. 'Fausta only likes pomaded aristocrats with mattress stuffing between the ears.'

'Thanks; I'll load on more attar – ' I hopped after her, brightening up as we bandied words. 'I feel sorry for the lady – '

'Leave her alone then! She's vulnerable; the last thing she needs is to find *you* with that soft look in your lying eyes, pretending you can't keep your hands off her – '

We were standing on a corner glaring at each other now. I tweaked at a strand of Helena's new hair. 'Been through a sheep dip, or are you starting to rust?'

'It's called *Egyptian Russet*. Don't you like it?'

'If you're happy.' I loathed it; I hoped she could tell. 'Trying to impress someone?'

'No; it's part of my new life.'

'What was wrong with your old life?'

'You, mostly.'

'I like a girl to be frank – but not that frank! Here's the court,' I growled. 'I'll nip in and tell the judge an Egyptian carrot wants him, then I'm off to flatter his sister with my Lydian arpeggios!'

Helena Justina sighed. She put her hand on my arm to stop me turning away.

'Don't disturb Aemilius Rufus; it was you I came to see.'

I waited until she let my arm go before I turned back.

'Well? What about?'

'It's hard to define.' The look of trouble in those fine, bright, wide-spaced eyes sobered me abruptly. 'I believe someone I am not supposed to know about is lurking round the villa rustica – '

'What makes you sure?'

'Male voices talking after Marcellus is supposed to be in bed, glances among the servants – '

'Is it worrying you?' She shrugged. Kowing her, she was more annoyed at being misled. But it worried me. I had the afternoon free, so I offered immediately: 'Are you going back?'

'I came with a steward who has errands for Marcellus – '

'Forget it. I'll take you.'

Just what she intended; I knew perfectly well.

We took the steward's mule, leaving a message that I would return it. I prefer my ladies to ride in front; young fruit insisted on sitting behind. The mule joggled, a situation I allowed because Helena had to cling on round my waist. Just after we turned into the Marcellus estate this scheme went awry. I could sense her growing restless so I was already reining in, but before I could lift her she skidded down the mule's flank in a swift rumple of white skirts around the longest legs in Campania – then she was sick, miserably, over a rail.

Stricken with conscience I fell off the mule too. Among all his bells and leather fringes I hastily found a water gourd.

'Oh I hate you, Falco! You did that deliberately . . . '

I had never seen her look so ill. It frightened me. I sat the lass on a boulder and gave her the gourd to sip. 'You'll feel better quicker if you just stop arguing – '

'No I won't!' she managed to flash up at me, with an honest grin.

Cursing myself, I wet my neckerchief and wiped her hot face and throat. She had that drained, dry-mouthed, white-gilled expression I recognised from being a poor traveller myself. I crouched over her anxiously, while she sat with her head in her hands.

When her breathing grew more level and she looked up ruefully, I paid a boy from the vineyard a copper to lead the mule on ahead to the house.

'We can amble on foot when you feel more yourself.'

'I'll try – '

'No; just sit quiet!' She smiled wanly, and gave in.

She was still poorly. If I had been a softer man I would have wrapped my arms around her. I tried not to let myself imagine that I was, or that she wanted it.

'Falco, stop looking like a little lost eider duck! Talk to me; tell me how you like living in Herculaneum?'

I sat back and obediently straightened my beak. 'I don't. It feels an unhappy house.'

'Rufus goes out too much; Fausta stays at home and mopes. Why did you go there anyway?'

'To earn some cash. And Aemilia Fausta seems a possible key to finding Crispus.'

'By seducing and spying – that's immoral!' she burst out.

'Seducing is a tiring way to do business, even for the safety of the state!'

'When you seduced me,' Helena demanded waspishly, 'was *that* for the safety of the state?'

Like true friends we had the knack of hurting one another down to a fine art.

I answered her in a black tone. 'No.' Then I left her to think about it. She flushed uneasily. I changed the subject: 'Aemilia Fausta knows about my work.'

'Oh, admitting your status is part of your seedy charm!' Helena insulted me, rallying again. 'Are you friends with her handsome brother too?'

I gave her a rascally glint. 'Would Rufus be more susceptible to my soft lying eyes?'

She looked at me oddly then went on, 'Can't you see that Aemilius Rufus took you into his house to keep an eye on you?'

'What's his interest?'

'To participate in reconciling the Emperor and Crispus himself – to help his career.'

'I thought he seemed evasive; yet his future looks bright enough – '

'He has lived too long away from Rome; he is very ambitious, but not well enough known.'

'Why was he away?'

'Nero. Anyone so good-looking posed a threat to the Caesarly ego; it was either self-exile or – '

'A trip to see the arena lions at state expense? Why *does* he look like that?' I scoffed. 'Did his mother meet a Macedonian vase peddlar behind a bush?'

'If it was his sister you'd be happy enough!'

I laughed briefly. 'If it was his sister she might be happier herself!'

Helena was still perched on her boulder but looked brighter. I rolled out on the ground, full length on my belly at her feet. I felt happy. Lying here in the sunshine, on good Vesuvius ploughland, with clear air in the lungs, someone pleasant to talk to, the Bay of Neapolis stretched away in a blue mist . . .

At Helena's silence I glanced up.

She had been overtaken by some mood of her own. She sat gazing out across the Bay, then she closed her eyes briefly, with an expression which was both pained and pleased at the same time.

It had nothing to do with my mission. She would have told me that.

Perhaps she was thinking about her handsome friend.

'It's growing hotter.' I hooked myself upright. 'I should get you indoors. Let's go.'

I started off too fast, because Helena had to slip her hand into mine to slow me down. I kept hold of her, whether she liked it or not, to cheer myself up.

It *was* hot, though pleasant walking. I was keen to march ahead and explore the villa, but in the country a man should always make time for a stroll with a lass. You never know when the demands of city life will provide another chance. You never know when the lass will agree.

We came through the vineyards where the half-ripe green bunches were already bending boughs. Our road doubled back. As we turned into the next slow climb upwards we caught sight of the villa. In the riding range on the terrace, a man was exercising two horses, turn and turnabout.

'Are those racers? Is there a trainer?'

'Bryon – that's him.' She paused. 'The stables here might be worth exploring . . . '

I hopped up on a boundary rail, clinging to a fig tree in the corner of a field. The Senator's daughter, who had no sense of propriety, put one sandal on the rail then pulled herself up too, hanging on to me. We watched the trainer press the horse he was riding fast down the course, then slow, turn, spurt ahead and pelt hard along another length. I had no interest in racehorses, but it gave me an excuse to hold Helena steady . . .

We turned to each other at exactly the same time. At that range it was impossible to ignore how intensely we both remembered what had happened in the past. I released her, before staying so close became far too difficult. Then I leapt to the ground and helped Helena down too.

She lifted her chin defiantly. 'I suppose you threw the spoons in the sea?'

'Certainly not! My father was an auctioneer; I know the price of spoons . . .' We were friends. Nothing could change it. Friends, allied by the love of intrigue; constantly arguing yet never quite as irritated with each other as we both professed. And the tension between us, both emotional and sexual, still felt decidedly permanent to me. 'Just now, what were you thinking of?' I ventured to ask.

Helena moved away from me quietly, shaking her head. 'Something I'm not sure about. Don't ask me,' was all she said.

XLVI

By the time we reached the house, Helena was looking dreadful again. She normally enjoyed such sturdy good health that this troubled me as much as it plainly embarrassed her. I insisted on staying beside her until she was installed on a couch in a long colonnade, with a tray of hot borage tea.

While the small flurry which our arrival caused was settling down I acted the visitor. Helena sent away the slaves. I sat with her, supping from a little bowl which I held between a thumb and two fingers like anyone respectable. (If it's not too strong I quite like borage tea.)

When my mouth was thoroughly scalded I put my bowl down then stretched, looking round. No sign of Marcellus, and few staff. The usual gardeners were raking out a big bank of mimosa. Their heads were well lowered over it. Somewhere indoors I could hear a woman scrubbing, accompanying herself with rasping song. I poured more tea through a pointed strainer for her ladyship, standing idly beside her afterwards as if I was merely watching the slow curl of the steam . . .

The great house seemed relaxed and quiet. Normal people going about their normal tasks. I touched Helena's shoulder quietly, then strolled off on my own like a shy man going to answer a natural call.

Seeing the racehorse trainer had aroused my interest. I walked round the outbuildings in the hope of finding him. The stables lay on the left as you faced out to sea. There was an old livery block, used for packmules and carriages. And a large new section, built about five years ago, with signs of recent activity. With the discretion of half a lifetime I managed to infiltrate myself indoors unseen.

There was no doubt, this was where Pertinax and Barnabas had once kept their bloodstock. The tack room contained one of the silver equine statuettes I had seen in the Pertinax house in Rome. Most of the stabling was empty now, presumably since his death. But two horses I was confident I recognised from that morning were sweating contentedly in adjacent stalls. They had just been rubbed down by a burly ostler who was now swabbing out the walkway between the rows.

'Hello!' I cried, as if I had permission to be there. The man leaned on his besom and gave me a shrewd look.

I strolled down to the two horses and pretended to take an interest. 'These the two Atius Pertinax had in Rome?'

I hate horses. They can tread on you, or lean on you, or roll heavily on top of you to break your legs and crush your ribs. If you offer them titbits they will gobble off your fingers. I treat them as cautiously as lobsters, wasps, and women who regard themselves as lively sexual athletes: horses, like any of those, can give you a nasty nip.

One was all right. He was really something special; even I could tell that. A proud-necked, sweet-spirited stallion with mulberry colouring. 'Hello, boy . . . ' While I was petting this beauty, I glanced at his stablemate. The ostler jerked his head with shared disgust.

'Little Sweetheart.' Someone had a sense of humour. Little Sweetheart was rubbish. He stretched his neck at me, jealous of his neighbour receiving attention, though he knew in this heady company a rapscallion who looked like an overworked bottle brush stood no chance.

'Bit of a character? What's this one called?'

'Ferox. He gets twitchy. Little Sweetheart calms him.'

'Ferox your champion?'

'Could be.' The stableman looked canny in a professional horsey way. 'He's five now, and pretty well furnished . . . You a racing man?'

I shook my head. 'I'm an *Army* man! When the legions want to go anywhere, they march on their own feet. If horseflesh is a real strategic necessity they hire in hairy short-legged foreigners, who can ride like hell in battle, know how to doctor the staggers, and will discreetly deal with dung. Works superbly. In my view, any system that works for the legions is good enough for a citizen in ordinary life!'

He laughed. 'Bryon,' he introduced himself.

'Name's Falco.' I went on fondling Ferox to sustain the conversation. 'You're the trainer! What are you doing mucking out? No stablelads?'

'No anything. All sold up.'

'When Pertinax took the ferry into Hades?'

He nodded. 'The horses were his passion. First thing the old man did: all the stock, all the staff – gone overnight. He couldn't bear them here.'

'Yes I heard he was cut up. What about these two?'

'Maybe he regretted it later. Ferox and the Sweetheart were sent to him from Rome.' I knew about that. When we cleared out the house on the Quirinal we found bills of sale for these two in Marcellus' name. I never saw the animals but I had signed the chitty for their transfer home myself. 'So what's your interest, Falco?' Bryon continued. He seemed friendly, but I could tell he was sceptical.

'You know Barnabas?'

'I used to,' he answered, without committing himself.

'I've got some cash that belongs to him. Has he put in an appearance here lately?' Bryon looked at me, then shrugged. 'I reckon,' I pressed on with a warning note, 'you would certainly have seen him – in view of the horses.'

'Perhaps . . . In view of the horses!' He agreed the hypothesis without giving an inch. 'If I do see him, I'll tell him that you came.'

I fended off Little Sweetheart, who was nuzzling insistently, and pretended to change the subject. 'Things seem quiet round here for a villa on Vesuvius in summer. Is no one staying at the house?'

'Only the family,' Bryon informed me in his straight-faced, stony way.

'And the young lady?'

'Oh she's one of them!'

This trainer had a shrewd idea I was someone without authority; he drew me firmly out of doors and began to walk me to the house. As we went by the livery stables I made sure I scanned every stall. Bryon finally lost patience with our good-mannered pretence. 'If you tell me what you're looking for, Falco, I'll tell you if we have it here!'

I grinned, unabashed. I was looking for the two horses that had followed me from Rome to Croton – not to mention their mystery rider, whom I deduced had been Barnabas.

'Try this then: two top-quality riding nags – a big roan that looks as if he was bred for the racetrack but just missed, and a squatter skewbald packhorse – '

'No,' Bryon said tersely.

He was right; they were not here. Yet the abruptness of his answer convinced me that at some time he had seen the two I meant.

He marched me back to the colonnade then backed off, seeming both disappointed and relieved as Helena Justina, the young lady who was one of the family, greeted me with her sleepy, unperturbed smile.

XLVII

When I strode back to Helena with my happy harpist's whistle, she had just been joined by her father-in-law. Making no reference to the retreating horse trainer, I apologised for my presence as I gave Caprenius Marcellus a vague explanation of events: 'I ran across Helena Justina, with a touch of the sun . . . '

The arrival of Marcellus put an end to my exploring. There was no help for it; I took my departure formally, with a calm nod to her ladyship – all I could do to answer the question in her dark, deeply inquisitive brown eyes.

Marcellus must have found my story easy to believe. Helena looked completely drained. I felt she needed more than a rest under a rug and a hot drink. She needed someone to look after her. The worst part was, my normally competent lady looked as if she thought so too.

As I rode the steward's mule back down the villa track I could hardly remember a word from her between when I brought her to the house and when I left. Only those eyes, which had settled on me with a stillness that made me hate leaving her.

Something was wrong. One more problem. One more buried relic to excavate as soon as I had time.

Damn the steward, waiting in Herculaneum for his mule; I stopped off and took dinner in Oplontis with my friends. Frankly, I thought they all seemed more relaxed, now I had pushed off to live elsewhere.

Helena's prophecy about the maid was correct. The daft chit had been sent to the slave market! Incredible. I hoped she found a more charitable mistress; I never saw her again.

Nothing was said to me. Next day I raised the matter with Aemila Fausta myself. She heard my views, then threatened to terminate my teaching post. I advised her to do it; she crumbled; I stayed.

My disgust was not simply because the girl had been attractive. After half a day with Helena I could barely remember what Fausta's maid was like. But I thought there must be better ways of keeping discipline.

I would not allow this set-to with Fausta to affect our professional relationship. She grew keener than ever to improve her musicianship.

She had found a new incentive: she told me that Aufidius Crispus was planning a huge banquet for all his friends on this part of the coast.

Rufus was going. He refused to take his sister; he told her he was escorting a girl he knew. Fausta seemed startled. I hoped that meant the girls her brother knew were unsuitable types; it promised more fun.

I had great hopes of the Crispus thrash. Partly for Aemilia Fausta, who was determined to gate-crash the event. And partly because she was taking her harp. So to beat time unobtrusively (and talk her past unfriendly doormen), the noble Aemilia Fausta was taking me.

XLVIII

Tonight I would meet him. Sometimes you know.

A member of my household who has a crisp sense of humour tells me whenever women feel that way the hero always turns out to have limp hands, a sneering mother, and a bladder condition which affects his private life. Luckily I never knew Aufidius Crispus well enough to hear about his family or his medical complaints.

He had taken a villa at Oplontis (hired it, leased, borrowed, simply pinched it for the night, who knows? – who *cared*, when the setting was gracious, the liquor was lavish and the beautiful after-dinner dancers were pretty well nude?). According to local custom, the villa had belonged to Poppaea Sabina, Nero's second wife. This Imperial connection held out a hefty hint of the ambitions of our host.

Poppaea's villa was the dominating feature at Oplontis. Probably the people who had lived in it managed to overlook the clutter of rude fishing huts beyond their boundary and thought their villa *was* Oplontis. People who inhabit such opulence find it convenient to ignore the poor.

For most of our stay this grand complex stood shuttered and dark. Arria Silvia tried to get in for a look round, but a watchman chased her off. As far as we could gather, when Poppaea married Nero this villa became subsumed into the Imperial estates, and after she died it stayed empty. There seemed a reluctance to do anything with the place, as if the waste of such a beautiful woman's life, and the cruel means of her death at Nero's hands, had struck even the Palace bailiffs with a sense of shame.

Most of the mansion was on two floors, with the building girdled by single-storey colonnaded walks and gardens on all sides. A wide terrace lay right on the seafront, leading to a grand central suite. The side wings must have contained over a hundred rooms, each decorated in such exquisite taste that as sure as eggs get broken they would be stripped out and renovated the next time the villa was occupied. It was ripe for refurbishment; by which I mean, it was lovely as it was.

I could never exist anywhere so huge. But it gave a spare-time poet plenty of scope to fantasise.

* * *

Dinner was held properly at the ninth hour. We arrived in good time. From the array of chairs congesting the Herculaneum road this was one of the largest functions I would ever be assisting at. The magistrate had set off ahead to collect his bit of fancy stuff, but Aemilia Fausta believed other people paid their local taxes for her personal convenience so she had commandeered an escort from her brother's official staff; they marched us briskly past the crowds, queue-hopping at public expense.

Most of the local quality, and some mere smut, were dining here courtesy of big-hearted Crispus tonight. The first people I spotted were Petronius Longus and Arria Silvia. They must have let themselves be netted to assist the great man's aim of extending very public hospitality on a wide social front. A true patron. Father figure to starveling clients from all ranks. (Buying in support from top to bottom of the voting tribes.)

Petronius would take his free bread buns and run. I happened to know that since Petro had been elected to the watch he had never cast a vote. He believed a man on a public salary should be impartial. I didn't agree but I admired him being so stubborn in his eccentricities. Aufidius Crispus would be an unusual politician if he had allowed for such morality in the voters he was courting.

Petro and Silvia did not speak to me at that juncture. They were inside, watching my progress with satirical smiles. I was still outside. I was hopping about in my best mustard tunic while my formidable female companion argued with the chamberlain at the door.

The man consulting the guest list knew his barley from his oats. This function was slickly organised. There was never any question of me barging us in bodily; if I tried any rough stuff, the heavy mob in studded wristguards who were lurking with a backgammon board behind the potted plants would fix us in a genteel arm lock and wheel us on our way.

Aemilia Fausta was a woman of few ideas but when she got one she recognised a treasure she might never possess again and she stuck to it. As she weighed in I felt seriously impressed. Tonight she was trussed up in mauve muslin, with her small white bosoms like two cellar-grown mushrooms arrayed in a greengrocer's trug. A castellated diadem sat rock steady on her pillar of pale hair. Bright spots of colour, some of it real, fired her cheeks. Determination to see Crispus made her as sleek and as wicked as a shark on the scent; the chamberlain was soon thrashing with the breathless desperation of a shipwrecked sailor who had spotted an inky fin.

'What host,' sneered Aemilia Fausta (who was a small woman, fairly bouncing on her heels), 'draws up a steward's dining list which includes himself or his hostess? Lucius Aufidius Crispus would expect you to know: I' announced the noble Fausta with unspeakable gall, *'am his fiancée!'*

The only thing that diminished this defiant gambit in my eyes was that for the lady it was simply the truth.

Beaten, the hapless flunkey led us in. I raised a fist to Petro, accepted a coronet from an extremely pretty flower girl, and then as the magistrate's sister whirled ahead I padded along behind, carrying her cithara. A clean-cut master of ceremonies weighed up the situation fast, then settled Fausta with a bowl of Bithynian almonds while he glided off to consult Sir. Surprisingly quickly he slid back. He assured Aemilia Fausta that her place was waiting in the private dining room, the elegant triclinium where Crispus himself would be presiding over the premier guests.

I don't know what I had expected, but the speed and good manners with which his castoff was made welcome provided an early hint that Aufidius Crispus possessed dangerous social expertise.

XLIX

The master of ceremonies started to apologise.

'Forget it. I'm just her harp teacher; no need to fiddle with your seating plans again – '

He promised to squeeze me in, but I told him when I was ready for any squeezing I would do it myself.

It was almost eating time, but I slipped out through the latecomers to scrutinise the flotilla of fabulous barges which had clustered against the spacious platform on the villa's seaward side. The *Isis Africana* took only a moment to find; she had been moored aloof from this nautical scrimmage, on her own, slightly out in the Bay. She was lying dark, as if everyone had already disembarked.

It was hardly a function where the host hovered on the doorstep in his best boots, waiting to shake hands; some of the hands he had invited were too clammy to touch. But Crispus must be in the house by now. I re-entered from the terrace to sneak an early look at him if I could.

I walked through the atrium. It was mainly red, painted with a mock colonnade of fluted yellow columns, through which massive double doors appeared, decorated with emblematic figures and set with azure studs, among distant perspectives of fanciful scenery, religious objects and triumphal shields. A connecting room brought me into a peaceful enclosed garden – live plants plus horticultural landscapes on the inner walls. Beyond that lay the grand saloon, which opened through two majestic pillars straight into the main gardens – a wonderful, typically Campanian effect. Most of the couches for visitors of quality had been set up in the saloon, so when I looked in noise and warmth and the perfume from scores of fresh garlands were spilling out into the summer night. Smaller reception rooms contained table space for the lower sort. None of this was what I wanted. Fighting back through the scrum, by a lucky guess I found the lavish kitchen suite; with, as I expected, the master dining room stationed alongside.

The triclinium at the Villa Poppaea was approached through two herm-like pillars where winged centaurs crouched on guard. It was a small room, painted in the ethereal architectural style which characterised the villa, and included a fine mural of a mock courtyard gate with winged sea horses writhing on its architrave below a shrine

181

to some patron god. On the back wall a particularly vivid painting of a bowl of figs caught my eye.

Tonight the room was piquant with fine, scented oils. The standard nine places, in couches of three, lay under graceful swags of embroidered cloth, beneath peacock feathers arcing over tall floral displays; peacocks in full display were also a motif in the decor of the house. I made a few mental notes of these gracious touches, in case I ever gave a dinner party at home.

I had arrived too early; Crispus was not there yet. The place of honour on the central couch still lay unoccupied.

I did see Aemilia Fausta, looking pleased with herself though tense, tearing at grapes on the left-hand couch – not quite the most exalted place. Two senators I failed to recognise were positioned more prominently, on either side of their host's empty place. A couple of women were flashing heavy jewellery, and there were two younger men fashionably arrayed in circular cheesecloth dinner gowns. One was our blond god Rufus, standing at the top of the room, talking to one of the senators. He had dumped the famous floozy on her own at the end of the table, just in front of me.

I knew her the minute I saw her. I gulped in a good eyeful before she turned and realised: long, pale feet, kicking each other fretfully as she was ignored by the magistrate; then a body that was slender and full at the same time, sheathed in some fine silvered cloth which looked as if it would slide wonderfully under a man's hands if he risked taking hold of her. Half a fortune in lapis lazuli beads circled her throat. Dark shining hair, curled at the front, then its heavy mass battened under a round gold net. That neat, deep-blue necklace and the close, golden cap made her look younger and sweeter; compared to the unashamed flamboyance all around, she had a compact, understated elegance. Tonight she was the best-looking woman in Campania, but people in Campania have garish taste and I was probably the only man who knew.

A slave tidied her sandals at the foot of her couch so she twisted round to thank him and saw me. I was lolling in the doorway with Fausta's instrument under my left arm and my right hand in her abandoned almond bowl. Until Helena looked back I had been munching my way methodically through the nuts.

Eyebrows I would have recognised across the width of the Circus Maximus shot up as the magistrate's escort glued her bonny brown eyes on me. I mouthed a silent, admiring whistle. The Senator's golden-capped daughter turned away (supplying an overhead view of a gorgeously haughty shoulder), with what she meant to be an expression of utter disdain.

She ruined the effect by preceding it with a distinctly sultry wink.

* * *

There was a flurry which heralded Crispus' approach, then I was hustled out. I shed the harp onto a slave as I went, ordering him to stow it at the back of Fausta's couch. (I had no intention of carting round someone else's cithara all night.) Accepting the situation, I let myself be pushed off to the public rooms. I would have liked to identify Crispus, but good timing is a crucial part of my work. Now, with his favoured guests chomping at the manger, was not the time to draw the big man's attention to my Emperor's communiqué.

I glanced into the saloon again but the appetiser course was already preceding formally and although there were one or two free places they were beside men who looked unfriendly or women with fat fingers and false hair. I ducked round a file of waiters shouldering trays of dressed endive, then foraged among the lower orders until I flopped down with relief between Silvia and Petronius.

'Avoid the mussel dumplings!' Silvia advised, hardly bothering to greet me. 'Lucius saw them half an hour ago, congealing well.' She shared my mother's views on serving food. And I was not surprised to find she had sent our lad into the kitchen even here. 'The top table are having ostrich but there won't be enough for us – '

'What's it going to be then, Lucius?' I asked in some hilarity. I did know his name was Lucius, though I only called him that if we were sensationally drunk. 'One of those does where a clever chef makes a ton of rock salmon look like forty different cuts of meat?'

Petro chuckled, before opening his mouth and dropping in Colymbadian olives; they were superb – huge fruits from Ancona, swum in amphorae of oil and herbs until they became infused with a fragrance you never find in the small, hard, brine-soaked Halmadian sort people normally eat.

Petronius assured me they had caught so many sea bass and lobster for this evening, the water level had sunk two inches in the Bay. Two annoying Campanian revellers were boasting about Baian oysters; we watched in silence, both of us remembering the oysters they dredge up in Britain from the cold, murky channel between Rutupiae and Thanet, and their dusky brothers from the north banks of the Tamesis Estuary . . . Petro tucked into the dinner wine with a wry face. It seemed fine to me, though I could tell he despised it. He had been tasting local vintages while I was away from Oplontis and enthused educationally about sparkling whites and robust young reds while I tackled the hors d'oeuvres, feeling jealous of having given up his company.

I was really missing Petro. This morose pang reminded me I had work to do. The sooner I did it, the sooner I could escape from Herculaneum back to my friends . . .

If the hired waiters were hoping to get off early, they hoped wrong. The invitees were planning on a long night. The plebs displayed cautious manners but the senators and knights and their ladies were piling into the viands, all eating twice as much as they would at home since this was free. The noise and the scents of sizzling wine sauces must have blown on the breeze to Pompeii, three miles away. The liquor slaves were skidding on the wet soles of their bare feet as they rushed round with refills, barely bothering to show the charcoal to the hot wine scuttles or measure the spice. There was no doubt Crispus was achieving what he wanted. It was the sort of ghastly communal occasion that everyone would remember later as a wonderful time.

After a couple of hours the Spanish dancing troupe arrived. Those of us around the bottom table redoubled the cheer we were just putting up as our main course dishes hove in sight. The waiters were doing their best, with gristly good temper, but it was a job and a half feeding such a throng, and there were the usual aggravating women who ordered up veal medallions in fennel sauce – *without the fennel, please!*

I guessed that the entertainers were timed to suit the nobs in the triclinium, who had their own swift fleet of carvers and carriers under supervision of a wily major-domo. Sure enough, when I went to ask the winged centaurs how matters were progressing, a great silver platter with one forlorn cinnamon pear was just coming out after the dessert course as a table tray of finger bowls swept in. I could hear the furious clack of Hispanic castanets, while one of those singers with no voice but a great deal of bravado was expressing anguish loudly in ferocious Spanish style. Through the portals I glimpsed a fiery girl with floor-length blue-black hair and not much in her clothes coffer striking attitudes which demonstrated her nakedness most attractively. I was so busy admiring her formidable fandango I forgot to look out for Crispus. Lackeys staggered past me under cornucopiae of fresh fruits, some so exotic I was unsure what their names were, then the doors slammed, and I was shooed away again.

I rushed back and in an undertone told Petro about the dancer; he whistled enviously at this bonus of my job.

Silvia had organised a main course for me. I managed to cram in a gingered duck wing, a potted salad, and a few mouthfuls of roast pork in plums, then I nipped back to the triclinium hastily. Things had moved on faster than I wanted. The host and most of his private party had dispersed. The two women with the jewellery were talking about their children, ignoring one of the younger men, before whom a different dancer with hypnotic stomach muscles was spiralling majestically.

Judging by the care with which the catering had been ordered, I reckoned my man had emerged now for some heavy social mingling. *Making himself agreeable*, as Helena Justina called it. Once they had eaten his dinner, people would feel even better about him if they saw him putting himself out to compliment them on their dress sense and enquire after their elder sons' careers. He would be moving round doing good work for himself; Aufidius Crispus was an operator on a determined scale.

I ducked out and started searching through the reception rooms, asking flushed waiters to point out Crispus if he was in sight. A perfume-sprinkler sent me to look for him in an inner peristyle garden, but no luck.

No one was there – except a quiet, solitary woman on a stone seat, looking as if she was waiting for someone. A young woman, in a slim dress and not much jewellery, with fine, dark hair fastened under a round gold net . . .

It was her own business if she had managed to fix up a treat for herself. I was not about to interfere and spoil her assignation. They only reason I hung around was that a man appeared. He clearly thought she was waiting there for him, and I thought the same. So I stopped, to see who he was.

I didn't know him. But after I had decided that, I stayed there anyway because Helena Justina was giving the impression that neither did she.

L

He emerged from a group of hibiscus bushes as if he had been up to something a well-brought-up young woman would rather not know. He was drunk enough to greet Helena as a marvellous discovery, yet not enough to be deflected by her frosty attitude. I assumed she could handle it; this swaying lecher was no worse a social menace than M. Didius Falco, droolingly affectionate – and a few brisk insults usually handled me.

This garden was decorated in a simple rustic style. I stood tight against a pillar which was painted with dark diagonal stripes; it was dusk now, so neither of them noticed I was there. He said something which I could not catch, but I gathered her reply: 'No; I'm sitting alone because that's how I want to be!'

The man swung nearer, puffing himself up tipsily. Helena ought to have slipped off straight into the crowd but she was obstinate, and perhaps the fellow she really had planned to meet in the garden seemed worth a few risks. He spoke again, and she insisted, 'No. I'd like you to go!'

He laughed. I knew he would.

Then she did get up. The pale, supple cloth of her gown swung from her shoulder brooches, trying to drape itself straight – emphasising where the lady beneath it was not.

'*For heavens' sake!*' Her bitter exasperation struck me at once – but he was far too fluthered with drink. 'My head aches,' Helena raged, 'my heart aches; the noise is making me dizzy and the food is making me queasy! I was sitting by myself because there is nobody I want to be with – especially not you!'

She tried to sweep by, but misjudged it. I was already moving when he caught her arm. Drunk or not, he was quick; his other hand was grappling brutally under her gown as I leapt the low wall which connected the rustic columns and covered the ground between us with a roar. Then I seized him by both shoulders and dragged him off.

There was a crack of heads, one of them mine. He was fairly athletic, and his energy surged unexpectedly, so he landed some punches. Root ginger repeated on me faintly, though I was far too angry to feel much else. Once his accuracy started fading I squared him up and demonstrated my disapproval with a series of unrelenting

186

blows in the parts of his body which my trainer had always advised me never to hit. After that I screwed his head under one elbow and hauled him to a sturdy well where I let a torrent from its fountain spew straight into his lungs.

While he was still on the healthy side of drowning, Helena's low voice warned, 'Stop it, Falco; you're killing the man!'

So I plunged him under a couple more times then stopped.

I propelled him through the colonnade to a corridor, where I sped him on his way with my party sandal in the small of his back. He sprawled headlong. I waited until I saw him starting to struggle upright, then strode back to Helena.

'Why were you skulking?' she accused by way of thanks.

'Coincidence.'

'Don't spy on me!'

'And don't expect me to let you be attacked!'

She was sitting on the rim of the well, hugging herself defensively. I put out my hand to her cheek but she drew back from another male assault; I flinched myself. After a moment she stopped shaking.

'If you still want to sit in the garden I'll stand guard.'

'Did he hurt you?' she asked, ignoring that.

'Not as much as I hurt him.' She frowned. 'He's upset you; you ought to have company.' She exclaimed; I bit my lip. 'Sorry; that was crass. I heard what you said – '

Then Helena Justina let out a whisper which sounded like my private name, snatched the hand she had recoiled from, and buried her face in my palm. 'Marcus, Marcus, I just wanted to be somewhere quiet so I could think.'

'What about?'

'Everything I ever do seems to turn out wrong. Everything I ever want becomes impossible . . . '

As I struggled to react to this, she suddenly looked up at me. 'I beg your pardon – ' Still gripping my hand so I could not escape, she demanded in her normal purposeful voice as if nothing else had happened, 'How are you getting on with Crispus? Have you talked to him yet?'

I confessed I had still not found him. So the noble young lady jumped from her wellhead and decided she had best come and help. I did mention about being sharp, and tough, and good at my job (et cetera). Before I got to the part about how I loathed being supervised, she had hurried me out of the garden and was coming with me whether I wanted her or not.

LI

I should never have allowed this. Her father would disapprove of his flower rushing about, and my sort of work is best done alone.

On the other hand, Helena Justina always did seem to find a plausible reason to ignore social conventions, and as we combed through the great reception rooms I certainly saved time having somebody who could identify the man I was looking for. Or not, in fact; because Crispus was never there.

'Is he a family friend?'

'No; my father hardly knows him. But Pertinax did. When I was married he came to dinner several times . . . ' Turbot in Caraway, no doubt.

As we went out into the spacious formal gardens which extended beyond the central features of the house, she slipped her hand through my arm. I had seen her like this before. Helena hated crowds. The bigger they were, the more her own sense of isolation grew. That was why she was clinging to me; I was still a menace, but I had a friendly face.

'Hmm!' I mused, as we stood at the far end of the garden among fine-scented roses, looking back towards the stupendous fluted pillars of the grand saloon. 'This would be nice work if we had time to enjoy it – ' I tilted my wreath to a more debonair angle, but Helena answered severely:

'We don't have time!'

She hauled me back indoors and we started to explore the smaller rooms. As we crossed the lofty atrium we passed one of the senators who had dined in the triclinium, already leaving the party with his wife. He nodded goodbye to Helena, with a grim glance at me as if I was just the sort of low-down plebeian rake he would expect to find with a senator's daughter twined around him at a party like this.

'That's Fabius Nepos,' Helena told me in an undertone, not bothering to untwine her arm just to save an old gent's blood pressure. 'Very influential in the Senate. He's elderly and traditional; not inclined to speculate – '

'Looks like we can assume he's one prospective collaborator who is going home early, unimpressed!'

Encouraged, we pressed on into a smaller hall which was decorated with illusionary perspectives of Corinthian columns, theatrical masks, a peacock to please the popular taste, and an elevated Delphian tripod to add a touch of culture for the rest. An extremely serious man with a beard was talking about philosophy. He looked as if he believed himself. The people who were privileged to hear his visionary dissertation looked as if they all thought they would probably believe him too – only nature had denied them the wherewithal to catch his drift.

I did. I thought it was tosh.

When we peeped back into the triclinium, Aemilia Fausta was sitting morosely by herself, plucking at her cithara. We ducked out before she spotted us, giggling together uncharitably. Later we discovered a long corridor set with stone benches for waiting clients, where Fausta's brother and a group of similar well-barbered aristos were standing round with winecups, watching some of the younger male waiters playing dice on their knees on the floor. Rufus looked surprised to see us, but made no attempt to reclaim Helena so I waved and we sped on.

She seemed in no mood to go sedately back to him. Her spirit was up now. She pushed ahead of me eagerly, sweeping open double doors and rapidly scanning the occupants as if she hardly noticed the ribaldry from the drinkers or the startling combinations of people who had wrapped themselves together for the purposes of pleasure. It was not, as I remarked at the time, the kind of party you would take your Great-aunt Phoebe to.

'I expect an aunt could cope with it,' Helena disagreed. (Thinking about my own Auntie Phoebe, she was probably right.) 'But let's pray your mother never finds out you came!'

'I'll say you brought me – ' I grinned suddenly. I had noticed a welcome alteration in her appearance. 'You've washed your hair!'

'A lot of times!' Helena admitted. Then she blushed.

In one colonnade the musicians who had come with the Spanish dancers were now strumming and fluting for their own amusement – about six times as well as they had played for the girls.

Not a good night for fountains. By one in a small tetrastyle atrium we saw the other senator from the triclinium, spread-eagled between two slaves while he was gloriously, obliviously sick.

'I don't know his name,' Helena told me. 'He had a lot to drink. He's the commander of the Misenum fleet – ' As he sagged between the slaves we watched for a moment, admiring the fleet commander's total abandonment.

After half an hour of fruitless search we both stopped, frowning with disgust.

'Oh this is hopeless!'

'Don't give up; I'll find him for you – ' The part of me that wanted to snort that I would find him for myself backed down happily before the part that was smitten with honest lust. When Helena Justina was bright-eyed with determination she looked adorable . . .

'Stop it, Falco!'

'What?'

'Stop looking at me,' she growled through her teeth, 'in that way that makes my toes curl!'

'When I look at you, lady, that's how I have to look!'

'I feel as if you were going to back me into a bush – '

'I can think of better places,' I said. And backed her towards an empty couch.

The annoying bundle wriggled out from under me just as for once I had her in a satisfactory clinch. I landed on the couch in the graceful position the Fates liked to see me in: flat on my face.

'*Of course!*' she exclaimed. 'He'll have a room! I should have thought of that!'

'What? Have I missed something?'

'Oh hurry, Falco! Get up and straighten your wreath!'

Two minutes later she had me back in the atrium, where she crisply extracted from the chamberlain directions to his master's dressing room. Three minutes after that we were standing in a bedroom with a dark-red painted ceiling, just off the seafront side of the house.

In the five seconds since we had stepped inside his borrowed boudoir, I had learned two things. Aufidius Crispus was wearing an ensemble which made his ambitions perfectly clear: his dinner robe was deeply dyed with the juice of a thousand Tyrian sea-shells to the luxuriant crushed purple which emperors reckon suits their complexions best. Also, his luck was better than mine: when we came in he had the prettiest after-dinner dancer pinioned on a bed with her rose behind his ear and half her breast in his mouth, while he was banging away at her Spanish tambourine with breathtaking virility.

I turned Helena Justina against my shoulder to shield her from embarrassment.

Then I waited until he had finished. In my business it always pays to be polite.

LII

The dancer slipped out past us, bearing her rose for reuse elsewhere. Evidently the incident had been rapid and routine.

'Beg your pardon, sir; did I put you off your stroke?'

'Frankly, no!'

Helena Justina sat quickly on a stool, more straightbacked than usual. She could have waited outside, though I was glad that she stayed to see me through this. Crispus glanced at her without much interest, then he settled in an armed chair, shuffled his purple folds back into order, plugged his head back through a laurel wreath, and offered audience to me.

'Sir! I'd thank you for inviting me to your highly select symposium, but I came with Aemilia Fausta, so 'invitation' is hardly the word!' He smiled faintly.

He was in his middle fifties, with a tireless, boyish look. He had a swarthy complexion with slightly heavy though good-looking features (a fact he was rather too aware of), plus a great array of regular teeth which looked as though he whitened them with powdered horn; he showed them at every opportunity, to emphasise what superb teeth they were and how many he still owned. Beneath the wreath, which he wore as if he was born with it, I admired the careful way his barber had layered off his hair. (Probably that same afternoon, judging by the fatty whiff of Gallic pomade which hung around the dressing room.)

'What can I do for you, young man? Who are you, first?'

'Marcus Didius Falco.'

He leaned on his chin thoughtfully. 'Are you the Falco who sent home my friend Maenius Celer with some colourful bruising and stomach cramps?'

'Could be. Or maybe your Celer just ate a bad oyster and bumped into a wall . . . I'm a private informer. I'm one of the dispatch boys who have been trying to deliver a letter to you from Vespasian.'

The atmosphere crackled as he sat more alert in his chair.

'"*I don't like you, Falco!*" Isn't that what I am supposed to say? Then you answer something like, "*That's all right, sir; I don't much care for you!*"' I could see at once that this would be nothing like convincing the chief priest Gordianus; Crispus was really expecting to enjoy our interview.

191

'I suppose you'll throw me out now, sir?'

'Why should I?' He was scanning me with some interest. 'I've heard you are an informer! What qualities does that need?'

'Oh, judgement, foresight, constructive ideas, acceptance of responsibility, reliability under pressure – plus the ability to shovel dung down a sewer before it attracts public notice.'

'Much the same as an administrator!' he sighed. 'Well, Falco, what's your mission here?'

'Finding out what you're up to – which is more or less self-evident!'

'Oh really?'

'There are plenty of public positions you could want. For all of them you need the Emperor's support – all except one.'

'What a shocking suggestion!' he told me pleasantly.

'Sorry; what I do is a shocking job.'

'Perhaps I should offer you a better one?' he tried, though with a latent humour in his tone, as if mocking his own attempt.

'Always open to suggestions,' I said, not looking at Helena. He smiled at me again, though I noticed no grand offers of employment rushing forth.

'Well, Falco! I know what Flavius Vespasianus has palmed off on Gordianus; what's he offering me?' The way he named the Emperor as if he were still a private citizen gave a clear indication of his disrespect.

'How do you know about Gordianus, sir?'

'For one thing, if the garland you are wearing was provided by me tonight, it came in a consignment I had shipped round the coast from Paestum.'

'Paestum, eh! Apart from a talkative garlandseller, who else is spreading rumours that Gordianus is going to Paestum?'

At my insistent return to the question I saw a glint in his eyes (which were brown enough to entice the women, though too close together to be classically correct). 'He told me himself. He wrote to me about his brother's death – ' Crispus stopped.

'Warning you!' Barnabas.

'Warning me,' he agreed gently. 'Have you come to do the same?'

'Partly, sir; also to negotiate.'

'What with?' he exploded, on a contemptuous note. (I remembered Crispus owned half Latium, in addition to his expensive dinner outfit and his natty sailing boat.) 'Vespasian has no money. He *never* had any money; it's what the man is famous for! All through his public career he was notoriously mortgaged to the hilt. As Governor of Africa – the most gracious post in the Empire – he ran out of credit so disastrously he had to trade in Alexandrian wet fish . . . What does he pay you, Falco?'

'Too little!' I grinned.

'So why do you support him?' the man purred. I found him easy to talk to, perhaps because I reckoned he would be difficult to offend.

'I don't, sir, particularly. Though it's true I would rather see Rome ruled by a man who once had to ask his accountant tricky questions before his steward could pay the butcher's bill than by some mad limb like Nero, who was brought up believing himself the son and the grandson of gods, and who thought wearing the purple gave him free rein to indulge his personal vanities, execute real talent, bankrupt the Treasury, burn half of Rome – and bore the living daylights out of paying customers in theatres!'

Crispus was laughing. I had never expected to like him. I was beginning to see what made everyone tell me he was dangerous; popular men who laugh at your jokes pose a threat which blatant villains can never command.

'I never sing in public!' Crispus assured me affably. 'A dignified Roman hires in professionals . . . You see, from my point of view,' he explained, taking time to convince me, 'after Nero died we saw Galba, Otho, Vitellius, Vespasian – not to mention various other pretenders who never even managed to edge their buttocks onto the throne – and the only thing which made any of them better than anybody else – for instance better than me! – was that they had the simple luck at the time to be holding public positions which provided armed support. Otho won over the Praetorian Guard, while the rest were all stationed in provinces where the legions they commanded were bound to hail their own governor to the skies. So if *I* had been in Palestine in the Year of the Four Emperors . . . '

He stopped. And smiled. And cleverly left any statement of treason unsaid.

'Am I right, Falco?'

'Yes, sir – up to a point.'

'What point?' he enquired, still perfectly pleasantly.

'Where your political judgement – which looks pretty shrewd – ought to tell you what we all have to accept: that a violent cycle of events has reached its natural conclusion. Rome, and Italy, and the Empire, are exhausted by the civil war. By popular consent Vespasian is the candidate who survived. So whether anybody else could, in theory, have challenged him is, in practice, no longer relevant. With all due respect to you, sir!' I declared.

At this juncture Aufidius Crispus rose in order to pour himself some wine at a pedestal table. I declined. He inflicted some on Helena without consulting her.

'This is not the woman you came with!' he commented satirically to me.

'No, sir. This is a kind-hearted lady who volunteered to help me find you. She's good at blind man's bluff.'

Helena Justina, who had not previously spoken, put down the winecup untasted. 'The lady Didius Falco came with is my friend. I shall never mention this conversation to Fausta but I do feel concern about what you intend for her.'

Crispus looked astounded by this female initiative, but soon managed to answer with the same frankness he had shown me: 'It might be tempting to reconsider my position there!'

'I can see that! Hypothetically, of course,' Helena challenged.

'Of *course!*' he interrupted in a laughingly suave tone.

'A man with his sights on the Palatine might reflect that Aemilia Fausta comes from a good family with one consul among her ancestors and a brother who promises to duplicate the honour. Her face would look dignified on the back of a silver denarius; she is young enough to bear a dynasty, sufficiently devoted to prevent any scandal – '

'Too devoted!' he exclaimed.

'Is that your problem?' I chipped in.

'It was. Indeed it is.'

'Why did you let her dine with you?' Helena hectored him.

'Because I see no reason to humiliate the lady. If you are her friend, try to explain to her that I could marry for policy – but *not* with such intensity on her side and such lack of it on mine.' He prevented himself from shuddering, but only just. 'Our marriage would be a disaster. For her own sake Aemilia Fausta's brother ought to give her to somebody else – '

'That would be extremely unfair to some other poor man.' Helena plainly thought him selfish. Perhaps he was; perhaps he should have tried to make a go of it – and plunged them both into domestic misery, like everybody else. 'What will you do?' she asked in a low voice.

'At the end of the evening take her home to Herculaneum on my ship. Tell her decently, in privacy, that I cannot oblige her. Don't worry. She won't be upset; she won't believe me; she never did before.'

His briskness closed the subject, though none of us objected to letting it rest. Aemilia Fausta's predicament embarrassed us all.

I got to my feet, and removed from my tunic the letter I had been carrying for so many weeks. He smiled, looking relaxed. 'Vespasian's billet-doux?'

'It is.' I gave it to him. 'Will you read it, sir?'

'Probably.'

'He wants me to take your reply.'

'Fair enough.'

'You may need time to think about it – '

'Either there is no answer at all, or I'll tell you tonight.'

'Thank you, sir. Then if I may, I'll wait in the colonnade outside.'

'Surely.'

He was businesslike about it. The man had talent. He had shown over the problem of Fausta that he possessed some compassion, which is rare. He also had good sense, a cheerful humour, the ability to organise, and an approachable style. He was quite right; he matched the Flavians. Vespasian's family had years of public service behind them, yet they continued to seem small-minded and provincial in a way this urbane, likeable character never would.

I did like him. Mainly because at bottom he refused to take himself seriously.

'There is one thing I wish to ask you, Falco.'

'Ask away.'

'No,' said Aufidius Crispus, glancing coldly at Helena. 'I want to ask you when this lady has withdrawn.'

LIII

Helena Justina shot us both a disparaging look, then slipped out of the room – like the dancing girl, but more aggressive and without a rose.

'Hates secrets,' I excused.

'You after her?' His eyes narrowed with that semiserious glint he used when he was amusing himself manipulating people. 'I can probably arrange it . . . '

'Nice present, but the lady won't look at me!'

He grinned. 'Falco, you're an odd sort for a Palace messenger! If Flavius Vespasianus has written to me personally, why send you as well?'

'Hiring in professionals! What did you wish to ask me? And why not in front of the lady?'

'It touches on her husband – '

'*Ex*-husband,' I stated.

'Pertinax Marcellus; divorced from her, as you say . . . What do you know about Pertinax?'

'Overambitious and underintelligent.'

'Not your type? I saw his death announced recently,' he murmured, giving me a speculative look.

'True.'

'Is it?'

'Well, you saw it announced!'

He stared at me as if I had said something that might not be genuine. 'Pertinax was involved in a project I know something about, Falco.' Crispus' own role as a plotter had never been proved and I could hardly foresee him admitting it. 'Certain people had collected substantial funding – I wonder who has it now?'

'State secret, sir.'

'Does that mean you don't know, or you won't tell?'

'One or the other. You say first,' I offered bluntly, 'why you need to know?'

He laughed. 'Oh come!'

'Excuse me, sir, I've better things to do than sit on a stool in the sun watching grapes ripen. Let's be frank! The cash was being hoarded in a pepper warehouse by a man who has apparently disappeared – Helena Justina's uncle.'

'Wrong!' Crispus shot back. 'He's dead, Falco.'

'Really?' My voice rasped as once again I smelt the decaying flesh of that body I had flushed down the Great Sewer.

'Don't play games. I know he is. The man wore a ring; a monstrous great emerald, rather low taste.' Even for his banquet Crispus himself had not troubled with jewellery, apart from one flat onyx signet ring, good quality but discreet. 'He never took it off. But I've seen the thing, Falco; I was shown it here, earlier tonight.'

I did not doubt it. He was talking about one of the rings which Julius Frontinus the Praetorian captain had wrenched from the swollen fingers of the warehouse corpse. The cameo which I had lost.

So while we were in Rome Barnabas had found it. And Barnabas must have been in Oplontis tonight.

Thinking quickly, I worked out that Crispus was hoping he could still get his hands on the sticky ton of bullion which the conspirators had assembled, and that he intended using it to further plans of his own. Half Latium and a fancy yacht might not be enough to secure the goodwill of all the provinces, the Senate, the Praetorian Guard, and the lively Forum mob . . .

In the hope of convincing him to abandon his plans, I declared what I had guessed: 'Curtius Gordianus wrote to warn you that the Pertinax freedman Barnabas has turned himself into a freelance killer? He was here tonight, wasn't he?'

'Yes, he was.'

'What was he after?' I queried, keeping my voice unsensational. 'Trying to bring you in as a backer for this chandlery lark of his?'

'I think you've lost me, Falco,' Crispus remarked, in his pleasant, winsome way.

He gazed at me. I let the subject drop, like a fool who had accidentally stumbled on to a clue, without understanding its significance.

I didn't understand it, that was true. But I was never the kind of amateur who would make his own uncertainty a reason to give up.

I had begun to suspect that wherever the grain importing fitted into this conundrum, Aufidius Crispus would be well to the fore of it. I wondered if he, and perhaps Pertinax before he died, had devised some private embellishment to the original conspiracy – an extra wrinkle, all their own. Was Crispus still hoping to pursue it? Had Barnabas come here tonight wanting to resurrect whatever fiddle Crispus had been intending with his master? And did frank, helpful, honest broker Crispus then decide that Barnabas would be better occupied telling me his life story in some dripping prison cell?

'You know Barnabas is wanted for the Longinus murder now? Are you turning him in, sir?'

I knew that under the affable exterior, Aufidius Crispus was a dangerous man, and like most of them, as quick to remove an embarrassment from among his own associates as he was to obliterate an opponent. Quicker, in fact. 'Try the Villa Marcella,' he suggested, without a second thought.

'I thought so! I was short of an excuse to search the place, but if that's a firm tip, I can pick the freedman up – '

'My tips are always firm,' smiled Aufidius in his elegant, easy-going way. Then his swarthy face hardened. 'Though I suggest, Falco, that you prepare yourself for a surprise!'

He had finished with me. He was holding Vespasian's unopened letter and I was anxious to leave him free to read that ancient piece of papyrus before the ink faded and beetles ate into it. I had the latch off the door when I stopped.

'About your friend Maenius Celer. I hit him because he was assaulting a lady.'

'That's Maenius!' he shrugged. 'He means no harm.'

'Tell that to the lady!' I rasped; Crispus seemed surprised.

'Camillus' daughter? She looked – '

'Immaculate; she always does.'

'Is this a formal complaint?'

'No,' I growled patiently. 'This is the explanation of why I hit your noble friend!'

'So, what's your point, Falco?'

I could never explain.

He was a clever, efficient operator. In a contest with the Flavians I might easily have given him my support. But I knew that stern, old-fashioned Vespasian (who agreed with me that the only point in taking women to bed was with their glad consent) would hold a grim view of jolly Maenius Celer and his so-called harmless escapades. I had found that men who shared my views on women made the best benchmates in politics. Which meant that Aufidius Crispus had just lost himself my vote.

There was nothing to gain by extending the conversation; I went straight out.

LIV

Helena had vanished. I wanted to find her, but I had told Aufidius Crispus I would wait in the colonnade.

For no obvious reason, I started walking along the veranda, away from the main body of the house. Only when I was beyond the sounds of other people, where a few desultory lamps lit the shadows, did I stop.

I stood still, hearing sea water rippling against a small pier thrust out into the Bay. From what Crispus had said about me being an odd messenger, I knew that however approachable he had appeared at our interview, he despised me. So long as Vespasian employed me, Crispus would despise Vespasian too.

The weight of my inability to influence him was suddenly too much. I lost all faith in myself. I needed a friend to console me, but now that Helena had taken herself off I was completely alone.

Sharp footsteps rang in the distance. Crispus emerged swiftly from his room. He was in front of the main building; I was in one wing, further back from the sea. I could see him but he was too far away to catch as he strode off.

I could have called out. There was no point. He made no attempt to look for me. He had reached his decision: Vespasian's letter would receive no reply. I had believed the man could be deflected from his purpose; but if so, it was evident that the messenger who achieved this tricky task would not be me.

I never give up that easily. I set off after him.

The scene indoors had grown disorganised during my absence. I found no one with sufficient command of their senses to ask which direction Crispus had taken. Thinking he might be collecting Aemilia Fausta, I headed back to the triclinium where I had seen her last. She was there, still looking lonely; he was not.

This time she spotted me. 'Didius Falco!'

'Madam – ' I stepped across the prone figures of several young gentlemen who had been having a better time tonight than their aristocratic constitutions could endure. 'Seen Crispus?'

'Not recently,' admitted Fausta, with a close look which implied suspicions relating to dancing girls. Feeling thwarted myself, I sat down to be sociable. 'You look depressed, Falco!'

'I am!' I leaned my elbows on my knees, rubbing my eyes. 'I deserve a rest; I want to go home; I need an affectionate woman to tuck me into bed with a beaker of milk!'

Fausta laughed. 'Nutmeg or cinnamon? In your milk?'

I laughed too, reluctantly. 'Nutmeg, I think.'

'Oh yes; cinnamon turns grainy if it stands . . . ' We had nothing in common. The pleasantries petered out.

'Seen Helena Justina?' I felt restless. I wanted to consult Helena about what had happened after she had left.

'Oh Helena went off with my brother. Something far too private to need any witnesses!' Fausta warned me in an arch tone as I started to my feet. A knot formed in my windpipe; I tried to ignore it. The magistrate's sister smiled at me with a silkiness that said she was a hungry sea anemone and I was a drifting shrimp. 'Helena Justina will not thank you if you intrude – '

'She's used to it. I worked for her once.'

'Oh Falco, don't be so innocent!'

'Why?' I forced out, still making conversation. 'What's her secret?'

'She sleeps with my brother,' Fausta proclaimed.

I did not believe her. I knew Helena Justina better than that. There were many men Helena might let her fancy light upon, but I was absolutely certain that brilliant, blond, rangy, successful magistrates – who ignored their escorts at dinner parties – were not her type.

At that moment Helena and Aemilius Rufus came together into the room.

And I believed it after all.

LV

He had his arm tightly round her. Either Helena needed support for some reason, or the magistrate liked holding her. I could not blame him; I liked holding Helena myself.

As Rufus billowed through the door, like a gorgeous crocus in his saffron dinner robe, he bent that golden head towards hers and murmured some intimacy. I could only escape from the room by smacking straight past them, so I stood where I was with my head tipped back. Then Helena exchanged replies with Rufus, who signalled to me.

I walked across, coolly.

Aemilius Rufus inflicted on me his easy-going, meaningless smile. I spared myself the trouble of making a mess of his mouth. No need to hurt my fist. If this was what the lady wanted, no point causing a scene. He had the rank (which did not bother me) but he also had the lady. I could only get the worst of it.

Helena stayed silent and downcast while Rufus took the lead: a strong woman letting herself be made submissive by a conventional man. She was wasting herself on him. Still, most of them do.

It was Rufus who spoke: 'I gather you act as Helena's bodyguard from time to time; she needs you now.' From his lazy manner, he was trying to disguise some disaster I was too low to be told about.

I hate being patronised. 'Too many prior commitments,' I refused him stubbornly.

Helena knew when I was angry, especially with her. 'Didius Falco!' she appealed to me formally. 'We have heard something here tonight; if it is true it's unbelievable. I must talk to you – ' A train of revellers suddenly crashed into the room, knocking the three of us sideways. 'Not here – ' she frowned in helplessness, above the influx of noise.

I shrugged. I wanted to leave anyway. If Crispus intended taking Fausta home on his yacht, he had left me a free agent for the rest of the night.

Rufus released Helena. 'I'll arrange for your chair.'

He left the room ahead of us. 'Found someone to ease your troubles, I see!' I sneered at Helena. In the lamplight her eyes had grown as dark as olives; they met mine in surging distress at my callous tone. Her unspoken reproach troubled me unexpectedly.

Helena walked quickly after the magistrate; I strode alongside. When we came into the atrium Rufus waved to say his orders were in hand, then went off in another group. Theirs must be a long-standing, casual affair, I reflected bitterly. She and I waited outside, where there was a sea breeze and more peace.

The air was cool, though still pleasant. Even I could admit the Bay of Neapolis was one of the most elegant quirks of geography in the Empire. Extremely civilised by starlight. I saw its fabled attraction. As the summer wavelets lapped a few paces away, I could even imagine why other daft people thought so highly of the sea.

It was a bland, beautiful night and I had nothing left to do with it but share the peace and the starlit scenery with the girl at my side – who had once been so sweet and soft and mysteriously friendly towards me but who tonight was herself: a senator's daughter and the mistress of a magistrate, completely cut off from a bug like me.

Her chair was too long coming.

'What happened with Crispus?' Helena enquired in a colourless voice when our silence became uncomfortable.

'I failed to convince him.'

'What will he do?'

'I can't tell.'

'He may not know himself.' She spoke quietly, frowning. I let her talk. 'This is what he's like. He makes up his mind on a whim, then he rapidly changes it. I can remember him talking about horses with Pertinax; after a long debate, when everyone had agreed how they were all going to bet, Crispus would immediately settle on some different horse of his own . . . ' She tailed off.

'Did he win?' I muttered, staring out to sea.

'No, that was the stupidity. He usually lost money. He could not even grasp how well Pertinax knew horses.'

Despite myself I was being drawn in. 'He mind losing?'

'No. Losing funds – or losing face – never frightens him.'

'This seems a gamble too. Something to do. He has no driving sense of injustice or ambition. At least Gordianus displayed some intensity! If the worst Crispus can complain about is that in Africa Vespasian ran short of cash, the man is certainly not driven by maniacal jealousy – ' Helena's stillness beside me was helping me crystalise the problem for myself. 'He could be won over. He has talent; he deserves a position. But the Emperor sent the wrong man to reclaim him. Crispus thinks I'm about as important as a ball of fluff in a lamb's tail; and he's right – '

'He's wrong!' Helena frowned, with only half her concentration. 'You can manage it.' Suddenly she turned to me, leaning against my side. 'Oh Marcus, I can't bear all this – Marcus, hold me! Please, just for a moment – '

I moved abruptly away.

'Other mens' women hold certain attractions – but excuse me, I'm not in the mood tonight!'

She stood straight as a spear, and I heard her deep, shocked breath.

I had shocked myself.

Time to leave. A chair in the Marcellus livery drew up nearby. Rufus was nowhere in sight.

'There were two things I needed to tell you,' Helena whispered fiercely. 'One I must deal with by myself! But I am asking you to go with me to the villa – '

'Why not your handsome friend?'

'Because I want you.'

'Why should I work for you?'

She looked me straight in the face: 'Because you are a professional and you can see I am afraid!'

I *was* a professional. She never forgot that. Sometimes I wished she would.

'All right. The usual rates,' I answered softly. 'The same rules as before: if I give you instructions don't argue, just follow them. And to do the job properly I need to know what frightened you – '

Helena said, 'Ghosts!'

Then she walked to her chair without a backward glance, knowing I would follow her.

It was a single chair. I had to stalk the two miles to the villa behind it, chewing over my anger about Rufus as I went.

Helena had four bearers and two fat little boys with torches, all of whom started looking at me as if they knew exactly why her ladyship had brought me along. Going up the mountainside there were plenty of places where we could pause to admire the panorama, and I ground my teeth as I sensed the bearers' contempt when we continued without stopping and they realised their mistake.

The house lay in silence.

'Let me go first – ' I was her bodyguard again, keeping her close to me as I helped her from the chair, glancing round behind us as we went into the portico, then stepping ahead through the house door before I steered Helena in herself. Because we were in the country there was no need to summon a porter; the great doors pushed open easily without bolts or bars.

'Come with me, Falco; it's vital that we talk – '

At intervals along the corridors small pottery lamps burned, though no one was about. Helena Justina hurried to the upper floor. We reached a heavy oaken door to what I guessed was her bedroom. As I put my hand on the latch I inspected her set face. I said briefly, 'I can't work in a bad atmosphere. Being rude to a client was unprofessional; I apologise.' Then I opened the door without waiting for an answer, and moved her in past me with a light touch of my arm.

There was a short corridor where a slave could sleep, though Helena was never the type to keep attendants by her all night. Beyond a closed curtain the bedroom was lit, but after I closed the door behind us the length of six paces lay dark. I said something conventional like, 'Can you see your way?' Then I found Helena in the darkness, turning back to answer me, so I had to decide rapidly whether to step back deferentially – or not.

The decision made itself. It was a long kiss, with a great deal of pent-up frustration on my side, and if I really thought she was sleeping with the magistrate you may wonder why I did it.

I was wondering myself. But I had no objection to showing the young lady that whatever she was obtaining elsewhere, she might find better value in the rough grip of her bodyguard . . .

Just as I was deciding I had convinced her, a metal lamp crashed over in the room.

LVI

Blazing with indignation, Helena reached the inner room first. I glimpsed someone scrambling out through a folding door: narrow ribs, thin legs, light hair and jaw-line beard, dressed in a white tunic, yet familiar. I ought to have caught him; we were equally surprised, though his lying in wait for the lady gave my anger a real edge.

I had to let him go. I had to, because when she rushed into her bedroom, Helena gasped and stumbled in a faint.

I managed to support her as she fell; she was unhurt. I lifted her onto the bed, caught up a handbell and shook it ferociously, then rushed outside to look. A long balcony ran the full length of the building with several stairs to ground level and doors into all the upper rooms. The man had vanished. I sped back to the indoor corridor and bellowed to raise the alarm.

Helena was already coming round. Muttering reassurance I stooped over her, unknotted her belt and unhooked her blue beads; she started protesting confusedly. She wore a fine chain too, which was twisting against her neck. I freed that, expecting an amulet.

Stupid: Helena drove off the evil eye all by herself. Hung on the chain was my silver ring. Instinctively she grabbed it back from me.

In response to my rumpus people started invading the room. I shoved my way out past them, leaving Helena to explain, then set off after our trespasser: I had no doubt it was Barnabas.

I hared round to the stables, convinced that was where he lurked. The trainer Bryon appeared, looking startled. He was muscular and a substantial weight, but before he knew what was happening I had him by both arms and had grazed his head pushing him backwards against a wooden post.

'Where is he?'

His eyes went automatically to the block where they kept the racehorses. I set off, running lightly across the yard. The high-strung champion, Ferox, reared up in panic and struck his hooves on the woodwork, though his bottlebrush companion whinnied at me with pleasure. I glanced round frantically. Then I knew: a short wooden staircase led up beside the rackety nag's stall to an overhead loft. I went up without a second thought. The freedman could easily have smashed in my skull as I pushed up the hatch; luckily he was not there.

'Oh *highly* salubrious!'

It was the best-appointed hayloft I ever saw: a fretted bed, an ivory table, a cupid with a superb bronze patina holding a conch-shell lamp, a shelf of flagons, the remains of a three-course meal on a silver table tray, olive stones scattered like rabbit droppings – an *untidy* man . . . No occupant.

The evil green cloak was hung on a peg, close beside his bed.

Bryon was calming Ferox when I descended the stairs.

'Well, I'm still looking for Barnabas – only now I know he's here!'

There was no doubt that the staff had been told to keep mum about the freedman's existence. Bryon scowled at me sullenly. 'He comes and goes. Mostly he goes; he's gone now.'

Ferox struggled wildly again, and Bryon complained I was frightening the horse. 'We can do this the easy way, Bryon – or not!'

'I don't know where he is, Falco – maybe talking with the old man. Discussing him is more than my life's worth – '

'From what I know of Barnabas, that's true!'

I stormed out.

I knew I had no hope of finding him, but if the old man and he were in open confederacy I reckoned the freedman would feel safe to remain on the premises.

I raged all through the farm frightening chickens, then searched the house. This time I meant everyone to realise I knew about him. I burst into empty salons, opened up attics, invaded the library. I turned over bedrooms, sniffing the air to judge whether anyone had recently been using them. I pawed the latrine sponges, counting how many were wet. I checked dining couches for dust or lack of it. Not one of the bleary-eyed slaves whom I rousted from their cubicles would be able to claim any longer that they did not know a thin man with a beard had been in their master's house, and that the Emperor's bad-tempered agent wanted him. They tumbled out and stood around half naked until the villa was a blaze of lamps: wherever he had hidden himself, he must be stuck there now.

I made them drag chests from inglenooks and turn over hogsheads that stood empty in corners. After my efforts it would take them a week to put the place to rights. There was not a bale of unwashed laundry I had not unroped with a stab of my knife, or a grain sack I had not kicked until it split. A bag of chicken feathers they were saving to stuff a mattress made a fabulous mess. Cats fled yowling from my path. The rooftop pigeons shuffled their feet in the darkness, and cooed unhappily.

In the end, I banged into the day room where Helena and

Marcellus were sitting together in silence, shattered by the devastation I had caused. Helena had a long woollen shawl wrapped tightly round her chest. I threw an extra stole across her knees.

'Did you find him?' asked the Consul, no longer pretending.

'Of course not. I'm a stranger; he must know your villa inside out. But he's here! I hope he's cramped in a bread oven with his face in the ashes and a loaf-rake poked in his ear! If he's taken to threatening your daughter-in-law, I hope someone lights the oven while he's there!'

I dropped on one knee beside Helena Justina. Marcellus must have seen the way I looked at her. I no longer cared. 'Don't worry; I won't leave!'

I could sense her suppressed anger as she addressed Marcellus over my head in a voice that shook with indignation. 'This is incredible!' It seemed as if she had been waiting for my support before she tackled him. 'I can hardly believe it – what was he doing in my room?'

'Foolishness. Did you recognise him?' the Consul asked guardedly.

'I should do!' blazed Helena. I had the odd sense that what she was saying meant more to Marcellus than to me. 'I suppose he wants to speak to me. I won't see him tonight when I'm tired and overwhelmed. Let him come tomorrow, and be properly announced – '

I stood up abruptly. 'Lady, this is not on!'

'Don't interfere, Falco!' The Consul flared up in ill-restrained anger. 'You have no business here; I want you to leave!'

'No; Falco is staying,' Helena returned in her steady way. 'He is working for me.' They fought over it in silence, but she had spoken so quietly he could see she was adamant.

The Consul shifted with irritation. 'Helena is in no danger here, Falco. No one will invade her privacy again.'

I wanted to rage that Barnabas was a killer, but decided not to make him doubly desperate by emphasising that I knew.

Helena gave me a faint smile. 'Tonight was a mistake, but not a threat,' she said to me. I stopped arguing. A bodyguard's role is to fend off attackers; explaining their filthy motives is for liberal philosophers.

I pointed out to Marcellus how weary Helena was, and in view of what had happened earlier, made no bones of the fact I intended to see her all the way to her room.

Helena's bedroom was full of servants. For her safety's sake I welcomed them. Besides, now things were so serious it was best not to play around with bright ideas like kissing her in corridors.

I brought her in, then winked chirpily at her. Making them *feel* safe was part of the first-class service I reckoned to give. 'Well, this is like old times!'

'I am so relieved you are here!'

'Forget it. You need protection. We'll talk tomorrow. But expect me to veto any suggestion of you seeing Barnabas.'

'I will if I have to – ' She hesitated. 'There is something about him you don't know yet, Marcus – '

'Tell me.'

'After I see him.'

'You won't. I'm not intending to let you be exposed to him again!' She took a furious breath, then subsided as her bright eyes clashed with mine. I shook my head tenderly. 'Ah lady! I can never decide whether you are my favourite client – or simply the most quarrelsome!'

She buffed me on the nose with her knuckles, like a pet who had been a nuisance. I grinned, and left her, still capped with the golden net that made her look so young and vulnerable. Maids flocked round to help her prepare for bed, and I managed to believe we were on good enough terms again that Helena Justina would happily have dismissed her women and kept me.

I prowled round on guard all night. She would expect that.

Barnabas put in no further appearances, though I kept up a steady tread, hoping he would hear my relentless patrol as I continued watching out for him.

LVII

Next morning I took Helena down to Oplontis and left her with Petronius and Silvia while I went back to Herculaneum to collect my things.

'You look disgruntled. I hope I'm not to blame!' Aemilia Fausta gurgled with girlish sarcasm. I had been up all night and the hour's sleep I had snatched while Helena was breakfasting had only made things worse. I had hitched a ride in a dung cart; I had the fly bites to prove it and felt too bilious to face an Aemilius luncheon of oozing pickled eggs.

Aemilia Fausta, who wanted the world to know she had been ferried home last night by the great Aufidius Crispus, pretended to apologise for leaving me in the lurch. 'I was unable to find you, Falco, to tell you my plans – '

'I knew your plans; Crispus told me his.' It was not the time for Fausta to indulge in badinage. 'Don't fret,' I growled. 'The place was full of women who were after me . . . Sailed home in the *Isis*, eh? I trust nothing scandalous occurred?'

Fausta heatedly denied it (which left the indelible impression something had). I could not imagine that any bachelor alone with her on a pleasure boat could allow himself to overlook the chance.

'Madam, make it your rule in future: just do what seems natural, and apologise to the musicians afterwards!'

Luckily at that point the kitchen erupted into one of its fits of clattering so she had to sweep off to play the mistress of the house. She looked like a woman who could shout at a kitchenmaid. I scowled after her, thinking about Helena Justina, who looked as though when she saw some stupid girl making a mess of cleaning a cauliflower, she would grasp the knife quietly and demonstrate the way it should be done . . . Then I thought that perhaps what Aemilius Rufus wanted from Helena was a wife to train his cook.

Loathing Rufus, I extracted my salary from the house steward, then found Fausta again to say goodbye.

'I shall miss my music lessons!' she admonished me gaily. She seized the cithara (which Crispus must have brought back on the yacht too, polite man) and started plectruming away like a Muse who had been given a lecture from Apollo on the need to keep her standards up. I commented on the nerve-racking vitality.

'Does this mean that Aufidius Crispus made things up?' I still hoped he had attempted to shed Fausta, but my heart sank; his behaviour with women was evidently as fickle as Helena had warned me it often was with horseflesh and might yet be over politics.

Fausta murmured in a prim voice, 'If Aufidius Crispus was to achieve the supreme honour there would naturally be a place for an Empress at his side . . . '

'Oh naturally,' I rasped. 'Someone gracious who will not object when he prods dancing girls with his princely staff of office! He won't achieve it – because I for one will be ripped to shreds by the Furies before I let him do it. Aemilia Fausta, if you want an honourable position you could achieve better by marrying someone like Caprenius Marcellus, especially if you presented him with a child – ' (This illustrates the low type of client I usually worked for.) I intended to leave Fausta's imagination to judge how the noble role of motherhood might be achieved in view of the Consul's poor health and advanced years, but she looked so complacent I spelt it out vindictively: 'Get his name on a contract then find yourself a charioteer or bathhouse masseur who will help you make an old man very happy – and set yourself up for a long and wealthy widowhood!'

'You're disgusting!'

'Just practical.'

Barracking her about Crispus had upset her equilibrium. Uncertainty swept over her again. Her head bowed towards the cithara, that pale hair in its faultless chignon looking like unyielding new lacquer on a hard stone bust. 'So you're leaving me . . . My brother tells me you are working for Helena Justina now.'

We stared at one another, both remembering the last time Fausta had mentioned her brother and Helena in one breath.

I brought out carefully, 'I think you made a mistake.'

'What was that?'

'Your brother,' I said levelly, 'does *not* tangle with your friend.' I was sure of it. The magistrate had let Helena leave the banquet with a wave from afar. He was the type who would. But I happened to know that if Helena had a lover she kissed him goodbye.

'Then it must be someone else!' Aemilia Fausta lost none of her spite. 'Perhaps,' she suggested, 'the man you have been hired to protect her against?'

The woman was ridiculous. I refused to waste effort arguing.

By that time, in any case, it had struck me that my new client had gone with me to Oplontis that morning a little too readily; I raced back there without more ado. I was right. Helena Justina had a mind of her own. The minute I had disappeared towards Herculaneum, she had made some excuse to Silvia and set off back to the Villa Marcella by herself.

No doubt about it: she was hoping to see Barnabas.

I found her at the villa on a daybed in the shade, pretending to sleep. I tickled her foot with a flower. She opened her eyes meekly.

'Either do what I say, or I give up the job.'

'I always do what you say, Falco.'

'Do it – and don't tell lies!' I refused to enquire if she had seen the freedman, and she did not volunteer. Anyway, there were too many servants about for a discreet chat. I stretched out under a box hedge. I felt desperately tired. 'I need to sleep. Wake me if you decide to shift from here.'

When I woke up she had gone indoors without telling me. Someone had fastened a flower at a ludicrous angle in the straps of my left boot.

I stomped in and found her.

'Lady, you're impossible!' I dropped the flower in her lap. 'The only thing this commission has to recommend it is I can forget about giving lectures on diatonic scales.'

'You give lectures on everything. Would you rather be in Herculaneum, teaching the harp?'

'No. I'd rather be here protecting you – from yourself, as usual!'

'Oh, stop harassing me, Falco,' she grumbled cheerfully. I grinned at her. This was wonderful: my favourite work.

I sat down a few feet away, where I arranged my expression to appear suitably diffident and was all set to fend off marauders if any were on the prowl that afternoon.

The one advantage being a harp teacher did have was that in order to demonstrate fingering you could position yourself right alongside the young lady who was employing you, and put both arms round her. I would miss that.

Probably.

PART FIVE
THE MAN WHO DID NOT EXIST

THE BAY OF NEAPOLIS
July

'Come here, my Galatea. What is there to amuse you in the sea? . . . Here by the stream all kinds of flowers are blooming on the turf. Here a bright poplar sways above my cave, and the dangling vines weave shadows on the ground. Come here, and let the wild waves hammer on the beach . . .'

Virgil, Eclogue IX

LVIII

But for one flaw the Villa Marcella could be recommended as a holiday spot. It was well appointed, had the best views in the Empire, and if you had the right connections it was free. All a visitor had to do was forget he was sharing these elegant acres with a calculated killer; although in that respect the villa was no worse than any two-as dosshouse on this flea-ridden shore, where the clientele were liable to knife you as you slept.

I had no intention of letting Barnabas stay on the loose. On the first day I went to the stables while Helena and the Consul were lunching safely among their platoon of slaves. But Bryon made no secret of it: 'He's gone off somewhere.'

A glance into the palatial hayloft confirmed this: the freedman's den looked untouched, down to the olive stones drying up on last night's dinner plate. But his cloak had been lifted from its peg.

'Where was he heading?'

'No idea. But he'll be back. What else can he do?'

'Something dangerous!' I exclaimed, with more force than I meant.

I spent that second night on a balcony seat outside Helena's room. I had not forewarned her, but a maid brought me a pillow; Helena knew.

We shared breakfast on the balcony, like relatives staying in the country; very odd. Then I tackled the stable again.

This time Bryon met me in the yard, looking concerned. 'He never came in, Falco; that's unusual.'

I cursed. 'Then he's skipped!'

The trainer shook his head. 'Not him. Look, I'm not daft. First he's here, but nobody is supposed to know. Then you come; now I reckon he's desperate – '

'Oh he is! I need the truth, Bryon – '

'Wait it out then. He'll be back.'

'He paid you to say that? You're protecting him?'

'Why should I? I was born here; I thought I was one of the family. My mistake! I was sold overnight. Then they bought me back, but only for the horses. A double shock, and not a word said to me about it either time. Oh, I always got on all right with him,' Bryon declared. 'But things will never be the same again. So believe me, he'll turn up.'

'You mean because he needs the old man?'

Bryon smiled grimly. 'No. Because of how badly the old man needs him!'

He would not explain.

He did come back. And I found him. But a lot happened first.

Helena Justina took the air that morning, accompanying the lad who renewed the wreath of flowers on the herm at the estate boundary. I had escorted them. Then two donkeys hove into view bearing Petronius Longus, Arria Silvia, and a basket which I could see was stuffed with picnic things: a prearranged rendezvous.

Petronius had been longing to take me drinking ever since we arrived. This was his opportunity. He must have imagined a holiday carnival would in some way help me.

I was annoyed. 'Don't be ridiculous! I'm tracking down a murderer; he could turn up any time. How can I go gadding up the mountain – '

'Don't be so stuffy!' Helena chaffed. 'I'm going, so you have to.' Before I could argue further she had sent the boy home, cajoled me onto a donkey, and hopped up behind me. She held onto my belt. I held onto my temper, just.

It was a still, hazy day with that vapoury, innocuous look which on the Campania coast means intense heat later. Petronius picked our route. My donkey was the awkward one, which increased the fun.

We rode up past the rich black ploughland on the lower slopes, then through the thriving vineyards which in those days covered the mountain almost to its summit, making Bacchus its natural patron god. Wild broom was still flowering as our way snaked higher and higher into the rarified air. Vesuvius then was much more majestic than now. It was twice the size, for one thing – a quiet, luxurious, richly farmed mountain, though there were ancient secret places on the peak where only hunters went.

Petronius Longus stopped for a tasting at a wayside wineseller's. I did not feel like drinking. I said I had always wanted to go up to see the gorges at the top of the mountain where Spartacus the rebel slave had held out against a consular army and nearly brought down the state; I too was in a fair old mood for bringing down the state.

Helena came with me.

We rode as far as the donkey could easily travel, way up among the tangled brushwood which I knew was frequented by wild boar. We both dismounted, tethered Ned, then set off to cover the final stint to the top. It was rough going; Helena stopped.

'Too strenuous for you?'

'I'm struggling – You go on; I'll wait with the donkey.'

She went back. I went on. I thought I wanted to be by myself, but I felt lonely as soon as she left.

I reached the summit quickly, had a look round, decided the historical research had not been worth the effort, and scrambled back down to Helena.

She had spread out a cloak and was sitting there with her sandals unstrapped, lost in thought. When she glanced round I deliberately let her see me making an inventory. She was wearing a pale-green gown which showed off the fact she was well worth showing off. Her hair was parted and twisted the way I had once liked it, above simple gold earrings. If she coloured her face it was subtle enough not to show. A pity I could not convince myself she had planned this neat effect for me.

'Did you reach the top? What was it like?'

'Oh, a cone-shaped peak with a huge rocky depression, and great fissures full of wild vines. That must have been how the rebel army made their escape when Crassus evicted them – '

'Is Spartacus a hero of yours?'

'Anyone who fights the Establishment is a hero of mine.' None of this was the point at issue so I sounded terse. 'Well, what is this merry jaunt about?'

'A chance to speak to you privately – '

'Barnabas?'

'Yes and no. I met him yesterday,' Helena confessed, her restraint admonishing my harshness. 'It was perfectly civilised; we sat in the garden, and I had honey cakes. He wanted to see me. He has no money, for one thing – '

That angered me. 'You were divorced from his patron. He has no right to sponge off you!'

'No,' she said, after an odd pause.

'You never gave him cash?' I accused.

'No.' I waited. 'The situation is complicated,' she told me, still in that washed-out voice; I continued to stare her out. 'But I may be short of funds myself – '

I could not envisage Helena in financial straits. She had inherited land from a female relation, then after her divorce her father had given her part of the dowry her ex-husband had returned. Pertinax himself had bequeathed her a small fortune in precious spice. So she was richer than most women, and Helena Justina was not the type to squander it on tiaras or to give away thousands to some seedy religious sect.

'Unless you want to flirt with a *very* demanding ballet dancer, I can't see you strapped for cash!'

'Ah well . . . ' She ducked the issue stubbornly. 'Now you tell me something. What happened at the Villa Poppaea that upset you so bitterly?'

'Nothing that matters.'

'Something about me?' she persisted.

I could never resist Helena's earnestness; I let out abruptly, 'Do you sleep with Aemilius Rufus?'

'No,' she said.

She could have answered, *'Of course not; don't be stupid.'* It would have sounded much stronger, though I would have believed her less.

I did believe her. 'Forget I asked. Look, next time you take honey cakes with Barnabas, I'll be behind the pergola.' Her silence jarred me. 'Lady, he's a fugitive – '

'Not now. Let me deal with him. Somebody has to bring him back to the real world – '

I was overwhelmed with fondness for her dogged way of doing things. 'Helena Justina, you cannot take every problem in the Empire onto yourself!'

'I feel responsible . . . ' Her face remained strangely remote as she argued with me. 'Don't you harass me, on top of all my other troubles – '

'What troubles?'

'Nothing. Do your work for the Emperor, then we can attend to Barnabas.'

'My work can wait; I'm looking after you – '

'I can do that myself!' she suddenly exploded, astonishing me. 'Always. I shall have to – as I fully realise!'

I felt my jaw harden. 'You're talking nonsense.'

'No, I'm speaking the truth! You know nothing about me; you never wanted to. Lead your own life how you choose – but how could you say what you did about Rufus? *How could you think that?*'

I had never seen Helena so hurt. I was so used to insulting her, I had failed to notice that for once her tolerance had snapped.

'Look, it was none of my business – '

'Nothing about me is any of your business! Go away, Falco!'

'Well that sounds like the sort of instruction I can understand!' I felt so helpless I lost my temper too. I thundered blackly, 'You hired me because I was good – too good to waste my time on a client who will never confide in me.' Helena made no answer. I walked over to the donkey. 'I'm going back. I'm taking the donkey. Are you coming with me sensibly, or staying on this mountain by yourself?' More silence.

I unhitched the animal and climbed aboard.

'Don't worry,' I said unpleasantly. 'If a wild boar steps out of the undergrowth, just roar at him the way you roar at me.'

Helena Justina neither moved nor answered me, so I started down the mountain without looking back.

LIX

I rode downhill for three minutes at a steady pace. As soon as the track widened, I reined in the donkey and drove him back again.

Helena Justina was exactly where I left her, with her face out of sight. Nothing had attacked her: only me.

When my heart steadied I walked over, then reached down and rubbed the top of her head gently with my thumb.

'I thought you had left me,' she said in a muffled voice.

'Is that likely?'

'How should I know?'

'I thought I *had* left you,' I admitted. 'I'm the sort of fool who would think that. If you just stay in the same place so I can find you, I shall always come back.' She choked on a sob.

I dropped on my haunches and wrapped both arms round her. I held her tight but after a few hot tears had trickled away under the neck of my tunic she grew quieter. We sat there, perfectly still, while I sent my strength flowing into her, and the strain I had been feeling for so long it had come to seem natural went running away too.

Eventually Helena mastered her misery and looked up. I hooked two fingers into her neckchain and pulled out my old silver ring. She coloured faintly. 'I used to wear it . . . ' She tailed off in embarrassment.

With both hands I snapped the chain apart; Helena gasped and caught the little circle of silver as it fell into her lap. I glimpsed the inscription: *anima mea*, 'my soul'. I grasped her left hand and replaced the ring myself. 'Wear it! I gave it you to wear!'

Helena seemed to hesitate. 'Marcus, when you gave me your ring to wear – were you in love with me?'

That was when I realised how serious things were.

'I made myself a rule once,' I said. 'Never fall in love with a client – '

She rounded on me in distress, then saw my face. 'Sweetheart, I've made a lot of rules, and broken most of them! Don't you know me? I am frightened you will despise me, and terrified other people will see you doing it – but I'm lost without you. How can I prove it? Fight a lion? Pay my debts? Swim the Hellespont like some lunatic?'

'You can't swim.'

'Learning is the hard part of the test.'

'I'll teach you,' muttered Helena. 'If you fall into any deep water, I want you to float!'

The water was pretty deep here. I stared at her. She stared at the ground. Then she confessed, 'That day you left for Croton, I was missing you so badly I went to your apartment to look for you; we must have passed one another in the street . . . '

Overcome, she ducked her head onto her knees again. I cackled with laughter, bitterly. 'You should have told me.'

'You wanted to leave me.'

'No,' I said. My right hand was cradling the back of her head, exploring a hollow which seemed purposely made to fit the ball of my thumb. 'No, my darling. I never wanted that.'

'You said you did.'

'I'm an informer. All talk. Mostly inaccurate.'

'Yes,' she agreed thoughtfully, raising her head again. 'Didius Falco, you do say stupid things!'

I grinned, then I told her some more.

Above the Bay, the sun broke free of that vaporous cloud cover, and a band of light ran swift as silk across the coastal plain and up the mountain where we were. Warmth flooded over us. The elegant ellipse of the coastline brightened; at its open end the Island of Capreae emerged as a dark smudge complementing the folds of the Lactarii range. Below us the small, white, red-roofed buildings of Herculaneum, Oplontis and Pompeii crouched along the shore, while on the linenfold slopes of the distant hills villages and farms tantalised the eyesight among the natural rocks . . .

'Hmm! Just the sort of spectacular vista where you bring a beautiful woman, and never once look at the view . . . '

As the sunlight hit us, I levelled Helena on her back and stretched myself alongside, beaming down at her. She started stroking my ear as if it was something wonderful. My ear could take more of that; I realigned my head so it was more readily available while I basked in her scrutiny. 'What are you looking at?'

'Oh, a thatch of black curls which never look combed – ' I happened to know Helena liked my curls. 'One of those long, straight, superior noses off an Etruscan tomb painting . . . Eyes that keep moving, in a face which never reveals what they have seen. Dimples!' she scoffed (driving her little finger into one of them).

I jerked my head, trapping the finger in my teeth, then pretended to eat it.

'Excellent teeth!' she added crossly, as an afterthought.

'What a wonderful day!' I had always liked warm weather. I had always liked Helena too. It was hard to remember there had ever seemed much point pretending otherwise. 'My best friend's happy getting drunk with his wife, so I can forget him. I'm lying in the sunshine up here, with you all to myself, and in a moment I shall be kissing you . . . ' She smiled up at me. A shiver ran all down my neck. Alone with me now, she seemed completely at peace. I too had relaxed to the point where I was ceasing to relax . . . Helena began to reach for me, just as I gathered her closer and kissed her at last.

Many seconds later I looked up gravely at the sky. 'Thank you, Jove!'

Helena laughed.

The green dress she was wearing was light enough to show that she was wearing nothing else. It was fastened along each elbow-length sleeve with five or six mosaic glass buttons twisted through embroidered loops. I undid one to see what would happen; Helena combed my curls with her fingers, smiling. 'Shall I help?'

I shook my head. The buttons were stiff, but stubbornness and other factors had taken hold by then so I winkled off three, working upwards; then I explored her arm, and since she seemed to like it I carried on unbuttoning to the top of the sleeve.

My hand slid from her wrist to her shoulder then down again, no longer on her arm. Her cool soft skin which never saw the sun shrank, then rose to my touch at her intake of breath; I had to fight to stop my fingers quivering.

'Is this leading somewhere, Marcus?'

'I hope so! Don't imagine I could get you on your own at the top of a mountain and not make the most of the chance.'

'Oh I never thought that!' Helena assured me quietly. 'Why do you think I wanted you to come?'

Then, being a practical woman, she undid all the buttons on the other sleeve herself.

A long time afterwards, when I was utterly defenceless, a wild boar strolled out of the undergrowth.

'Grrr!' said the Senator's daughter amiably, over my naked shoulder.

The wild boar snuffled, then turned round with a disapproving snort and ambled off.

LX

When Petronius Longus stopped snoring and roused himself, conflicting emotions fought in his face. He took in the fact we had come down the mountain in a very different mood from when we had left. While he was sleeping Helena and I had finished his wine (though that did not matter at the price here); now she and I were tangled together like puppies in the shade. As a man with a hard grasp of the social rules, Petronius was visibly torn.

'Falco, you'll have to be careful!'

I tried not to laugh. In ten years of watching my contorted relationships, this was the first time Petro had bothered to give me brotherly advice.

'Trust me,' I said (It was what I had told Helena. I blocked out how at the crucial moment when I tried to restrain my efforts, she had cried out and would not let me go . . .)

Petro growled, 'For heavens' sake, Marcus! What will you do if there's a mistake?'

'Apologise to her father, confess to my mother, and find a priest who keeps his prices down . . . What do you take me for?'

My shoulder was aching, but nothing could make me shift. The joy of my life had her head on my heart and was profoundly asleep. All her troubles had been drained away; her tranquil lashes were still spiky from her helpless tears afterwards. I could easily have wept myself.

'The lady might see things differently. You ought to stop this!' Petro advised perversely, now that his expedition up the mountain had ensured I never could.

His wife woke on the bench beside him. Now I watched Silvia interpret the scene: Helena Justina tucked against my side with her knees under mine; Helena's hand clasping my own; her fine hair, crumpled by my arm; the depth of her sleep; my own unsmiling peace . . .

'Marcus! What are you going to do?' she insisted in a worried undertone. Silvia liked everything to be neat.

'Finish my commission, and put in a claim for payment as rapidly as possible . . . ' I closed my eyes.

If Silvia thought we had started something scandalous she must have blamed me for it, because when Helena awoke the two of them went off together to wash their faces and reorganise themselves. When they came back it was with the secretive, satisfied air of two women who had been gossiping. Silvia had her hair wound on the nape of her neck the way Helena usually wore hers, and they had knotted Helena's with ribbon. It suited her. She looked as if she ought to have been doing something typically Athenian on a black-figure vase. I would have liked to be the free-spirited Hellene lying in wait to catch her just around the vase handle . . .

'This is confusing,' Petro joked. 'Which one was mine?'

'Oh I'll take the one with the topknot, if you like.'

He and I exchanged a look. When one of two friends is married and the other stays a bachelor, rightly or wrongly the assumption is that you operate by different rules. It was a long time since Petro and I had been out together on such easy terms.

Anyone who knew Petronius and his interest in wine also knew that he would seize on this opportunity to make a few purchases for domestic use. True to his usual thoroughness, once he found a crisp white at a few coppers an amphora (with a *pétillance* he described to me lovingly, as connoisseurs do), Petronius Longus acquired as much as he could: while I left him on his own he had bought a culleus. Seriously. A huge barrel as tall as his wife. At least twenty amphorae. Enough to put a thousand flasks on the table if he kept an inn. (More if he watered the drink.)

Silvia was hoping I would dissuade him from this mad bargain, but he had already paid. We all had to wait while he burned his name in the cask then made complicated arrangements for coming back with Nero and the cart, which was the only way he would ever get his culleus away from here. Silvia and I asked how he intended to transport his family home now (not to mention where they would live, if their house was full of wine), but he was lost in euphoria. Besides, we knew he would manage it. Petronius Longus had done stupid things before.

Eventually we rode back.

I had the one with the topknot. She sat in front, intensely quiet. When we reached the villa letting her go was almost impossible. I told her again that I loved her, then I had to send her in.

Petronius and Silvia had tactfully waited at the estate entrance while I took Helena up to the house. When I rode back with the hired donkey they stayed politely silent.

'I'll see you when I can, Petro.' I must have looked grey.

'Oh Jupiter!' Petronius exclaimed, swinging down from his mount. 'Let's all have another drink before you go!' Even Arria Silvia forbore to complain.

We broke into a wineskin, sitting under a pine tree in the dusk. We three drank, not too much but with a certain desperation now Helena had left us.

Afterwards I walked up to the house, reflecting that love was as hard on the feet as it was on the pocket and the heart. Now I noticed something I had missed before: a chink of harness under the cypress trees led me to two rough-coated, saddle-sore mules, tethered away from the track with nosebags on. I listened, but caught no other sign of life. If revellers – or lovers – had come up the mountain from the coast, it seemed odd that they should travel so far onto a private estate for their happy purposes. I patted the animals, and went on thoughtfully.

By the time I arrived at the villa again, it was an hour since I had brought Helena back.

Any murderer or coffer-thief could have got into that house. The servants who greeted Helena had long disappeared. No one was about. I went up, confident at least that her bedroom would be well staffed; a safety measure I had insisted on. It meant I myself could only expect five minutes being polite to her but I was looking forward to a silly charade in front of other people, playing her surly bodyguard, all gristle and grim jokes . . .

Reaching Helena's room I opened the heavy door, slipped in and closed it silently. It was an open invitation; I had to fix a bolt on the door. The outer space was dark again, with the same lights beyond the curtaining.

She had company. Someone spoke, not Helena. I should have left. I was asking for every kind of disappointment, but by then I felt so desperate to see her that it carried me straight into the room.

The green dress lay folded on a coffer; her sandals were tumbled askew on a bedside rug. Helena had changed into something darker and warmer with woollen sleeves to the wrist; her hair was plaited on one shoulder. She looked neat, grave, and impenetrably tired.

She had come home so late she had her dinner on a tray. She sat facing the door, so when I batted in through the curtain her shocked eyes watched me frantically absorb the scene.

There was a man with her.

He was sprawled in a chair with one knee over its arm, casually scoffing nuts. Helena seemed more sullen than usual as she chewed at a chicken wing, though she was getting on with it as if the presence of this person in her bedroom was commonplace.

'Hello,' I stormed angrily. 'You must be Barnabas! I owe you half a million bits of gold – '

He looked up.

It was certainly the man who had attacked me in the warehouse, and probably the one I had glimpsed harassing Petro in the ox cart on the Capua Road. Then I stared at him harder. After three months of chasing the man in the green cloak, I finally discovered who he really was. The freedman's old mother in Calabria had been right: *Barnabas* was dead.

I knew this man. He was Helena Justina's ex-husband; his name was Atius Pertinax.

According to the *Daily Gazette*, he was dead too.

LXI

He looked healthy for a man who had been murdered three months before. But if I had any choice in the matter, dead was how Atius Pertinax would soon be. Next time I would arrange it myself. And make it permanent.

He wore a very plain tunic and a new jaw-line beard, but I knew him all right. He was twenty-eight or nine. Light hair and a spare build. He had pale eyes I had forgotten and a sour expression which I never would forget. Permanent bad temper tightened the muscles round his eyes and made his jaw clench.

I had met him once. Not when I tailed him to the Transtiberina; the year before. I could still feel his soldiers pulping my body and hear his voice calling me savage names. I could still see his pasty legs below a senatorial toga, striding from my apartment where he had left me lying beside a broken bench, helplessly spitting blood on my own floor.

He was a traitor and a thief; a bully; a murderer. Yet Helena Justina was letting him lounge in her bedroom like a lord. Well he must have sat with her like this a thousand times, in that grand, tasteful, blue-and-grey room he allowed her in their house . . .

'My mistake. Your name's not Barnabas!'

'Is it not?' he dared. I could see him still wondering how to react to my sudden arrival.

'No,' I responded quietly. 'But officially Gnaeus Atius Pertinax Caprenius Marcellus is mouldering in his funeral urn – '

'Now you see the problem!' Helena exclaimed.

I wondered how she could bear to sit there eating until I noticed how she was nibbling at her chicken bone, showing her teeth as if she despised his predicament too much to let it interfere with her appetite.

I strode into the room. Apart from the fact I was intent on arresting him, it was a good old Roman custom that in the presence of your moral superior you leapt to your feet. Pertinax tensed, but sat tight.

'Who the hell are you?' He had made too much noise before too. 'And who gave you permission to enter my wife's room?'

'The name is Didius Falco; I go where I like. By the way – she's not your wife!'

226

'I've heard about you, Falco!'

'Oh you and I are old acquaintances. You once arrested me for the pleasure of it,' I reminded him, 'though I like to think I have the character to rise above that. You destroyed my apartment – but I helped dispose of your house on the Quirinal in return. Your Greek vases did well,' I smiled annoyingly. 'Vespasian was pleased with those. Your Praxiteles *Cupid* was a disappointment though – ' I knew Pertinax had paid a lot for it. 'A copy; I expect you realised . . . '

'I always thought it had big ears!' Helena told me conversationally. Pertinax looked peeved.

I hooked a footstool forwards with my heel and squatted where I could cover Helena yet still fix him. She coloured slightly beneath my quiet scrutiny; I found myself wondering if Pertinax realised I had been her lover – with a passion I was proud of – a few hours before. A glance at him told me: it never crossed his mind.

'So what happened?' I wondered thoughtfully. 'In April this year the Praetorians burst in to question you – ' He listened with an exaggerated, weary look as if I was being ridiculous. 'Barnabas was dressed up in your senatorial stripes; the short-sighted Praetorians whisked *him* off to jail. He would expect a nasty beating when they found out, but no worse. Poor Barnabas definitely shook hands on a bad bargain that day. One of your fellow plotters decided to silence their luckless jailbird – '

Pertinax sank back, his thin shoulders hunched. 'Cut it, Falco!'

I was fascinated by those nuts. Some of the shells fell loose on a table as he spat them ineffectively back at the bowl; most dropped onto the striped Egyptian floor rug.

'You soon realised your fellow plotters were being picked off by the Palace.' I let him absorb this, watching him again. Bryon the trainer had called him desperate, but to me he looked merely unpleasant. In fact I found Pertinax so offensive, the hairs on my neck prickled at sharing the same room. Yet he was one of those men who seem quite unaware of their own obnoxiousness. 'If you reappeared you were a marked man. Your half-brother was dead. You took his identity in order to claim his corpse from the jail. You buried him, and paid him the last respect of telling his mother the truth, even though a wrong word from that batty old basket in Tarentum might expose you. Then you realised that you and Barnabas were so alike you had a first-rate, possibly permanent, disguise. So you have foolishly stuck yourself, honourable sir, only one step up from slavery!'

Pertinax, whose manners were as uncouth as you would expect in a Calabrian who had been given more luck in society than he ever deserved, cracked another nut. If he had been a commoner my ex-posing his story would be the first step to jail; he knew as well as I did that a consul's son could stare me out derisively. For several reasons, all of them personal, I would have liked to smash my fist through his pistachios – after he had eaten them.

Helena Justina had finished her meal and tidied her own tray. She went down on her knees, collecting the shells Pertinax had scattered, like a wife trying to prevent their servants noticing what a boor her husband is. Pertinax, like a husband, let her do it.

'You don't exist!' I reiterated in his direction as cruelly as I could. 'Your name has been sponged off the Senatorial list. You have less social standing than a ghost.' Pertinax moved restlessly. 'Now all your attempts to contact your fellow conspirators are going awry. Tell me, did Curtius Longinus meet his fate because when he saw you in Rome again, alive, he threatened to expose you to gain Vespasian's goodwill for his brother and him?' He made no attempt to resist the charge. It could wait. 'Crispus too has plans of his own now, in which you do not feature,' I harassed him as my anger grew. 'You saw him at Oplontis. You tried to coerce him, but he gave you the brushoff; am I right? Your dining couch was reassigned to a woman – Aemilia Fausta, who had not even been invited – then Crispus pointed me straight at you, hoping I would get you off his neck. Aufidius Crispus,' I emphasised, 'is another double-dealer who would cheerfully see you strangled, Pertinax!'

Helena was still on the floor, sitting back on her heels.

'That's enough,' she interrupted quietly.

'Too near the knuckle, lady?'

'Too strong, Falco. What will you do?'

Good question. The ex-Consul was unlikely to allow me to drag his precious son off the estate.

'Suggest something,' I offered, ducking it.

Helena Justina folded her hands in her lap. Always ready with a plan: 'The easiest solution is to leave the conspirator Pertinax at peace in the Marcellus mausoleum. *I* think my husband should put his past mistakes behind him, and start life afresh.' Although Helena was trying to help him, Pertinax sat biting his thumb contemptuously. He had nothing to contribute.

'As Barnabas?' I queried. 'Fine. His children will count as full citizens; his descendants may be senators. A freedman can use his talents; assemble a fortune; even inherit from Marcellus, if Marcellus can bring himself to cause a social upset by doing it. You are a wonderful lady; it's a wonderful solution, and he's a lucky man to have you to support him like this. Just one problem!' I grated in a changed voice. 'Pertinax the conspirator is supposed to be dead – but *Barnabas* is wanted for arson and a senator's premeditated death.'

'What are you saying, Falco?' Helena glanced quickly between the two of us.

'Aulus Curtius Longinus died in a fire at the Little Temple of Hercules. I'm saying, "*Barnabas*" lit the fire.'

I had never told Helena the details. She was shocked, yet remained acutely logical. 'Can you prove that?'

Pertinax finally troubled himself to interject unpleasantly, 'The lying bastard can't.'

'But Falco, if you wanted to pursue it,' Helena reasoned, 'there would have to be a trial – ' You could tell those two had been married by the way that she ignored him. 'A trial would force recent events into the open – '

'Oh plenty of adverse rumours will fly!' I agreed.

'Curtius Gordianus will be embarrassed over his priesthood in Paestum; Aufidius Crispus has been promised the past may remain confidential – '

I laughed softly. 'Yes; they lose any chance to back out of their plot discreetly! Helena Justina, if your ex-husband adopts your suggestion I might support him to the Emperor.' I would sooner have prepared him a legionary ambush: a ditch across his path some dark night, set with barbed stakes viciously peeled back like lilies . . . but producing him as a penitent would earn me greater favour. 'So now he has to decide what he wants.'

'Yes, he must.' Her eyes left me, and fell rather disparagingly on him. He looked at her without expression. Knowing his real identity, I understood why Helena felt so troubled. He was alive, minus his property. So he was demanding back the legacy he had bequeathed to her. At least that; perhaps much more.

I had a sense of them wrangling, though I may have imagined it.

Helena Justina climbed to her feet carefully, holding one wrist behind her as if she had backache.

'I should like you both to leave now.' She rang a bell. A slave came in immediately, as though when Pertinax was here swift service was expected.

'I'll go with you,' I said to him. I had no intention of letting him out of my sight.

'There's no need, Falco!' muttered Helena swiftly. 'He cannot leave the villa,' she insisted. 'He has no identity – nowhere to go.'

'Besides,' Pertinax weighed in, with a dreary attempt at nonchalance, 'your filthy associates harry me if I try!'

'What does that mean?'

'Don't you know?'

It was Helena who enlightened me in a troubled voice. 'Two men have been following Gnaeus everywhere. He went out riding yesterday and they prevented him from coming home all night.'

'What were they like?' I asked him curiously.

'One built like a gladiator, and a runt.'

'Means nothing to me. You managed to shake them off?'

'They were on commercial mules; I had a decent horse.'

'Really?' I did not tell him I had found the two mules here tonight on his father's estate. 'I work alone. I had nothing to do with it.'

If Helena thought I would leave a man in her bedroom she could think again. But Pertinax shrugged a goodnight to her almost at once, then sneered at me and went out onto the balcony.

I followed him as far as the folding door and watched him down the stairs and on his way, a thin figure strutting with a little too much confidence. From the far side of the garden court below he glanced back once. He would have seen me, a solid black shape in the doorway, outlined from behind by the bedroom lamps.

I came back in, fastening the catch on the folding door. With her servants now present, Helena and I were not free to speak openly, but I could see that sharing the secret was a heavy relief. I confined myself to commenting, 'I might have known he would be someone who makes a mess with his food, and has never learnt to close a door when he goes out!' She smiled wearily.

I said goodnight and went to my own room. There were people looking after her. Helena was safe tonight.

Not so true of Pertinax. When he looked back towards the house and scowled at me, he had missed something else: two dark figures emerging from the darkness beneath the balcony.

One like a gladiator, and a runt . . . They must have heard me up above them. And as they, slipped across the courtyard like twisted shadows on a badly polished handmirror they must also have realised that I was bound to see them too.

When Pertinax set off walking again, they silently made after him.

LXII

Nothing else transpired, but it seemed a long night.

That resentful tick would never surrender quietly. Helena Justina had a high sense of duty; he still made her feel responsible for his plight. So sooner or later Pertinax and I faced a private reckoning.

As my initial shock wore off, I remembered what I had heard about their marriage. Helena had led a solitary life. She slept alone in that beautiful room while Pertinax had his spacious quarters on a different wing, with Barnabas as his confidant. For a young, ambitious senator, taking a wife was an act of state service which he endured to win fools' votes. Having done it, Pertinax expected his marital rights, but begrudged her his time.

No wonder senators' wives run after gladiators and other low life forms. Pertinax should count himself lucky that his had the good manners to divorce him first . . .

Next morning I ambled about the villa looking for something to happen. I found the ex-Consul in a large garden at the back of the house, discussing asparagus with one of the staff.

'Seen your son this morning?' I hoped Pertinax had had a heavy weight dropped on his head by the two intruders during the night. But Marcellus disappointed me.

'Yes, I have. Falco, we need to talk . . .'

He said a few words about wilt to the gardener then we strolled, slowly because of the Consul's infirmity, among the formal flowerbeds. They had the usual profusion of urns, fountains, birdbaths and statues of Cupids with guilty expressions, though the Consul's landscape gardener was a passionate shrub man at heart. He had double quantities of box and rosemary planted out in scroll shapes; his trellises and stone borders were almost invisible under enthusiastic daphnes and rampaging quince. Everywhere lattices sagged under jasmine; huge mulberry trees were lovingly tended in formal parterres. Of the twelve species of roses, I counted at least ten.

'What are your intentions?' Marcellus asked bluntly.

'My instructions just don't cover this. The Emperor will expect me to consult before I act.' We had paused, staring into the sunlit depths of a lengthy fishpool which placidly reflected his gaunt frame and my shorter, more sturdy one. I crouched down, admiring an unusual variegated periwinkle. 'Mind if I pull a shoot off this?'

'Take what you like.'

I jerked away a runner that looked ready to reroot itself; the Consul watched in amusement. 'Family failing, sir! So, about your son, I can't see you letting me rope him to a donkey's tail. Even if I did, it's pointless if the Emperor then tells me he cannot possibly offend such a prominent man as yourself by locking up your heir. Domitian Caesar plotted too. Treating your son less leniently would be illogical.'

That was a gamble, but the Emperor did prefer easy solutions and an offer of an amnesty might make Marcellus cooperate.

'And why,' he broached, eyeing me cannily down that massive nose of his, 'are you questioning an accident at the Temple of Hercules?'

'Because it was no accident! But I can count the beans in a pod. Any decent barrister should be able to convict *Barnabas*, but it will be hard to find a prosecutor able to stand up to the smooth-chinned, quicksilver lawyers who will rush to make their reputations defending a consul's son.'

'My son is innocent!' Marcellus insisted.

'Most murderers are – if you ask them!' The Consul was careful not to let his annoyance show. 'Sir, Helena Justina's suggestion seems the best plan to me – '

'No; it's out of the question! My son needs to resume his own name and status – a way must be found.'

'You intend to stand by him whatever the outcome?'

'He is my heir.'

We took a turn under a pergola.

'Sir, rehabilitation may be difficult. What if Vespasian reckons bringing the dead back to life raises too many questions? Since your fortune provides an obvious motive for fraud, he might find it more convenient to announce, *"here's a wicked freedman hoping to profit by his patron's death"*!'

'I will vouch for his real identity – '

'Ah well, sir! You are an elderly man in poor health who has lost the heir he doted on. Naturally you *want* to believe he is still alive – '

'*Helena* will vouch for him!' the Consul snapped. I grinned.

'How true. And how fortunate for him!'

We both stood for a moment, smiling at how if Helena ever saw a mix-up she went flying in to speak out with the truth.

'They should never have separated!' the Consul complained bitterly. 'I knew I should not have allowed it. Helena never wanted a divorce – '

'Helena Justina,' I agreed coolly, 'believes in marriage as a contract of close companionship to last for forty years. She knew,' I said flatly, having given myself a nervous twinge, 'she did not have that with your son.'

'Oh they could do!' Marcellus brushed it aside. 'My son has great promise; something must be done for him – '

'Your son's a common criminal!' This was true, though unhelpful. I added more mildly. 'I reckon Vespasian's old-fashioned respect for a patrician name will protect Pertinax Marcellus; he'll survive to tend your ancestors' death masks. One more criminal in the Senate makes no difference after all!'

'A jaundiced view!'

'I speak as I see. Consul, I've sampled the Herculaneum holding cell; it's crude. If I let Pertinax remain in your custody, will you honour the parole and keep him on the estate?'

'Of course,' he said stiffly. I was not convinced Pertinax would stick to it, but I had no choice. Marcellus could call on scores of slaves to prevent an arrest. The ugly armed cavalry Pertinax had commanded when he tried to intercept me at Capua the day I arrived with Petro was probably estate blacksmiths and drivers, got up in iron hats.

'He will have to answer the charges against him,' I warned.

'Possibly,' replied the Consul offhandedly.

I felt utter frustration at his air of self-assurance; we were discussing treason and murder, but I had completely failed to impress on him how serious the situation was.

I gathered I was dismissed.

I found Helena on her balcony. I ran up and beamed at her; she was reclining with a beaker of cold water, sipping it uncertainly.

'Off colour?'

'Slow to wake up . . . ' She smiled, with a private gleam that gave me a tickle in my throat.

'Look, the problem of Pertinax will depend on dispatches now. Don't expect an early adjudication from a gang of Palace clerks – '

Helena gazed at me, assessing my reaction to last night's discovery. After a moment I muttered, 'How long have you known?'

'Since the night of the banquet.'

'You never said!'

'Are you jealous of *Pertinax*?'

'No, of course not . . . '

'Marcus!' she chided gently.

'Well what do you expect? When I walked in last night, I assumed he had come for the same reasons as me.'

'Oh I doubt it!' she laughed, in a dry tone. I was still sitting on the balcony parapet digesting this when someone brought me a messenger.

It was a slave from Herculaneum; Aemilius Rufus wanted to see me. I guessed this would be about Crispus. I had lost interest in Crispus – except for the fact that he was one quarry Vespasian had agreed to pay me for and I was desperate for cash.

I dismissed the servants while I tried to decide. Helena urged, 'It could be important; you ought to go.'

'Only if you stay with Petro and Silvia until I get back.'

'Gnaeus will never hurt me.'

'You don't know that,' I scowled, irritated by her use of his familiar name.

'He needs me.'

'I hope not! *What for?*'

By then I was so agitated she had to confess. 'This is bound to upset you. The Consul has convinced him he ought to remarry me.' She was right. I was upset. 'You would ask! Listen, Caprenius Marcellus has two great aims: salvaging a public career for Gnaeus, and obtaining an heir. A grandchild would secure the estate – '

'I don't want to hear this. You appal me sometimes; how can you even speak of it?'

'Oh, a girl does need a husband!' Helena suggested ironically.

It was completely unfair. I shrugged, struggling to express my own lack of status, and contacts, and cash. Then hopeless rage took over. 'Well you know what to expect from that one! Neglect, disinterest – and probably worse now! Did he beat you? Don't worry; he will!' Helena was listening with a set face as I crashed on like a loose heifer in a melon patch.

'Well, you're a man. I'm sure you know!' she retorted stiffly. I jumped down from my perch.

'You do what you want, my darling! If you need to be respectable, and you think that's the way, you go back to him – ' I lowered my voice, restraining myself because she needed to remember this: 'But any time you've had enough of it, I'll come and fetch you out of it.' I was off along the balcony. '*That's* called loyalty!' I threw back insultingly.

'Marcus!' she pleaded; I set my back and refused to answer her.

Halfway down the estate road I saw Pertinax. He was schooling his horses on the riding range; even at a distance he looked thoroughly absorbed. He had both the racers out. He kept one in the shade while he was galloping the other. It was far more deliberate than the young mens' light recreation for which that tree-shaded area had been first designed. He was working them professionally. He knew exactly what he was doing; the procedure was a joy to watch.

Little Sweetheart was snuffling in the grass for poisonous plants that would give him belly ache. Pertinax was on the champion, Ferox. If he had been alone, I would have fought him then and settled everything, but Bryon was with him.

Bryon, who was leaning on a post eating figs, stared at me

curiously but with his master there I did not speak. Pertinax ignored me. The sombre skill with which he was galloping Ferox seemed to emphasise the advantages he would always have over me.

There was fresh mule dung under the cypress trees, but the two animals I found there last night had gone. I had a feeling I would soon see them again.

I had marched all the way to the highroad before a boy caught up with me.

He only had to run as far as the herm. I was sitting on a boulder, cursing myself for quarrelling with Helena, cursing her, cursing *him* . . . desperately worrying.

'Didius Falco!'

The lad had fish pickle spilt down his tunic, a skin problem it was better not to think about, and badly grazed, dirty knees. But if he had been fainting on a podium in the slave market I would have mortgaged my life to save him from cruelty.

He handed me a waxed tablet. The writing was new to me, though my heart leapt. It was short, and I could hear Helena's aggravated tone in every word:

He never hit me; though I always felt he might. What makes you think I could choose someone like that, after I had known you?
Don't fall in any water. HJ

Back at home on the Aventine I sometimes found love letters lying on my doormat. I never kept incriminating correspondence. But I had the feeling that in forty years time when my pale-faced executors were sorting through my personal effects, this was a letter they would find wrapped in linen, tucked down the side of my stylus box among the sealing wax.

LXIII

The fact he had asked me to visit him did not mean that Aemilius Rufus troubled to be at home when I arrived. He was in court all day. I had lunch at his house, politely hanging round for him. Rufus wisely ate out.

I perched on one of the knife-edged silver seats, leaning against its unyielding horsehair cushions with the pensive expression of a man who cannot get his bottom comfortable. I was wriggling about beneath a frieze of King Pentheus being torn to shreds by Bacchantes (nice relaxing subject for a waiting room) when I heard Aemilia Fausta going out; I stuck fast in my stuffy nook, avoiding her.

Eventually Rufus deigned to return. I popped my head out. He stood talking to a link boy, a good-looking Illyrian slave who was squatting on the front step cleaning out the wickholder of an interesting lantern; it had rattling bronze carrying chains, opaque horn sides to protect the flame, and a removable top which was pierced with ventilation holes.

'Hello, Falco!' Rufus was staggeringly agreeable after his lunch. 'Admiring my slave?'

'No, sir; I'm admiring his lamp!'

We exchanged a whimsical glance.

We adjourned to his study. This at least had some character, being hung with souvenirs he had picked up on foreign service: peculiar gourds, tribal spears, ships' pennants, moth-eaten drums – the sort of stuff Festus and I hankered after when we were teenagers, before we moved on to women and drink. I declined wine; Rufus himself decided against, then I watched him becoming sober again as his meal took effect. He threw himself sideways onto a couch, giving me the best view of his profile and the glints in his golden hair that shimmered in the sunlight coming through an open window. Thinking about women and the sort of men they fall for, I hunched glumly on a low seat.

'You wanted to see me, sir,' I reminded him patiently.

'Yes indeed! Didius Falco, events certainly liven up when you're around!' People often say this to me; can't imagine why.

'Something about Crispus, sir?'

Perhaps he was still trying to use Crispus to do himself some good, because he sloughed off my question. I quelled my next thought: that his sister had made some obnoxious complaint to Rufus about me. 'I

236

have had a visitation!' he complained sulkily. Magistrates in dull towns like Herculaneum expect a quiet life. 'Does the name Gordianus mean anything to you?'

'*Curtius* Gordianus,' I classified carefully, 'is the incumbent elect for the Temple of Hera at Paestum.'

'You keep up with the news!'

'Good informers study the Forum *Gazette*. Anyway, I've met him. So why did he approach you?'

'He wants me to arrest someone.'

A long core of stillness set like cooling metal down the centre of my chest. 'Atius Pertinax?'

'Then it is true?' Rufus asked warily. 'Pertinax Marcellus is alive?'

'Afraid so. When the Fate was snipping his thread, some fool jogged her elbow. Is this what you heard at the banquet?'

'Crispus hinted.'

'Crispus would! I was hoping to play off Crispus and Pertinax against one another . . . So were you, I dare say!'

He grinned. 'Gordianus seems set on complicating things.'

'Yes. I should have expected it.' This new move by the Chief Priest fitted his stubborn intensity. I could envisage him after I had left Croton, brewing to the boil as he mourned his brother's death. And now that the magistrate had mentioned Gordianus, I remembered those two familiar shadows I had observed the previous night – and identified them. 'He has two lookouts keeping Pertinax under day-and-night surveillance.'

'Does that mean you have seen him?'

'No. I've seen them.'

The magistrate eyed me, uncertain how much I knew. 'Gordianus span me a weird tale. Can you shed any light, Falco?'

I could. So I did.

When I finished Rufus whistled softly. He asked sensible legal questions then agreed with me; the evidence was all too circumstantial. 'If I did place Pertinax Marcellus under arrest, more facts *might* emerge – '

'A risk though, sir. If some widow without two sesterces to rub together had put this case to you, you would decline to hear it.'

'Oh, the law is impartial, Falco!'

'Yes; and barristers *hate* to earn a fee! How did Gordianus know Pertinax was hereabouts?'

'Crispus told him. Look, Falco, I shall have to take Gordianus seriously. You are an Imperial agent; what is the official view?'

'Mine is that if Gordianus forces a trial it will raise a bad smell all the way from here to the Capitol. But he might succeed despite the lack of evidence. We both know the sight of a grief-stricken brother calling out for justice is the sort of sentimental scene that makes juries sob into their togas and convict.'

'So I *should* arrest Pertinax?'

'I believe he killed Curtius Longinus, who may have threatened to expose him, and later he tried to kill Gordianus too. These are serious charges. It sticks in my craw to grant him a pardon simply because he is a consul's adopted son.'

Aemilius Rufus listened to my grounds for action with the caution I should have expected from a country magistrate. If I had been the victim of a malicious prosecution based on flimsy evidence, I might have commended his thoroughness. As it was, I felt we were wasting time.

We talked round the problem for another hour. In the end Rufus decided to throw it over to Vespasian: just the sort of negative compromise I despised. We stopped the next Imperial dispatch rider who came through town. Rufus penned an elegant letter; I tore off a terse report. We told the horseman to ride all night. Even at the rate they travel the earliest he could arrive in Rome was dawn tomorrow, but Vespasian liked reading his correspondence at first light. Thinking of Rome, I was buffeted by homesickness, and wished I had dashed off with the message to the Palatine myself.

'Well. Nothing else we can do now,' the magistrate sighed, swinging his athletic torso into a sitting position so he could reach a tripod table and pour us wine. 'May as well enjoy ourselves – '

He was not the type I choose for a companion and I wanted to leave, but writing reports gives me a strong urge to get drunk. Especially at a senator's expense.

I almost suggested we went out to the baths together, but some lucky fluke stopped me. I hooked myself upright, stretched, and hopped over to fetch my wine; once in possession I condescended to sit on his couch to facilitate clinking cups like the cronies we weren't. Aemilius Rufus favoured me with his relaxed, golden smile. I buried myself gratefully in his Falernian, which was immaculate.

He said, 'I'm sorry I never saw much of you when you were tutoring my sister. I have been hoping to put that right – '

Then I felt his right hand fondling my thigh, while he told me what beautiful eyes I had.

LXIV

I have only one reaction to approaches like that. But before I could crump my fist against his handsome Delphic jawbone he removed his hand. Someone he could not be expecting came into the room.

'Didius Falco, I'm so glad I caught you!' Bright eyes, clear skin, and a swift, light step: Helena Justina, the darling of my heart. 'Rufus, excuse me, I came to see Fausta but I gather she is dining out . . . Falco, it's much later than I expected, so if you are going back to the villa,' she suggested serenely, 'may I travel under your protection? If that suits your own plans, and is not too much trouble – '

Since the magistrate's wine was the very best Falernian, I drained my cup before I spoke.

'Nothing is too much trouble for a lady,' I replied.

LXV

'You might have warned me!'

'You were asking for all you got!'

'He seemed such a gentleman – he caught me by surprise . . . '

Helena giggled. She was heckling me through the window of her sedan chair while I walked alongside grumbling. 'Drinking wine with him, snuggling on one seat with your tunic up over your knees and that doe-eyed, vulnerable look – '

'I resent that,' I said. 'A citizen ought to be able to drink where he likes without it being interpreted as an open invitation to advances from men he hardly knows and doesn't like – '

'You were drunk.'

'Irrelevant. Anyway I was not! Lucky you came to see Fausta – '

'Luck,' rapped back Helena, 'had nothing to do with it! You were away so long I started worrying. I passed Fausta actually, going the other way. Were you glad I came?' she suddenly smiled.

I stopped the chair, brought her out, then made the bearers walk ahead while we followed in the twilight and I demonstrated whether I was glad.

'Marcus, why do you think Fausta was heading for Oplontis? She had discovered that a certain someone will be at Poppaea's villa again, treating the commander of the fleet to dinner again.'

'Crispus?' I groaned, and reapplied myself to other things.

'What's so special about the Misenum prefect?' wondered Helena, unimpressed by the distractions I was offering.

'No idea . . . '

'Marcus, I shall lose my earring; let me take it off.'

'Take off anything you want,' I agreed. Then I found myself being drawn into considering her question. The damned Misenum fleet commander had adroitly intruded himself between me and my romantic mood.

Ignoring the British squadron, which is almost beneath the notice of anybody civilised, the Roman Navy orders itself in the only way possible for a long narrow state: one fleet based over at Ravenna to guard the eastern seaboard, and another at Misenum in the west.

Answers to several questions were suggesting themselves now.

'Tell me,' I broached thoughtfully to Helena. 'Apart from Titus and the legions, what was the key feature of Vespasian's campaign to become Emperor? What was worst in Rome?'

Helena shuddered. 'Everything! Soldiers in the streets, murders in the Forum, fires, fever, famine – '

'Famine,' I said. 'In a senator's house I suppose you managed as normal, but in our family no one could get bread.'

'The corn!' she responded. 'It was critical. Egypt supplies the whole city. Vespasian had the support of the Prefect of Egypt, so he sat all winter in Alexandria, letting Rome know that *he* controlled the grain ships and without his good will they might not come . . . '

'Now suppose you were a senator with extraordinary political ambitions, but *your* only supporters were in deadbeat provinces like Noricum – '

'*Noricum!*' she chortled.

'Exactly. No hope there. Meanwhile the Prefect of Egypt still strongly supports Vespasian, so the supply is assured – but suppose this year, when the corn ships hail in sight of the Puteoli peninsula – '

'The fleet stops them!' Helena was horrified. 'Marcus, we must stop the fleet!' (I had a curious vision of Helena Justina sailing out from Neapolis like a goddess on a ship's prow, holding up her arm to stop a convoy in full sail.) She reconsidered. 'Are you really serious?'

'I think so. And we're not talking about a couple of sacks on the back of a donkey, you know.'

'How much?' demanded Helena pedantically.

'Well, some wheat is imported from Sardinia and Sicily; I'm not sure of the exact proportions, but a clerk in the office of the Prefect of Supply once told me the amount needed annually to feed Rome effectively is fifteen billion bushels – '

The Senator's daughter permitted herself the liberty of whistling through her teeth.

I grinned at her. 'The next question is, whether Pertinax or Crispus is now the prime mover of this abominable plan?'

'Oh that's answered!' Helena assured me in her swift, conclusive way. 'It's *Crispus* who is entertaining the fleet.'

'True. I reckon they *were* in it together, but now Pertinax has taken to assaulting all and sundry, Crispus views him as a liability . . . The corn ships leave for Egypt in April – ' I mused . . . Nones of April – *Galatea* and *Venus of Paphos*; four days before the Ides, *Flora*; two days before May, *Lusitania, Concordia, Parthenope,* and *The Graces* . . . 'It takes three weeks to get there and as much as two months to sail back again against the wind. The first ones home this year must be overdue – '

'That's a problem!' Helena muttered. 'If this fiasco takes to the water, you'll be stuck!' I thanked her for the confidence, and quickened my step. 'Marcus, how do you think they are planning to proceed?'

'Hold up the ships when they arrive here, then threaten to sail them off to some secret location? If *I* was doing it, I'd wait until the Senate sent some stiff-necked praetor to negotiate, then start emptying the sacks overboard. The vision of the Bay of Neapolis being turned into one vast porridge bowl would probably produce the right effect.'

'On the whole,' said Helena with feeling, 'I'm glad it's *not* you doing it! Who asked you to investigate the corn imports?' she asked me in a curious tone.

'No one. It was something that I stumbled on myself.'

For some reason Helena Justina hugged me and laughed.

'What's that for?'

'Oh, I like to think I've cast my future into the hands of a man who is good at his work!'

LXVI

I decided to raid Poppaea's villa while Crispus was there.

Ideally I would have slipped inside the place on my own. My expertise as an informer would lead me straight to the diners at the moment when they concluded the sordid details of their plan; then, equipped with hard evidence, M. Didius Falco, our demigod hero, would confront them, confound them, and single-handedly clap neck-irons on the lot . . .

Most private informers will boast of such ideal episodes. My life had a crankier pattern of its own.

The first problem was that Helena, Petronius and Larius, who were all highly inquisitive, came too. We arrived like second-rate temple drummers, too noisy – and too late. As we stood on the terrace debating how best to get in, the supper party streeled out past us. There was no chance of extracting a confession from any of them – or the slightest sense.

Crispus himself led the exodus, feet first and face down; he knew nothing about anything. The dispassionate slaves who were bringing him to his skiff had simply lifted the dinner table he had fallen across, limbs akimbo, then bumped him outside on it like a finished dessert course, with tonight's limp wreath hung on one of the handles and his shoestraps through another. It would be a long time before his honour woke up, and he would not make a good subject for interview at that point.

His guests had been the commander from Misenum, plus a group of trireme captains. The navy was made of really stern stuff. During the recent civil wars we had had a bad outbreak of piracy in the Black Sea, but here on the west coast things had stayed peaceful since Pompey's day. The Misenum fleet had little to do but cope with the many claims on their social life. Round the Bay of Neapolis there were parties every night, so the navy spent most evenings infiltrating private functions in search of free drink. Their capacity was enormous and their expertise at steering a course home afterwards while singing jolly songs in fabulously obscene versions made sober men blench.

When they first emerged from the house, half a dozen trireme captains were pretending to be hunting dogs. They were nipping each other, yowling, yapping, begging with their front paws, panting with their tongues out, sniffing at the moon and at the insalubrious backside of whoever was in front. Their delight in their own silliness was a joy. Their fleet commander circled these splendid fellows on all fours, baaing like a Lactarii sheep. They all milled around like Greek comedians whose producer had failed to plot their moves on stage, then the situation somehow gelled of its own accord; they surged up a gangway with heavy arms on each others' shoulders, locked in a loving chain like blood brothers, lifting their knees as they danced. One nearly fell overboard, but at the summit of his arc over the water his comrades used centrifugal force to swing him back, chorusing a wildly soaring whoop. Trailing its gangplank, their transport disappeared.

The evening seemed more melancholy after they had gone. Petronius said his respect for the navy had trebled on the spot.

We were leaving when Helena Justina remembered her friend. I wanted to abandon Fausta, but was overruled. (One reason why an informer should work alone: to avoid being dragged into good deeds.)

The lady was lurking in the atrium, weeping copiously. She had been at the amphorae. This would only seem a good idea to a wine merchant with sinking profits (if such a man exists).

All around her the caterers were tidying up, ignoring the dishevelled spectre sobbing on her knees. I could see Helena stiffening. 'They despise her! She's a woman, behaving stupidly, but worst of all, she has no man to look after her – '

Larius and Petro stepped back shyly, but Helena had already forced a slave to stop and explain. He said Fausta had made another indomitable foray into the villa, halfway through the meal. The banquet had been a racy one: all male, with all-female entertainment . . .

'And Aufidius Crispus,' cried Helena haughtily, 'was entwined with a Spanish dancing girl?'

'No madam . . . ' The slave looked sideways at Petro and me. We grinned. 'Two, actually!' He was happy to go into details but Helena hissed through her teeth.

Evidently Fausta had simply crumpled and withdrawn, in the kind of abject grief that was her well-known speciality; Crispus probably never even saw her. Now she was stuck out here in an unoccupied villa, while the caterers had pushed all the empty amphorae off a jetty into the sea and were about to leave.

Helena made a lively fuss until someone brought the lady's chair. Fausta's bearers tonight were an ill-matched set of Liburnian slaves, one with a limp and one with a set of venomous neck boils. 'Oh, we cannot leave these ninnies in charge of her!' Helena declared.

Without admitting liability, Larius and I managed to insert Fausta into her chair. The slaves lurched her as far as the inn at Oplontis, but while we were discussing what to do next she slipped off and scampered onto the beach proclaiming a curse on men, naming the parts which she wished to wither and drop off them in such detail that it made me queasy.

I had had enough of her whole family. But to please Helena, I agreed to waste more of what could otherwise have been a pleasant evening and somehow deal with her . . .

With luck, some bandit in need of a scullion to warm his broth would kidnap Fausta first.

I insisted on putting Helena in her own litter back on the road to the villa. This took quite a long time, for reasons that are nobody's business but mine.

By now most of the coast lay in darkness. When I returned to the inn Fausta had disappeared. Although it was so late, I found Larius talking poetry to the nursemaid Ollia on a bench in the inn courtyard; at least he had progressed from Catullus to Ovid, who has a better outlook on love and, more crucially, on sex.

I sat down with them. 'You been philandering, uncle?'

'Don't be ridiculous. No senator's daughter would enjoy being bedded on the bare ground among a lot of curious spiders with a pine cone in her back!'

'Really?' asked Larius.

'Really,' I lied. 'What coaxed Aemilia Fausta away from the sand hoppers?'

'A kind-hearted, off-duty watch captain. He hates to see noblemens' sisters sitting drunk on beaches.'

I groaned. Petronius Longus was always a soft touch for a sobbing girl. 'So he threw her over his shoulder, stuffed her into the chair while she declaimed what a nice man he was, then he marched off her pathetic entourage to Herculanem himself?'

Larius laughed. 'You know Petro!'

'He won't even bother to ask for a reward. What did Silvia say?'

'Nothing – very pointedly!'

It was a beautiful night. I decided to hitch up Nero and meet Petro with transport home. Larius decided to keep me company; then, because they were young and illogical, Ollia came as company for him.

When we reached the magistrate's house the door porter told us Petronius had arrived with the lady but since she was none too stable in her party shoes, had helped her indoors. Rather than risk fending off suggestions for fun with Aemilius Rufus, we waited in the cart.

Petro, who was a long time coming out, seemed surprised to find us there. We were all napping, so he swung into the front seat and took up the reins. He was the best driver among us anyway.

'Watch that magistrate!' I warbled. 'His Falernian is decent but

I wouldn't want to meet him behind a bathhouse pillar in the dark . . . His sister give you much trouble?'

'Not if you ignore the usual *"Men are disgusting; why can't I get one?"* stuff.' I said some hard words about Fausta, though Petronius maintained the poor little thing was rather sweet.

Larius was nodding off on Ollia's comfortable shoudler. I had a better woman to think about than some louse of a magistrate's fool of a sister so I huddled in a corner and went to sleep too, lulled by the cart's gently creaking motion through the warm Campanian night.

Ever good-natured, Petronius Longus hummed to himself quietly as he drove us all home.

LXVII

Two days later the magistrate tried to arrest Atius Pertinax. It was Petro's daughter's birthday so I had slipped down to Oplontis with a gift. After my spurning him, Rufus made no attempt to warn me. So I missed the action.

There was not much to miss. Rufus should have followed my advice: since the Villa Marcella was orientated seawards, the discreet approach was down the mountain from above. But when orders to apprehend Pertinax arrived from Vespasian, Aemilius Rufus grabbed a troop of soldiers and dashed up the main estate road, prominently visible to the house.

Marcellus gave him a frosty greeting and permission to search, then sat in the shade to wait for the idiot to discover the obvious: Pertinax had fled.

Once the furore had subsided, Helena Justina followed me to Oplontis with the tale.

'Gnaeus rushed off riding with Bryon. Bryon, in all innocence apparently, came back later with both horses, to say the young master had decided to go for a cruise – '

'He has a boat?'

'Bryon left him on Aufidius Crispus' yacht.'

'Does Crispus know there is an arrest warrant?'

'That's unclear.'

'Where was the yacht?'

'Baiae. But Bryon saw her sail.'

'Brilliant! So the illustrious Aemilius Rufus has flushed Pertinax onto the fastest thing between Sardinia and Sicily . . . '

Rufus was useless. I would have to charter a ship and look for the *Isis Africana* myself. It was too late in the day now, so at least I could enjoy one more evening with my lady first.

Silvana was the birthday girl (Petro's middle daughter; she was four), and tonight the children were joining our evening meal. We were delayed, however, because we had hit one of those joyful family crises without which no holiday is complete. Arria Silvia found the nursemaid Ollia in floods of tears.

Two brisk questions about Ollia's personal calendar revealed that my prophecy about the fisherboy must be correct. (He was still hanging around every day.) Ollia denied it, which clinched the verdict. Silvia gave Ollia a slap round the head to relieve her own feelings, then instructed Petronius and me to sort out the inconvenient lobster catcher, now that it was too late.

We found the young gigolo preening his moustache by an old lead-stocked anchor; Petro got an arm up his back rather further than his arm was meant to go. Of course he claimed he never touched the girl; we expected that. We marched him to the turfy shack where he lived with his parents and while the youth sulked Petronius Longus put the whole moral issue in succinct terms to them: Ollia's father was a legionary veteran who had served in Egypt and Syria for over twenty years until he left with double pay, three medals, and a diploma that made Ollia legitimate; he now ran a boxers' training school where he was famous for his high-minded attitude and his fighters were notorious for their loyalty to him . . .

The old fisherman was a toothless, hapless, faithless cove you would not trust too near you with a filleting knife, but whether from fear or simple cunning he cooperated eagerly. The lad agreed to marry the girl and since Silvia would never abandon Ollia here, we decided that the fisherboy had to come back with us to Rome. His relations looked impressed by this result. We accepted it as the best we could achieve.

The news that she was to be made an honest woman by a sly tyke with a seaweed moustache set Ollia off crying again, as well it might. Larius, from whom we had kept the sordid details in view of his artistic nature, was glowering at me frantically.

'Ollia's slipped up with her bit of whale blubber,' I enlightened him. 'She's just realised *why* her mother always warned her: she'll spend the next fifty years paying for this mistake. When he's not out after the women he'll be lying in bed all day, shouting for his dinner and calling her a dozy slut. Now you will appreciate why women who can afford it are prepared to risk abortionists' drugs – '

Larius got up without a word and went to help Petronius order the wine.

Helena Justina, who had been talking to the children while Silvia was calming Ollia, shot me the long, cool glance of a senator's daughter who had glimpsed life on the seamy side and decided this too was something any woman who could afford it would spend serious money to avoid.

We managed to make a good night of it, in the desperate way people do when the choice is between dogged survival or sliding under the morass.

As soon as Petronius reappeared with trays of bread and wine flasks the strain began to evaporate. The affectionate touch of his great hands on frazzled heads soothed everyone as he got us organised. Finding myself near Silvia, who did have more troubles than usual that night, I jollied her along with a hand on her knee (the table was so narrow that people sitting opposite were practically on your lap). Silvia kicked Petro, thinking it was him, so without bothering to look up from his mullet he said, 'Falco, keep your hands off my wife.'

'Why do you behave so badly, Falco?' Helena grumbled at me publicly. 'Put your hands on the table and if you must be offensive, ogle at me.'

I wondered morosely whether Helena was so short with me because she was worried about Pertinax being on the run. I watched her, but she knew I was doing it; her pale face resolutely gave nothing away.

It was one of those nights when a troupe of country dancers came, which soon cheered us up with something to scoff at. Anywhere in the world you can see these tired performers: the girls with scarlet ribbons and tambourines who turned out on close inspection to be a mite older than they first appeared; the bright-eyed little card with a fiendish grin and savagely hooked nose who frenetically played the panpipes; the aloof, balding character tootling a solemn flute of a kind unknown to musicologists. Shepherds down from the hills, or the innkeepers' relations, who knows? It was a summer job – a little money, a few drinks, some thin applause, whistles from the locals, and for us the educational extra of slipping out to the latrine and finding one of the dancers leaning on a wall eating a stick of salami – looking less colourful, less cheerful, and decidedly less clean.

These were as good, or as bad, as they ever are. They whirled and glided and kicked their booted heels with just a touch too much disinterest (considering they expected us to put money in the hat), though the girls did smile steadily as they touted round baskets of roses afterwards, cursing under their breath at the big, black-haired young man who was supposed to wring the cash from us. *He* showed a particular yen to sit down for a drink out of someone else's flagon and take the weight off his quaint dancing pumps. While he was talking to Petronius, I put my arm round Helena and reminisced how in the old days it always turned out that my elder brother Festus knew the flute player, so the children in our party would be given a free instrument from the sad musician's bundle of home-whittled sticks, instead of us having to pay for them . . .

Petro leaned over to Helena. 'Once he sounds off about his brother, whip his winecup away!' She did. I let her, because while she was doing it she smiled at me so fondly I felt weak. Petronius chivalrously handed her a walnut. It was one of his accomplishments that he could crack a walnut shell so skilfully he brought out the kernal intact: both halves, still held together cunningly by their papery flange. After she ate it she let her head loll on my shoulder, and held my hand.

So we all sat under a vine trellis into the evening, with the glint of the dark sea beyond a stone abutment, while men in skimpy tunics thumped up the dust in a fine haze over the hibiscus leaves. Ollia had a stomachache and my poor Larius had heartache. I was thinking about my search for Atius Pertinax tomorrow. Helena was smiling dreamily. Petronius and Silvia decided that their holiday had done them as much good as it ever would, and it was time to go home.

None of the new flutes would play. (They never do, but Petro and I would never learn.)

We all walked slowly back to the inn, and because it was Silvana's birthday we made a ceremony of putting the children to bed. I did not know what I would have to go through before I saw Helena again, so I had drawn her to one side for a private farewell. Someone called upstairs that I had a visitor. Petronius winked at me and went down to deal with it.

One of the children, who had reached the stage of being as naughty as they dared, scampered after him in her undershift. Twenty seconds later, even over the hubbub upstairs, we heard her screams.

I was first down the corridor and first down the stairs. Petronilla stood rooted in the doorway, still screaming. I picked her up. There was nothing else to do.

Petronius Longus lay sprawled face down in the inn courtyard with both arms outstretched. A savage blow had felled him, struck at the most dangerous, tender area of his neck. The blood which oozed so slowly from the wound said everything.

For one long moment I held his child, and simply stood, unable to move. There was nothing I could do for him. I knew he was dead.

LXVIII

Among the pounding feet that followed me down, Silvia's sandals whispered, then she shot past me like a breath and onto him before I could snatch her back. I thought she gasped, *'Oh my baby!'* but that must have been a mistake.

I pushed the child into someone's arms then ran out and tried to persuade Silvia to leave him. Helena Justina squeezed in alongside me and knelt by his head so she could gently check for a breath or a pulse.

'Marcus, come and help me – he's alive!'

After that she and I worked as partners. Life held some hope again. There were things to do.

Larius tore off on a donkey in search of a doctor. Ollia, with surprising sense, extricated Silvia. I did not want to move Petro, but it was growing darker every minute and we could not leave him out there. Helena commandeered a room on the ground floor – paid for it, I think – then we carried him in on a hurdle.

He should have been dead. A smaller man would have been. *I* would be. Presumably some villain who specialised in pointless gestures now thought I was.

He was deeply unconscious, so deeply it was dangerous. Even if he ever woke, he might not be himself. But he was a big, fit man with the physical strength to match; there was stamina and determination in everything he did. Larius found a doctor who salved the wound, reassured us that Petronius had not lost much blood, and said all we could now do was keep him warm and wait.

Helena soothed the children. Helena made Silvia comfortable with blankets and cushions in Petro's room. Helena saw to the doctor, shooed off the sightseers, and reassured Ollia and Larius. I even saw her with Ollia, feeding the children's kittens. Then she sent a message to the villa that she was staying here.

I went round the inn, as Petronius used to every night.

I stood on the road outside, listening to the darkness, hating whoever had done this, plotting revenge. I knew who it must have been: Atius Pertinax.

I looked in on the stables and fed Nero hay by hand. Indoors again in the room where Petro had been taken, Silvia rocked gently, nursing Tadia in her arms. I smiled, but we did not speak because the children were asleep. I knew Silvia blamed me. For once we had nothing to quarrel about: I blamed myself.

I snuffed all the tapers except one, then sat with him. Tonight his features contained strange hollows. Under the bruises from his headlong fall his face seemed so lacking in colour and emotion it was like another man's. I had known him for ten years; we had shared a barracks at the back of the world in Britain and a tent on forced marches during the Iceni troubles. Back in Rome afterwards, Petronius and I had split more wine jars than I cared to remember, scoffed at each others' women, laughed at each others' habits, exchanged favours and jokes, rarely squabbled except when his work clashed with mine. He was a brother to me, where my own had been almost too colourful to tolerate.

He never knew I was there. Eventually I left him, with his two elder daughters curled asleep against his side.

I walked upstairs, watchful and conserving my resources. I turned up the mattress on his bed and found, where I knew it would be, Petro's sword. I stood it beside my own bed.

In our other room, Helena was talking to Ollia and Larius; I looked in to say goodnight, needing to count heads. I managed to croak at Helena pompously. 'This is very inadequate, but thank you for staying. It would be chaos without you. I don't mean to burden you with our troubles . . . '

'Your troubles are my troubles,' Helena replied steadily.

I smiled, unable to cope with it, then jerked my head at Larius. 'Time for bed.'

But Helena was persuading Ollia to confide in her and Larius seemed part of the seminar, so after I had left them the murmur of their voices continued for some time.

It was the third hour of darkness. I was lying on my back, with folded arms, studying the top of a window recess on the opposite wall as I waited for the day and my chance to extract my revenge. A board creaked; I expected Larius but it was Helena.

We knew each other so well we never spoke. I held out my hand to her, and made space on the awful bed. She blew out her lamp and I damped it to stop the wick smelling, then I thumbed mine too.

Now I was lying on my back with my arms folded, but this time they were folded tight round Helena. Her cold feet found a place to warm themselves under one of mine. I have a clear recollection of how we both sighed at that moment, though I cannot say which of us fell asleep first.

Nothing happened. There is more than one reason for sharing a bed. Helena wanted to be with me. And I needed her there.

LXIX

For the next three days I scoured the Bay in a hired vessel from Pompeii, a slow ship with a dull captain who could not, or would not, grasp my urgency. Once again I was searching for the *Isis Africana* and once again it seemed a waste of time. Every night I went back to the inn, exhausted and morose. Petronius started to regain consciousness late the first day, deeply quiet and puzzled at his own condition, yet essentially himself. Not even his gradual recovery comforted my bitter mood. As I expected, he could remember nothing about the attack.

On the third day I wrote to Rufus, offering to join forces. I told him what had happened, and named the new charge against Pertinax: attempted murder of a Roman watch captain, Lucius Petronius Longus. They boy who took my message returned, asking me to visit the Aemilius house. Larius drove me in Nero's cart.

Rufus was out. It was his sister who wanted to see me.

I met Aemilia Fausta in a cold room where the heavy shadow of a walnut tree outside fell across the open shutter. She looked smaller and thinner than ever. Her pallor was increased by the unflattering tones of an insipid aquamarine gown.

I was annoyed. 'I expected your brother. Did he get my letter?' Anticipating my reaction, she nodded guiltily. 'I see! But he'll manage the hunt without me?'

'My brother says informers have no part in civic life – '

'Your brother says too much!' I let her see I was angry; I had wasted a journey, and lost a day of my search.

'I am sorry,' Aemilia Fausta interrupted carefully, 'about your friend. Was he badly hurt, Falco?'

'Whoever hit him wanted to crack someone's skull apart.'

'His?'

'Mine.'

'Will he recover?'

'We hope so. I can't say more.'

She was sitting bolt upright in a wicker chair, a long fringed scarf twisted across her lap. She had a numb expression and her voice sounded colourless.

'Falco, is it certain the attacker was Pertinax Marcellus?'

253

'No one else has a motive. Plenty of people dislike me; but not enough to want me dead!'

'My brother,' she went on, 'believes it is an advantage that Crispus and Pertinax are together now – '

'Your brother's wrong. *Pertinax* has lost all sense of morality; these wild attacks – and there have been others – show the full extent of his breakdown. *Crispus* just needs his big ideas trimmed.'

'Yes, Falco,' Fausta agreed quietly.

Giving her a thoughtful scrutiny I said, 'Vespasian disagrees with his politics, and *you* don't like his private life – but that does not affect his potential for public service.'

'No,' she acknowledged, with a sad smile.

My scalp tingled expectantly. 'Are you offering me some information, lady?'

'Perhaps. My brother has arranged to meet Crispus with a view to arresting Pertinax. I am frightened what may happen. Sextus can be impetuous – '

'Sextus? Oh, your brother! I gather Pertinax is unaware they have arranged this friendly rendezvous?' I wondered if Aufidius Crispus had now made his choice: to secure Vespasian's favour by handing over the fugitive. (Or whether he was simply shedding himself of an embarrassment before he made his own bid for the throne.) Meanwhile, in some way he would probably bungle, Aemilius Rufus was attempting to snatch Pertinax so he could roll into Rome covered with glory . . . In this high-flown project I noticed nobody was planning any active role for me. 'Aemilia Fausta, where is the meeting?'

'At sea. My brother left before lunch for Misenum.'

I frowned. 'He would be wise not to trust the fleet. Crispus has close associates among the trierarchs – '

'So,' confided Aemilia Fausta, more drily, 'has my brother!'

'Ah!' I said.

Darting off at a tangent, the lady abruptly enquired, 'Is there anything I can send to help your friend and his family?'

'Nothing special. Thanks for the thought . . . '

As in most things, Fausta seemed to expect rebuff. 'You think it's none of my business.'

'Correct,' I said. A thought crossed my mind which I dismissed as disloyal to Petronius.

I could see that Aemilia Fausta would be just the type to jump straight from her passionate infatuation with Crispus to a single-minded crush on anyone so foolish as to listen to her troubles. This scenario was no new one. Being a big, tolerant type (who loved something dainty to cuddle on his knee), my tentmate Petronius had left in his wake many fervent little ladies who regarded him as their saviour for reasons I was too embarrassed to enquire about. He usually stayed friends with them. So he would not want me to quarrel with Fausta on his behalf.

I suggested, 'There is something you can do, in fact. Petronius could survive a journey now; I need to get him home. Could you lend the family a couple of decent litters to travel comfortably? Even better, persuade your brother to supply an armed guard? He'll see the point. Then I can send Helena Justina back to the city in safety too . . . '

Fausta nodded gratefully. 'Now, I need to move swiftly. "At sea" you say. Can you be more specific about this rendezvous?'

'Will you promise me Aufidius Crispus will be safe?'

'I never give promises that are outside my control. But my commission was to save him for Rome . . . So, where is the meeting?'

'At Capreae,' she said. 'This afternoon. Below the Imperial Villa of Jove.'

LXX

I needed a ship, fast.

I raced from the house. Outside, Nero, who had no shame, was making friends with a couple of lacklustre cheapskate mules who had been parked against a portico in a haze of flies. I knew the mules. Larius was leaning on a wall in the shade, chatting to their riders: a sinister hulk who was not safe on the streets and a whiskery midget with a furtive face. They both wore white tunics with green bindings; the livery was all too familiar: the Gordianus steward and his shrimpy sidekick.

'Larius, don't associate with strange men!'

'This is Milo – '

'Milo's bad news. Come on; we need to move. Gallop Nero to the seafront so I can commandeer a boat – '

'Oh, Milo's got a boat on the seafront – '

'That so?' I forced myself to sound polite.

Milo smirked at me. He gave me a pain in the head; the only consolation was that it could not be half as bad as the headache I had once given him with a certain piece of porphyry. 'Find out!' he threatened with a leer: Croton etiquette again.

'Let me ask politely: show me your ship and I promise not to tell Gordianus you refused to cooperate! Let's go – the magistrate's sister has come up with a lead on Pertinax – '

At the south end of town sea walls pierced with sturdy arches provided a vantage point where the citizens of Herculaneum on their way to the Surburban Baths could stroll above any shipping which braved their fierce waterfront regulations to tie up picturesquely on the wharf. The harbour facilities were not exactly throbbing with cranes and unloading pulleys, but provided a berth for the occasional tentative craft. Milo's shrimp took charge of Nero and the mules. 'He's good with animals – '

'That must be why he tags along with you!'

The ship Milo indicated was a chunky piece of timberwork called the *Sea Scorpion*. The crew were on watch for trouble and had seen us approaching; a sailor was ready to pull in the gangway as soon as Larius, Milo and I tumbled aboard.

The familiar unkempt, heavy shape of the Chief Priest Gordianus was waiting on deck, snuggling his huge webby ears in a long cloak as if since his brother's death he felt unable to get warm. He still looked unhealthily grey, though his bald skin had acquired patches of rose-coloured sunburn.

We shook hands like army commanders in the middle of a war: the same sense of a great deal having happened since we last met, and the same faint tinge of jealousy.

'Good to meet up with you, Falco! All well?'

'I've had some narrow shaves. Pertinax has just tried to murder me the same way he attacked you . . . Tell me, how did you discover he was still alive?'

'You were right, my brother had written to warn me. He had left the letter with his banker; after you left Colonna it came to me.'

'Any news of your wounded deputy, sir?' I was half prepared for the answer. Gordianus raised his eyes to heaven: the stand-in priest was dead. Another charge against Pertinax, though as usual without proof.

We put out across the Bay with a brisk breeze in the *Sea Scorpion*'s favour. Gordianus asked if I recognised the ship. I thought not, and I was right because in fact I had never seen her, but when he called out to the captain to make for Capreae, I realised I *had* heard of her. The captain was a friend of mine: a lively, beady-eyed little fellow in a curly hat like an upturned field mushroom, who had been standing by rather sheepishly, waiting to be recognised . . .

'*Laesus*! This would be a happy moment on a better day!'

I introduced my nephew, who was craning to get an artistic perspective on my friend from Croton's strange two-sided face. Larius slouched up shyly, a suspicious beanpole in a grimy tunic, still wearing his satchel from when we were selling lead. Then I glanced sharply between Gordianus and the sea captain. 'Did you two know each other all along?'

Gordianus laughed. 'No; we met when I needed a charter to bring my household from Cape Colonna to Paestum. Your name came up later, and I heard about your adventures together then.'

'Bit of luck falling in with somebody reliable!'

'True. Laesus will stay until this business is settled. He helped me find Aufidius Crispus; then when Crispus confirmed the truth about "Barnabas", Laesus worked with Milo keeping track of Pertinax.' We leaned back against the ship's rail, as the crew adjusted the mainsail for a long haul out along the Surrentum coast. 'Tell me what you think of this man Rufus?' Gordianus abruptly asked. 'It struck me he had rather a casual attitude.'

'Oh, he's intelligent, and hard working in the community.' I knew better than to criticise a fellow senator to Gordianus merely for enjoying old wine and young waiters. On the other hand, the bungled attempt to arrest Pertinax was unforgiveable. 'His shambles at the Villa Marcella speaks for itself.'

Gordianus humphed. 'Self-centred and immature!' was his terse verdict on the magistrate. It explained why he had opted to continue his private search for Pertinax even after raising an official hue and cry.

Something struck me and I turned to Milo, who was slouching by the mainmast forestay. 'If you were trailing Pertinax, you must have been there when he bludgeoned my friend at the inn!' He was. Milo always made me angry – but never so angry as this. 'Jupiter and Mars! When Petronius Longus came to the doorway, why didn't you shout?'

'We had heard Pertinax ask for you!' Milo jibed unpleasantly. 'Sorry we couldn't stay to help; we followed him back to the yacht . . . '

I had to walk away by myself to the far end of the ship, to stop myself feeding the steward to the porpoises in shreds.

The journey out to Capreae always seems further than it looks. The sour old Emperor Tiberius chose himself a good sanctuary; plenty of time to prepare visitors a grim welcome before incoming ships berthed.

I was not seasick, though I thought about it uneasily.

'You all right?' Larius asked solicitously. I explained that making kind enquiries of people who had queasy stomachs never helps.

Larius, who loved ships and never felt ill at sea, leaned on the rail beside me, enjoying his trip. As the endless cliffs of the Lactarii peninsula eased slowly past he squinted against the breeze, happily absorbing the spray and the sunlit ocean scenery.

'Uncle Marcus, Helena suggests I ought to talk to you.'

'If it's about your bloody wall painting, I'm not in the mood.'

'It's about Ollia.'

'Oh, it's a joke!' He gave me a disapproving look. 'Sorry! Go on then.' Larius, the shocking romantic, adjusted his pose like a figurehead braving the storms of life, with his limp hair blowing back from his forehead and a stalwart expression. A sea trip brought out the worst in him.

'Ollia is not having a baby; that was Silvia's mistake. As a matter of fact, there was never anything between Ollia and the fisherboy – '

'Goodness!' I scoffed. 'Then why didn't she deny it? Or him?'

'They both did.'

True. 'So what's the real story?'

'He kept hanging around and she didn't know how to get rid of him. Everyone else had the wrong idea about it – '

'Except you?' I hazarded.

Larius blushed. I hid a smile. He went on earnestly. 'Ollia was too frightened of Silvia to explain.' I grinned. 'The fisherboy never wanted her – '

'So what was his angle?'

'He wants to go to Rome. To better himself.' I let out an expression of contempt. 'Oh he's all right,' Larius muttered. 'Petro says he has tried so hard we ought to take him anyway. My father would have him as an oarsman; it gives a let-out for me . . . '

'In order to do what, sunshine?'

'To be a wall painter in Pompeii.' I told Larius if he wanted to be so stupid I was still not in the mood.

I had a good look at him; he seemed to have filled out to a more easy-going figure while we were away. He dropped the fresco painting plea, but I had the impression that was only because it was all fixed anyway.

'Well, give Ollia my congratulations on her escape from mother-hood – '

'About Ollia – ' Larius began.

I groaned, trying not to laugh. 'I can guess. Ollia has decided her great dream is a poetry-reading lank with ochre paint in his fingernails?' Larius hid his hands but I was pleased to see he stood up to me.

They had one of those sweet, neat plans young people so rashly inflict on themselves. Larius insisted on describing it to me: home to Rome; explain to his mother; back to Pompeii; learn his trade; earn enough to hire a room with a balcony –

'Vital equipment for a bachelor on his own!'

'Uncle Marcus, why are you always so cynical?'

'I'm a bachelor blessed with a balcony!'

Then they would get married; wait two years while Larius saved more money; have three children at two-year intervals; and sedately spend the rest of their days deploring the raggedness of other peoples' lives. There were two possibilities; either they would grow out of each other and Ollia would run off with a sandalmaker – or, knowing Larius, he would manage the whole daft scheme.

'Helena Justina found out all this? What does she think?'

'She thought it was a good idea. Helena gave me my first commission,' Larius told me with a sly look. 'I drew her a still life: you, fast asleep with your mouth open.'

'She never kept it?'

'Oh yes! She wanted a souvenir of her holiday . . . '

I said nothing, because a sailor gave a cry: Capreae.

When we set out the day had been overcast. Passing Surrentum the shoreline cliffs had been a shadowed mix of dark-green vegetation and honey-toned rocks against the hazier colours of the mountain range behind; the sea was a rippling pewter grey, slightly threatening beneath the sullen sky. Now, as we approached the island which lay like the double hump of two basking whales, the cloud cover thinned. Only the frothy white triangle which often hovers above Capreae still served as a marker from afar.

We sailed on in bright sunlight, over a blue sea of gemstone intensity.

The island seemed to rush nearer at a faster speed. From the main harbour a small regatta of pleasure boats streamed out, their sails making a line of dark-red dots in apparently haphazard chase. If the *Isis Africana* had been among them we should never have picked her out, but as Curtius Gordianus gave Laesus directions we left the little boats far to one side while we pressed in close to the sheer crags. Slowly we explored these deep secluded bays where access could only ever be by water. Sometimes dark cave mouths gaped in the rock wall above. All round the island there was plenty of activity from fishing and excursion boats, though none disturbed the limpidly bright lagoon where the *Sea Scorpion* finally crept in and found the *Isis* moored.

Crispus and Pertinax were bathing. It was a strangely relaxed scene.

We sailed closer without fuss, and Laesus dropped anchor. The swimmers were watching us. Keeping his face hidden, Gordianus hailed Crispus cheerfully, like some old friend whose arrival today was a happy coincidence. We saw Crispus float on his back as if he were considering, and possibly cursing, us; then he set off to his yacht with a lazy overarm stroke, following Pertinax who had started swimming at once. Once it became clear they were not weighing anchor the Chief Priest and I were rowed across to them, taking Milo, in a skiff.

When we clambered aboard, Aufidius Crispus was towelling off on deck, a squat, muscular figure covered in dark hair. Pertinax had disappeared into the galley, as if to dress in privacy; perhaps he hoped we were casual visitors who would not stay. Crispus pulled on a loose red tunic whose metallic braid was well tarnished from frequent exposure to salt spray. He shook water from his ears with a vigour I remembered him applying to other things.

'What a surprise!' he said, with no surprise at all on his swarthy jowls. He was expecting the magistrate, but accepted we had come to take over the arrangement, for he called out robustly, 'Gnaeus! Come out here; I want you to meet some old friends!'

Since there was little else for it, Atius Pertinax shuffled on deck. He wore a white tunic already belted, and his usual tight expression. When he recognised Gordianus his river-water eyes became guarded. Reluctantly he grinned; then slouched closer, offering to shake hands.

Remembering his brother, Gordianus had frozen. He could not bear the proffered handclasp. I stepped forward myself.

'The name's Falco,' I announced, as our quarry jerked his head in annoyance and shock. 'I'm supposed to be dead – but so are you.' Then I stood to attention and formally announced: 'Gnaeus Atius Pertinax Caprenius Marcellus, also known as Barnabas, in the name of Vespasian Augustus you are under arrest! I am taking you into custody and transferring you to Rome. You have the right to a trial by your equals in the Senate, or you may exercise every citizen's privilege and appeal to the Emperor himself. To do that,' I informed him with relish, 'you must prove who you are first!'

'What are the charges?' Pertinax blustered.

'Oh, conspiracy against the Empire, murder, religious arson, assault on a Roman watch captain – and intending to murder me!'

LXXI

Pertinax looked as if he was really seeing me at last. Yet his arrogance was barely dented. I think he failed to grasp how for the second time since their plot had failed *he* was threatened with a jail term, while his associates were coolly abandoning him. I almost pitied his plight – but when someone wants to kill me, my better nature fades.

I stood with my feet planted slightly apart, aware of the shifting deck beneath them, and the fragility of the *Isis* after the *Sea Scorpion's* workaday bulk.

Pertinax shot a wizened glance at Crispus, evidently supposing he would be arrested too. Crispus shrugged, and failed to enlighten him. I nodded to Milo. Since the skiff we had come across in was too small to take more than three, Milo transfered first to the *Sea Scorpion* with the prisoner, then sent it back empty for Gordianus and me.

While we waited none of us spoke.

The skiff came creeping back towards the yacht. Crispus exchanged courtesies with Gordianus, wishing him well for his position at Paestum. They both ignored me with a sort of polite deference, as if they were at a highly important banquet and had spotted a happy weevil winking out from a bread roll.

I myself was in no mood for self-congratulation. The sight of Atius Pertinax only made me feel sour. Until I landed him in a very solid jail cell, I would not relax.

I sent Gordianus down into the skiff first.

'Well, thanks for the delivery, sir!' The yacht rolled, such a delicate craft that the motion disturbed my balance; I grabbed at the rail. 'You can rely on Vespasian's gratitude.'

'I'm glad,' smiled Crispus. Here on his yacht in his holiday clothes, he looked older and shabbier than when he was fired with confidence at the Villa Poppaea – though more like a man you could go out with on a fishing trip.

'That so?' I asked levelly. 'So I can rule you out of any wicked schemes I've found involving Egyptian grain ships?'

'Dropped it,' Crispus admitted, frankly enough apparently.

'What – no joy from the fleet?'

He made no attempt to repudiate the plan. 'Oh, the commander and the trierarchs will drink with anyone who pays for the liquor –

but the marines all think of themselves as soldiers. Give your man his credit, Falco; Vespasian has the army's full loyalty.'

'They know Vespasian is a good general, sir.'

'Well, let's hope he makes a good Emperor too.'

I studied his face. Helena was right; he took his losses casually, however large the stake. If they *were* losses. The only way to find out was to give him his head, then watch him.

As I swung over the rail ready to descend, Crispus steadied my arm. 'Thanks. I meant what I said; I imagine you can ask Vespasian for whatever post you want,' I promised, still trying to salvage him.

Aufidius Crispus flashed a sly glance down at the skiff where Gordianus had slewed in the bow in his usual lumpish style. 'I'll need more than a damned priesthood then!'

I grinned. 'Ask away! Good luck, sir; see you in Rome . . . '

Perhaps.

So far recapturing Pertinax seemed too easy. I ought to have known. The Fate who controls my destiny has a sinister sense of fun.

The *Sea Scorpion*'s skiff had rowed us halfway to its mother ship when a newcomer appeared in the lagoon. Gordianus glanced at me. It was a trireme from the Misenum fleet.

'Rufus!' I muttered. 'Trust him to turn up in his rosebud wreath when the banquet is already breaking up!'

The newcomer had glided up in silence but as soon as we spotted her they started the drum. On the side we could see, eighty oars dipped. As the rowers took their time from the drummer, sunlight flashed once off the shields and speartips of the squadron of marines who lined the trireme's fighting deck. She was steely-blue and grey, with a proud flash of scarlet round the horn on her nose. A vividly painted eye gave her a swordfish ferocity as she streamed forwards, lethally propelled by three huge banks of oars. Behind me I heard barrel-chested Bassus, the bosun of the *Isis*, utter a warning shout.

In our skiff the sailor who was rowing paused uncertainly. Though triremes are the navy's workhorses, and common enough in the Bay, to see one speeding at full thrust still stopped the breath. Nothing on water was so beautiful or dangerous.

Gordianus and I watched her come towards us. I realised she was passing dangerously close. We were terrified. We glimpsed her jaws – the heavy timbers cased in bronze that formed her ram; that ever-open, evilly serrated mouth just above the water line. She passed so near we heard the grumble of the thole pins and saw water streaming off the blades as her oars rose. Then our own rower flung himself prone and we all clung to the skiff as huge combers from the trireme's wake buffeted our tiny craft.

We waited, knowing a trireme can turn on her own length. We waited for her to impress her terror on the Crispus yacht then swirl to a halt, dominating the lagoon. Helpless in her path, like a highly decorated piece of flotsam, the *Isis Africana* waited too. But the trireme did not stop. Just before impact, Aufidius Crispus took his last whimsical decision. I recognised his red tunic as he dived.

With that fatal flaw in his character, he had made the wrong decision yet again.

He went straight under the trireme's starboard blades. Only the top tier of oarsmen, those on the outrigger who could see the blades, would have known he was there. I glimpsed his torso once, churning hideously. Oars locked. A couple snapped. The rest ruffled on without pause, like the fluted fin on some gigantic fish, as they drove the great ship's slender keel straight into the yacht. The ram took her in full snarl. There was no doubt it was deliberate. The trireme ran into the *Isis* with one fierce stroke, then straightway backed oars: the classic manoeuvre to hook out her victim's shattered timbers as the two ships wrenched apart. But the *Isis* was so small that instead of pulling free, the trireme hauled the yacht's rumpled carcass backwards too, impaled on its nose.

Everything went quiet.

I noticed that the trireme was called *Pax*. In the feckless hands of an incompetent, small-town magistrate, it was hardly apt.

Our boatman had lost his oar; he swam for it, leaving us rocking on the turbulent sea. When we pulled him back aboard he turned the skiff towards the trireme, and we braced ourselves for recovering what we could.

By the time we pressed near enough, the choppiness was settling. The crew of the *Isis* were clinging to lines and being slowly brought on board the *Pax*, while marines swarmed over the mighty bronze ram, hacking off what was left of the yacht. Splintered shards of the beautiful toy skirled on the bay. We could hear screams from within a juddering fragment of the hull where a crewman was trapped; although the marines fought to save him, the timbers broke away and took him to the bottom before they managed it. Sickened, Gordianus and I left them to it and hauled ourselves up a rope ladder over the light-boned hull of the trireme to confront the magistrate. We came aboard in the stern. Rufus made no attempt to meet us, so we both walked the huge length of the ship and came up to him just at the moment when a group of marines, aided by the grim-faced bosun Bassus, dragged what was left of Aufidius Crispus in over the rail.

Another corpse.

This one thudded on deck streaming wet, with that thin, crimson poignancy fresh blood takes on when mixed with sea water. Yet another corpse, and yet again no need for it. I could tell Gordianus was as angry as I was. He wrenched off his cloak, then he and I wrapped the battered body in it; he spoke one harsh word to Aemilius Rufus before he turned away: 'Waste!'

I was less restrained.

'What was the point of that hideous manoeuvre?' I raged, making free with my contempt. 'Don't tell me Vespasian ordered it – Vespasian has better sense!'

Aemilius Rufus hesitated. He still possessed those startling looks, but the confident air which had once impressed me seemed a tawdry gift, now I had watched him in action and learned he was one more aristocrat with erratic judgement and a total lack of practical intelligence. I had seen it in Britain during the Great Rebellion, and here it was at home: yet another second-rate official with fool's gold in his pedigree, sending good men to the grave.

He made no answer. I expected none.

He had been scanning the rescued crewmen, trying to hide his agitation because he could not see the one man we all knew he was looking for. His elegant, fair-skinned face revealed the moment when he decided not to approach Gordianus – an irascible elder senator, who would give him short shrift. I had the honour instead.

'Rather unfortunate! But it solves the problem of Crispus – '

'Crispus was not a problem!' My terse answer unsettled him.

'Falco, what's happened to Pertinax?'

'Feeding the Baian oysters, if it was up to you! Oh, don't worry; he should be safe on the *Sea Scorpion* – '

I ought to have known better.

When we all turned to the rail and looked for my old friend Laesus and his sturdy merchant ship, we discovered that the *Sea Scorpion* had slipped her anchor during the mêlée. She was already far away from us, heading south for the open sea.

LXXII

There were still pieces of wreckage to untangle from the trireme, and broken oars to pull in. Even then we ought to have caught up. But as we set off in pursuit, we ran into the regatta I had seen earlier as we first sailed towards the island. The *Sea Scorpion* had already positioned herself the far side of this line so our great craft had no choice but to pick its way diagonally through the little boats, none of whom understood that we were involved in a chase. Their owners were senators' sons and equestrians' nephews, and once we had disrupted their race these high-spirited youths decided it would pay us back if they dodged their zippy yachts round us like mad minnows pecking at a waterlogged bread roll.

'Oh for heavens' sake!' roared Gordianus. 'Pertinax must have overpowered Laesus somehow, and now he's making off!' A thought struck him. 'He's got Milo – '

'Never mind Milo,' I uttered in a hollow voice. 'He's got my nephew Larius!'

The trireme carried a sail, but it had been lowered for action so we lost precious minutes raising her mast again and setting the canvas aloft. Meanwhile, the merchantman was running for the end of the peninsula. The breeze which had carried us out to Capreae was still sending her along at a good five knots as she made for the headland. Then she turned in around the Amalfi coast, and we lost sight of her.

'How could he manage it?' Gordianus fretted.

'Well-placed friends!' I said grimly. 'Your ally and mine, the trustworthy Laesus, must have been in league with Pertinax from the start!'

'Falco, what do you mean?'

'I mean we're victims of a Calabrian clique. When I first met Laesus in Croton that was no coincidence; he must have been there to meet Pertinax. I thought he looked shocked when I said Pertinax had died! Once Laesus discovered what I was there for, I'm damn sure he tried to poison me. Then when Pertinax attacked your deputy at Colonna, I'll bet the *Sea Scorpion* took him off. When Laesus conveniently agreed to take you to Paestum, he was marking you for Pertinax – '

'But why?'

'They both come from Tarentum. They must have known each other long before Marcellus adopted Pertinax. Tarentum is the sort of crooked Calabrian town with unshakeable local loyalties.'

I remembered with a sinking feeling that Laesus had admitted he used to sail to Alexandria: Pertinax must have asked him here for his knowledge of the corn ships' annual run. Crispus was dead, but now Pertinax was on the loose with full knowledge of his colleague's plan to blackmail Rome. Pertinax, whose adopted father had filled him with ludicrous ideas of his own worth . . .

On the face of it, compared to a candidate with heavyweight talents like Crispus, Pertinax posed no threat to the Empire at all. But I happened to be more cynical. Think of Caligula and Nero: Rome has a habit of taking lunatic would-be emperors to its heart.

The magistrate Aemilius Rufus came up: more trouble.

'We'll soon overtake,' he boasted. Wrong as usual. We never caught the *Sea Scorpion*. When we finally made it round the headland towards Positanum, the sea was full of litter from her decks, but the ship had disappeared.

There was no point in hurrying; they reefed our sail.

Then a marine yelled. The *Pax* rowed up nearer and gently stopped. Some of the sailors were there, clinging to driftwood; we pulled them in. Then I let out a hoarse sob of relief. Grinning weakly, but so tired he could not speak, I recognised my nephew floating on his back. He was desperately struggling to subdue a half-submerged figure who was thrashing stupidly: 'Milo!' cried Gordianus. 'Falco, your brave young nephew had saved my steward!'

I muttered that Larius had never showed much sense.

We must have missed quite a party. When Milo saw Atius Pertinax grinning in triumph as he was greeted by the sea captain, the steward ran amok. In the process of being overcome he was beaten and roped up with fishing lines. Meanwhile, my nephew stood by looking innocent; the sea captain suggested to Pertinax keeping Larius as a hostage.

'Did he, by Jupiter! But how did you get in the water, Larius – and where is the ship?'

Larius assumed his expression of playful nonchalance. 'Oh I could see the *Sea Scorpion* needed a new coat of pitch so I guessed she was pretty barnacled. I pretended to feel seasick and went below decks. I had a chisel in my satchel from when we were selling lead, so I just set to in the bilges. The worms had nearly done the job anyway; she was so spongy one good storm would have claimed her as a wreck. I soon punched her hull full of more holes than a wine strainer – '

'Then what happened?'

'What do you think? She sank.'

* * *

While my sister's boy was being treated like a hero, I discovered that when the *Sea Scorpion* had started to wallow everyone had leapt overboard. Those who could swim, did. Milo was still tied up. My nephew's tricky conscience made him save the steward: no small task for a fourteen-year-old lad. Even when Larius edged a floating spar half under them, buoying up fifteen stone while Milo wrestled around in panic took a determined effort. By the time we found them, my boy looked pretty limp.

We rowed the *Pax* as close to the rocks as possible, and took bumboats ashore. We picked up a few more soggy crewmen, but both Laesus and Pertinax had made good their escape. They had been spotted heading up into the Lactarii Mountains together. Aemilius Rufus took the trireme into Positanum and made a great fuss organising a search.

He had no success. Trust him.

I stayed in the port below the steep little town and bought a meal to revive Larius. Milo stuck to him too, with pathetic gratitude, but if I was hoping he would repay us by digging into his pocket for a flagon I was wrong. Once things quietened down around us, Larius murmured privately, 'Pertinax has a bolt hole he uses, back towards Neapolis – he said something to the sea captain about hiding up.'

'On the farm!'

The quiet voice came from Bassus. We had pulled that big, breezy man from the water after the trireme had sunk the *Isis*, just before he was submerged under the weight of his own gold amulets. Here he had been drinking heavily in silence: mourning the loss of his employer, the yacht, and especially his livelihood. I signalled him to join us. The bench sagged dangerously under his bulk as he huddled in with Larius, Milo and me.

'You been to this farm, Bassus?'

'No, but I heard him complaining to Crispus that it was grim. That was his excuse for coming aboard with us – '

'Bassus!' Bassus, who was already drably sozzled, frowned as he dimly deciphered that my appeal was made to him. 'Bassus, give us a clue about this hideaway.'

'He said it was a farmhouse – and it stinks.'

Then Milo contributed, 'Must be that run-down dungheap.'

'You know it?' I rounded on him urgently. 'You tailed him there? Can you find it again?'

'No hope, Falco. He was dashing all over the mountain that night, trying to shake us off. It was dark and we lost ourselves – '

'What mountain? Vesuvius? Near his father's estate?'

Larius laughed suddenly – a quiet, confident chortle deep in his throat.

'Oh no! Oh Uncle Marcus, you really will not like this – it must

be the one where that man chased you: the one with the pretty girl
– and the big friendly dog!'

As soon as he said it, I guessed Larius was right.

Without more ado we drained our cups, dragged ourselves upright
and started outside. I asked the bosun, 'You with us, Bassus?' But, deeply
depressed by the loss of the *Isis*, Bassus said he would stay in Positanum
with the drink.

He came with us to the door though. As we reeled in the sudden
sunlight that glanced off the harbour, I heard him let out a chuckle
ironically. 'That's fate for you!' Then he pointed southwards out to
sea. 'Here they come . . . '

Bearing slowly towards the Amalfi coast was the most amazing
vessel I had ever seen. The Royal Barge of the Ptolemies was supposed
to be larger, but I had never been privileged to gawp at the Egyptian
fleet. This one was a monster. If her deck was less than two hundred
feet in length, the shortfall could not be more than any lad on the
Tiber waterfront could spit. When she docked she must tower above
everything else like the multistorey apartments in Rome. Across the
beam she was forty feet easily. And the depth of her hull, labouring
so heavily, was probably even more than that.

To power this immense bulk she had not merely the normal square
sail but a fabulous arrangement of red topsails as well. Far behind her
I could just make other dark smudges, apparently motionless on the
horizon, though they too would be heading towards us, low in the
water beneath their huge cargoes, at an inexorable pace.

'Bassus! Whatever in Hades is that?'

He squinted at her thoughtfully as she loomed imperceptibly
nearer the rocky coast. '*Parthenope*, probably . . . but could be *Venus
of Paphos* – '

I knew before he said it: the first of the corn ships had arrived.

LXXIII

Now I was thinking fast.

'Bassus, I can appreciate your loyalty to Crispus. As a matter of fact I had a good opinion of him myself. But he's gone. And unless we do something, Atius Pertinax – who is a different kind of leech on the Empire altogether – will be hijacking the grain ships and threatening Rome.'

The bosun was listening in his normal, impervious way. Desperate not to sound overhasty I confessed to him, 'I can't do this alone. I need your help, Bassus, or the game's over. You've lost the man you sailed for, and you've lost your ship. Now I'm offering you a chance to gain a heroic reputation and earn yourself an honorarium . . . '

Through the drink he thought about it. Drink apparently made Bassus a mellow, amenable type. 'All right. I can live with being a hero. So we need to think up a plan – '

I had no time to waste being diffident. I had been mulling over this problem since I first came to Campania. I already had a plan. Without making a fuss about my forethought and ingenuity, I explained to Bassus what I thought we ought to do.

I left him in Positanum to make contact with the grain ships as they arrived. Once most of the pack had gathered in the Bay of Salernum, still out of sight of the fleet at Misenum, he would let me know.

When the magistrate took his borrowed trireme back again round the headland, I asked him to drop my small party at Oplontis – though I did not tell him why. Gordianus knew. He had set himself the task of escorting the body of Aufidius Crispus to Neapolis, so now it was just Larius, Milo and me. Larius had done his bit for the Empire that day; I left him at the inn.

Milo and I went to the farm.

As we approached tentatively through the trellised arch we found the same smell and the same air of sour neglect. At first I was pleased to see that the dog was missing from his chain; then I realised it might mean he was roaming loose. When we got there it was dusk; after a long hot day the waft of ill-tended animals and old dung was stomach curling. Milo hung back.

'You're useless,' I told him cheerily. 'Trust me to lumber myself with

270

you. Milo, big dogs are like bodybuilders – perfect cowards until they smell fear.' There was heavy perspiration on the steward's objectionable face, and I could smell his fear myself. 'Anyway, he hasn't found us yet . . . '

We tackled the pungent outbuildings before we broached the house. In the split-boarded midden that passed for a stable we discovered a sturdy skewbald horse I recognised.

'Pertinax had this gypsy as his packhorse when he was following me down to Croton! I wonder if the bastard's ridden off somewhere on the roan?'

I led the way, biffing at blue flies, and we were nearing the house when we both stopped dead: intercepted by the guard dog.

'Don't worry, Milo; I like dogs – '

I did, but not this one. He was growling. He would be. I deduced this was not a mutt who would scamper off if someone looked him in the eye and shouted boo.

He was as tall as a man if he stood on his hind legs, one of those browny-black creatures they breed for aggression, with a neck like an ox and small, mean ears. Milo gave him a few pounds but both the dog and I were aware Fido weighed as much as me. I was the kind of bite-sized titbit this bully liked for a target; the hound was staring cold-bloodedly straight at me.

'Good boy, Cerberus!' I encouraged him steadily. Behind me I heard Milo gurgle. What I needed was a poisoned chicken; but since Milo had watched Petronius have his skull split I was perfectly willing to let him be the bait instead.

I murmured to Milo, 'If you've got a bit of rope on you, I'll put him on a lead.' The dog had other plans. The rumble in the canine's throat assumed a more ominous note. I applied myself to calming him.

I was still talking when he sprang.

I rammed one elbow in his chest and braced both feet while I tried to hold his head and fend him off. I could smell dead meat on his breath, and his dentistry was unbelievable. I should have shouted at him fiercely; you have to dominate a mobster like that. I never had the chance.

'Stand back, Milo – '

Same old Milo: give him an order and he did the opposite. Luckily for both of us, Milo's idea of taming a dog was to grab him from behind, then jerk up his snout, twist it sharply, and break his neck.

We stood in the yard, frankly quaking. I admitted to Milo that I reckoned we were quits.

Laesus was in the house. I found him; Milo disarmed him of his seaman's knife.

We dragged him outside, backwards. The sad side of his face

splashed down in a cowpat; the happy half could see what Milo had done to the mountainous dog.

'Falco!' he gasped, trying to grin in his old friendly manner. At first I went along with it.

'Laesus! I've been hoping to meet up with you again, old friend. I wanted to warn you, next time you drink saffron pottage at your favourite eating house, watch out for the belladonna they add to the broth!'

Grinning at the thought of someone poisoning my pottage, Milo pushed the sea captain's face deeper into the dung.

'I lost my ship!' Laesus complained. As a sailor he could cope with fishiness, but close contact with the joys of agriculture was making poor old Laesus lose his nerve.

'That's a tragedy. You can either blame my nephew – or put it down to having gobbled up my sacred goat!' He groaned and tried to speak again but Milo was enjoying himself the way he liked best: showing off how powerful he was, punishing someone unpleasantly. 'Where's Pertinax, Laesus?' I demanded.

'I don't know – ' Milo demonstrated to Laesus the points on his body where pressure is unbearable. I winced, and looked away.

I told Laesus what I had worked out about Tarentum loyalties. 'I should have remembered Calabrians stick together like this farmyard muck! I suppose you rescued me in Croton market because even in Bruttium an Imperial agent dead in the Forum might attract attention. You preferred to polish me off privately – and it's lucky for me you failed! I wondered why you pressed me so hard to sail with you to Rhegium afterwards; no doubt I would have jumped overboard with fishing weights in my boots. Gordianus was lucky he had Milo in attendance while he was on your ship. Now where's Pertinax? Tell me, or you'll do worse than eat manure; Milo will be spreading the fields with what's left of you!'

Milo lifted the sea captain by his neck and his heels, far enough for him to gasp the words: 'He found a message here that his father has been taken ill. But – '

'But what?' I snarled.

'He said he might be visiting his ex-wife on the way!'

LXXIV

We had a quick scout round the farm, but the occupants must have scarpered. All we found were more evil odours, ants in the cheese press, and busy flies. Then, as we picked our way out along the rutted track, we ran into the black-chinned villain who had chased me that first day.

Milo was encumbered with Laesus, who saw this as his chance to escape and began struggling furiously. I took on the farmer. He was fresh, and I had made the mistake of letting myself relax. We circled ominously. He was missing the cudgel this time but I could tell from his stance that violent country wrestling was his speciality; I preferred games of skill. We grappled briefly, and the next moment I was lying on my back with all the breath knocked out of me. But I was fit after my holiday; so I scrambled up for the next throw, more wary this time.

It never came. There was a flash of white, an unexpected scurry, and before I could tackle him the farmer had collapsed headlong. A goat had knocked him flying – a goat whose wild eye and eager expression looked somehow familiar . . . I said, 'Your stock's well trained!' Then I gave the floored yokel a tap on the forehead that left him cold. He would wake up with a furious headache to find us long gone.

The animal that flattened him let out an impassioned bleat, then launched at me. I struggled to stay upright, fending off the attentions of yet another old friend from Croton I had never expected to encounter again.

Laesus looked self-conscious. 'Every time we got the fire lit she ran off. She's nothing but trouble, Falco; you can have her back – '

And so we left that filthy hideaway: Milo dragging Laesus on one piece of rope, and me holding another string to lead my sacred goat.

When we arrived in Oplontis I put Milo in charge of escorting the sea captain to a berth in the Herculaneum jail. My personal grudge dictated I go for Pertinax myself. Milo understood that; pursuing grudges was a hobby of his own.

Although Helena Justina was still at the inn, Larius assured me in an undertone there had been no sign of Pertinax. I reckoned I knew why. That snob would never expect a senator's daughter to stay in such deplorable surroundings solely to help stricken friends; he would assume she still lived at the villa. Yet even if he did know we had her, we could frighten him off now. Aemilia Fausta had been as good as her word. She had already sent transport for our invalid and his family – plus an armed guard from Herculaneum who were so excited at the prospect of action they intended to stab first and ask questions afterwards.

I drew Larius to one side.

'I'm going up to the villa rustica. I don't know what I'll find. I need you to look after the people I'm responsible for. I want them all to leave Campania. I don't like the way Pertinax is preoccupied with Helena; it's not safe. If I tell her the truth, she'll argue. So we'll say that Petronius Longus is being whisked back to Rome under armed guard because he is a material witness, and I'll ask Helena Justina to go too – '

'To supervise?' grinned Larius; I chortled back abstractedly.

'Yes; she'll like that . . . ' Then I looked at him properly. 'You were a good lieutenant on this trip. I could use you, Larius. Drawing the Battle of Actium three times a month is soul-destroying. You ought to be using your grit and initiative – and be showing off to girls! Want a job as my assistant back in Rome?'

My nephew laughed. He told me frankly that he had more sense.

I got them away that night. The cavalcade left in a resinous tang of torches: a rapidly convened train of baggage and querulous children, led by Larius and Ollia's fisherboy driving Nero with Petro's culleus of wine. We had certainly assembled a quaint batch of souvenirs. Milo's shrimp took charge of my goat, who was being sent with Nero to live on Petro's cousins' farm.

When it came to the point, my plans crumbled: face to face with Helena I told her the truth.

'Yes, I see.' She always had a quiet response to a genuine emergency, though obedience to my instructions had never featured much in our relationship. 'Marcus, is it still your intention to put Pertinax under arrest?'

'He has two deaths now to answer for, plus the attack on Petronius. Whatever his old father thinks, Pertinax is no longer simply a conspirator who can hope for an amnesty. After his arrest on the *Isis*, he must know it himself. But that only makes him more desperate.'

'I was so hoping we could find a way to make things right for him – '

'I hate you to defend him!'

Helena held me by the shoulders, looking miserably anxious. 'Marcus, I had more loyalty to you after four minutes in your arms than I felt towards him after four years of marriage – though that does not mean I have no loyalty to Pertinax at all.'

I caught her face between my hands. 'Helena! You have to let him go!'

'I know that,' she said slowly.

'I don't think so! When you reach Rome, stay indoors and if Pertinax tries to contact you, you *must* refuse!'

'Marcus, promise me one thing: don't kill him.'

'I don't want to kill him.' She said nothing. 'Helena my love, someone may have to.'

'If it has to be done, let somebody else be responsible. Marcus, don't forget that whatever you do, you and I will always have to live with it – '

'That 'always' was a hard one to resist. Suddenly I was seeing her in closer focus, as I had not done since Petronius had been attacked. 'If I leave him free to murder again, I shall have to live with that!'

Helena Justina gave a long, ironic sigh. 'Then I shall have to bury him.'

'Duty's a wonderful thing!'

There were tears in her eyes. 'And what am I do to if he kills you?'

'He won't,' I said harshly. 'I can promise you that!'

I stopped her talking, as I held her tighter and smiled tenderly into her anxious eyes, shutting out all thoughts of Pertinax. She was holding me in a way that reminded me how badly I wanted her. She looked exhausted. She had been here at the inn with me for almost a week, uncomplaining and supportive even when I dragged in at night too far gone to eat the meal she had saved for me, let alone to provide any demonstration of my love.

'We've been living together here,' I acknowledge ruefully. 'And I've been too preoccupied even to notice it!'

'Ah well!' smiled Helena in her dry, practical way. 'I had always assumed that was what living with you would be like!'

I promised, 'One day we'll do it properly.'

Helena Justina studied me, standing very still. 'You know that's what I want,' she said.

Then I kissed her, trying not to let it seem like the last kiss I might ever give her, and Helena kissed me – so sweetly and for so long I almost dreaded that she thought it was.

Everyone was waiting for us. I had to let her go.

LXXV

At the Villa Marcella I was met by Gordianus.

'I thought you were on funeral duty, sir.'

'Too anxious to relax. Where's Milo?'

'Herculaneum; incarcerating the sea captain. What's the situation here?'

'Caprenius Marcellus has had a stroke – '

'Don't believe it! As an invalid that old man is as genuine as a reluctant wife claiming a headache – '

'It's true, Falco; the doctor says another will finish him.'

'Pertinax?'

'No sign. But his father is convinced he will come.'

'Just you and me then, sir, sitting at the Villa Marcella, waiting it out . . . '

Us, waiting for him at the villa. And Pertinax out there somewhere, waiting for the grain ships to arrive from Alexandria.

Strokes were something I knew. My Great-uncle Scaro, an eccentric old rascal, not least for being fond of me, had several (though in fact my amiable uncle died from choking on home-made false teeth). I went in to inspect Marcellus for myself.

The diagnosis was correct. It's grim to see an intelligent man so drastically struck down. The worst aspect was that his slaves were terrified. So he was not only paralysed and robbed of proper speech; he had the added indignities of being treated like an idiot and seeing his servants afraid to deal with him.

I had nothing else to do, so I set about interpreting. At least when he wanted a drink or his pillows raised he could be made comfortable more quickly. I sat with him; read to him; even – since I was handy and it saved fuss – helped the poor old devil to his sickbed commode. The range of my work never failed to amaze me. Here I was: a trireme smash yesterday; a dogfight today; now a consul's nurse.

'You're doing well!' Gordianus commented, looking in.

'I feel like his wife. Next thing, I'll be complaining about my dress allowance and the Consul here will call my mother an interfering witch.'

'What's he saying now?'

'Ah . . . he wants to change his will.'

The Consul dribbled agitatedly. 'Helena . . . Gnaeus!'

I asked, 'You want to leave your estates to Helena, so she can hand them on to Gnaeus?' He lay back, satisfied. I folded my arms, letting him see I was unimpressed. 'Lucky you trust the lady! Most of them would snatch your money, then run off with the nearest low-rank muscleman who has a hint of disreputable promise in his smile - '

He started mouthing anxiously again. I let Gordianus calm him. Anyone who tried to use Helena to help Pertinax lost my sympathy.

After Gordianus left us I sat looking fiercely at Marcellus, while he glared indignantly at me. I said conversationally, 'Helena Justina will never remarry your son!'

Caprenius Marcellus continued his bleak, accusing stare. I could see he knew now just what I was telling him.

The ex-Consul had finally realised *which* sturdy member of the gutter-clogging classes had managed to subvert his daughter-in-law.

We waited four days. Then a discreet message from Bassus in Positanum informed me that enough corn transports had assembled to initiate the next stage of my plan.

I went down to Oplontis for a friendly chat with the driftwood-featured father of Ollia's fisherboy. That evening I watched the tuna boats sail out with their bobbing lanterns, in the knowledge that wherever they were casting their nets the word would spread: Aulus Curtius Gordianus, a distinguished priest (we all know priests!) who had inherited his brother's maritime villa on the cliffs near Surrentum, was celebrating his legacy with a private party for his masculine friends. It was supposed to be a closely guarded secret; there was talk of a spe-cialist dancer with extraordinary proportions being brought specially from Valentia – and he was laying in *huge* quantities of wine.

The specialist dancer never progressed beyond a promise, but in other respects Gordianus threw himself into this enterprise with a flair which suggested he must have had unlikely adventures in his youth. It was a starlit night, but he laid on tremendous bonfires so that any gate-crashers could find him more easily. When the loud trierarchs of the Misenum fleet made land with their commander, the good Gordianus merely sighed like a man who preferred to avoid trouble, and let them find their own way to his casks.

There was just enough food to make people persuade them-selves they could tolerate more drink than their real capacity. There were fine wines and heavy ones, new wines and vintages which Gordianus reckoned his brother had been maturing for as much as fifteen years. There appeared to be no organisation; anyone could get at it . . . A host who was so careless, instead of trying to fend the happy trierarchs away from his liquor, caught them off guard: they gave themselves philosophical advice about how to

avoid getting headaches – then for once even the navy drank itself
insensible.

An hour before dawn I left the disgusting proceedings and climbed
slowly up the path behind the house until the lights of the party had
disappeared behind. Straining my eyes northwards and out across
the ocean, I thought I could just make out huge ghostly shapes,
like windmills walking on the water, tacking immeasurably slowly
to and fro beyond Capreae. I knew they were there, and I hoped I
really had seen them. Either way, I could relax: a good consignment
of the fifteen billion bushels that were needed to feed Rome next year
was safely going home.

I went back to Oplontis straightaway.

While the old man was still sleeping I searched the house and
grounds. Pertinax was nowhere to be seen. I found Bryon, and told
him I had thwarted the young master's plan.

When I had slept off part of my hangover, I prowled round to the
stables again; they seemed even more deserted now. Missing Bryon, I
stood still in puzzlement, then I risked letting rip a shout. Faint thuds
started up in the livery stable block. I hared inside and soon found the
trainer, fastened up in a tack room.

'Oh gods, what happened to you?' Big as he was, Bryon had
received a thorough pounding. He had a split mouth he could
hardly croak through, and bruises it hurt to contemplate. The cruelty
was familiar. 'Don't tell me: Pertinax! He enjoyed doing that . . . '

I helped Bryon outside, wetted his neckerchief in a trough, and
applied it where the damage looked worst.

'Caught him in the loft – told him what you had said about his plan – '

'And he turned on you? Bryon, count yourself lucky you escaped
alive. Where is he now? In the house with the old man?'

'He's gone, Falco.'

I doubted that; Pertinax was too desperate for cash. I dragged
Bryon with me and hurried indoors. But the attendants assured me no
one had visited Marcellus. I strode into the sickroom, making Bryon
come too.

'Tell the Consul what happened to you, Bryon!'

For a moment this vigorous outdoor type hung back in the
presence of an invalid; then he rallied. 'I came on the young master
and warned him the Emperor's agent had scuppered whatever he had
planned. I told him he should stop running and face the charges against
him – '

'So he jumped you, battered you, and then locked you up? Did
he ask about his father's health?'

'No. But I told him the Consul had had a bad attack, and I told him,'
stated Bryon in the same level voice, 'the Consul had been calling out
for him.'

'You made sure he knew – but he left?'

'Oh yes,' said Bryon quietly, not looking at the Consul. 'He left. I've heard him clatter off in a fury on that roan of his often enough.'

I rounded on the bed where the Consul lay motionless, with his eyes closed. 'Better face facts, sir! Atius Pertinax has given up on you. Give up on him!'

Seeing him lying there, we lost all sense of his immense height. His commanding presence seemed to fade even as I watched. Even his huge nose shrank from its ludicrous domination of his old, lined, suffering face. He was one of the wealthiest men in Campania, but everything he valued had now gone. I signalled to Bryon, and we quietly left the room.

The ex-Consul would make no more attempts to redeem Pertinax. Illness and betrayal had succeeded where I had failed.

Pertinax was an excellent rider, and he knew this location. I took a horse out myself to warn the magistrate's searchers to watch closely for the roan, but he must have already slipped through. We had no idea where he might be heading – Tarentum possibly. We had lost him. I returned to the house.

When your nearest relations are spiking you so callously, the last thing you want and the first thing you get is inquisitive neighbours on a social call. Aemilius Rufus was now in with Marcellus, paying his respects. His sister, who had come with him, was walking on the terrace.

She was wearing black, with heavy veiling folded back while she patrolled the colonnade alone and gazed sadly out to sea.

'Aemilia Fausta! I'm sorry about Crispus. I would tell you it ought never to have happened, but that makes the tragedy worse. There was nothing I could do.'

I felt she had expended all her grief on her reluctant lover while he was alive; now he was dead she accepted my condolences decisively. I said in a low tone, 'In future, when you read some court poet's bucolic account of how the crowds at Misenum and Puteoli turn out every year to cheer the incoming grain ships, you can smile to remember what no one ever says: in the consulship of whichever two nobles are holding office *this* year, the transports' annual arrival went unmarked . . . '

'Is it all over?'

'Ships in the night! There may be stragglers still to come, but Vespasian can look after them once I've made my report.'

She turned to me, as she drew her black mantle into a closer frame for her fair-skinned face. 'Crispus was a man with special gifts, Falco. You will be proud to have known him.'

I let that pass. After a moment I smiled, 'Strong colours suit you.'

'Yes!' she agreed, with her new capable laugh. 'Didius Falco, you were right. My brother offends me, I won't live with him now. Perhaps

I *shall* marry a rich old man, and when he's gone enjoy myself as a widow, in strong, dark colours, being overdemanding and shouting at people – or playing the cithara very badly by myself.'

I suppressed the thought that this honourable lady had been strolling here in the Consul's stately portico reckoning up the value of his fabulous estate.

'Aemilia Fausta,' I responded gallantly, 'on my word as a harp teacher, you play very well!'

'You always were a liar, Falco,' she said.

She married the ex-Consul; we arranged it the next day. Curtius Gordianus took the auguries and concocted the usual lies about 'good omens for a long contented partnership'. Grief and ill health made Caprenius Marcellus incoherent so it was me who interpreted his marriage vows. No one was so impolite as to ask what occurred on the wedding night; nothing, presumably. Naturally the bridegroom altered his will, leaving everything to his new young wife, and any children they might have. I helped him write his will too.

I never saw Aemilia Fausta again, though I heard of her from time to time. She lived a blameless, vigorously happy life as a widow, and died in the eruption of Mount Vesuvius. Before then Fausta had nursed Marcellus devotedly. He managed to live long enough to know that his estates and the honour of his famous ancestors were both secure: nine months after they were married Aemilia Fausta gave birth to a boy.

I saw her son once, years later. He had survived the volcano and grown into a strapping youth. Someone pointed him out. He was in a chariot, leaning on the front rail with one elbow while he waited patiently for a hold-up in the road ahead to clear. For someone with more money than anyone deserves, he looked a decent lad. He had brown hair, a broad, calm brow and an untroubled expression which seemed vaguely familiar.

His mother had named him Lucius; after Crispus, I suppose.

There was one other event which I cannot omit. It was Bryon who broke the bad news to me. The day after the wedding, I was preparing to leave when Bryon confessed. 'Falco, I know where Pertinax may be.'

'Where? Spit it out!'

'Rome. We had Ferox and the Sweetheart entered in their first race, at the Circus Maximus – '

'Rome!' Rome: where I had sent Helena Justina to be safe.

'I had a word with the new mistress,' Bryon went on. 'She seems to know her mind! Ferox is still to be sent for the race. She also told me, the Consul is making a special bequest to you; he likes you, apparently – '

'You amaze me. What's the gift?'

'Little Sweetheart.' I never have much luck in life, but that was ridiculous. 'Her ladyship says, will you please take him with you when you go?'

Every citizen has the right to decline inconvenient legacies. I nearly declined this.

Still, I could always sell the nag for sausage meat. For all his faults of character, he was well fed and free from visible disease; there were plenty of hot-piemen selling worse things from trays along the Via Triumphalis and in front of the Basilica.

So I kept him and saved my fare home, struggling all the way up the Via Appia on this cock-eyed, knock-kneed, self-willed, pernickety beastie who now was my own.

PART SIX
THE HOUSE
ON THE
QUIRINAL

ROME
August

LXXVI

Rome: the mere hum of the city convinced me Pertinax was here.

Even in August, with half its citizens absent and the air so hot that taking a breath braised your liver and lungs, my return to Rome brought the thump of real life to my veins after Campania's debilitating glare. I soaked in its vivid atmosphere: the temples and fountains, the astonishing height of the gimcrack apartments, the arrogance of the sophisticated slaves who barged along the highroad, the drips on my head where my road dived under the gloom of an aqueduct – stale garments and fresh tempers, a sweet tang of myrrh among the sour reek of brothels, a fresh hint of oregano above the old and indelible reek of the fish market. I throbbed with childish delight to be back in these streets I had known all my life; then I grew more subdued as I recognised the sneer of a city which had forgotten me. Rome had lived through a thousand rumours since I left, none of them concerning me. It greeted my reappearance with the indifference of a slighted dog.

My first problem was disposing of the horse.

My brother-in-law Famia was a horse doctor with the Greens. I won't call it lucky, because nothing that sodden sponge Famia ever did was good news. The last thing I wanted was being forced to beg a favour from one of my relations, but not even I could keep a racehorse in a sixth-floor apartment without arousing adverse comment from other people in the block. Famia was the least obnoxious of the husbands my five sisters had inflicted on our family, and he was married to Maia, who might have been my favourite if she had refrained from marrying him. Maia, who in other respects was as sharp as the copper nails priests bang into temple doors at the new year, never seemed to notice her own husband's disadvantages. Perhaps there were so many she lost count.

I found Famia at his faction's stables, which like all of them were in the Ninth district, the Circus Flaminius. He had high cheekbones with slits where his eyes should be, and was as broad as he was tall, as if he had been squashed from above by a bushel weight. He could tell I was after something when I let him rant for ten minutes about the poor performance of the Blues, whom he knew I supported.

After Famia had enjoyed himself slandering my favourites, I explained my little problem and he inspected my horse.

285

'He a Spaniard?'

I laughed. 'Famia, even I know Spaniards are the best! He's as Spanish as my left boot.'

Famia brought out an apple which Little Sweetheart guzzled eagerly. 'How does he ride?'

'Terrible. All the way from Campania he's been chaffing and chomping, even though I tried to give him a gentle time. I hate this horse, Famia; and the more I hate him, the more affectionate the clod-hoofed fool pretends to be – '

While my horse was eating his apple and belching after it, I took a good look at him. He was a dark-brownish beast, with a black mane, ears and tail. Across his nose, which was always poking in where it wasn't wanted, ran a distinctive mustard band. Some horses have their ears up spry and straight; mine constantly flickered his lugs back and forth. A kind man might have said he looked intelligent; I had more sense.

'You rode him from Campania?' Famia asked. 'That should harden his shins.'

'For what?'

'Running, for instance. Why – what will you do with him?'

'Sell him when I can. But not before Thursday. There is a beauty called Ferox running – worth a flutter, if you ask me – my fool was his stablemate. I've promised their trainer mine can go to the racecourse; they reckon he calms Ferox down.'

'Oh that old story!' Famia responded in his dour way. 'So yours has been declared too?'

'What a joke! I suppose he'll soothe Ferox as far as the starting gates, then be pulled out.'

'Give him an outing,' Famia encouraged. 'What can you lose?'

I decided to do it. There was a good chance Atius Pertinax would turn up to see Ferox perform. Attending the Circus as an owner myself was one way to ensure I could gain access wherever I needed it behind the scenes.

I shouldered my luggage and set off for home. I hauled my stuff round the back of the Capitol, mentally saluting the Temple of Juno Moneta, patron of my much-needed cash. This brought me into the Aventine at the starting-gate end of the Circus Maximus; I paused, thinking briefly of my pathetic nag, and more seriously of Pertinax. By then my bags were dragging on my neck, so I stopped at my sister Galla's house for a rest and a word with Larius.

I had forgotten Galla would be furious about my nephew's future plans.

'You promised to look after him,' she greeted me ferociously. Fending off her younger children, four dedicated scavengers who could instantly spot an uncle who might have presents in his backpack,

I kissed Galla. 'What's that for?' she growled at me. 'If you're looking for dinner there's only tripe!'

'Oh thanks! I love tripe!' Untrue, as all my family knew, but I was ravenous. Tripe was all there ever was at Galla's house. Her street possessed a tripe-and-trotter stall, and she was a lazy cook. 'What's the problem with Larius? I sent him home fit, sane and happy, in possession of a fat little girlfriend who knows what she wants from him – plus a famous reputation for saving drowning men.'

'A fresco painter!' Galla jibed in disgust.

'Why not? He's good at it, it fetches in the money, and he'll always be in work.'

'I might have known if there was a chance of him being pushed into something stupid, I could rely on you! His father,' complained my sister pointedly, 'is *extremely* upset!'

I gave my sister my opinion of the father of her children, and she mentioned that if I felt like that I was not obliged to loaf on her sun terrace eating her food.

Home again! Nothing like it. Spooning in the unctuous offal, I smiled quietly to myself.

Larius turned up, not before I was ready for him, and helped me with my luggage the rest of the way: a chance to talk. 'How was the journey, Larius?'

'We managed.'

'Petronius find it hard going? Is he all right?'

'You know him; he never makes a fuss.'

My nephew seemed rather tight-lipped. 'What about you?' I persisted.

'Nothing worries me either. Are you going to ask about your ladylove?'

'As soon as I have a rest and a trip to the bathhouse I intend to see my ladylove for myself. Why? If there is something I should know first, come out with it!'

Larius shrugged.

We had reached the Ostia Road. I was nearly back on my own midden. I halted in the loggia of a cold-meat shop; it was closed but the smell of smoked hams and preservative herbs lingered tauntingly. I screwed the neckbraid of my nephew's tunic angrily round one hand. 'The word is, Pertinax may have come to Rome. Is it something about him that you don't want to say to me?'

'Uncle Marcus, nothing happened.' He shook me off. 'Helena Justina was unwell some of the time, but Silvia looked after her. Anyone can be a poor traveller – '

I had once journeyed fourteen hundred miles in Helena's calm, uncomplaining company; I knew exactly how good a traveller she was. I felt my mouth twist. I wondered what I had come home to. Then, before I let myself start guessing, I swung up my baggage and started down the narrow alley that led to the old familiar odours of Fountain Court.

After Larius left me, I stood out on my balcony. Our tenement stood halfway up the Aventine Hill, and its one great advantage was a fabulous view. Even when I closed my dry, tired eyes there was plenty to absorb: creaking carts and barking watchdogs; distant cries from river boatmen; leery wineshop choruses and wavering temple flutes; screams from young girls, from either terror or hysterical amusement, it was impossible to tell.

Down there, Rome must be harbouring plenty of fugitives. Men running from their mothers; their debts; their business partners; their own inadequacy. Or like Gnaeus Atius Pertinax Caprenius Marcellus: running from Fate.

LXXVII

I wanted to see Helena, but a small knot of doubt had started tightening inside me.

It was still evening when I took my travel-grimed body for a bathe. The gymnasium I often went to stood near the Temple of Castor; its clients were mostly dining at this hour – decent men who did not object strongly to eating in with their families, or whose idea of entertainment out was a plain three-course meal among old friends with light music and pleasant talk. Glaucus the proprietor would be at home himself by now. I was glad, because Glaucus would certainly make free with snide comments about the havoc two months in Campania had wreaked on my physique. As soon as he saw me he would want to bash me back into shape. I was too tired to let him start tonight.

The bathhouse usually stayed open until after dinnertime. It was well lit, with pottery lamps lining all the corridors, yet at this time of night the place assumed a certain eeriness. There were attendants lurking somewhere who would scrape you with a strigil if you wanted to shout out for them, yet most people who came at dusk managed alone. Many clients were middle-class grafters with proper jobs of work. Designers of aqueduct systems and harbour engineers who sometimes worked late at emergencies on site. An academic type who had lost all sense of time in the library at the Portico of Octavia and then come here stiff and bleary-eyed. Men in trade, arriving from Ostia after an afternoon tide. And one or two offbeat, freelance freaks like me, whose weapon training Glaucus personally supervised and who worked at odd hours for reasons which his other customers politely never asked about.

I left my clothes in the changing room, hardly glancing at the stuff on other pegs. I had a good scrape in the hot room, swilled off, then pushed through the heavy retaining door to relax in the dry steam. Someone else was already there. I nodded. At this hour it was traditional to pass in silence, but as my eyes became accustomed to the humidity I recognised the other man. He was in his fifties, with a pleasant expression. He too was slumped in private thought, but knew me just as I took in his vibrant eyebrows and spiked, boyish hair: Helena's papa.

'Didius Falco!'

'Camillus Verus!'

Our greeting was unforced. He took an affectionate view of my rough-and-ready attitude, and I liked his shrewd good humour. I realigned my exhausted frame alongside.

'You've been in Campania, I heard.'

'Just got back. You're late, Senator!'

'Seeking refuge,' he admitted, with an honest grin. 'I'm glad I've seen you here tonight.'

I lifted an eyebrow, with a definite feeling I was waiting for bad news. 'Something special, sir?'

'Didius Falco, I am hoping,' declared the Senator with significant formality, 'you can tell me who has done me the honour of making me a grandfather.'

A long trickle of perspiration had already started from the damp curls at my hairline; I let it run, slowly across my left temple, then with a sudden rush past my ear, down my neck and onto my chest. It splashed off, onto the towel across my lap.

'Do I take it this is news to you?' the Senator asked levelly.

'True.'

My reluctance to believe that she could keep back something so vital clashed against vivid memories of Helena fainting; unwell; turning back from climbing Vesuvius; worried about money . . . Helena crying in my arms for reasons I had never found out. Then other memories, more intimate and more intense. 'Evidently not my business to know!'

'Ah,' said her father, accepting this bleakly. 'I'll be blunt: my wife and I assumed it was.' I said nothing. He began to look more doubtful. 'Are you denying that it is possible?'

'No.' I never doubted that Camillus Verus had guessed my feelings for his daughter early on. I adopted professional banter as a temporary defence: 'Look, a private informer who leads a lively social life is bound to find women who want more from him than he bargained for. So far I never had any difficulty persuading a magistrate they were vexatious claims!'

'Be serious, Falco.'

I drew a harsh breath. 'I don't suppose you want me to congratulate you, sir. I don't imagine you are congratulating me . . . ' If I sounded irritable, that was because I was starting to burn with a furious sense of injustice.

'Would it be so terrible?'

'Just terrifying!' I said, which was the truth.

The Senator gave me a stressful smile. I already knew he thought enough of me to think that if I was what his daughter wanted, the two of us were capable of managing, even without the usual domestic trappings of money to pay the baker or parental support . . . He dropped a hand onto my arm. 'Have I upset you?'

'Frankly, I'm not sure.'

Camillus then tried to draw me in as his ally. 'Look, there is no point me trying to protest my senatorial rights like some old-fashioned censor. This is not illegal – '

'And it's not helpful!' I exclaimed.

'Don't say that! There was enough harm done when Helena was married to Atius Pertinax; that was a mistake which I have promised myself never to repeat. I want to see her happy.' He sounded desperate. Of course he loved his daughter more than he should – but then, so did I.

'I can't protect her from herself!' I stopped. 'No, that's unfair. She never ceases to amaze me with her clear-eyed good sense – ' Her father started to protest. 'No, she's right, sir! She deserves a better life than she could ever have with me. Her *children* deserve better; as a matter of fact, so do mine! Sir, I can't discuss this.' For one thing, she would hate to know we were doing it. 'Can we change the subject? There is something else we need to consider urgently. You mentioned Atius Pertinax, and he's the crux of it. Have you heard what the situation is?'

He let out an angry expression; Camillus Verus had no time for his son-in-law. Most fathers feel that, but in his case he was right: his daughter *was* too good for the man, who *was* contemptible.

He knew Pertinax was still alive; I warned him that the fugitive might have transferred himself to Rome.

'With hindsight, sending Helena here was none too wise. But I know your views, sir. Until I can apprehend him, will you ensure she stays safe at home?'

'Of course. Well . . . as far as I can. But her condition should stop her rushing about,' he reminded me unavoidably.

I paused. 'Is she well?'

'No one tells me anything,' her father complained. When he spoke of his womenfolk Camillus Verus always adopted a downtrodden pose, as if they took the traditional view of a paterfamilias: someone who was there to pay the bills, make a lot of noise no one listened to – and be led by the nose. 'She looks peaky.'

'Yes, I noticed that.'

We exchanged a tense glance.

We finished our bath together, went through to the changing room and dressed. At the top of the gymnasium steps, we clasped hands. If Helena Justina's father was as shrewd as I suspected, he could tell from my face how bitter I felt.

He hesitated awkwardly. 'Will you be coming to see her?'

'No.' One way or the other, that made me out a sewer rat. A lonely occupation. 'But tell her – '

'Falco?'

'Forget it. Better not.'

The father of his future grandchild should be the happiest man in Rome. What price the pathetic candidate who had it made plain he was not required to acknowledge his position?

Well be reasonable. Nobody could expect such a high-born Roman lady – *father in the Senate, two brothers on active service, adequate education, passable face, property worth a quarter of a million in her own right* – to own up that she had allowed herself a dalliance with a low-bred, uncivilised brigand from the Aventine like me.

LXXVIII

It was late. It would soon be dark. I had the restless feet of a man who needed to visit his ladyfriend but could not bear to go. The obvious alternative was to plough into a wineshop and drink so deep I would only have to worry whether anyone good-natured would point me in a homeward direction afterwards, and if they did, whether I could stagger as far as my apartment or fall down dead drunk in the road.

I went to the Palace instead.

They kept me waiting. I was so angry at Helena's secrecy that for once the last thing I wanted was time to think. I hunched on a couch, growing more and more devastated by the injustice, until I was in two minds to storm off home and get drunk on my own balcony. The moment I decided to do it a flunkey called me in. I could not even enjoy myself getting annoyed because as soon as he saw me Vespasian apologised.

'Sorry, Falco. Matters of state.' Chatting with his concubine, no doubt. 'You look glum!'

'Oh, thinking about women, sir.'

'No wonder then! Want a cup of wine?' I wanted it so badly it seemed safest to decline.

'Enjoy your trip?'

'Well I still get seasick, and I still can't swim . . . '

The Emperor gave me a thoughtful look as if he could tell I was feeling cynical.

I was far too tired, and not in the mood; I made a bodge of narrating my report. Other people, more important people, had told him most of it anyway. Going over the sorry details of how Aufidius Crispus was pointlessly drowned felt like a waste of time.

'The Censor published the news as "an unfortunate boating accident",' the Emperor grumbled angrily. 'Who commanded the trireme that's in need of steering practice?'

'The Herculaneum praetor, sir.'

'Him! He turned up in Rome; I met him yesterday.'

'Showing his profile round the Palace, in the hope of a fancy foreign post! Sextus Aemilius Rufus Clemens – ' I proclaimed. 'Good old family and a wealth of mediocre public service to his name. He's an idiot, but how can he lose? Now Crispus is dead, when it comes to awarding honours I assume this hasty-handed trierarch takes precedence over me?'

'Grit your teeth, Falco: I don't issue contract bonuses when senators get drowned.'

'No, sir. As soon as the ships crashed, I guessed *I* would be slapped down for it!'

'Rufus has been extremely helpful with advice about the fleet,' the Emperor reproved me with his fiercest growl.

'Oh, I can do that, Caesar: the Misenum fleet needs an overhaul: more discipline and less drink!'

'Yes. I had the impression Rufus fancies wielding an admiral's baton himself – ' I was furious, until I caught the Emperor's glint. 'In future the Misenum fleet prefecture is reserved for trusted friends of mine. But I shall certainly give this fellow a chance to prove himself with the perils of command; he must be ready for a legion – '

'What? In a spectacular front-line province where his incompetence can flower more visibly?'

'No, Falco; we all have to accept that a public career involves serving a turn in dismal holes abroad . . . '

I started to grin. 'What have you dug up for Rufus, sir?'

'Somewhere landlocked; that should spare us the benefits of his nautical expertise: Noricum.'

'Noricum!' Crispus' old province. Nothing ever happens there. 'I think Crispus would approve of that!'

'I hope so!' smiled Vespasian, with deceptive gentleness.

Our new Flavian Emperor was not a vindictive man. But one of his attractions was a private sense of fun.

'That all, Falco?'

'All I can hope for,' I croaked wearily. 'I would nag you for a bonus for coercing Gordianus, but we went through that – '

'Not at all. I put you down for it. Is a thousand enough?'

'A thousand! That would be a good reward for an after-dinner poet who had coined a smooth ten-line ode! Rich pickings for a theatre lyre player – '

'Never believe it! Lyre players nowadays demand at least two thousand before they shift offstage. What does a man like you need money for?'

'Bread and a bottle. After that my landlord mostly. Sometimes I dream of changing him. Caesar, even I might like a home where I can turn round to scratch myself without taking the skin off my elbow. I work to live – and my life at the moment distinctly lacks elegance!'

'Women?'

'People always ask me that.'

'I wonder why! My spies tell me,' Vespasian threatened jovially, 'you came back from Campania richer than you went.'

'One duff racehorse and a sacred goat! The goat has gone into retirement but next time you break a molar on a gristly meat rissole, say hello to Falco's horse – Rome is richer too,' I reminded him. 'By a good part of fifteen billion bushels that could have gone astray . . .'

He seemed not to hear me. 'Titus wants to know this horse's name.'

Brilliant. I had only been back in Rome six hours, but news of my ghastly windfall had reached the Emperor's elder son! 'Little Sweetheart. Tell Titus Caesar to save his stake! I'm only running the nag as a favour to the bookmakers, who say they have been short of laughs lately – '

'That's honest for a horse owner!'

'Oh sir, I wish I had the nerve to steal and lie like other people, but conditions in jail are notorious and I'm frightened of the rats. When I want a laugh I tell myself my children will be proud of me.'

'What children?' whipped back the Emperor aggressively.

'Oh Caesar, the ten little Aventine urchins I cannot afford to acknowledge!'

Vespasian shifted his big, square-bodied frame while his brow creased and his mouth compressed in the way he was famous for. I always knew that when his mood altered and he stopped baiting we had reached the crux of the interview. The lord of the world tutted at me gently like a great cuddly uncle who was letting himself forget how much he disapproved of me.

'What you accomplished with the grain ships was excellent. The Prefect of Supply has been requested to report on a suitable level of reward – ' I knew what *that* meant: I would never hear anything about it again. 'I shall give you a thousand for Gordianus – and I'll make that ten if you can also settle Pertinax Marcellus without publicity.'

Miserly; though on Vespasian's scale of public remuneration, madly generous. I nodded.

'Pertinax is officially dead. There will be no need to announce it in the *Daily Gazette* again.'

'What I would really like,' the Emperor suggested, 'is some proof of his guilt.'

'You mean, it may have to come to trial?'

'No. But if we deal with him *without* a trial,' Vespasian commented drily, 'perhaps there is even more reason to have some evidence!'

I was a republican. Finding an Emperor with moral values always startled me.

At this late stage, proof against Pertinax was a near impossibility. The only one of his victims who had ever survived was Petronius Longus and even he had nothing to tell a court. That left as our only material witness Milo, the Gordianus steward. Milo was a slave. Which meant we could only accept *his* evidence if it was extracted under torture.

But Milo was the sort of stupid stalwart whose response to the challenge of a professional torturer would be to grit his teeth, brace his mighty muscles – and die before he broke.

'I shall do my best to find something!' I promised the Emperor solemnly.

He grinned.

I was leaving the Palace, with the sardonic taste of this interview still pursing my mouth, when someone in a doorway greeted me derisively.

'Didius Falco, you disreputable begger! Thought you were wearing yourself out on the women around Neapolis!'

I wheeled cautiously, ever on my guard in the Palace environs, and recognised the grim presence. 'Momus!' The slave overseer who had helped with the dispersal of the Pertinax estate. He seemed grubbier than ever as he grinned through half-toothless gums. 'Momus, the widespread assumption that I fill all my free time fornicating is beginning to get me down! Has somebody been saying something I might want to dispute?'

'Plenty!' he chaffed. 'Your name seems to crop up everywhere these days. Have you seen Anacrites?'

'Should I?'

'Keep your head down,' Momus warned. There was no love lost between him and the Chief Spy; they had different priorities.

'Anacrites never bothered me. Last I saw, he was demoted to book-keeping.'

'Never trust an accountant! He keeps bouncing in saying he wants to examine you about a certain lost consignment of Treasury lead – ' I groaned, though I made sure I did so under my breath. 'The word is that Anacrites has booked a pallet in the name of Didius Falco in a long-term cell in the Mamertine.'

'Don't worry,' I told Momus, as if I believed it. 'I'm in on it. Prison is just a ruse to escape the indignant fathers of all the women I have deceived . . . '

He grinned, and let me go. Pausing only to shout after me, 'By the way, Falco, what's this about a horse?'

'He's called Hard Luck,' I answered. 'By Short Commons, out of Come to Grief! Don't bet on him; he's bound to break a leg.'

I strode out of the Palace on the north side of Palatine Hill. Halfway back to my own sector I passed an open winery. So I changed my mind, turned into it, and got drunk after all.

LXXIX

I was woken by the sound of a very brisk broom.

This told me two things. Someone thought it was their duty to wake me up. And last night I did find my way home. When you fall down in a gutter people leave you there in peace.

I groaned and grumbled a few times, to give warning I might emerge; the broom fell silent huffily. I hauled on a tunic, decided it was dirty, so covered the stains with a second one. I washed my face, rinsed my teeth and combed my hair, all without achieving any improvement in how I felt. My belt was missing and I could only find one boot. I stumbled out.

The woman who made it her business to keep my apartment in order had been working quiet miracles for some time before she started that stuff with the broom. Her familiar black eyes seared me with piercing disgust. She had done the room; next she would tackle me.

'I came to make you breakfast, but it had better be lunch!'

'Hello mother,' I said.

I sat down at the table because my legs were objecting to holding me up. I assured my mother it was good to be home, having a decent lunch prepared for me by my loving ma.

'So you're in trouble again!' snarled my mother, undeceived by flattery.

She fed me lunch while she washed out the balcony. She had found her new bronze bucket for herself. She had also found my spoons.

'Those are nice!'

'A nice person gave them to me.'

'Have you seen her?'

'No.'

'Have you seen Petronius Longus?'

'No.'

'What are you planning today?'

Most men who do my job have the shrewd sense to free themselves from the attentions of their curious family. What client wants to employ an informer who has to tell his mother every time he ventures out?

'Someone to find.' My strength of mind had been weakened by the lunch.

'Why are you so irritable? What do you want this poor fellow for?'

'Murder.'

'Oh well,' sighed my mother. 'There are worse things he could have done!'

I inferred that she meant things done by me.

'On second thoughts,' I muttered, washing the spoon I had eaten my lunch with, then wiping it with a cloth as I had been instructed by Helena, 'I'll go to a wineshop instead!'

I refused to admit to a hangover, but the thought of more liquor did have a vinegary effect on my insides. Belching painfully, I went to visit Petronius.

He was moping at home, still too weak to patrol the streets yet, and fretting that in his absence his deputy was obtaining too much sway among the ranks. The first thing he said was, 'Falco, why is the Palace fraud squad after you?'

Anacrites.

'Misunderstanding about my expenses – '

'Liar! He told me what commodity was named on the warrant.'

'Oh did he?'

'He tried to bribe me!'

'To do what, Petro?'

'Turn you in!'

'If we're talking arrests – '

'Don't be stupid!'

'As a matter of interest, how much did he offer?'

Petronius grinned at me. 'Not quite enough!'

There was no chance that Petronius would ever cooperate with a Palace spy, but Anacrites must be well aware he only had to spread the whisper that there might be money in it and the next time my landlord Smaractus was sending round his rent squad, some penniless runt on an Aventine backstair would think of fingering me. Getting out of this pickle looked likely to involve personal inconvenience of some sort.

'Don't worry,' I said lamely. 'I'll sort it out,' Petronius laughed bitterly.

Arria Silvia came in to supervise us, a penalty of Petro being stuck in his own house. We talked round the subject of their journey home, my own journey, my ludicrous racehorse, and even the hunt for Pertinax, all without mentioning Helena. Only as I was taking my leave did Silvia's patience break: 'Can we assume that you know about Helena?'

'Her father informed me of the situation.'

'The situation!' echoed Silvia, in high old indignation. 'Have you seen her?'

'She knows where to find me if she wants to see me.'

'Oh for heavens' sake, Falco!'

I caught Petro's eye and he said in a low voice to his wife, 'Better leave it. They have their own way of doing things – '

'Hers, you mean?' I grated at them both. 'She told you, I gather?'

'I asked her!' Silvia ranted accusingly. 'Anyone could see the girl is having a terrible time of it – '

I was afraid of that.

'Well think yourselves honoured; she never told me! Before you start condemning me, consider how I feel: there was *no* reason why Helena Justina should keep this to herself! And I know perfectly well why she preferred not to tell me – '

Silvia interrupted in horror, 'You think someone else is the father!'

The thought had never crossed my mind. 'That,' I stated coolly, 'would be one possibility.'

Petronius, who was very straightforward in certain respects, looked appalled. 'You never believe that!'

'I don't know what I believe.'

I did know. What I really thought was worse.

I gave them one last glance as they stood there, both furious, and both allied against me. Then I left.

Convincing myself I might not be this baby's father was insulting to Helena and demeaning to myself. Yet it was easier than the truth: look at what I was. Look at how I lived. I could not blame her for an instant if Helena Justina refused to bear a child of mine.

She had, without me knowing it, already told me what she planned to do. She would 'deal with it'; I could still hear her saying so. That could only mean one thing.

I filled in the rest of that afternoon by accepting I had a hangover, and going home to sleep it off.

LXXX

Lying in bed is never entirely wasted. Somewhere in that void between convincing yourself you are awake and then ages later rousing yourself, I devised a plan for picking up the trail on Pertinax. I dug out a tunic I used to like; it had been mauve once but was now unappealingly light grey. I went to the barber's for a really good shearing. Then, merging anonymously into the throng, I set off.

At the magic hour just before dinner I crossed the Tiber on the Aurelian Bridge. I was alone. No one knew where I was going, or would notice if I failed to return. None of the people who might once have cared to do so would be bothering to remember me tonight. So far, curing a headache had been the most productive aspect of my day.

Days change. In my case, usually for the worse.

Smoke from a thousand bathhouse furnaces drifted across the city. It caught my throat, calling to life the unhappy rasp that was already lurking there. By now, Helena Justina would know I was back in Rome, aware of her plight. Her father was bound to have told her how deeply hurt I felt. As I expected, she made no attempt to contact me. Not even though I had made it easy for her by spending most of the day at home in bed.

Crossing the river, I listened to the ripple of refined applause from a performance in Pompey's theatre – not the ripe jollity of a satyr play or even the gasps and cheers that greet arthritic monkeys on tightropes. Tonight it must be something old, possibly Greek, probably tragic, and definitely reverent. I was glad. It suited my mood to think of other people suffering: three hours of sombre stuff from the chorus, a tight little speech or two from a principal actor fresh out of elocution class, and then, just as you get to the good bit with the blood, your honeyed dates fall down into the row in front, so you have to bend forwards to grab them again before some shopkeeper with enormous buttocks sits back and squashes them – and as you lean down to get them you miss the only excitement in the play . . .

Tough. If you want entertainment, stay in and pick fleas off a cat.

The Aurelian Bridge was not the most straightforward route to where I was going, but tonight was for choosing long ways round and losing my way. Cursing blind beggers. Bumping old grandmothers into the gutter. Stepping in games of draughts chalked on the pavement while the players were still using them. Losing face. Losing grace. Hurting my toe trying to kick a hole in the stubborn travertine parapet of an ancient bridge.

The Transtiberina fills up by night. During the day it disgorges its populace over the river to hawk contaminated pies, damp matches, sinister green necklaces, good-luck charms, curses, the use of the salesman's sister for five minutes in the crypt of the Temple of Isis at half an as a go (and if you catch something incurable, don't be surprised). Even the solemn, dark-eyed children disappear from the streets of their own sector to play their special kind of tag – lifting purses from unwary pockets around the Cattle Market Forum and along the Sacred Way (where nothing is sacred nowadays, though perhaps not much ever was).

At night back they all come, like dark effluent seeping silently into the warrens of the Fourteenth. The thin men swinging armfuls of belts and rugs. The hard-eyed women who fix you with demands for their twisted sprigs of violet or cracked bone amulets. Those children again, with their sad, beautiful, vulnerable expressions – and unexpected catcalls of obscene abuse. By night the Transtiberina swells even more richly with the exotic. Above the warm aura of oriental flavourings rises the murmurous music of foreign entertainments carried on behind barred doors. Hard gambling for small sums, but a lifetime's misery. Casual lechery being served at a high price. The thump of a tabor. The shiver of tiny brass bells. To the walker a shutter swinging stealthily overhead in the dark is as dangerous as the door which flies open abruptly, spilling light, and a manic knifeman, onto the street. Only an informer with the kind of brain disorder that needs his doctor to send him on a six months' sea cruise with a huge bottle of purgatives and a fierce course of exercise, goes into the Transtiberina alone at night.

Still, in I went.

These places never look the same a second time. When I finally found the street I wanted it was as small and as narrow as I remembered, but the wineshop had put two tables outside and in the blank grey walls that faced the alley one or two lockups I had never even noticed during the siesta had now pushed back their wooden fronts for the evening trade. I strolled up to a pastryshop, then leaned against its awning pole as I gnawed my way through a hunk of their handiwork and considered the deadly stodginess of foreign cakes. It was spherical, about half the size of my fist; it had the hard-packed consistency of my sister Junia's home-made meatballs, but all the flavour of an old horse-blanket. As it went down, which it did very slowly, I could feel my startled guts expressing moral outrage every inch of the way. I could have dumped it in a drain, but it might have caused a blockage. Anyway, my mother had brought me up to hate wasting food.

I had plenty of time to pretend I was chewing through my sweet-meat, savouring one or two little hard bits that were either nuts or well-roasted woodlice who had sidled into the cake dough. Mean-while I discreetly eyed up the first-floor window of the room which the so-called freedman Barnabas had once leased.

The window was too small and the housewalls were too thick to see much, but I could just make out the shadow of at least one person moving about inside. An unusual stroke of luck.

I was licking my fingers when the street door opened suddenly and two men came out. One was a chatty scallywag with an inkpot hung on his belt who looked like a scribe on piecework. The other, ignoring his companion's flow of natter as he glanced surreptitiously up and down the alley, was Pertinax.

He had learned to look around him, though not to see; if I was near enough to recognise him – the light, ruffled hair and the pinched nostrils in that agitated face – then even in a scalped hairstyle and a new-coloured tunic he should have known me too.

On the threshold they shook hands and went their separate ways. I let the inkpot pass me, heading off the way I had come myself, then I prepared to go after Pertinax. It was lucky I was slow. Two men who had been playing a sluggish game of soldiers at one of the tables outside the wineshop pushed away the board and counters and then stood up. Before Pertinax reached the streetcorner, they also began to move – after him, and just ahead of me. They too separated: one speeded up until he overtook Pertinax while the other loitered behind. As the man who was dawdling reached the corner he met another quiet figure in the wider street beyond. With sudden intuition I had stepped into a doorway. When numbers two and three joined forces I was near enough to overhear their low exchange.

'There he goes. Critus is front marker – '

'Any luck with Falco?'

'No, I wore myself out checking his haunts, then heard he had spent all day at home – I missed him. I'll stick with you; the simplest way to catch Falco is with this one as bait – '

The back markers split up to opposite sides of the street and went on again. These must be Anacrites' men. I let them all go.

An added complication. Now I would have to make Pertinax aware that he was being tailed. Unless I could persuade him to shake off his Palace minders, there was no way I could get at him without being arrested myself.

All in all, it seemed an ideal moment for another drink.

LXXXI

At night the wineshop had a packed, rancid atmosphere. Its customers were paviours and stokers, muscular men in their working tunics who had big thirsts and shed their sweat readily once they sat still. I moved in among them extremely politely, edging my way past brawny backs to the counter. I ordered a flagon from the ugly old madam, and said I would wait outside. As I guessed, it was the daughter who came out with it.

'What's a pretty girl like you doing in this shack?'

Tullia gave me the smile she kept for strangers as she organised the jug and beaker from her tray. I had forgotten how attractive this wineshop barmaid was. Her huge dark eyes looked at me sideways, assessing whether I might be susceptible, while I seriously wondered too. But tonight I stayed cold, with a lean core of sadness: the sort of sinister fish flirty girls who know their business alway avoid.

Tullia knew; as she flounced off I grasped her dainty wrist.

'Don't go; stay here with me!' She laughed, with practised artistry, trying to buff me off. 'Sit down, sweetheart – ' She peered at me closer to see how drunk I was, then recognised I was manically sober.

'Hello, Tullia!' Alarmed, her eyes went to the curtained doorway for help. 'I've lost something, Tullia; has anybody handed in a large green cameo ring?' She remembered why she knew me. She remembered I might not be in a healthy mood. 'The name's Falco,' I reminded her softly. 'I want to talk. If you call out your big friends, you will find yourself over the river, having this chat with the Praetorian Guards instead. *I* have the advantage that I quite like pretty girls. The Praetorians are famous for not liking anyone.'

Tullia sat down. I grinned at her. She was not reassured.

'What do you want, Falco?'

'Same as the last time. I'm looking for Barnabas.'

Someone looked out of the doorway. I reached for an empty cup from another table and with a comfortable expansiveness poured Tullia a drink. The head disappeared.

'He's away,' Tullia tried, her tone too guarded for it to be the truth.

'That's interesting. I knew he went to Croton and Cape Colonna – ' I could tell these place names were new to her. 'Then he picked up the same sunny glow as me in Campania. I noticed the tan when he went out just now, but I'm not keen on talking to him in the presence of a group of Palace spies.'

The fact that 'Barnabas' was in trouble did not surprise the barmaid in the least. That his trouble involved the Palace frightened her.

'You're lying, Falco!'

'Why should I? Better warn him, if he's a friend of yours.' She looked shifty. I weighed in at once. 'Are you and Barnabas keeping company?'

'Perhaps!' she said defiantly.

'Regular?'

'Maybe.'

'More fool you!'

'What does that mean, Falco?' From the narrow way Tullia asked this I could see I had caught her interest.

'I hate to see a beautiful woman throw herself away! What has he promised you?' She said nothing. 'I can guess! You go along with it? No. You look as if you've learned by now not to trust anything you hear from men.'

'I don't trust you either, Falco!'

'I knew you were intelligent.'

With a shimmer of cheap earrings Tullia fetched a light from the other table so she could watch me more closely. She was a tall girl, with a figure which in a better mood would be a pleasure to watch.

'He's not serious,' I warned.

'He offered to marry me!'

I whistled. 'He's got taste! So why the doubts?'

'I think he has another woman,' Tullia announced, leaning on her pretty elbows and fixing me.

I thought about his other woman in an offhand way. 'Could be. There was someone in Campania he was hanging round.' I fought to keep my face neutral. 'I suppose if you asked him he would only deny it – unless you had some evidence . . . Why don't you do some detective work? Now he's out,' I suggested, 'you could investigate his room. I dare say you know how to get in?'

Naturally Tullia knew.

We crossed the street together and climbed sordid stairs which hung together merely by a lath or two. As we went up my nostrils clenched against the stench of a huge unemptied nightsoil vat in the well of the building. Somewhere a heart-broken baby wailed. The door to the Pertinax apartment had shrunk in the summer heat so it hung aslant on its hinges and needed to be lifted bodily.

The room was bare of character, partly because unlike his Campanian hayloft no one had filled this with artefacts for him, and partly because he had no personality anyway. There was a bed with one faded coverlet, a stool, a small cane table, a broken coffer – all stuff that came with the room. Pertinax had added only the normal filthy plate he lived with when there was nobody to wait on him, a pile of empty amphorae, another pile of laundry, a pair of extremely expensive boots with the mud of that farm on Vesuvius still unscraped on their toestraps, and some open baggage packs. He was living out of his luggage, probably from idleness.

In my helpful way I offered to look round. Tullia hovered in the doorway, keeping a nervous eye out for movements below.

I found two interesting items.

The first was lying on the table with the ink barely dry – documents drawn up that evening by the scribe I had seen with Pertinax. I replaced the parchment wretchedly. Then, because I was a professional I continued to search. All the usual hiding places appeared to be empty: nothing under the mattress or the floor's uneven planking, nothing buried in the dry soil of the flowerless window box.

But deep in the empty coffer my hand found something Pertinax must have forgotten. I nearly missed it myself, but I was bending low, taking my time. I brought out a huge iron key.

'What's that?' whispered Tullia.

'Not certain. But I can find out.' I straightened up. 'I'll take this. Now we'd better go.'

Tullia blocked my path. 'Not until you tell me what that writing is.'

Tullia could not read; but she had realised from my grim face that it was significant.

'It's two copies of a document, as yet unsigned – ' I told her what they were. She went pale, then she reddened with anger.

'Who for? Barnabas?'

'That is not the name the scribe has written. But you're right; it's for Barnabas. I'm sorry, sweetheart.'

The barmaid's chin lifted angrily. 'And who is the woman?' I told her that too. 'The one from Campania?'

'Yes, Tullia. I'm afraid so.'

What we had found was a set of marriage certificates, prepared for Gnaeus Atius Pertinax and Helena Justina, the daughter of Camillus Verus.

Well a girl does need a husband, as the lady said.

LXXXII

'Is she attractive?' Tullia forced herself to ask me as we hurried down into the dark little street.

'Money always is.' Pausing to check for observers, I asked nonchalantly, 'What was *his* attraction – good in bed?'

Tullia laughed derisively. I took a deep, happy breath.

Safely in the gloom of the wineshop, I grasped the girl by her shoulders. 'If you decide to ask him about this, make damn sure you have your mother with you!' Tullia was staring at the ground stubbornly. She probably knew already that he could be violent. 'Listen, he'll tell you he has a reason for that document – '

Abruptly she looked up. 'Getting the money he talks about?'

'Princess, all Barnabas can ever get now is a freedman's grave.' She might not believe me, but at least she was listening. 'He will tell you he was married to this woman once, and needs her help to acquire a large legacy. Don't fool yourself; if he ever gets the legacy, there's no future for you!' The barmaid's eyes took on an angry glint. 'Tullia, he already has an Imperial posse tailing him – and he's rapidly running out of time.'

'Why, Falco?'

'Because according to the Encouragement of Matrimony laws, a woman who stays single more than eighteen months after divorce *cannot* receive legacies! If he wants to inherit anything using his ex-wife, he'll have to move fast.'

'So when were they divorced?' Tullia demanded.

'No idea. Your friend with his eyes on the cash was the husband; better ask him!'

Having laid my bait, I nodded farewell and pushed through the brawny clientele to the outer door. Outside, two customers had come across my abandoned flagon and promptly tucked in. I was all set to express my indignation when I noticed who they were. At the same moment the two freebooters, who were Anacrites' watchdogs, recognised me.

I backed indoors, gestured expressively to Tullia, then barged through the crush and opened the door she had used to let me out when I had been there before.

Ten seconds later the spies burst indoors after me. They stared round wildly, then spotted the open door. The paviours parted tolerantly to let them run over there, then closed once more into an impenetrable pack.

I hopped up from behind the counter, waved at Tullia, and skipped out the front way: the oldest dodge in the world.

I made sure I disappeared by a route that would avoid spy number three if he was back in the main street.

When I tramped across the river again it was too late to do any more. The first rush of delivery carts was already petering out; the streets were busy with waggons of wine barrels, marble blocks and fish-pickle jars, but the initial frenzy that always occurs after curfew had passed. Rome was becoming more watchful as late-night diners braved the dark byways to go home, accompanied by yawning torch-bearers. An occasional solitary walker sneaked through the shadows, trying to avoid attention in case robbers or deviants were breathing nearby. Where there had been lanterns hung on loggias they were now flickering out – or being doused deliberately by housebreakers who wanted a dark run home later with their swag.

It seemed probable that my own apartment was being watched by the Chief Spy, so I went to my sister Maia's house. She was a better provider than any of the others, and better tempered with me. Even so it was a mistake. Maia greeted me with the news that Famia would be really glad to see me, because he had brought home to dinner the jockey he had persuaded to ride my horse in Thursday's race.

'We had calf's brain custard; there's some left, if you're interested,' Maia informed me. More offal! Maia had known me long enough to know what I thought about that. 'Oh for heavens' sake, Marcus, you're worse than the children! Cheer up and enjoy yourself for once . . . '

I threw myself into it with all the jollity of Prometheus, chained to his rock on the mountainside, watching for the daily raven to fly in and peck his liver out.

The jockey was of previously unblemished character, but that didn't mean much. He was a tick. And he thought I was his new sheep. But I was used to brushing off parasites; the jockey was in for a surprise.

I forget what his name was. I made a point of forgetting. All I do remember is that he and that wastrel Famia expected me to pay far too much for the runt's pitiful services, and that considering I was giving him a chance to ride his heart out in the city's premier stadium, with Titus Caesar in the president's box, it ought to have been the jockey who paid me. He had a mean size, and a seamed, truculent face; he drank too much, and from the way he kept looking at my sister, he expected the women to drop at his feet.

Maia ignored him. One thing I could say about my youngest sister was that unlike most women having made one ghastly mistake in life at least she stuck with it. Once she married Famia, she never felt the necessity to complicate her problems by having crass affairs.

Fairly early on in the process of allowing the jockey to drink Famia and me out of pocket I disgraced myself. I had been sent to fetch a wine flask, but I slipped off to see the children. They were supposed to be in bed, but I found them playing chariots. Maia was bringing up her children to be surprisingly good-natured; they could see I had reached the flushed and niggly stage, so they lured me into the game for a while and one told me a story until I nodded off, then they all tiptoed out leaving me fast asleep. I swear I heard Maia's eldest daughter whisper, 'He's settled! Doesn't he look sweet . . . '

She was eight. A sarcastic age.

I had originally intended to hole up at Maia's until any spies had gone home to their own sleazy burrows, then slide back to the Falco residence. I should have done it. I shall never know whether anything would have been different if I did. But there must be a chance that if I had gone to my own apartment that night instead of bedding down at my sister's, it would have saved a life.

LXXXIII

August.

Sultry nights and steamy tempers. A few hours later I was awake again, too hot and too wretched to relax. A bad time of year for men with troubled spirits and women who were enduring difficult pregnancies. I thought about Helena, making my heartache worse as I wondered whether she too was lying sleepless in this sticky heat, and if so, whether she was thinking of me.

Next morning I woke late. Maia kept a peaceful house.

Tossing all night in my clothes never bothered me. But I had taken against the washed-out tunic I'd put on yesterday. I became obsessed with the hope of changing this dull rag for a livelier shade of grey.

Since I could not risk colliding with Anacrites' scabs at my apartment, I persuaded my sister to go there instead.

'Just call in at the laundry. Don't go up; I don't want them to follow you home. But Lenia's bound to have some clothes of mine to collect – '

'Give me the money to settle your account then,' ordered Maia, who had a good understanding of the customer relations Lenia enjoyed with me.

Maia was gone a long time. I went out in yesterday's tunic anyway.

My first task was to check with the Censor the date of Helena's divorce. The record office was closed because it was a public holiday, a frequent menace in Rome. I knew the watchman, who was used to me turning up out of hours; he let me in by the side entrance for his usual modest fee.

The document I wanted must have been deposited early last year, because afterwards Helena had gone to Britain to forget about her failed marriage, which was where she met me. Knowing that, I found the paperwork in an hour. My wild stab had been unerringly accurate: Helena Justina had shed her husband eighteen months ago. If Pertinax wanted her to marry him within the time limit for inheritance, he had just three days left.

Next I walked around the Aventine, hunting for the man who might identify the big iron key I found hidden in that chest. This was my own sector, though among one-man byways where I rarely went. Eventually

I bumped round a corner where some slack-mannered basket weaver had piled giant hampers and panniers all over the pavement, lethal to passers-by. I stubbed my toe on the kerb while I was looking out for the antisocial caneware, then came across a fountain where a river god was contemplating the sad rivulets that trickled from his navel as morosely as he had been three months before. Kneeling in the lichen, I scooped up a drink then started banging on doors.

When I found the right apartment, its burly, black-bearded occupant was at home, relaxing after lunch.

'I'm Didius Falco. We met once . . . ' He did remember me. 'I'm going to show you something. I want to know where it belongs. But only tell me if you feel sure enough to repeat it in a court of law.'

I produced the iron key. The man held it in one hand and gave due consideration before he spoke. It was nothing special: the straight sort, with a large oval handloop and three plain teeth of even lengths. But my potential witness ran his forefinger over a faintly scratched letter 'H' which I had noticed myself on the widest part of the stem. Then he looked up, with those deep, dark, beautiful oriental eyes.

'Yes,' said the priest of the Little Temple of Hercules Gaditanus sadly. 'That is our missing Temple key.'

At last: hard evidence.

Seeing the priest wiping off his beard with a dinner napkin reminded me I was short of sustenance myself. I had a bite in a cookshop, then strolled along the river walk, thinking about my discoveries. By the time I returned to Maia's house I was more optimistic.

Maia had been to Lenia's, come home for lunch, then vanished to visit my mother, but she had left a bundle of my garments, most of which I recognised dismally; these were all the tunics I had never bothered to pick up from the laundry because they had sleeves unstitched or lamp-oil burns. The most decent was the one I had worn when I disposed of the warehouse corpse. I had dumped it on Lenia afterwards, where it had been waiting to be paid for ever since.

I sniffed at it, then pulled myself into the tunic, and was pondering my next move against Pertinax when Maia came home.

'Thanks for the clothes! Was there any change?'

'Comedian! By the way, Lenia said somebody keeps trying to find you – and since the message is from a woman, about an assignation, you may want to know – '

'Sounds promising!' I grinned cautiously.

'Lenia said . . . ' Maia, who was a pedantic messenger, prepared a faithful recitation. '*Will you meet Helena Justina at the house on the Quirinal because she has agreed to talk to her husband and wants to meet you there?*' Are you working on a divorce?'

'No such luck,' I said, with foreboding. 'When am I go to?'

'That could be a snag – the servant mentioned this morning. I would have told you at lunchtime, but you weren't here – '

I spat a short exclamation, then shot from my sister's house without waiting to kiss her, thank her for yesterday's custard, or even explain.

The Quirinal Mount where Pertinax and Helena had lived when they were married was unfashionable, though people who rented apartments in this pleasant, airy district were rarely doing so badly as they complained. While Vespasian was still a junior politician his youngest child Domitian, the scorpion's sting in the Emperor's success, had been born in a back bedroom in Pomegranate Street; later the Flavian family mansion had been there before they fixed up a palace for themselves.

I felt odd, coming back to the place where I had worked thinking Pertinax was dead. Odd, too, that Helena regarded her old home as neutral ground.

Since our house clearance, the building itself remained unsold. It was what Geminus would call a property 'waiting for the right client'. By which he meant, too big, too expensive, and with a nasty reputation for harbouring ghosts.

How true.

There was a porter from the Palace payroll whom I had installed to guard the mansion until its freehold was transferred. I expected him to be fast asleep at the back of the house, but he answered my urgent banging almost at once. My heart fell: that probably meant he had been roused from his normal slumbers by previous activity today.

'Falco!'

'Has a man called Pertinax been?'

'I knew he was trouble! He claimed to be a buyer – '

'Oh Jupiter! I told you to keep out passing speculators – is he still here?'

'No, Falco – '

'When was it?'

'Hours ago – '

'With a lady?'

'Came separately – '

'Just tell me she didn't leave with Pertinax.'

'No, Falco . . . '

I squatted on the porter's stool, held my temples until my temper cooled, then made him go calmly through what had occurred.

First Pertinax himself had conned admission. He started walking round quietly, just like a prospective purchaser, so since there was nothing to steal the porter left him to it. Then Helena arrived. She asked after me, but came in without waiting.

At that point she and Pertinax seemed like a couple – probably, the porter deduced, virtual strangers whose marriage their relations had recently arranged. They walked upstairs, where the porter heard them arguing – nothing out of the ordinary when two people view a house: one always loves the outlook while the other hates the amenities. My man kept his head down, until he heard voices more sharply raised. He found Helena Justina in the atrium, looking badly shaken, while Pertinax was bellowing at her from the landing above. She ran out straight past the porter. Pertinax rushed after her, but at the street door he changed his mind.

'Did he see something?'

'The lady was talking to a senator outside. The senator could see she was upset; he helped her into her chair, urging the bearers to hurry – '

'Did he go with her?'

'Yes. Pertinax hung in the doorway, muttering, until he saw them leave together, then he made off too – '

My first thought was that the senator must have been Helena's father, but I learned differently almost at once. Violent knocks announced Milo, the dog-taming steward.

'Falco – at last!' Milo gasped, out of breath despite his fitness. 'I've been looking for you everywhere – Gordianus wants you at our house urgently – '

We wheeled out of the Pertinax house. Gordianus also had a mansion on the Quirinal; on the way Milo told that the Chief Priest had brought himself to Rome, still out for vengeance from his brother's murderer. Since the Quirinal was such a respectable district, after last night's sticky heat Gordianus had risked an unattended morning stroll. He had spotted Pertinax; followed him; watched Helena arrive; then saw her rush out. All Milo could tell me was that immediately afterwards Gordianus himself took her home.

'You mean to his house?'

'No. To hers – '

I stopped dead.

'When his own, with all his servants, was only three blocks away? He, a senator, walked all across the city to the Capena Gate? Why the urgency? Why was the lady so distressed? Was she ill? Was she hurt?' Milo had not been told. We were within sight of the street where he said Gordianus lived, but I exclaimed, 'No, this is bad news, Milo! Tell your master I shall come and see him later - '

'Falco! Where are you rushing off to?'

'The Capena Gate!'

LXXXIV

That nightmare journey all across Rome took another hour.

I planned the best route I could round the southern side of the Palatine, though it meant clambering through the grounds of Nero's Golden House. The Golden House was in limbo – too extravagant for the Flavians – so I found a whole convention of surveyors crowding the lake area, trying to decide what our respectable new Emperor should do with it. Vespasian himself had a grand idea that this prime site should be returned to the people, the Flavians' gift to Rome for all posterity . . . So here were the designers, about to wish on us a fifteen-year construction site for their new city amphitheatre. The last thing I wanted as I struggled to reach the Camillus house was having my way impeded by a swarm of dreary architects in peculiar-coloured tunics, planning yet another forgettable Imperial monument. It strikes me the happy Roman mortar mixer who developed the use of concrete has a lot to answer for.

At last I reached the peace of the Capena Gate. As usual, the door porter refused to let me in.

I argued; he shrugged. He looked like a king and I felt like a lout. He stood inside; I stayed out on the step.

By then I was so hot after my gallop, and so anxious, that I grabbed the young pervert by the front of his tunic, then flung him against the doorpost and banged my way in. Falco: ever ready with the subtle touch.

'If you know what's good for you, sonny, you'll learn to recognise the friends of the house!'

A sharp female voice demanded what the commotion was. I was whisked into a reception room, face to face with the noble Julia Justa, the Senator's highly irritated wife.

'I apologise for breaking in,' I said tersely. 'There seems no other way I can pay my respects – '

Helena Justina's mother and I had failed to strike up a friendship. What I found most unnerving (since, to put it bluntly, her mother did not like me) was that where Helena had inherited expressions and intonations from her father, her looks came from her mother's side. It was always odd to see the same intelligent eyes as hers viewing me so differently.

I noticed that Julia Justa, who was a well-dressed, well-mannered woman, with a face that had benefited from the best oils and cosmetics a millionaire's wife could buy, looked pale and strained today She also appeared to have some problem deciding what to say to me.

'If,' began Helena's mother slowly, 'you are visiting my daughter – '

'Look – I heard something that disturbed me; is Helena all right?'

'Not entirely.' We were both standing. The room seemed incredibly stuffy; I was finding it hard to breathe. 'Helena has lost the child she was expecting,' her mother said. Then she regarded me with a pinched expression, uncertain what to expect from me – yet certain it would be something she did not like.

It was quite unacceptable to turn my back on the wife of a senator in her own home, but I took a swift interest in a dolphin statuette that served as a lamp. I never like other people seeing my emotions until I have inspected them for myself.

The dolphin was a slick little clown, but my silence was worrying him. I returned my formal attention to the Senator's wife.

'So, Didius Falco! What have you to say about this?'

'More than you think.' My voice sounded tinny, as if I had spoken into a metal vase. 'I'll say it to Helena. May I see her?'

'Not at present.'

She wanted me out of the house. Good manners and a bad conscience both dictated a speedy departure. I never had much truck with good manners: I decided not to shift.

'Julia Justa, will you tell Helena I am here?'

'I cannot, Falco – the doctor has given her a strong sleeping draught.'

I said in that case I had no wish to inconvenience anyone, but unless Julia Justa vividly objected I would wait.

Her mother agreed. She could probably see that if they put me out of doors I would only cause speculation among their noble neighbours by lurking out in the street like a seedy creditor.

I waited three hours. They forgot I was there.

Eventually, the door opened.

'*Falco!*' Helena's mother surveyed me, startled at my sticking power. 'Somebody should have seen to you – '

'Nothing I wanted, thanks.'

'Helena is still asleep.'

'I can wait.'

At my grim tone, Julia Justa came further into the room. I answered her curious gaze with a hard, bitter stare of my own.

'Madam, was today's event an accident of nature, or did your doctor give your daughter something to help things along?'

The lady considered me with Helena's own angrily perturbed dark eyes. 'If you know my daughter, you know the answer to that!'

'I do know your daughter; she is extremely sensible. I also know

Helena Justina would not be the first unmarried mother who had a solution to her predicament wished on her!'

'Insulting her family will not help you to find out!'

'Excuse me. I've spent a long time thinking. Always a bad idea.'

Julia Justa let slip a slight sigh of impatience. 'Falco, this is achieving nothing; why are you still here?'

'I have to see Helena.'

'I must tell you, Falco – she never asked for you!'

'Did she ask for anyone else?'

'No.'

'Then no one else will be offended if I wait.'

Then Helena's mother said that if I felt so strongly I had better see Helena now, so that for everybody's sake I could go home.

It was a small room, the one she had had as a child. It was neat, and convenient, and when she had returned to her father's house after her divorce she must have asked for it back because it was nothing like her grand apartment in the Pertinax house.

In a narrow bed, under a natural linen coverlet, Helena lay motionless. She was drugged so deeply there was no chance of waking her. Her face looked completely colourless and plain, still in the exhaustion of her physical ordeal. With other women in the room I felt unable to touch her, but the sight of her dragged out of me, 'Oh they should not have done this to her! How can she know anyone is here?'

'She was in pain; she needed rest.'

I fought against the thought that she might need me. 'Is she in danger?'

'No,' her mother said, more quietly.

Still sensitive to atmosphere, I noticed that the white-faced maid who was sitting on a coffer had been crying earlier. I found myself asking, 'Will you tell me the truth; did Helena want the child?'

'Oh yes!' her mother answered immediately. She disguised her annoyance, but I glimpsed the bad feeling that must have surged around this family before today. Helena Justina would make no one an easy relative; she did everything in her own stubborn high-minded way. 'That may have placed you in a difficult position,' Julia Justa suggested to me in a thin voice. 'So this must be quite a relief?'

'You seem to have me well weighed up!' I answered narrowly.

I wanted Helena to know that I had been with her today.

I had nothing else to leave, so I tugged off my signet ring and laid it on the silver tripod table at the side of her bed. Between the pink-glass water beaker and a scatter of ivory hairpins, my worn old ring with its dirty red stone and greenish metal looked an ugly chunk, but at least she would notice it and know whose grimy hand she had seen it on.

'Don't move that, please.'

'I shall tell her you came!' Julia Justa protested reprovingly.

'Thank you,' I said. But I left the ring.

Her mother followed me from the room.

'Falco,' she insisted, 'it *was* an accident.'

I would believe what I heard from Helena herself. 'So what happened?'

'Is it your business, Falco?' For an ordinary woman – or so she seemed to me – Julia Justa could pack a simple question with heavy significance. I let her decide. She went on stiffly, 'My daughter's ex-husband asked to meet her. They quarrelled. She wanted to leave; he tried to stop her. She broke free, slipped, and hurt herself running downstairs – '

'So this is down to Pertinax!'

'It may well have happened anyway.'

'Not like this!' I burst out.

Julia Justa paused. 'No.' For a moment we seemed to have stopped sniping. Her mother agreed slowly, 'The violence certainly increased Helena's distress . . . Were you intending to come again?'

'When I can.'

'Well that's generous!' cried the Senator's wife. 'Didius Falco, you arrived a day after the festival; I gather that is usual for you – never around when you're really wanted. Now I suggest you stay away.'

'There may be something I can do.'

'I doubt it,' said Helena's mother. 'Now this has happened, Falco, I imagine that my daughter will be quite content if she never sees you again!'

I saluted the Senator's wife graciously, since a man should always be good-mannered to a mother of three children (especially when she has just made a highly dramatic statement about the eldest and sweetest of her children – and he intends to insult her later by proving her wrong).

Then I left the Camillus house, remembering how Helena Justina had begged me not to kill Pertinax. And knowing that when I found him, I probably would.

LXXXV

I walked straight to the Transtiberina and up to his room. I was completely unarmed. It was stupid. But all his personal property had gone; so had he.

Across the street the wineshop was doing a hectic trade, but with a stranger serving. I asked after Tullia and was brusquely informed: 'Tomorrow!'; the waiter could hardly find time to account for her. Men were always calling for Tullia, I expect.

I left no message; no one would bother telling that busy young lady that yet another healthy male with a hopeful expression had been hanging round for her.

After that I spent a lot of time walking. Sometimes I was thinking; sometimes I just walked.

I crossed back to the city, pausing on the Aemilian Bridge. Downstream, the desultory river slapped past the triple peperino arch of the main exit from the Great Sewer. At some time in the past three months a bloated corpse, for which I had responsibility, must have swirled out down there, anonymous amidst the dark storm water that carried him away. And now . . . Did you know, only emperors and stillborn babies have the right to be buried in Rome? Not that it would have been relevant for our poor scrap of life. I had a wry idea what informal arrangements were made for the relics of early miscarriages. And perhaps if I had been a different man, with a less neutral view of the gods, I might have heard in the sound of the Tiber lapping past the Cloaca Maxima the cruel, punishing laughter of the Fates.

Hours after I had left the Transtiberina I turned up at Maia's house. She took one look at me, then fed me, kept away the children, kept away Famia with his wine flask, and steered me to bed. I lay in the darkness, thinking again.

When I could bear no more, I let myself sleep.

Pertinax could be anywhere in Rome but the next day was Thursday, and Thursday marked his champion's run in the Circus Maximus; I knew where to find him then – somewhere among the two hundred thousand spectators who would be cheering Ferox on: *Easy!*

Famia, who liked to enjoy an occasion by making himself sick with excitement from the crack of dawn, tried to drag me out early, but if

I spent all morning in the full glare of the stadium, I would be useless for anything. Once you have seen one opening procession winding into the arena, you can miss a few. What's another presiding magistrate with a smug expression leading the parade in his four-horse quadriga, when there are men to catch who murder priests, batter fathers of young families, and cut off the lives of unborn children before their parents have even had a chance to quarrel over what their names might be?

When I left my sister Maia's house, I took a detour by way of Galla's where luckily I found Larius.

'Excuse me, young sir, I want a hack artist!'

'Be quick then,' he grinned. 'We all have to go to the Circus to cheer a certain horse . . . '

'Spare me the honour! Look, do me a thumbnail sketch – '

'You modelling for a grotesque medallion on a Celtic drinking pot?'

'Not me.' I told him who. Then I told him why. Larius drew the portrait without another word.

The loss of the unborn is a private grief. To lighten the atmosphere I ragged him not to waste his money gambling on my horse. 'Don't worry,' agreed Larius frankly. 'We'll cheer yours – but the cash is on Ferox today!'

I walked to the Capena Gate. No one in the Camillus family was receiving visitors. I sent in my respects, with the distinct feeling the door porter would not deliver them.

I noticed a flowershop, so purchased a huge bunch of roses at an equally imposing cost.

'They came from Paestum!' wheezed the florist, excusing it.

'They would do!' I cried.

I sent in the roses for Helena. I knew very well that she would rather have had a flower I grew on my balcony, since she was a sentimentalist, but her mother looked like a woman who would appreciate the cost of a grand bouquet.

Helena must have been awake now but I was still refused admission. I left, with nothing but the memory of her white face yesterday.

Since nobody loved me I went to the races.

I arrived at noon; the athletics were on. Filling the outer vaults was the usual scene of deplorable commerce, a strange contrast to the delicacy of the paintings and gilt decoration which adorned the stucco and the stonework under the arcades. In the cookshops and liquor stalls the hot pies were lukewarm and greasy, and the cool drinks came in very small containers at twice the price you would pay outside. The loose women were plying for hire noisily, vying with the bookies' touts for spectators who were still trickling in.

Only I could attempt to snare a villain in the largest stadium in Rome. I entered by one of the gates on the Aventine side. I had the president's box on my far left above the starting gates, the glittering imperial balcony immediately opposite me against Palatine Hill, then the apsidal end with the triumphal exit away to my right. The dazzle off the first two tiers of marble seats was sizzling hot by then, and even in the lull at lunchtime I was met by a wall of sound.

In the old days, when men and women sat higgledy-piggledy together and the Circus Maximus was the best place to find a new love affair, I would have stood no chance of finding anyone without his seat number. Even now that the Augustan regulations had segregated people respectably, the only rows I could eliminate for certain were those allocated to women, boys with their tutors, or the priestly colleges. It was a fair bet Pertinax would not risk taking his place on the lower podium, where fellow senators would recognise him. And knowing what a snob he was, he would avoid the top gallery, which was frequented by the lowest orders and slaves. Even so, the Circus filled the whole valley between the Cattle Market Forum and the old Capena Gate; it could seat a quarter of a million, not to mention the hordes of auxiliary workers busily toing and froing on legitimate tasks, the aediles looking for bad behaviour in the crowd, the pickpockets and pimps keeping an eye out for the aediles, the perfumesellers and garland girls and wine toters and nut merchants.

I did start to work along one block, scanning the crowds as I fought round the gangway which divided the first and second of the three tiers of seats. Staring up sideways soon made me dizzy, and the massed faces merged into one indistinguishable blur.

This was no way to find a bug in a sack of barley. I nipped down the next stairway back into the arcades, then passed among the booths and the knots of prostitutes, showing everyone the little plaque Larius had drawn for me. When I reached the business end of the stadium I found Famia, who introduced various other people to whom I also exhibited my sketch of Pertinax.

After that the only decent thing was to make a show of inspecting my brother-in-law's efforts to turn out my racehorse handsomely.

With his tail tied high and his ragged mane plaited, Little Sweetheart looked as good as he ever would, though still a disaster. Famia had found him a saddlecloth, though he would have to manage without the gold fringes and pearl-encrusted breastbands his rivals were tricked out in. To Famia's disgust, I insisted that even though he was bound to lose sensationally, if this was the only time in my life I could field my own racehorse, I would run the Sweetheart for the Blues; Famia made a stink, but I was adamant.

Ferox looked a million in his glossy mulberry coat; you could shave in his flanks. He was attracting plentiful attention as he and the Sweetheart waited side by side in the Cattle Market Forum; the buzz among the bookmakers was scintillating. Ferox would be running in the colours of the Marcellus-Pertinax faction, the Whites.

I acted up as an owner for a while, allowing the punters to jibe at me for the faith they assumed I placed in my gangling scruff, then Famia and I went off for lunch.

'You betting, Falco?'

'Just a flutter.'

Famia would think it bad form for an owner to back another horse, so I did not tell him Larius was putting fifty gold sesterces on Ferox for me: all my spare cash.

When we came back to the Circus they had started the horse races, though from our place on the card we had another hour to wait. I went to check that the Sweetheart was keeping Ferox calm, in order to safeguard my wager. While I was petting Ferox, I noticed a small, nervous, stuffed-vineleaf vendor hopping about: clearly a man with a gastric disturbance – or something significant to say. He said it to Famia, though they were looking at me. Money changed hands. The vineleaf tray skedaddled, then Famia came across.

'You owe me ten denarii.'

'See me tomorrow when I call in my bet!'

'Your man is in the second tier, on the Aventine side, near the judges' box; he's put himself level with the finishing line.'

'How can I get near him unobtrusively?' Famia cackled that with my well-known ugly visage it would be impossible. But he was useful: five minutes later I had slipped through one of the dark stalls at the starting gate end, and squeezed myself through the double doors.

Noise, heat, smells and colour assaulted me. I was in the arena, right down on the track. I had a bucket and a shovel. I waited until the riders passed, then wandered out across the sand, making a desultory scoop at the ground as I crossed the diagonal starting line. I reached the central barrier, the *spina*, feeling that I stood out like a pimple on a barrister's nose – but Famia was right: nobody ever notices the slaves who sweep up dung.

They were running one of those show pieces where bareback riders stand astride two horses at once – dramatic, though comparatively slow. The trick is to have the horses well trained, and to keep a good rhythm; my brother could do it. (My brother was the flashy, athletic type with a streak of blatant stupidity; he tried anything that risked his neck.)

Standing up against the marble podium, the huge size of the Circus was breathtaking. The width across was half the length of a normal stadium, and from the white chalk of the starting line the far end seemed so distant I had to squint. Immediately above me as I ambled up the length of the spina, towered magnificent shrines and statues; Apollo, Cybele, Victory. For the first time I appreciated the workmanship on the great gilded bronze screen which stood between the senatorial seats and the arena itself. Beyond them yawned two tiers of marble

terracing and a third tier of wood, then the closed-in upper gallery
with standing room only. As I made a random pass with my bucket,
I noticed how the sand had a glistening mica rim near the podium
and the spina, where coloured chippings from past gaudy occasions
had worked to the edges of the track. They never have awnings at the
Circus; you could frizzle up an omelette on the sand. Everywhere had
a constant odour of warm horseflesh above the lunchtime garlic and
ladies' cologne.

The spina was ornamented with mosaics and gilt, against which I
must have appeared a small, dark dot, like some tiresome, meandering
bug. In the space of two races I shuffled up as far as the huge red
granite Egyptian obelisk which Augustus had set in the very centre of
the spina; then I edged on nearer to the finishing line and the judges'
box. This was where the seats were always most warmly packed. At
first the mass of faces melded into one great fudge of humanity, but
as my confidence grew I began to see details: women shuffling their
footstools and hoisting their stoles over one shoulder, men red-faced
and bilious in the sun after lunch, soldiers in uniform, children
squirming restlessly or fighting in the aisles.

There was a break between races, filled with tumblers and acrobats.
Spectators moved about. I squatted against the podium, dry-eyed in
the dust, while I began a methodical survey of the second tier. It took
me twenty minutes to find him. As I did I thought he spotted me too,
though he looked away. Once I pinpointed him, it seemed impossible
that I could have missed his bad-tempered physiognomy before.

I sat still and went on searching. Sure enough, two rows lower down
and ten places along I found Anacrites himself. Some of the time
he was watching Pertinax, but mostly he stared round at the other
seats. I knew who *he* was looking for! At the far end of the row
where Pertinax was sitting and again higher up were two spies I
recognised who formed a triangle with Anacrites, penning in the man
I wanted and keeping him safe from me. None of them looked at the
arena while I was crouching there.

I stood up. So did Pertinax. I started to cross the track towards the
gilded screen. He moved along the row of seats. He had seen me. I
knew it, and so did Anacrites, though he could not work out where I
was. Stumbling over other peoples' feet, Pertinax reached a gangway.
Even if I climbed over the screen, in among the indignant nobility on
their marble thrones, he would be off down the stairs and out of
the nearest vomitarium long before I got near. Meanwhile Anacrites
suddenly shouted to one of the aediles' heavy squad and gestured
unmistakably at me. I was not only losing Pertinax, but about to be
arrested myself.

Then another shout aroused me, amid pounding hooves. I looked
up into the huge grinning teeth of a beribboned black stallion bearing
straight down on me. Trick saddlemen: this time two men in barbarian

trousers, linking arms as they stood upright on a single horse. With a fiendish cry and a wild flash of eyeball one leaned out sideways as the other balanced him. They scooped me up like a disreputable trophy. We shed the second rider then careered on, with me as terrified ballast waving my dung shovel and trying to look as if this mad ride was the best fun I had ever had.

The crowd loved us. Anacrites hated it. Not being a fool who fancied himself as a horseman, so did I.

We swept right round the three conical goal posts and the altar of Consus at the end of the spina, slewing at a nerve-racking angle as we turned. Then we sped back along the whole length of the stadium on the far side. In a screech of polished hooves I was dropped at the starting gates. Famia dragged me in.

'Jupiter, Famia! Was that idiot a friend of yours?'

'I told him to look out for you – we're on soon!'

My brother-in-law seemed to be assuming I was interested in the progress of my own cockeyed horse.

We were next. There was a shift in the atmosphere; word had it this was a race to watch. Famia said big money was riding on Ferox. The champion did look special – that high-stepping gait, the powerful build, and the deep-purple sheen on his wonderful coat. He looked like a horse who knew this was his great day. As I watched Bryon mounting their jockey, he and I exchanged a good-mannered nod. It was then that I noticed someone, someone not studying Ferox but intently scanning the crowd which was inspecting him. Someone looking for Pertinax, without a doubt.

I muttered to Famia, 'Just seen a girl I know – '

Then I slipped through the crowd while my brother-in-law was still grumbling how he would have thought that on this one occasion I could leave the women be . . .

LXXXVI

'Tullia!'

'Falco.'

'I was looking for you yesterday.'

'*I* was looking for Barnabas.'

'Will you see him again?'

'Depends on his horse,' the barmaid said dourly. 'He thinks he has a winner – but he left his bets with me!'

I drew Tullia by the arm right across the Cattle Market Forum to the shade and quiet beside that little round temple with the Corinthian columns. I had never been in it or noticed who its divinity was, but its neat structure had always appealed to me. Unlike the more brash temples further from the river, this lacked the usual swarm of seedy trade and seemed an improper place to be propositioning a big-eyed young girl in her sparkly-hemmed holiday gown.

'I have something to suggest to you, Tullia.'

'If it's filthy, don't bother!' she whipped back warily.

'Had enough of men? Then how would you like to make a great deal of money for yourself?'

Tullia assured me she would like that very much. 'What money, Falco?'

If I said half a million she would not believe me. 'A lot. It should go to Barnabas. But I reckon you deserve it more . . . '

So did Tullia. 'How do I get it, Falco?'

I smiled quietly. Then I explained to the barmaid how she could help me corner Pertinax, and obtain for herself a fortune that was as pretty as her face.

'Yes!' she said. I love a girl who does not hesitate.

We walked back to the horses. Little Sweetheart was gazing about him as if all this was wonderful. What a comic. The first time Famia put up his jockey, my wonderful animal shrugged him straight off.

'Which one's that, Falco?' Tullia enquired.

'Little Sweetheart. He belongs to me.'

Tullia chuckled. 'Good luck, then! Oh - I'll give you these!' She handed me a leather pouch. 'His betting tokens. Why should Barnabas have the benefit? In any case,' she told me, 'he was afraid to use his own name in case it was recognised – so he used yours!'

If that was his sense of humour, I guessed that it must have been Pertinax himself who had named my horse.

Since Ferox was carrying all my spare savings, I did want to see the race. So when Titus Caesar, whom I had met previously in the course of my work, sent me an invitation to join him in the president's box, I shot up there in a trice.

It was the one place in the Circus where I knew there could be no chance of Anacrites interrupting me.

Titus Caesar was a younger, more easy-going version of his Imperial papa. He knew me well enough not to be surprised when I burst into his presence with a toga bundled under one arm instead of arrayed in the immaculate drapes most people adopted at public meetings with the Emperor's son.

'Sorry, Caesar! I was helping out with a dung shovel. They're a bit short-staffed.'

'Falco!' Like Vespasian, Titus tended to look as though he could not decide whether I was the most appalling subordinate ever to be wished on his retinue, or his best laugh today. 'My father says you're claiming Little Sweetheart is sausage meat – I reckon that makes him a certainty.'

I laughed, uneasily, as I hastily robed myself. 'Caesar, the odds against my poor bag of bones are a hundred to one!'

'Could be a killing here!' Titus winked at me happily.

I told Titus I assumed he was old enough not to bet his purple livery on a shag-tailed besom like mine. He looked thoughtful. Then the curly-haired Caesar adjusted his wreath, stood up to give the crowd someone to roar at, and solemnly let fall the white kerchief to start our race.

It was a novice sprint for five-year-olds. There were ten declared, but one refused the starting box. Until Ferox put in his late appearance on the racecard, the favourite had been a big grey Mauretanian, although other people reckoned the clever money was on a compact little black chaser with Thracian blood. (It was well sweated up, and looked like a windblower to me.) Our Ferox was a Spaniard; there could be no doubt of it. Everything from the proud set of his head to the hungry gleam in his eye spoke quality.

When the slaves hauled the ropes and the starting gates swung out in unison, the Mauretanian was already stretching his neck as the horses crossed the starting line. Ferox was close behind him. Little Sweetheart had been crowded out by a brown horse with a white sock and a spiteful squint, so he was last.

'Ah!' murmured Titus, in the tone of a man who has pledged his last tunic to his bookmaker and is wondering if his brother will lend him one. (His brother was the mean-tempered Domitian, so probably not.) 'A back marker, eh? Tactics, Falco?' I glanced at him, then grinned and settled down to watch Ferox race.

Seven laps provide a lot of opportunity for casual conversation of a knowledgeable kind. We worked our way through the fact that it was a useful field and that the grey Mauretanian was in great heart but seemed in need of an outing so might not finish a principal. White socks was running wide round the goal posts, while the little black Thracian looked a lovely horse, an easy mover with a very consistent stride.

'Generous and genuine!' boasted a guardsman who had bet on him, but the Thracian had given all he had by the third lap.

Seven circuits when your savings are in the balance seem a long time.

By the time they lifted down the fourth of the wooden eggs that count off the laps, complete silence had fallen in the president's box. It was starting to look like a two-horse race: Ferox and the Mauretanian. Ferox ran in an interested manner, cantering easily with his tail straight behind him. He had grace and he had elegance. He ran with his head up to give him a good view of any horses in front. He could run as fast as anything on the track, but quite early on I began to suspect that our beautiful mulberry stallion actually *liked* something to watch in front of him.

'I think yours is pulling up,' Titus suggested hopefully, trying to be polite. 'Perhaps he'll come from behind.'

I answered gravely, 'He's left himself a lot of work to do!'

Little Sweetheart was eighth instead of ninth – but only because a perky russet had made a mistake, had come down on his nose and been pulled out.

I watched mine for a moment. He was terrible. Old mustardface ran with the most ungainly action. Even to his owner, who was trying to be charitable, that horse looked as if he had made an appointment at the abattoir before he came out. His head stayed down as if his jockey was strangling him. As he travelled forward his back legs, which were slightly out of rhythm with the front, kicked up behind at every stride and seemed to hesitate. Thank the gods he was not a hurdler. My baby would have been the kind who looks six times at every jump as he makes his approach, then hangs in the air halfway over so your heart is in your mouth.

At least his tail flew out at a jaunty angle that I rather liked. He was so bad I was starting to wish I had bet on him out of loser's sympathy.

By the sixth lap, Ferox was challenging strongly in second place. Still.

Little Sweetheart had just realised the horse immediately in front of him now was the white sock who had jostled him at the start, so he redeemed himself by passing it; he got a bit close but fiddled through all right. This time Titus refrained from comment. Sixth place in a field of seven (following a collision, there was a loose horse, a daft ginger thing, now): nothing to raise a shout about. Especially with only a lap and a half to go.

The roar of the crowd was increasing. I saw the Sweetheart twitch his ears. Out at the front things were starting to happen. A muddy grey in third place had been running on his own for so long he nearly went to sleep. A spotted nag no one had given a thought to made a temporary challenge, causing Ferox to increase his stride, though he kept his favourite position at the big Mauretanian's shoulder. My palms were wet. Ferox was second: he would be second in every race he ever ran.

Everything I ever did in life seemed to go wrong. Nothing I ever wanted seemed attainable. Who said that? . . . Helena. *Helena, when she thought that I had left her, and knew that she was going to have our child . . .* I needed her so badly I almost spoke her name. (I might have done it, but Titus Caesar had always looked at Helena in a speculative way that worried me.)

The field was well strung out now. There was a good twenty lengths between first and last as they went past the judges for the sixth time. The spectators were cheering Ferox, all certain he would sprint for it on the final lap. As the front runners rounded the posts I knew in my bones he never would.

They were halfway down on the far side from the judges – little more than half a lap to go – when I and most of Rome discovered something new: my horse, Little Sweetheart, could run as if his mother had conceived him in a conjunction with the wind.

They were running towards us. He was wide, so even with the rest of the field in front of him I saw his mustard nose lift. When he started his run, it was unbelievable. The jockey never used his whip; he just sat tight while that fool of a horse decided it was time to go – and went. The crowd opened their hearts to him, though most were losing money with every stride. He was the permanent tailender, the endless no-hoper – yet he streaked past the field as though he was just going for a rollick in the sun.

Ferox came second. Little Sweetheart won. He was leading at the finish by three lengths.

Titus Caesar clapped me on the shoulders. 'Falco! What a wonderful race! You must be extremely proud!'

I told him I was feeling extremely poor.

It took me hours to get away.

Titus rewarded my jockey with a heavy purse of gold. I had a present too, but mine was a fish: Titus promised me a turbot.

'I know you're a trencherman – ' He paused, with polite anxiety. 'But will your cook know what to do with it?'

'Oh, the cook can visit his auntie!' I assured him blithely. 'I always attend to my turbots for myself . . . '

In Caraway Sauce.

Two people made a killing. One was Titus Caesar, who could reliably expect that as the elder son of a great Emperor he would find himself a favourite with the gods. The other, for which I shall never forgive him, was my pernicious, devious, close-mouthed, horse-doctoring brother-in-law Famia.

They had a big family party, the rest of them. I had to endure it, knowing this would be the one night of my life when other people would be glad to buy my wine for me, but I needed a clear head. All I can remember of the ghastly entertainment is Famia carousing, and my three-year-old niece playing with Tullia's useless gift to me of the Pertinax betting tokens . . . Marcia, spreading the sad little bone disks all around her on the floor while people ineffectually told her to stop eating them.

As soon as I could I went to see Gordianus. He had little to add to what I already knew about events on the Quirinal yesterday – but I had news for him.

'Sir, a Transtiberina barmaid will be bringing you a document later this evening. It has to have an alteration made to it first.'

'What is it?'

'A marriage contract. Coming to you from the bridegroom. He thinks his bride has asked to inspect it, prior to the formalities. Tomorrow you and I have an appointment with Atius Pertinax.'

'How's that, Falco?'

'We are arranging his wedding,' I said.

LXXXVII

The day we married Atius Pertinax was refreshingly clear, after rattling rainshowers in the night.

My first task was to nip down to the Cattle Market Forum to buy a sheep. The cheapest I could get which would be acceptable to the five gods of matrimony was a little mottled fellow, who looked perfect enough for the purposes of religion, though a puny sort of lamb if we had wanted a pot roast in red wine sauce. However, we would not be needing the gods to remember our sacrifice gratefully for long.

Next a rancid garlandseller at the Temple of Castor shucked off some tired wreaths onto me. My sister Maia loaned us her wedding veil. Maia had worked the looms at a cloakmakers before she married; the weaver had had a soft spot for our Maia so her saffron veil was a distinctly superior length of cloth. Maia lent it out to poor girls on the Aventine; it had done duty at many an unstable coupling before it adorned the Pertinax bash. My mother would have baked us a must cake, but I left my mother out of this.

When I met up with Gordianus, leading my woolly contribution, he joked, 'I hope you see today as a rehearsal for a wedding of your own!'

The sheep, who was on my side, let out a sickly bleat.

We met Tullia in the Forum of Julius, on the steps of the Temple of Venus Genetrix.

'Will he come?' demanded the priest excitably.

'He was in the wineshop last night, looking for me. My mother gave him the message and collected the contract off him; she thought he believed her . . . '

'If he fails to show,' I said calmly, 'we all go home.'

'We could lose him,' grumbled Gordianus, worrying as usual, 'if he hears that his father has remarried anyway!'

'Aemilia Fausta promised me her marriage would not be publicly announced,' I reassured him. 'Don't worry until we have to. Let's go!'

Sunlight glanced on the golden roofs of the Capitol as we all left the Forum and turned north.

It was a small bridal party, as we had promised Pertinax: the bride, the priest, the priest's assistant with his box of secret implements, and a very large flautist tweedling a tiny flute. The priest's assistant was in military boots, but was hardly the first callow youth who had followed his religious calling unsuitably shod.

We left the flautist (Milo) on guard outside. Admitting our meagre procession, the door porter peered closely at the assistant priest (me – heavily veiled for 'religious purposes'); I gave him the price of a good dinner and warned him to lose himself. As he left he announced that the bridegroom had already arrived. He could have been arrested at once but we still had to go through with the wedding; I had promised the bride.

Atius Pertinax, alias Barnabas, stood in the atrium. He had honoured the occasion by coming clean-shaven in a toga, but instead of a bridegroom's air of worried ecstacy he had his normal surly face. He looked slightly ill when he saw Gordianus, but probably the fact of his talking to Helena outside the house that day confirmed the explanation Gordianus grimly gave: 'I would prefer to have no part in your affairs, Pertinax – but I have known the lady many years and she begged me to officiate.'

'We can omit the formalities!' snarled Pertinax, tight-lipped. I noticed a slight quiver beneath the refulgent saffron, though the bride maintained her modest silence. A tall, graceful girl, who moved well, glimmering in my sister's magnificent veil; it was fine enough for her to see her way, though it completely hid her from view.

'Very well. In marriage, as in death,' pronounced Gordianus sombrely, 'ceremonial can be optional. To satisfy the gods, the law and society, all you require is a sacrifice, a contract, and the bringing of the bride to her husband's house. The bride is already conducted here – unusual, but not an impediment. In the absence of her relations the lady had elected to give herself – '

'Trust her!' said Atius Pertinax. Those present who knew Helena Justina saw no reason to contradict. 'Shall we get on?'

Wreaths were handed round glumly. With impressive despatch, Curtius Gordianus covered his head and set up a portable altar in the empty atrium. The watchman had started the fountain before he slipped away – a single elegantly festive touch.

After a perfunctory prayer, the priest called his white-veiled assistant to lead forward the sheep. A second later poor lambkin was dead. Gordianus made a neat, untroubled job of it. His time at Cape Colonna had given him a good eye with the sacrificial knife.

He studied the organs, which looked distinctly seedy, then turned to the bride and announced without the slightest shade of irony, 'You will lead a long, happy and productive life!'

Pertinax looked nervous now, not without reason. If marrying for the first time is a drastic gamble, doing it twice over must seem utterly ludicrous. The priest had brought his contracts; Pertinax was induced to sign first. The priest's assistant carried the documents to the bride, who inscribed her name with maddening slowness while Gordianus engaged Pertinax in talk.

Signing the contracts completed this basic ceremony. Curtis Gordianus let out a short, grim laugh.

'Well! Time for the happy bridegroom to kiss his lucky bride . . . '

There were four yards between them when she lifted her veil and Pertinax braced himself for Helena's usual cool, reasoning contempt. He met a younger, brasher prettiness: huge dark eyes and tiny white teeth, clear skin, tinsel earrings, and an air of perfect innocence that was flagrantly false.

'Tullia!'

'Oh dear!' I exclaimed sympathetically. 'We seem to have brought his honour the wrong bride!'

As he started towards her, I threw off my white veil.

'Falco!'

'Always check a pre-written contract just before you sign it, sir. Some villain may have altered a critical element! Sorry; we lied about Helena Justina wanting to read through the documents, but then we had already lied about Helena agreeing to marry you – '

Tullia gathered up her skirts and scurried for the door. I whipped open the mysterious box which the priest's assistant carries at any wedding. In our family the joke is that the youth keeps his lunch in it – but I had a sword.

'Don't move! Gnaeus Atius Pertinax, I arrest you in Vespasian's name – '

His lip curled, revealing a dog tooth unattractively. 'Trust you!' Then he turned his head and let out a screeching whistle. 'Two can cheat, Falco – ' There was rush of feet, and out from a corridor burst half a dozen tall, bristly-chinned warriors in scale-armour trousers and glistening bare chests. 'Every bridegroom wants his own witnesses at his wedding!' jeered Pertinax.

His supporters were not rushing forwards with the aim of flinging nuts. Pertinax had obviously given them orders to kill me.

LXXXVIII

Luckily I had not expected the victim of a trick wedding to respond with graceful oratory. My first reaction was surprise. My next was to get my back to the wall, my blade up, and my eye on them.

From a man of his type, something of this sort was inevitable. Heaven knows where he found them. They looked like German mercenaries, big, long-haired, flaxen braggarts, originally hired by the dead Emperor Vitellius – now stranded in Rome after the civil war, with their fare home drunk in the stews along the Tiber and a new, more fastidious Caesar who would not be employing foreign auxiliaries within Rome.

They were heavy in the belly from too much beer and black pudding but they could fight, especially with the odds in their favour at any easy six to one. Some grim auxiliary captain on the Rhine frontier had put these hulks through several years of legionary drill. Their weapons were the huge, flat-bladed Celtic type which they swung over their heads and at waist height while I, with my short Roman stabbing sword, was hard-pushed to duck in underneath. Beneath my priestly costume I had a leather jerkin and arm guards – not enough against six skirling maniacs who were enjoying themselves with the threat of slicing off my salted crackling like a Black Forest pig.

Pertinax laughed.

'Keep smiling,' I seethed, watching the Germans. 'I'll deal with your gutteral lap dogs, and then I'll come for you!'

He shook his head, making for the exit. But Tullia was there first. Her terror of him, now he knew she had deceived him, made her foot fleet and her hand sure. She darted down the porter's corridor, past the two empty cubicles, and dragged open the huge, metal-plated door. Out rushed Tullia – and in thundered Milo instead.

At the sight of our humourless monster Pertinax skidded to a halt and turned about. I saw him run lightly to the staircase. I was trapped, hard-pressed by half a dozen heavy blades whose force when they touched down wrenched the power from my wrist as I desperately parried them. It was Curtius Gordianus who took off after Pertinax – an ungainly, sack-like figure fired with the long-nurtured hope of vengeance, who blundered upstairs at an alarming pace. He was wielding the small, sharp knife he had used in the ceremony, still wet from the throat of our sacrificial sheep.

Milo was considering what he should do, all bovine stupidity: my favourite thug.

'Do me a favour, drop your flute and grab a sword, Milo!'

Milo acquired a sword by the simple method of seizing the nearest mercenary, lifting the wild man off his feet, and crushing him until his eyes bulged and he limply dropped the blade.

'Cuddle a few more!' I gasped, managing to disarm the next while my boot made an imprint on his ragged chain-mail trews which if he was one for the women he would bitterly regret.

Now Milo and I could set ourselves back to back and work away from the wall. The opposition circled more widely, but we had more time to watch for them. When two charged from different directions we ducked by common agreement and let them impale themselves with an ugly crunch.

The crude fencing practice lasted less time than I thought. The last two who could run dragged off the wounded. To disguise their connection with the Pertinax house, Milo and I threw the dead outside in the street gutter opposite, like the dirty dregs of some drunken brawl the previous night.

'You caught it, Falco?'

Nothing hurt yet, but I was dripping badly: a long cut, down my left side. After five years as an informer I no longer felt the need to faint at the sight of my own blood but this was the last thing I wanted today. Milo was urging me to seek medical attention but I shook my head.

We hurried back, to look for Gordianus. No one answered when we called. I locked the street door and took the key. I found the spigot and turned off the fountain; as the water hung and then dropped, a nerve-racking silence fell throughout the empty house.

We stalked upstairs, constantly listening. One by one we flung open doors. Empty salons and deserted bedrooms. Dust undisturbed on pediments. Woozy flies flinging themselves against closed windows in warm solitude.

Gordianus was in the last room of the first corridor we explored. He had slumped against the marble dado and we thought he must be dead. Not so; only despairing.

'I had him – I got my knife in him – but he attacked me and I bungled it . . . '

Checking him over for physical damage, I muttered sympathetically. 'There's a world of difference between despatching something woolly at the altar, and taking human life – ' Pertinax had belted the Chief Priest viciously against a wall. Not much surface bruising, but at his age shock and exertion were taking their toll. He was having such difficulty breathing I worried for his heart.

I joined Milo in carrying the priest downstairs, and hurriedly let them out together. 'Milo, you look after him.'

'I'll come back – '

'No. What's here is mine.'

He helped make a pressure pad and bind up my side with the white veil I had worn at the ceremony. Then I watched him and Gordianus leave.

This was how I wanted it: Pertinax and me.

Inside the house again I relocked the door behind me. Pertinax probably had his own key when he had lived here, but it was no use to him now. When I act as an executor, the first thing I do is fix new locks.

I walked from the door slowly. One of us might leave that way eventually. It was the only door. This was a rich man's mansion. Rome was alive with cat burglars, and this gem of a property had been built for multimillionaires with treasures to protect. The external walls were completely blank for security. The windows faced inwards. All the light which flooded in came from internal courtyards and the open roof of the atrium. What happened in the streets outside belonged to another world.

He was here. So was I. I had the key. Until I found him, here we would both stay.

I started to search. There were scores of rooms and in some places there were passages where he could slip past me, so I had to patrol some areas twice. It took a long time. My wound started to burn and bother me. Blood was oozing through the cloth. I trod quietly, to avoid warning him and to conserve my own strength. Gradually I covered every room. And in the end I remembered the one place I had missed; so I knew where he must be.

I walked slowly down the red corridor for a second time. My boots slipped unwarily on the shining, level tessellation of the passageway floor. I stepped between the two plinths where basalt portrait busts had once stood, and into the elegant azure and grey bedroom that had once been a private haven for the lady of the house. The warm, deep blue of the wall panels welcomed me graciously. I felt like a lover, treading an accustomed secret route.

I noticed a small, rust-coloured smudge staining the geometric pattern of the silver and white mosaic. I knelt, with some difficulty, and touched it with my finger. Dry. He had been hiding here a long time. Perhaps he was dead.

Hauling myself upright, I dragged my tired feet over to the wooden folding door. It was closed. But when I opened it, from the far side of Helena's garden his angry eyes met mine.

LXXXIX

I limped to a stone border and edged myself painfully into a half-sitting position facing him. 'Couple of wrecks!'

Pertinax grimaced, eyeing up my own condition as he struggled to ease himself. 'What happens now, Falco?'

'One of us will think of something . . . '

He was in the shade. I was in the sun. If I moved to avoid it the fig tree would block my view of him. So I stayed.

He was the fidgety, hasty type; I had plenty of time. He fell silent watching me from that taut, narrow face.

'Your wife's garden!' I carolled, looking round. It was a small peristyle, full of muted sunlight and rich greenery. On one side of the colonnade, a worn stone seat with lion's paws. Low, sculptured hedges, with the faint scent of rosemary where I had crushed bushes as I found somewhere to perch myself. A thin trail of laburnum. And a small statue of an urchin pouring water – a ragamuffin in a patched tunic – who looked as if Helena might have chosen him herself.

Helena's garden. A good-tempered, mature little courtyard, as quiet and civilised as she was. 'This is a peaceful, private place for a talk,' I told him. 'And a good, private place for a man who doesn't exist anyway to die . . . Ah, don't worry. I promised your wife – your *first* wife – not to kill you.' I let him relax, then put iron in my voice: 'I'm just planning a series of hard, non-fatal blows that will persuade you staying alive is so painful you will finish off yourself!'

The priest had made a decent start of it. Better this way; some deaths need time.

He was on the ground, sideways to me, leaning on one hand. Almost no position was comfortable. He had to twist into the hasp of the wicked religious knife Gordianus had prodded into his ribs. He wanted to hold it firm. If he pulled it free, the rush of blood might bear his soul away. Some men would take the risk; I would have done.

I said, 'A military surgeon could safely get that out of you.' Then grinned, to let him know I would never let a surgeon into the house.

He was white. So was I, probably. Tension does that.

He thought he was going to die. I knew he was.

* * *

334

My eyes drooped. I saw him move, hopefully. I opened my eyes again, and smiled at him.

'This is pointless, Falco.'

'*Life* is pointless.'

'Why do you want me dead?'

'You'll see.'

'*Today* was pointless,' Pertinax mused. 'Why the trick with the barmaid? I can repudiate the marriage as soon as I want – '

'Got to get out of here first, sir!'

He thought about the marriage bitterly, ignoring me. His old restless bad temper jerked behind those pale, turgid eyes. His face had grown gaunt with his obsessions – that sense of outrage, not at his own failure, but at the world's refusal to give him recognition. His was a soul inching into madness. But he was not mad yet. I judged him still capable of answering for his crimes.

'Did my wife arrange this?' he demanded, as if the sunshine of sudden understanding had flooded him.

'Your *first* wife? She has the brains, but is she that vindictive, sir?'

'Who knows what she would do!'

I knew. In any situation I could make a fair guess: look for the obvious, then look for the oddest deviation from it and there would be Helena. Helena, making her quaint choice appear to be the only course anyone with any culture and moral fibre could take. He had owned her for four years whilst she struggled to do her duty by them both – yet he did not know the first thing about that eccentric mixture he called his wife.

'Helena Justina wanted to help you. Even when she knew you were a traitor and a murderer – '

'Never,' he stated briefly. 'This was the one thing I asked her to do for me . . . ' He watched me easing the bloodstained cloth around my ribs. 'We could help each other, Falco. Neither of us stands much chance alone.'

'Mine's a scratch on the surface. You're bleeding internally.'

Whether he was or not, the threat frightened him.

'Your wife's no fool,' I said, taking his mind off his terror of death. 'She told me, in Campania, "*Every girl needs a husband*".'

'Oh she does!' exclaimed Pertinax. 'Did she tell you she picked up a pregnancy?' He said it as if he meant a heat rash she had caught on holiday.

'No,' I replied calmly. 'She never told me that.'

'My father found out while she was staying in his house.' Remembering how she had looked sometimes in Campania, that was allowable. Anyone who knew Helena's normal stamina should have realised without being told. Including me.

Although he was in the shade, Pertinax was sweating heavily; he blew out his cheeks. I suggested, 'I suppose it was your father's idea to use the situation; to rescue Helena's reputation – to offer a respectable name for her child?'

'I'm starting to think he wants a grandchild even more than he wants to do something for me!'

'Have you quarrelled with him?'

'Possibly,' he squeezed out.

'I saw him after you left Campania. I thought his attitude had changed.'

'If you must know, Falco, my father made it a condition of standing up for me that I should re-establish relations with Helena Justina – and when she rejected the favour he blamed me . . . He'll come round.'

'Did she ask for this favour?'

'No!' he retorted in his most contemptuous tone.

'You surprise me!' I said softly. I let him settle, then put to him, 'This unlooked-for infant of hers must have a father somewhere.'

'You tell me! In fact I wish you would. If Helena Justina has slipped up with her father's driver it's irrelevant, but if she's involved with a man of quality I can put pressure on. You were her bodyguard; if you did the job properly you must know what pools she has been dandling her fingers in.'

I smiled faintly. 'You can assume, sir, that I do my job properly.'

The sunlit air was motionless in the small courtyard. Light gleamed broadly off the open-palmed leaves of the fig. Heat tingled a clump of scratchy lichen on the old stone seat and thrummed along the pierced walling where I sat.

'Ever see Helena Justina flirt with another man?'

'No one who got past me, sir.'

Pertinax spat with exasperation. 'The proud piece refuses to tell me – and you're no help!'

'What's it worth?'

'So you do know? Nothing,' he snarled abruptly. 'I'll find out for myself!'

'Thrash it out of her?' Pertinax made no answer. Something made him look at me more carefully. I asked softly, 'Does this man bother you?'

'Not in the least!' His defiance faded slightly. 'When I told her she was a fool not to take my offer she admitted she found it impossible to forget we had been married – but someone had a claim on her . . . '

I let out a long low, suggestive whistle. 'That's tough! Some sly double-dealer with an eye on her bank box must have persuaded Helena Justina that he is in love with her.'

He stared at me, as though he could not decide whether I was being satirical.

My side was aching more than I could easily tolerate.

'Talking of well-stocked bank boxes, I have some news for you,

Pertinax. Caprenius Marcellus had decided that placing his hopes in you is the short road to a long disillusionment. When you left without seeing him, he made other arrangements – '

'Arrangements? What arrangements?'

'Same as you today; he got married.'

His first reaction was disbelief. Then he believed it. He was too crazed even to feel hurt; I could see him immediately planning ways to extricate himself. The busy thoughts of a madman were moving in his sick eyes; I interrupted relentlessly: 'Marcellus was extremely fond of Helena. With her help you might have held him – but Marcellus had realised the truth. Oh, in many ways she will always be tied to you! The very high-mindedness you despise her for ensures that. She hated being divorced. But anyone who could offer Helena a refuge from her own sense of failure was bound to supersede you easily enough. Accept it,' I warned him steadily. 'You lost Helena Justina the way you failed at everything else you tried.' Before he could insult me in return I went on, 'I know why she rejected you. Marcellus knew.' I straightened my spine as I sat there, bracing myself against the hot pains in my side. He lay, half reclining in the damp shade against the far wall, refusing to ask me. I told him anyway.

'You think such a lot of yourself, Pertinax!' Whether I was making any impression on him or not, I had now convinced myself. The insults flowed much faster after that. 'You were useless – she soon did better once she was free of you. I expect you think you know her very well, but I doubt it! For instance, in all the years you were married to her, did you ever once discover that when a man has made Helena a happy woman, she cries in his arms?'

The truth came home.

'That's right,' I said. 'You lost her for the oldest reason in the world – *she found a better man!*'

Pertinax jerked with fury. As he started to come at me, the palm he was leaning on slipped and slid outwards. His bare arm scraped full length on the loose gravel path. I made no attempt to move. At the critical moment I had my eyes closed, but I heard the soft hiss of escaping air as the sacrificial dagger pierced his lung.

He died at once. So I knew that as he fell forwards the Chief Priest's knife had pierced his heart.

XC

When my own heart had stopped pounding I slowly stood up. Helena's garden.

One day, however long it took, I would give her another garden, where there would be no ghosts.

I dragged my feet to the street door, feeling stiff and sour-spirited. Fumbling, I got the key in the lock and fell out into the sunny glare of the street. A small curly dog with a stump of a tail was nosing the sheet which some neat-minded Quirinal steward had flung over the bodies of the two German mercenaries while the refined people of the district sat in their houses complaining.

I clucked at the little dog; he wagged his rump like a conspirator.

'Falco!'

A hired chair stood in the shade of a portico. Beside it, sitting on a step, was the barmaid Tullia.

'Good of you to wait!' Not entirely altruistic on her part: I still had her marriage certificate stuffed in my belt. I handed over the contract and told her I had left her new husband conveniently dead.

'Take this document to my banker. The money I promised is a legacy left to his freedman Barnabas by Atius Pertinax; as the freedman's widow it's yours. If the banker should query the signature on the contract, just remind him slaves adopt their patron's names when they are liberated formally.'

'How much is the money?' Tullia demanded briskly.

'Half a million.'

'Don't joke about it, Falco!'

I laughed. 'Truth! Try not to spend it all the first week.'

She sniffed, with the wariness of a natural businesswoman. This petal would clutch her cash with a sure grip. 'Can I take you somewhere?'

'Corpse to dispose of – '

Tullia smiled gently, pulling me by the arm to her sedan chair. 'I was his wife, Falco. Leave me to bury him!'

I let a small puff of laughter crease past my throat. 'Duty's a wonderful thing!'

338

She took me where I asked, to my gymnasium. She leaned out and kissed me goodbye.

'Careful – too much excitement will finish me, princess!'

I watched her settle back inside the chair, with all the gravity of a woman who knew exactly how she would order the remainder of her life. There would be, I thought, very few men.

She leaned out as the chair pulled away. 'Cashed your bets yet, Falco?'

'Ferox lost.'

'Oh, the *bets* were on Little Sweetheart!' Tullia informed me laughingly, drawing the curtains to hide her – now she was a wealthy lady – from the crowd.

I staggered in to let Glaucus patch me up, while I dismally remembered my last sight of those white bone disks . . .

'What in Hades happened to you?' demanded Glaucus, ignoring the sword cut and considering my glum face.

'I just won a fortune – but my niece has eaten it.'

Glaucus my trainer was a sensible man. 'Then put the child on a chamberpot – and wait!'

We had a discussion about whether bone dissolves in stomach acids, but I won't bother you with that.

He got me clean, and promised I would keep upright if I went steadily. Then I hired a chair myself, as far as the Capena Gate. I sat, dreaming of the new apartment I could now afford if any of the betting tokens were retrieved from Marcia . . .

Nothing is ever easy. As I paid off the bearers at the end of the Senator's street, I noticed a group loafing outside a cookshop: Anacrites' men. They had worked out that sooner or later I would try to see Helena. If I approached the house, my convalescence would be in a prison cell.

Luckily I was no slouch as a lover: I knew where to find the Senator's back gate.

When I crept in like a marble-thief, Camillus Verus himself was standing with his arms folded, staring at the carp in his gloomy pond.

I coughed. 'Nice evening!'

'Hello, Falco.'

I joined him making faces at the fish. 'I ought to warn you, sir, when I leave here I am liable to be arrested in the street.'

'Give the neighbours something to talk about.' The tunic Glaucus had lent me only had one sleeve; Camillus twitched an eyebrow at my bandaging.

'Pertinax is dead.'

'Tell me?'

'Some time. Before I can remember, I shall have to forget.'

He nodded. A carp shoved his snout up to the surface but we had nothing to give him so we just stared back guiltily.

'Helena has been asking for you,' her father said.

He took me indoors, as far as the atrium. The statue I had sent him from the Pertinax house now had pride of place. He thanked me as we both gazed at her, with a peacefulness that would have been unlikely if we had been surveying the real thing.

'I still wonder,' mused Camillus, 'if I should have ordered marble – '

'Bronze is best,' I said. I smiled at him, so he would know it was intended as a compliment to his daughter: 'More warmth!'

'Go and see her,' he urged. 'She won't talk, and she won't weep. See what you can do . . . '

Her mother and a gaggle of maids were crowding the bedroom. So was a man who must be the doctor. My roses were by Helena's bed, my signet was on her thumb. She was busy ignoring good advice with a set, stubborn face.

I leaned in the doorway like a professional, looking mean and hard. She saw me at once. Helena had a strong face, which took its softness from whatever she was feeling. Whenever that sweet face lit with relief, simply at seeing me walk into a room alive, the mean, hard look became difficult to sustain.

I went on helping the doorframe to keep itself upright, trying to find the sort of tasteless ribaldry she would expect. She spotted the bandages.

'Trust you,' she said, 'to turn up looking bloodstained when there's someone else's doctor to give you a free salve!'

I shook my head slightly, to say I was just scratched. And her eyes answered that whatever I had done to her, she was glad I was here.

Most of my work has to be done alone, but it would be good to know that when a job was over, I could come home to someone who would scoff at me heartily if I showed any tendency to boast. Someone who would actually miss me if I failed to make it home.

Remaining in the room while a lady was examined was obviously indelicate. Luckily the doctor was leaving. I blocked his path.

'The name is Didius Falco. I live off the Via Ostiana, above the Eagle Laundry in Fountain Court.' He looked puzzled. I said, 'Send your bill for professional services to me.'

Within the room, the women of the house fell suddenly still. They all looked at Helena. Helena was looking steadily at me.

The doctor was Egyptian in origin. He had a square head, with eyebrows that met in the centre above a straight, strong nose. He looked distinctive, but was very slow. 'I understood that the Senator – '

'The Senator,' I explained with forbearance, 'is the father of this lady. He gave her life, nourishment, education, and the good humour that smiles in her honey-brown eyes. But on this occasion, I will pay your bill.'

'But why – '

'Think about it,' I said gently.

I took him by the elbow and propelled him from the room.

Think about it. No, don't think. The child was yours. Ours. Think, Marcus. Think about that.

I held open the door. Amidst a flutter of female consternation, Julia Justa somehow drained the room of its irrelevant occupants. I was aware of hurried movement behind me; then the door closed.

Silence. Helena Justina, all eyes. Helena and me.

'Marcus . . . I was not sure if you would come again.'

I tipped my chin, in a travesty of my debonair normal self. 'I told you, fruit, just stay where I can find you, and I'll always come back . . . Just promise me,' I said quietly. '*Promise* me, Helena, that the next time you will tell me.'

In this silence now were all the world's pain and grief. Helena's eyes were finally filling with her unshed tears.

'I was working,' I went on carefully. 'I had a lot of things to think about. But I want it understood, Helena - if I had known you needed me, I would have dropped everything – '

'I know!' she said. 'I knew that. Of course.'

That was it then. Really I had known the reason all along.

'I thought,' she began after a moment, with her voice little more than a whisper so I knew she was almost unable to go on. '*I thought there would be plenty of time –* '

'Oh my love!'

She was reaching for me even before I began to move. In three strides I had crossed the room. I set one foot on the step, twisting onto the high bed, then at last Helena was locked in my arms, so tight I could hardly feel the deep despairing sobs she so badly needed to release. When I finally loosened my grip to cradle her more kindly, Helena's hand spread protectively on me, where I was hurt. Neither of us spoke, but we both knew. Where her face was pressed to my scratchy cheek most of the tears were hers, but some were my own.

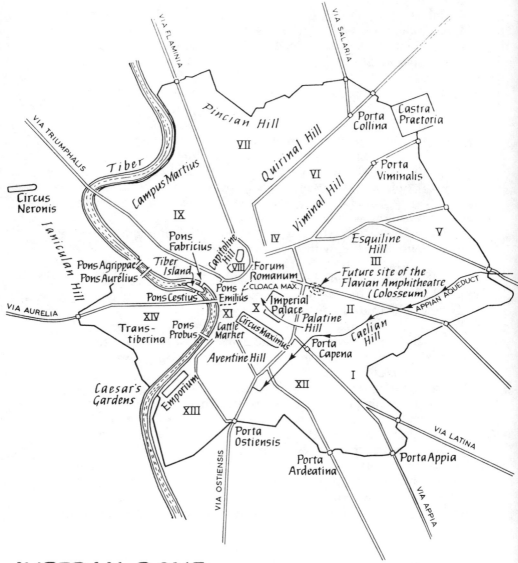

VIA FLAMINIA

VIA SALARIA

VIA TRIUMPHALIS

Pincian Hill

Tiber

Porta
Collina

Castra
Praetoria

Campus Martius

VII

Quirinal Hill

Circus
Neronis

IX

VI

Viminal Hill

Porta
Viminalis

Ianiculan Hill

Pons
Fabricius

Tiber
Island

Capitoline Hill

VIII

IV

Esquiline
Hill

V

Pons Agrippae
Pons Aurelius

Pons Cestius

Pons
Emilius

Forum
Romanum

III

Future site of the
Flavian Amphitheatre
(Colosseum)

CLOACA MAX.

APPIAN AQUEDUCT

VIA AURELIA

XIV
Trans-
tiberina

Pons
Probus

Cattle
Market

XI

X

Imperial
Palace

II

*Palatine
Hill*

II *Caelian
Hill*

Circus Maximus

Porta
Capena

Caesar's
Gardens

Emporium

Aventine Hill

XII

I

XIII

Porta
Ostiensis

VIA OSTIENSIS

Porta
Ardeatina

Porta Appia

VIA LATINA

VIA APPIA

·IMPERIAL ROME·

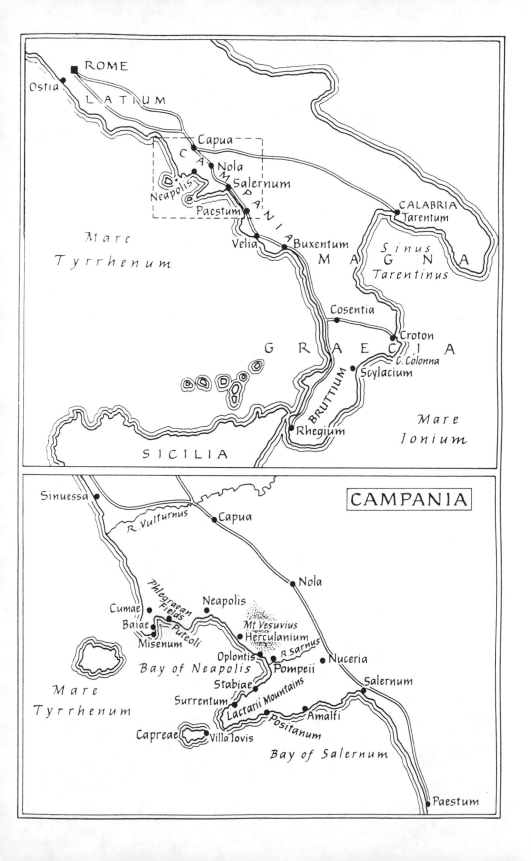